W9-AXF-632

SPEAK TO ME IN THE VOICE OF THE NORTH WIND
WITH THE WILLIWAW'S ANCIENT SOUL
OF KAH LITUYA'S TALES AND EXPLORER'S SAILS
AND SOURDOUGHS AND MOUNTAINS OF GOLD
LET ME BREATHE THE BLUE AIR OF GLACIERS
'NEATH THE SKY OF THE NEWLY BORN SPRING
AND REMEMBER THE TLINGIT TRADERS
AND HONOR THE LONG WINTER DREAMS
LET ME HEAR THE CALL OF THE EAGLE
IN THE FORESTS WHERE THE SALMON RUN
AND STAND ON THE SHORES OF MAJESTIC GRAY FJORDS
IN THE ARMS OF THE PALE ARCTIC SUN
LET ME WALK IN DENALI'S SHADOW
WHERE THE SITKAS SNARE PASSING CLOUDS
AND GAZE ACROSS COTTON GRASS MEADOWS
AS GHOSTS FROM THE FAR MOUNTAINS HOWL
SPEAK TO ME IN THE VOICE OF THE NORTH WIND
WHEN BOREAS UNVEILS HIS SOUL
AND THE AURORA'S CHARMED LIGHTS
DANCE THROUGH THE NIGHT ~
WITH THE SPIRITS OF "ICE" AND "COLD"
T.M.

INSIDE PASSAGE

~ CANADA

BRITISH COLUMBIA

PACIFIC OCEAN

QUEEN CHARLOTTE SOUND

VANCOUVER I.

PRINCE GEORGE

PRINCE RUPERT

KAMLOOPS

VANCOUVER B.C.

VICTORIA

BELLINGHAM

EVERETT

MACKENZIE R.

PROVIDENCE

FORT SIMPSON

NAHANNI BUTTE

WATSON LAKE

FORT NELSON

PEACE RIVER

McLENNAN

SLAVE LAKE

WILLISTON LAKE

DAWSON CREEK

GRAND PRAIRIE

BEAR LAKE

MACKENZIE

TAKLA LDG

ALICE ARM

HAZELTON

BABINE LAKE

SMITHERS

BURNS LAKE

FT. ST JAMES

FRASER R.

FOX CREEK

JASPER

PORTLAND CANAL

MINCOLITH

TERRACE

KITIMAT

MARILLA

QUESNEL

BLUE RIVER

KEMANO

SWANSON BAY

KIMSQUIT

WILLIAMS LAKE

GATE STRAIT

ARISTAZABAL I.

BELLA COOLA

CHARLOTTE LAKE

TATLA LAKE

MALAKWA

CHASE

ROSE HARBOUR

WAGLISLA

NAMU

CALVERT I.

WINDHAMS

CHILKO LAKE

CLINTON

LILLOOET

VERNON

KELOWNA

PENTICT

OLIVER

THURLOW

PORT HARDY

CAPE SCOTT

KELSEY BAY

POWELL RIVER

BOSTON BAR

WHISTLER

SQUAMISH

HOPE

CAPE COOK

GOLD RIVER

COURTENAY

STRAIT OF GEORGIA

NOOTKA

NANAIMO

TOFINO

UCLUELET

CAPE FLATTERY

OLYMPIC

N

INSIDE PASSAGE

A COREY LOGAN NOVEL

BURT WEISSBOURD

A VIREO BOOK **V** RARE BIRD BOOKS
NEW YORK LOS ANGELES

THIS IS A GENUINE VIREO BOOK

A Vireo Book | Rare Bird Books
453 South Spring Street, Suite 531
Los Angeles, CA 90013
rarebirdbooks.com

FIRST HARDCOVER EDITION

All of the characters and events in this story are imagined, as are many of the
Seattle locations. Seattle is, of course, real, though the author has created an
imaginary landscape in and around Capitol Hill.

Publisher's Cataloging-in-Publication data

Weissbourd, Burt.
    Inside passage : a Corey Logan novel / Burt Weissbourd.
    p. cm.
    ISBN 9780985490232

1. Bainbridge Island (Wash.)—Fiction. 2. Inside Passage—Fiction. 3. Sailing—
Fiction. 4. Murder—Fiction. 5. Mystery fiction. I. Title.

PS3623.E43265 I57 2013
813.54—dc23   pcngoeshere

For Ben, Emily, and Jenny

PROLOGUE

IN 1987, THE FORMER USSR supplied roughly a quarter of the world's uncut diamonds. Not surprisingly, corrupt Russian government officials began to smuggle rough diamonds to California and sell them on the black market to cutters in Antwerp and Israel. Before long, the Russian mob was selling the uncut gems to cutters all over the world.

SEPTEMBER 1989

LESTER BURRELL WAS A method-of-payment specialist. He was an expert in gems, drugs, various contraband currencies, and laundering. Whenever he could, Lester worked with diamonds. He would use them to pay for weapons smuggled through the Eastern Bloc arms markets for terrorists. Or to buy classified military technology to sell to North Korea. He was always the middleman.

So it was unexpected for Lester to be partnered with a Russian seller of stolen state-owned rough diamonds. Nevertheless, in 1989 Lester found himself in a bungalow at the Miramar Hotel in Santa Barbara with his Russian partner, a gangster named Yuri. The declining hotel was between the beach and the railroad tracks. Kids liked to put coins on the tracks. Lester liked to knock them off with his cane.

The Russian gangster had worked with Lester on lucrative three point arms deals. Most recently, it was Afghan drugs for stolen Soviet weapons. Diamonds had been the method of payment. Yuri trusted Lester, especially when it came to diamonds. He even liked the outdated suits Lester wore on his king-sized frame. Yuri said they reminded him of home. So he listened carefully when Lester proposed he steal fifteen million dollars of state-owned diamonds. Lester further proposed that they take the rough diamonds to Canada where he knew a diamond cutter who could launder the stones.

Yuri had the stones in a Nike gym bag. He had spread a sample on the formica kitchen table where they were being inspected by Lester and his diamond guy, Nick Season. Lester deferred to the guy, which surprised Yuri. The guy wanted to weigh and inspect each of the stones. So Yuri was cooling his heels—he had already counted the cars of two trains that went by out loud—while Lester and Nick inspected diamond after diamond. Yuri liked that Lester was so thorough.

When Nick Season was satisfied, he stood and stretched. He walked around the table, pensive.

"Good," Nick finally said, and came around behind Yuri.

Yuri was thinking Nick was too good looking for a diamond guy, and he didn't look Jewish. Still, Lester knew what was what. Yuri would already be dead if Lester hadn't bailed him out of a broken-down arms deal. The man he answered to would have squashed him like a bug. Boris would be going crazy right about now, throwing his vodka bottles at the wall. Good. Fuck you, Boris.

Nick put a hand on Yuri's shoulder, interrupting his musing. "Very nice."

Lester poured shots of tequila, one for each of them. Nick was adjusting his belt while Lester raised his glass to Yuri. Then Nick had the buckle in his right hand. Attached to the buckle, somehow concealed under the belt, was a thin icepick-like instrument. In one easy motion, Nick thrust the pick through Yuri's right eardrum. In one ear and out the other. Just as quickly, the pick was withdrawn. And Yuri lay dead on the tabletop.

Lester made a churlish sound. "Nice," was all he said.

"Al's waiting in Seattle. He'll take you to Vancouver." Nick left.

Lester lifted Yuri's head by the hair, looked at his lifeless face. "Nice," he said again.

ONE

MAY 2010

COREY LAY IN BED, liking the briny sea breeze, even the kelp smells. Each morning she took this time to quiet herself. The tightness was still there, though, at the back of her neck. Gingerly, she cracked a trace of a smile. Today the sky was dishwater white; the sea, gray. Blake Island was washed out, dark, dreary, and shrouded in fog. She missed the lush fir-green that came with sunshine, the splendid, somehow reassuring sight of Mount Rainier, topped with glistening snow, looming large beyond the island. It didn't matter. She had a window, an open window.

Six days earlier Corey Logan had earned her release from FCI Dublin, the Federal Correctional Institution in Dublin, CA. She had done twenty-two months. A condition of her release was three years of probation or "supervised release." Her probation officer, Dick Jensen, had all kinds of discretionary power, so she intended to be a model supervisee. She could do that.

What she couldn't imagine was her psychiatric evaluation, today's business. Before she went to prison, there had been a dependency adjudication for her son Billy in the State Court system. She was his sole guardian, and when she was arrested, Child Protective Services had taken him from her. She had been unable to regain his custody before being sentenced and sent to prison. In order for her to get him back now, she had to go to dependency court to petition for his return. The dependency court required a psychiatric evaluation, parenting classes, and drug testing. She had taken her parenting classes at the pre-release center. The drug testing was a formality; she didn't do drugs. Now she had to find a psychologist or a psychiatrist on the court approved list who would do the evaluation and let the court know that she was a "fit parent." Next week she would see Billy, who had turned fifteen while she was in prison. Thinking of Billy made her neck tense up again, even her throat got tight. When she lost custody, they put him in foster homes, moving him often, never telling her why.

That made the shrink even more important.

Corey stared out the window, trying to put Billy out of her mind. Her buoy was wobbling in the wake from the Bremerton ferry. Her eyes settled on her handsome wooden boat.

The *Jenny Ann* swayed gently at the red and white buoy she had anchored yesterday morning. Her friend Jamie had bought the 1936 hardtop Chris-Craft back for her at auction. Luckily, her boat was old, used, and tainted by the drugs found on board. Still, Jamie had paid $13,400, almost all the money Corey had.

As a child, she and her mom had lived aboard more often than not. In those days the thirty-six-foot wooden cruiser with the green and white trim was called Poseidon.

When her mother died from skin cancer that had spread to her lungs, Corey was seventeen. She was on her own, the last of the Logans. She had painted her mom's name on the boat herself.

Corey got out of bed and slipped on sweatpants and a Murder City Devils t-shirt. She flashed on Billy telling her it was weird for a grown up to like that band.

She went from her small bedroom with its tiny bath to the larger room that was her kitchen, living, and dining room. A floor-to-ceiling brick fireplace separated her bedroom from the great room. She made coffee, then took her diary from behind a chimney brick. It was bound in worn, nut-brown leather, and she liked the way it felt in her hands. Corey sat at the old plank table in front of her hearth. She rubbed a dark spot in one of the maple planks, then made her morning entry:

Six days. I still wake up scared. Glass-in-the-gut, bone-scraping fear. Nick Season is my waking nightmare. I imagine him killing Al. I hear him threatening Billy. I feel his pick rising through the

*bottom of my jaw then into the roof of my mouth. The window
helps. I stare at the sea and I begin to remember who I am. This
is my last chance. I have to stay focused. All I want is to get my
boy back. Nothing else matters...*

Corey imagined being with Billy again. She could picture little
things he did—like tapping his fingertips against the tops of his
thighs to the music that was forever playing in his head. He would
be a handsome young man now. And he would know his way
around; she had made sure of that. She had been on her own too,
and she had taught him what was what. He still needed his mom,
though. Anyone could understand that. She wondered why she
had to see a psychiatrist at all.

———

NICK SEASON STUDIED HIS reflection in a mirror mounted inside his
office closet door. He was built like a boxer, a middleweight with a
nose that had never been broken and deep black eyes that women
noticed. There were splashes of gray at his temples now, and he
combed his hair straight back. The gray was just the right touch,
he thought, to offset the coolness that occasionally flashed in his
eyes. As a young undercover cop, he had let his splendid black
mane grow long, and his girlfriend at that time said he looked like
a Greek warrior, fierce and merciless. It was the kind of double
meaning thing she would say, trying to tell him he was insensitive
but afraid he might break her jaw. Nick was just twenty-five then
and—he could see it now—still learning to pull the strings on
attitude.

His collar was open, and he adjusted the square Greek cross—
his father's legacy—that he wore on a chain around his neck. The
silver cross was small, and he liked it centered on his chest. When
he was satisfied, Nick practiced his smile. It showed perfect white
teeth, softened his sculptured Mediterranean features, and made
him look younger than his fifty-four years. He won people over
with that smile: this lawyer had a heart.

For the hell of it he took a fighter's stance, then he was
feinting, jabbing left, shadow boxing. Just like that, he was back
on Corey Logan.

He stepped up his shadow boxing. It didn't take his mind off Corey—she was a maddening itch you couldn't scratch—so he sat down at his desk and buzzed Lester, just once.

Minutes later Lester Burell, his chief legal investigator and the only man he trusted, set the heavy brass handle of his antique wooden cane against Nick's desk. Because of a game foot, Lester always carried the cane. It went nicely with his crew-cut gray hair, lantern jaw, and his large, gold wire-rimmed glasses. Lester stood, looking down at him. He was six feet four, and his cheap, double-breasted suit hung loosely on his large frame. Lester's craggy face revealed even less than his rheumy, raisin-colored eyes.

"Corey fuckin' Logan?" Lester asked.

Sometimes Nick thought Lester could read his mind.

He stared out his window. Nick could see Safeco Field, the Mariners' light-as-a-feather gem, and the Seahawks' broad-in-the-beam football stadium right next to it, like a beached whale. He turned back. "Talk with her probation guy. Pay her a visit. Be yourself." As an afterthought, Nick tried his smile on Lester.

Lester didn't seem to notice. Then, out of nowhere, the big man snapped, "I hate the mouth on that cooze."

"That can only help." Lester, Nick knew, would put her heart in that mouth. It had to be done. Later this month Nick planned to announce his candidacy for state attorney general. Corey Logan was the cloud in that otherwise clear blue sky.

"She worries me," he added, mostly to himself. In fact, starting today, Corey Logan was a worry he intended to manage.

———

THE FERRYBOAT RIDE FROM Bainbridge Island to downtown Seattle takes thirty-five minutes. It was a thing you could count on, Corey knew, pretty much every time. If the ferry was late, it meant the fog was so thick you could catch it in a jar. She thought it was a beautiful ride, even on a cloudy day. When the sky was clear, snow-capped Mount Rainier dwarfed Tacoma in the south, the Olympics rose in the west, and the Cascades framed downtown Seattle to the east. On those days she felt like most things were possible, even now.

Dr. Abraham Stein's office was near Pioneer Square, an older part of downtown and a tourist destination. It was a short walk from the ferry, and Corey liked the old brick buildings, the street life, the tired-looking bars, even the tourist shops and galleries sprinkled among renovated one-time buck-and-a-quarter hotels. The entrance to Dr. Stein's dusty brick building was under the viaduct. On the first floor there was a luckless-looking pet store, an antique furniture emporium, and this hole-in-the-wall Chinese take-out. Not what she had expected.

She checked herself out in the restaurant window. Jeans, washed and pressed last night, her tan cotton shirt tucked in. She was lean and her breasts were full. Her curly black hair was cut short. She could just make out the patch of freckles that spread across her nose. She looked good, she decided, except for the work boots, her only shoes. Corey spit into her palm. She raised first one foot then the other onto the door step, polishing her boots as best she could. As an afterthought, she adjusted her watch to cover the tattoo on her wrist, a bracelet braided with turquoise and red strands. The doctor's office was on the third floor. She looked at the elevator and chose the stairs. She could smell sweet and sour pork, or chicken, she wasn't sure which.

The waiting room was beige, quiet and tiny. Some magazine she had never heard of—*Atlantic Monthly*—lay on a dusty coffee table. She sat on a brown corduroy couch. It faced another door. No receptionist. A button-sized light near the inner door was on. The light went off. A burly guy with bushy salt-and-pepper eyebrows opened the door and offered a meaty hand. He was about her age, thirty-eight, maybe a couple of years older, and off-looking, like he didn't get out much.

"Abe Stein," he said.

She stood, took his hand. His handshake was firm but formal. "Corey Logan," she said.

He didn't meet her eyes. She couldn't tell if he was shy, or what. Dr. Stein didn't care how he looked, she could see that much. His tweed sport coat had a hole in the pocket where something had burned through. His brown wool tie was loose at the collar and hung askew. He showed a large palm, ushering her into his office.

She had supposed that he had let the waiting room go because the office was so great. The office, however, was a plain, badly-lit room, with nothing but this oversized dark oak table and two mismatched chairs sitting right in the middle. On her side of the table there was a worn leather chair, some kind of heirloom. On the far side there was a contemporary high-backed desk chair. Papers were in piles on the table, held down with blackened pipes, pipe racks, and ashtrays. Two open cans of Diet Coke sat on his side of the phone. Beyond the table, wooden blinds covered the windows. Below the blinds the windows were cracked open. She turned. On the wall behind her were two dissimilar paintings. One was colorful and modern. The other, a black and white portrait of a bearded man with glasses in a black suit.

When the doctor offered her the chair, he gave her a polite little half-smile. She decided to stand, keeping her options open.

Dr. Stein leaned his backside against his table, facing her, waiting. Corey toed the carpet; she wasn't saying boo. No, not until he made some kind of an effort. When he finally spoke, his voice was soft, tentative, as if he was choosing his words carefully.

"We can stand if you'd prefer."

She shrugged. He was watching her now.

After a long silence, he spoke again. "Are there questions you'd like to ask?"

She tried to think of a question. How about, why was he wearing a wool jacket on such a warm day? She shook her head.

He took a pipe from his desk. Even the outside of the bowl was charred. "Do you mind?" he asked, still watching. His eyes were pale blue, and they were smart eyes.

Corey waved her hand, okay. She wondered what kind of shrink violated the smoking ordinance at the first meeting.

Abe struck a wooden match. He held the match over the bowl and inhaled until smoke began to plume. When he was satisfied, he dropped the match into an ashtray behind him. "Normally—," he hesitated. "Often, I begin by explaining what I do."

The guy talked so softly, she had to lean forward to hear him.

"Would that be helpful?"

Corey was watching the match, still burning near a pile of papers where it landed when it slid from the ashtray.

"Is something wrong?" he asked when she didn't say anything. He was still watching her, intent. His brow was furrowed, and his eyebrows almost touched, like a "V."

Maybe it was the expression on her face—is this a bad dream?—or perhaps he smelled smoke. Whatever it was, Dr. Stein finally turned to see that his papers had just caught fire. He picked up a can of Diet Coke and doused the flame. Like it was no big thing. A little pool puddled on his desk.

The doctor had just set his stuff on fire. In his own office. And he was used to it. How was a guy like that ever going to evaluate her? How was he going to understand what it was like for her? What it was like to be her? Without a word, she turned and walked out the door, closing it behind her. The button-sized light was on, and a crabbed-faced schoolgirl who had taken her place in the waiting room shot her a withering look.

———

MORGAN CHANDLER'S HAND RESTED on the back of Billy's neck. She was making little stroking motions with her fingers. They were at a coffee place off Pike Street, the Blue City Café, where Morgan and her friends hung out drinking complicated coffee drinks. She said it was "sort of sixties," whatever that meant.

For a laid-back place, Billy thought it was pricey. His friends didn't mind. He didn't know where their money came from, but they always had it. When he scored for them, they would pay in advance. Cash.

Betsy, the café's proprietor, and raconteur, liked to tell anyone who would listen how, in 1988, she had signed a long-term lease on a hunch. That first year she ran a coffee counter—flanked by a tattoo parlor and a biker bar. Now, the main floor walls were exposed fir posts. Secondhand dark oak tables and chairs contrasted nicely with the fir mullions in the windows. There were well-worn, comfortable couches against the walls. In one corner she had built herself a modern kitchen with a tall glass counter where customers could order exotic coffees or choose from an eclectic menu. In an alcove, there was a rack with publications such as *The Stranger, Capitol Hill Times, Seattle Gay News, Skill*

Shot: Seattle's Pinball Zine, and other carefully chosen alternative periodicals.

"Nice game, Billy," a pretty ninth grader said as she walked by.

"Thanks." Billy raised long arms over his head, stretching. He was dark-haired like his mom, and lanky. He looked casually around the café, sizing up who was with whom and what was what. He still wore his select soccer team sweatshirt. He would hide it before he went "home," the worst place he had been since the King County juvenile detention center or "juvie." His foster mother had given him a fucking brown banana for breakfast this morning after he had washed all the sheets she took in for money from some old peoples' home.

The ninth grader turned. "Come to the girl's game Friday?"

"I'll try," he offered. The best thing about his high school was soccer. Because he was good at it, he had been invited to play on the Chargers, an AAU select team. So now he knew all these kids from Olympic. Two of the Chargers starters were a big deal at Olympic. They ruled on who was in and who was out. And these boys wanted to be his friend. They knew that he went to public school, that he knew his way around Capitol Hill and the "Ave," and that he could get drugs—all of which they thought was cool. They didn't know where he lived, or how he scored his dope, or that his mom was a convicted felon.

"She likes you," Morgan whispered, bringing him back.

"I like you," Billy whispered and gently kissed her lips. He especially liked how she was so sure of herself. And how she always knew what was the next big thing. Sometimes he was right there. Say with music, a thing he knew about. Other times he just didn't get what she and her friends were talking about. They would totally lose him on computer software, or new apps, or $75 designer t-shirts that he thought came from Value Village. Morgan said it didn't matter. What did matter was that she liked him. She had decided that he was really hot—kind of "radical," whatever that meant—and with these people, somehow that made it so. He wasn't exactly sure why she thought he was so sexy. Or why she thought it was cool to know funky streets like Pine, or sleep under the freeway. He made a steeple with his long fingers, thinking now about the evening. She would want to do something edgy, maybe get high and check out the Ave, and he would be out late. He would work it out so one of the guys would invite him to stay over. If he had to, he would stay at a squat he knew near the U.

So what if his foster mother got mad. So what? His real mom was out now, and she could deal with his foster mother. Or try to anyhow. It was about time his mom got the picture. Thinking about her made him tense up. She had really fucked things up. So he had learned to live without her.

TWO

IT WAS SWEET AND sour pork. Yeah, she was sure of it. Corey walked up the stairs toward Dr. Stein's office—again. She had tried the other names they had given her. One of them was a prune-faced female psychologist who made her look at inkblots and talk about whatever came to mind. Mostly what came to mind were prison memories. And they were hard to talk about. She talked about them though. About the violence. How it was part of life. Twice she had hurt people. And both times, afterward, it was hard to breathe. Even now it made her sweat whenever she talked about it. She still felt out of control, stunned by what she had done.

When she finished talking, the woman wanted to know if she had always had a problem with violence. When she tried to explain that she had never been violent, that she wasn't violent now—that her mom had taught her to stick up for herself, that was all—the woman went on for quite a while about how they could work on it together.

"How long?" Corey asked.

"Say twice a week for as long as it takes."

"So a week or two?"

The psychologist nodded. "Perhaps a year or two."

"No." She shook her head. "That can't be right."

And that was that.

The next one was another psychiatrist, smooth—not at all like the pipe smoker—and full of himself. He talked like he had this special understanding of her. He had decided that she was volatile. He wanted her to take this drug, Depakote, to stabilize her moods. When she explained that she had always been a little feisty, and that she would cheer right up when Billy came home, the guy said he couldn't recommend anything until she took a mood stabilizer for at least six months.

And that was that.

So she was back to sweet and sour pork. The little light was on in the waiting room. She figured that it went on when the office door closed, so you would know not to interrupt. She wondered why he didn't just lift one of those motel "do not disturb" signs, leave it on the waiting room door. Too cheesy, she guessed. The guy's mind didn't work like hers, she was thinking. The light went off, and there he was. Same wool jacket. His hair was too long and mussed up, like an orchestra conductor's. She walked right into the office before he could make that little gesture with his palm.

Corey sat in the leather chair and looked at her work boots. This was going to be hard, she realized. She waited, unsure what to do. The silence lasted a long time. She inspected every thread of the faded gray rug around her feet.

"Perhaps." Dr. Stein paused. "Perhaps you'd prefer to see someone else?" he finally asked.

Right, that's why she was sitting in his worn-out old chair.

"They are supposed to give you other choices...other names."

The guy slowed down between words, like he wasn't born here. She glanced up. His eyes were on her now. Locked on. The bushy brows were furrowed in that "V," she remembered; and now that "V" seemed to laser those locked-on pale blue eyes right into her head. How could an out-of-it guy you could hardly hear be so intense?

"You've already seen them."

Intense and smart.

He came around the desk and waited for her to look up again. His eyes were kind now. The lines on his brow had rearranged themselves so that he seemed more relaxed.

"We'll do the best we can," he said.

She looked down and thought about that. Finally, she offered, "Thanks." And looked his way again.

He was leaning against the edge of his table, reviewing her file.

He could use a new, lightweight jacket, she decided, and his hair needed cutting too.

Eventually he set the file down, lifted one of his blackened pipes, a question.

She shrugged. "Your landlord know about this?"

"He lives in Hong Kong."

"You got a fire extinguisher?"

His laugh was a low rumble. "I prefer Diet Coke."

The guy was trying to make a joke, she decided. "No problem."

"I'm absent-minded," he explained. "Not a good quality for a pipe smoker."

Absent-minded? Lost in space was more like it. She liked his rumbly laugh, though. And she liked that he had explained.

For maybe half an hour, he asked the routine questions. Easy stuff—address, phone numbers, medical history, more or less the bare bones facts of her life. It made her feel a little more comfortable, almost like she could talk to this guy.

When she finally settled into her chair, he lit a fresh pipe. Then he leaned toward her. "Can I ask some more difficult questions?" It came out kind of tentative, as if he was afraid she might say no.

She thought about saying speak up, but didn't. "You've read my file. Do your worst."

"That's actually a good idea," Abe said.

The "actually" pissed her off.

"It says here," he tapped her file with the stem of his pipe, "that you stabbed a woman in prison."

"Yeah. She came at me with some kind of knife."

"You stabbed her with a pencil."

"What I had."

"They never found a knife."

"So?"

"You're sure she had a knife?"

"Mister, how can this ever work if you don't believe what I tell you?"

He looked at the ceiling, took a puff. "Point taken."

Corey wasn't done. She touched the scar on her neck. "You think I did this to myself?"

"What happened to her knife?" he asked, his voice flat.

She decided to give him a chance, tell him the whole story. "Okay. It was about seven at night. I was finishing up my shift in the laundry, folding sheets. Two of them came at me from behind. The one gal had a shank, like the pointy part of a screwdriver, filed sharp, and duct-taped to a piece of wood. She cut me. I had this pencil I used for the laundry list. I stuck it into her neck. I didn't even think about it. Agh."

Her face tightened, an involuntary reflex. "She went down, bleeding, you know…" She was frowning now, trying to get this right. "You ever kill an elk, or a deer?"

He shook his head.

Corey nodded. Dumb question. She was starting to sweat. "Anyway, the woman I stabbed started gasping and shaking. The other one went for the shank. I scrambled over the table. I was bleeding pretty badly. Next thing I know, my one friend is there. She's got me down on the floor, and she's standing over me with a long mop handle. This other gal takes one look at Suze, that's what we called my friend, and she backs off. Before I know what's what, Suze's gone and I'm being cuffed. The one that got away must have grabbed the shank."

"Who's Suze?"

"Great big girl. I listened to her stories. We got to be friends."

Abe was taking notes. "I see." And after a short silence, "Why were they trying to hurt you?"

"They weren't trying to hurt me, they were trying to kill me."

"But why?"

Nick Season was why. But she couldn't tell him that. Un-unh. Not ever. Corey closed her eyes, massaged the bridge of her nose with thumb and forefinger. When she was back on track, she opened her eyes. "Have you ever been inside a prison at night?"

"No."

"Guy doing your job, he should spend a night inside." She hesitated. "People kill each other in prison over little things. I don't know what I did. Maybe it was just a mistake…some kind of unmeant insult, or a gang deal. Happens all the time."

"How did you feel after you stabbed her?"

Every shrink she saw asked her that. What did he think she would say…"great?"

She looked right at him. "She was on her knees, making throaty noises, with this pencil sticking out of her neck. How do you think I felt? Out of control. Afraid. Relieved it was her and not me. Mostly, I felt like screaming. But when I opened my mouth, no sound came out." Her shirt was sticking now, under her arms and at the small of her back.

He set down his pipe, glanced at his watch. "I'm afraid we have to stop."

Now? She had just done the hard part. "Why?"

"I schedule forty-five minutes for a session. An evaluation usually takes three or four sessions."

"How can you get me started talking about stuff like that then just turn it off?"

"I'm sorry. I thought you knew how I worked. There are time constraints. I should have explained."

"That's not right. Do you think it's easy to talk about this? It makes me sweaty and cold at the same time."

"We can continue for another few minutes—"

She interrupted. "I haven't even talked about Billy, my son. I'm worried about him."

He checked a calendar. "Can you come tomorrow? Say eleven-thirty?"

"I guess." She wanted to tell him that he wasn't getting this, that he was screwing it up. Instead she said, "The picture." She pointed at the colorful abstract painting behind her. He hadn't bought that picture. "Your mother give you that?"

"How did you know?" he asked.

"A hunch." She stood. He directed her out through a door she hadn't even noticed. It opened right into the hallway. Weird, one door for coming, another for going. She recalled the schoolgirl's scornful look. Corey wondered if she would ever get this right.

———

NICK CHECKED HIS SMILE, working with a hand mirror he kept in his desk. He flashed on Corey Logan. The woman was worming her way into his mind, a nagging, nasty, waking dream.

He hit a button on his phone, then two numbers.

When Lester picked up the phone, Nick could hear him breathing. No greeting, nothing. He wondered if he waited long enough, Lester might say something. Not likely.

"Corey Logan?" Nick finally asked.

"Her probation guy's got a history. I'm on it."

"Speed up the program. Put Riley on it." Riley was a hot-shot P.I. and sometime bounty hunter. Hiring Riley made this a big deal.

"And her kid?"

"Suggest what we're capable of. Give her a taste." Nick cracked his knuckles. "I've got a bad feeling," he added, mostly to himself. Nick knew that feelings didn't mean much to Lester, one way or another. He, on the other hand, paid attention to his worries.

Nick sighed; he had reason to worry. Corey Logan had threatened him, written down what she knew, then set it up so it would be released to the newspaper if anything happened to her. It had to be a bluff—she had no evidence. Still, he would be a politician soon, and then the press wouldn't need proof… so it was more of a threat than she knew. What it was…it was a stain, a debasement, hovering just out of reach, poised to soil his candidacy. She did that after two women tried to kill her in prison. She wasn't stupid.

He wondered, yet again, how much Al had actually told her. His cousin was smart enough, and careful, but she had him on some kind of short, good-father leash. What was that about? Pussy-whipped. That was all he could think of. Which was okay, except several years ago Al had dug up some dirt in L.A. and tied Lester to the Russian diamonds. It was a fluke, a one-in-a-million deal. Al was checking out known diamond traders from the eighties on some case he had caught, and he recognized Lester, the same man Nick had paid him to ferry to Vancouver, B.C. twenty years earlier. This was the kind of thing only Al could have put together. No evidence, but still.

Nick sat back, troubled. Maybe two years now, this had been worrying him. He stopped himself before he started going over and over the same things. The bad worries could suck the juice right out of you.

And he could see how the bitch was working her way under his skin, little by little.

THREE

COREY WAS WATCHING BILLY'S house. She was in her car across the street trying, unsuccessfully, to keep a lid on her excitement. The house was shabby, an eyesore in a transitional neighborhood. She tried to imagine Billy living in this house. She felt suddenly apprehensive. Corey checked her watch: it was time, three o'clock. But where was Sally, the caseworker from Child Protective Services? She was supposed to be here too. Trying to be patient, she stared at his house and worked at waiting—going over, for the umpteenth time, Billy's sorry foster care history.

Billy lived in this group home along with four other foster children and one of their babies. He had started in an individual home, but after five months his foster parents decided they didn't want to keep him. She wasn't sure why. Six months later he was moved from his second foster home.

Until they found another foster placement, the state had kept Billy in the King County juvenile detention center for eleven days: a nightmare, she was sure. He finally got placed in this group home, in yet another school district where they made him repeat the ninth grade because he had fallen behind.

Corey winced; she wasn't at all sure what to expect. Billy had visited her only once, sixteen months ago. Her friend Jamie had driven him fourteen hours each way. It hadn't gone well. Since then, she wrote him long letters at least twice a week. He responded to her letters sporadically, and his replies were short and often unfocused. His letters stopped coming at all almost a month before she was released. Starting today, she was allowed to see him once a week for two hours. Sally, the caseworker, was "monitoring the reintroduction of the family unit." Sally was okay, except that she always seemed too busy.

Corey couldn't wait another minute. When she stepped out of her pickup and crossed the street, she could see that the group home needed a new roof and some hard work in the front yard. She walked up three steps to the iron outer door. She could feel her pulse, pounding in her ears. The basement windows had rusty wire-mesh grills dotted with cobwebs. A teenaged girl answered when Corey rang. She carried a baby on her hip.

"I'm Corey Logan, Billy's mom," Corey said. She could hear a television somewhere in the house.

The girl left the iron door closed, shouting over her shoulder. "Billy here?"

"How would I know? He thinks this is a damn motel. He'll do extra loads if he comes home late."

"Yeah, right, that'll work good," the teenage girl muttered to herself. Corey guessed she was sixteen. She was eating a candy bar. Her acne was pretty bad. "He's not here."

"I was supposed to meet him here," Corey explained.

The girl shrugged, closed the inner door and went inside.

In prison there were times when she would lose her bearings and turn on herself, savagely self-critical. She did that now, blaming herself for all of the things that had gone wrong for Billy and certain that he must hate her. At these times, Corey felt as though she was being sucked under freezing cold water. She had learned to weather these episodes, to let her feelings run their course. Still, it was a long, bad moment. After it passed, she summoned her strength. She rang the doorbell, then she rang it again.

A wiry Caucasian woman reopened the inner door. Her body looked forty, though her hard, pallid face was older. Her red-rimmed eyes were tired.

The woman wiped a strand of hair from her forehead. "Why are you still here?"

"I'm Billy's mom."

"Billy, huh. He's never here when you need him."

"I was supposed to meet him here at three o'clock."

"Well, now you get the picture. Sorry." She closed the door.

Corey moved toward her car, panicky. Inside, she locked the door and carefully dialed Sally. She said yes, she would hold. She closed her eyes and wiped out her thoughts about Billy's foster home, her confused feelings about well-meaning Sally, and even her worries about her missing son. Corey kept her eyes closed, her cell phone to her ear. She would keep her head clear and empty until Sally picked up. She knew how to wait. When Sally came on, Corey started right in, pleasant enough. "Do I have the wrong day or something?"

"Is this Corey? Corey Logan?"

"Right. Sorry."

"Hey. Billy left me a message. He couldn't make it. I didn't know where to find you."

"What?"

"Look, he doesn't have to see you at all."

"What?"

"Let's try again next week."

"I can't wait another week. He's my son."

"I'm sorry. I'll talk with him. Do what I can. Okay?"

"Thanks," Corey said, breathless.

————

IT WAS LATE. COREY couldn't sleep. She sat at her worn plank table, her back to the smoldering fire, writing in her diary:

"Where's Billy. Why wasn't he there to see me? My ideas about that scare me. I have to find out. Right away. And who is that woman he lives with? And the girl with the baby? How many other kids live there? What have I done?"

She closed the book, hid it behind the chimney brick, then went into her bedroom and laid down on the bed. She would find Billy tomorrow, after her time with the doctor. She would try not to think about these things until she saw her son, talked with him. When she had finally put Billy out of her mind, Corey slept.

———

IT WAS 7:30 A.M. The tide was out, and Corey was poking around the tide pools, killing time before taking the ferry to Dr. Stein. Her rocky beach was part of the Blakely Shelf, a rock formation that stretched under Puget Sound. The shelf revealed its hiding places—its shallow crevices, its nooks and crannies teeming with sea life—when the tide was low. She had already seen sea stars, a small flounder, tiny black eels, sculpins, and a Dungeness crab.

She sat on a partially submerged rock, watching a sea anemone swaying gracefully in the water between her knee-high rubber boots. She was working to keep the demons back, wanting to feel okay about herself before seeing Dr. Stein. She slowly turned her head north, toward the little cedar cabin her mother had built and the fancy new house next door. Her dad William Logan had died at sea four months before she was born. His troller went down in the Ouzinkie Narrows between Kodiak Island and Spruce Island, Alaska. He left the Bainbridge property behind—her mom always said that he left it for his daughter. Three years ago she, Billy, and Al, had painted her mother's cedar cabin white. Now the paint was peeling, worn by wind and rain.

The owner of the new house had sent a balding real estate agent to offer money for her mom's cabin, to tear it down. She said no.

When the guy came again, Corey shut the door in his face.

Later she was sorry she had done that. He was doing his job, and he had no way of knowing what this cabin meant to her. What it was, she decided, was that she wasn't used to getting her way with people. She didn't expect them to understand what she was saying. So she didn't say much. She needed her energy for other things, like Dr. Stein. At least he tried to listen, even when he didn't understand. She believed he was working hard and that he thought about what he did. Except at certain times—she could see it come on—when he seemed distracted, preoccupied. It made him miss some things, like setting that fire. Corey caught herself. That wasn't her problem. She would make him see that she could be a good mom. She could do that. He could do that.

Corey took the steep old wooden staircase that switch-backed up the bank toward the cabin. She went slowly, looking down, reminding herself to replace the unstable, weatherworn steps. She was checking out a wobbly tread when her hand hit something hard—a piece of wood, a cane. She saw him then, an outsized man in a shabby suit, staring down at her from the landing through those oversized, gold-rimmed glasses that made his weird, cloudy eyes even bigger. Nick's man. Lester Burell. He had set his cane to block her way. Since her arrest, Lester had visited her twice. After those visits she knew two things: Lester had a reptile's thick skin, and a reptilian heart. She thought about running, but she couldn't move. She felt cold—on her skin, inside her bones.

Lester tapped his cane against the stair railing. "You get one chance."

Corey didn't respond. She didn't even look at him.

Lester didn't seem to notice. "You work for me. Whatever I need."

She wanted to throw up. "Why are you here?" she asked, instead. "I haven't said anything. I won't bother Nick."

Lester ignored her. "Chance to redeem your execrable self—" Another tap, and a mean smile. He nodded. "Show your good intentions…"

She looked out to sea.

He nodded again, as if she had said something, then continued. "I went ahead and squared it with your PO. Dick liked the idea." He cleared his throat, an attention-getter. "And it could help you get your boy back. Might be the only way. We agreed on that."

Corey tensed up, every single muscle. The lizard sonofabitch had talked with her probation officer. About Billy. She wanted to grab his ankle and pull, watch him tumble down the stairs onto the rocky beach. She waited, staring at the sea.

Lester went on, his voice gravelly, "Here's how I look at it." He waited until she turned back, then he lifted his large left palm, held it out. "In my pocket, or…" He raised his right palm, lowering his left, as if weighing two objects on a balancing scale. "Off the radar screen. Poof!" He blew across his right palm. "Gone." He held both palms at the same level. "Works either way."

Lester hawked up a wad of phlegm, lobbed it onto the beach—he was plainly finished here—then he climbed the steps and walked toward his car. Corey shifted, took slow breaths. She watched his back, his odd walk—a war wound. He had been a mercenary, he'd told her once. She knew that twenty years ago Nick had paid Al to ferry this man to Canada on his boat. Now, Al was dead and Lester was Nick's grim messenger.

She hadn't spoken with Nick himself since that harrowing night at King County jail. She still remembered the exact time—10:13 P.M.—when she finally made bail. Al, she assumed, had been contacted. She was in a bad dream. Al would help her sort it out, wake her up. When she stepped into the waiting area, her bad dream turned to a sweat-soaked, screaming nightmare. Right there, sitting on a bench next to Billy—engaging him in lively conversation—was Al's cousin, Nick Season. Nick waved. He looked like a million bucks.

"Hey, Corey," Nick said. "What a rough deal. We have to talk."

She ignored him, hugged Billy and looked anxiously at her friend Jamie, who sat on Billy's far side. She asked her son, "Where's dad?"

"We couldn't find him anywhere." Billy frowned. "It's really weird."

"We called everyone we could think of," Jamie explained. "Even the Bainbridge police. They can't find him either. No one knows where he is."

The pieces of the day's puzzle were coming together for her.

She remembered stepping away from them. "Who posted my bail?" Corey asked, afraid of the answer.

"I did." Nick took her arm, plainly concerned. "Let's talk privately."

"Wait here," she told Billy as Nick led her outside. He took her down Jefferson to a door stoop.

She felt like she was underwater, drowning.

Nick used his handkerchief to clear a place for Corey to sit on the stoop. He sat beside her. "Perhaps I can help," he offered.

She studied Nick's handsome face, his perfect black eyebrows, his sure black eyes. "Where's Al? What happened?"

"Al's gone," Nick said, as if talking to a slow child. "He's not coming back."

"Who did this? Did you—"

"Listen carefully, please," Nick interrupted softly. His voice was calm. "Here's what happened: You and Al were selling confiscated drugs that Al stole from the evidence locker. You hid them on your boat. Twenty kilos went missing. You sold ten already. Someone found out. Al ran with the money. He just disappeared. You're going to jail."

"Like hell."

Nick squeezed her arm. His grip was like a vice. "You're not listening. Here's the point. I don't want you to miss the point." His voice was still soft. He gave her a second. She saw the veins in his neck throbbing. "I like your son. Nice boy. I'm worried about him though. A young fella without his dad." Nick leaned in, so close she could smell his cedar-scented aftershave. "He could disappear too."

She slapped him hard enough to leave a handprint on his cheek.

Expressionless, Nick tightened his grip. Then he pulled her up the stairs to the dark entryway. With his right hand, Nick freed his brass belt buckle. A thin, icepick-like instrument was attached to the buckle, housed under his belt. In one fluid motion, Nick had the pick through her lower jaw, piercing the roof of her mouth.

Corey gasped. She stood on her tiptoes, head back, leaning against the brick wall. Blood was pooling in her mouth. The way the muscle in his jaw was working, she thought he might kill her.

"Remember this," he went on, his voice raspy and cold. Her toes hurt, and she could feel the pick working its way deeper. "Tomorrow. During your trial. When you're in prison. Remember this one thing." He raised the pick, like punctuation—if she came off her toes, it would impale her brain—then he spoke into her ear, enunciating each word. "You plead out. You do your time. You cross me…you say one word…I'll kill your boy. Sure as sunrise."

Nick slid the pick out. He stepped into a shadow, then he was gone. She huddled in the corner where the door met the brick wall. She held her arms tightly, trying to stop shaking. Then she was on her knees, biting down on her knuckle, tears running down her cheeks. Blood trickled from the corner of her mouth.

Corey held her arms that same way now, watching Lester drive his Mercedes up her steep dirt drive.

———

AT 11:30 P.M. SHE was back in the same worn leather chair. Her neck was tight, like a coiled spring, and her muscles, even her bones, ached. If she tried to talk about Billy now, who knows what could come out of her mouth. So she told the doctor that she would talk about Billy next time, since she hoped to see him for the first time later that day. He said that was fine and that he hoped her visit would go well. He was nice about it, and she wanted to offer something. So Corey told him, truthfully, that she loved her son and that she had let him down. She had to fix that, she explained. She didn't tell him that Billy had missed their first meeting. Nor that she planned to find him this afternoon for an unauthorized visit. It bothered her that she was deceiving this man, though she wasn't sure why.

Corey glanced at the quiet doctor. He was back in her file, puzzled, trying to figure who knows what.

"So you were arrested for smuggling marijuana once before," he eventually noted.

She put on her game face. "That's not right. I was nineteen years old. I had this great souped-up wooden cruiser. It was easy to bring a little bit down from Canada. Make some extra money. We're talking hundreds of dollars here. That's not smuggling. That's a hobby."

"I see."

He didn't, though, she could tell. "All I got was a warning, and I had to do community service."

"But then they found…what…ten kilos on your boat?"

"A set-up. Seventeen years later. I hadn't sold dope in years. For christsakes, I was living with a customs agent."

"A customs agent?"

"Is there an echo in here?"

"Tell me about that."

"Years ago he worked Roche Harbor. I used to stop there. I was just twenty-one. We both had family from Greece. One thing

35

led to another. Then he got moved to L.A. Seven months later Billy was born. When I told him about his son, he was angry at me for having the baby. He didn't want the responsibility. I told him that Billy was my responsibility, that I expected him to stay in L.A. Maybe three years ago, Al shows up again. He had grown up. We got together. Billy had just turned twelve." And for almost a year, they tried to be a family. They had done all right too. Billy, especially.

"Where is Al now?" he asked.

"He disappeared the morning I was busted."

"Just took off?"

Dead. Nick Season's inhuman work. She hadn't thought about it when Al told her Nick owed him money. She didn't ask questions when Al said it was for some favor he had done years ago. It never occurred to her that Al, a small fish in any big pond, was about to brace a great white shark. Corey looked over at Dr. Stein. He was waiting, not in any kind of hurry. She didn't think she ever really loved Al, but he was Billy's dad. "I guess so," was all she could think to say.

"Was Al selling marijuana?"

"Al? Al Sisinis?" she asked. But before he could answer, she said, "No."

He was back in the file. "It says here that the marijuana they found on your boat was from an evidence locker at Customs."

"That doesn't mean Al was selling it."

He looked up. "Did you keep marijuana on your boat?"

"Okay, we kept some dope on the boat—never more than an ounce—for personal use. And maybe Al was skimming off a bust he made. I don't know." That's where everyone, especially the investigating officers, stopped listening to her story. "Someone else stole twenty kilos from that same shipment and planted ten on my boat along with a sawed-off twelve gauge."

"So you believe you were set up?"

Corey looked right at him. "Believe? I know I was set up. Someone wanted me to go to prison." That's all she could tell him. Nothing she could prove, either.

"Why? Who would do that?"

Nick Season is who. "I dunno."

"You pled guilty."

"So? So what? That's a deal. What does that have to do with anything?"

"Many of my evaluees believe they're innocent. Some are, some aren't." Abe paused. "I can't always tell."

"I was innocent," she said softly. "There's nothing to 'tell'."

He made that "V" with his eyebrows. "Did you have a bad lawyer?"

"He was all right. But I never had a chance."

"Did he tell you to plead guilty?"

Stein was like a pit bull. She caught herself starting to lose it. "Let it go," was all she said, slow and clear.

"I can't, Corey. What I do is try to understand why you do what you do. I may even be able to help."

Help? Nick sent her a card every year on Billy's birthday. "I don't need your help. I'm out. And there are some things you just aren't ever going to understand. You want my trust? Well, mister, that's a two-way street. So when I say let it go, you've got to trust me on that."

He made a note on his yellow legal pad.

———

CoREY SAT IN HER black pickup across the street from Jackson High School. She was checking out the kids as they came pouring onto the street, milling around, texting, grouping up at the bus stop or in the parking lot. They were young, uncertain, and scraggly, these high schoolers with their colorful Nikes and wild hair. Some of the girls had nose or eyebrow rings, and a lot of the guys were sagging their pants or their baggy warm-ups. A gangly boy caught her eye from afar. He was tall and somehow familiar. It was his walk, and the headphones. Was that Billy? Yes! He was tapping his fingertips against his thigh. My God, he had to be three inches taller. His hair was long, and kind of wild. He was walking alone, confident-looking, carrying a worn book bag over his shoulder. Billy was handsome, like his dad, and he looked like he could take care of himself. She teared up, relieved and proud.

Just like that, Billy was inside a bus and on his way somewhere. She followed the bus, unsure what else to do. On Pike Street, west of Twelfth Avenue, she saw him step down. He continued west, walking down the hill toward the water. His step was a little livelier, and he had done something to his hair—tied it back in a ponytail. He wore a hooded blue sweatshirt now, though he left the hood down. He seemed at ease here, eyeing the kids who roamed this edgy street.

This was her first time in the Pike-Pine corridor in two years. Corey took in the funky cafés, the gay bars, the music clubs, the ethnic restaurants, a hip sex shop, even a witchcraft bookstore. She had forgotten the spiked collars, vivid tattoos, and the occasional facial piercing. This was an offbeat, colorful world that drew more than its share of young people who wanted, for whatever reason, that second look.

It surprised her that Billy was here. At fifteen, she had started working after school at the wharf, canning fish. Summers, she would fish with her mom. She was in the twelfth grade when her mother died, leaving her just enough money to get through high school. The summer after she graduated, Corey shipped out on a seiner to fish in Alaska. She was eighteen, and she had fished or repaired boats or tended bar or worked odd jobs at the docks ever since. She hoped that her son would be the first Logan to go to college. Billy stopped in an alcove to light a cigarette. She grimaced, then reminded herself that she had smoked as a teenager too.

Corey considered driving up beside him, honking, but that didn't feel right. She tried to pull over, but in this neighborhood there was never a parking place. Billy turned right toward Pine. When she made the turn, he was gone. She realized that he must have stepped into the coffee place down the block. A hand-painted wooden sign out front said Blue City Café.

She parked in front of a fire hydrant. From her spot she could see inside the café's large mullioned window.

Billy was sitting at a table near the front with three other kids: two girls and a boy. One of the girls had her hand on Billy's neck, and she kissed him, meaning it. Cigarettes. A girlfriend. Okay. But something was off. These kids looked different from Billy. Why?

She watched a crew of four girls and three guys move two tables together and settle in.

And then she had it. They dressed like street kids—ripped jeans, even the old band t-shirts. But their clothes weren't raggedy or old. No, they paid for this look. These kids were washed and coiffed and, in their own way, poised. Fresh out of the box, ready for whatever. None of these young people were in foster care. In fact, she would bet these kids didn't even go to public school. They were thoroughbreds, on some kind of fast track.

Two guys stopped by Billy's table to talk with him. These guys were big shots. They had that unmistakable look—indifferent, above it all. She could see other kids watching them, looking for clues. They high-fived Billy before moving on. Everything about this picture was wrong.

She used her cell phone to call the café. A woman behind the coffee bar picked up the phone. "I'm looking for Billy Logan," Corey explained. "He's the tall kid in the blue sweatshirt with little white letters on the front."

"Ma'am, there are maybe four guys in here wearing that sweatshirt."

She looked again. "Okay, right. Table by the window. With the blonde girl wearing silver sequins under the torn leather jacket."

The woman behind the counter looked around, found the sequins. "That's Morgan. Is Billy her friend on the left?"

My right, your left. "That's him."

The lady came around the counter with a portable phone. She handed it to Billy. He shook his head—there must be some mistake—but she had turned back to work.

When he had the phone to his ear, Corey said, "Billy, I'm outside. I wasn't sure what to do. I need to see you right away."

She could see him through the window, standing now, turning away from his friends. "What are you doing here?"

"Come out and turn left, you'll see the truck."

"It's not my time to see you."

"Billy, either you come out, or I come in."

"Thanks. Thanks a lot."

She watched him say something to his friends, then return the phone. He came out the door and walked to the truck. He was pouting when he opened the door and stuck his head in. "Why are you here?"

"Why?" she repeated. "Are you kidding?"

"You messed things up for me, big time. I'm doing okay now. Don't mess me up again."

"I'll try not to," she said gently, aware how wound up he was. She put a hand on the seat beside her. "Please sit. I want to talk with you. I need to."

"If I do, will you leave me alone? Let me go back to my friends?"

She thought he looked wary and vulnerable. "Yeah. Sure."

He hopped into the truck, closed the door, and sat against it, looking out the window.

Corey wanted to cry. "Billy, I'm sorry."

"Yeah, right." He continued to stare out the window.

"What happened?" she asked. She could see he was biting down on his lower lip. "What happened?" she asked again.

Billy kept staring out the window.

When he didn't respond, she touched his arm. "It's me. Whatever happens to either of us, I'm still your mom."

He finally said, "It's no big deal."

Right. His dad would have said that. "It is to me."

"What's that?" he asked, turning, pointing to her scar.

She touched it. "In prison, two women tried to kill me. One of them cut me with a shank. That's—"

He raised a hand, interrupting, "I know what that is, mom."

Okay. At least he called her mom.

Billy was looking at her scar. She watched his face soften, some kind of sea change.

She hesitated, unsure what was coming. What she remembered about being a teenager was the mood swings. Great mercurial changes because a boy didn't notice her, or a sunrise was particularly nice. Hormones. She was wondering how she would have felt if her mom was in prison, if someone had tried to kill her there, when he finally broke the silence.

"Trouble follows you," he said. A fact.

She put her arm around him. He leaned forward, head in his hands.

"And you?" she eventually asked.

After a minute Billy lifted his head. "It was fucked up."

She waited. When he settled back beside her, she could feel her eyes well with tears.

He looked straight ahead, out the windshield. "At the first place they locked me in the basement if I broke any of their rules. They had rules like 'No talking,' 'No excuses,' 'No eye contact.' They said if I told Sally, or if I wrote you, they'd tell her I was locked up for stealing, and I'd go to jail. The second place, it was…I dunno…it was bad. They locked me out at night if I was late. Then I had to sleep wherever. I finally ran away. In juvie I got beat up twice. One time it was pretty hard." He was working on his lip again. "And other stuff, you know."

Other stuff? Jesus. What? And what had she done? She felt a great wave of worry building. She held on, eyes closed. When it broke, Corey let it wash over her. There would be better, easier, times for these questions. "What about now?"

"In this group home, at least I can come and go as I please, so long as I do the laundry she takes in. I play on this soccer team, the Chargers, and I met all these kids from Olympic. Those kids." He pointed toward the café.

"How much do they know?"

"Not much."

Something about this was off, but it wasn't today's business. She took a cell phone from her purse and handed it to him. "I want you to have this. My cell number is programmed in." She showed him where. "They can't keep you from talking with me on the phone. Call me anytime, about anything. I'm this close…" She held her thumb and forefinger so they were almost touching. "To getting you back. Please help me with this. Pretty soon you'll be able to stay the night at the cabin."

"Thanks for the phone," he said.

"I know you don't believe me, but I'm working on it."

"Yeah."

There was a startling bang on the roof of the pickup. Metal against metal. Then another. Corey turned, and there was Lester, bringing the brass handle of his cane down on the truck roof.

"No parking, " he said, flashing some kind of badge. "Move along."

"Get the hell away from me!" she yelled through the window.

"Move along, lady." He brought the cane down again. When she opened the door and stepped out, he moved in closer. "Visiting day? Your case worker know about this? Your probation guy know?"

Lester loomed over her, a craggy colossus. His breath smelled of garlic. He wore an old-fashioned brown suit. She stood her ground, found his rheumy raisin eyes. "I'm not bothering anyone. So back off, creep."

Lester winked at Billy, as if she hadn't said a word. Then he made a pistol with his thumb and forefinger, pointing it over her shoulder at Billy's head. "Pow," he hissed, as he set his cane down on Corey's instep. She gasped, turning away.

"In my pocket?" he asked, his cheek next to hers, his skanky garlic breath in her face.

When she turned back, Billy was gone.

FOUR

EVERY SUNDAY, DR. ABE Stein's mother, Jessica "Jesse" Stein, hosted a brunch at her Capitol Hill home. Her house had been built in 1921, and architecture students from the U still came to see the stonework that bordered the steep slate roof. It sat high on the hill, on a quiet stretch of Twenty Second Street, with views of Lake Washington and the Cascades. Jesse had been a kingmaker in Democratic Party politics, locally and nationally, for twenty-odd years. In 1995, Teddy Kennedy came to brunch, and her Sunday events became a local political institution.

Sam Lin, Abe's elderly Chinese driver, eased Abe's burgundy-colored '99 Oldsmobile with the neat white trim up onto the curb across the street from Jesse's house. Sam barely slid the big Olds forward between two cars. "Frontward parallel parking," Sam explained. Sam's daughter, Lee, prepared Abe's tax returns. Three years ago Abe had told Lee that he needed a driver. Long before that, she had wanted her father to do something besides give her advice. So now Sam shared his insights with Abe. "I tell you this, buddy," he gamely offered. "In my country, there is no crime. In this country, everyone's a criminal—lawyers, politicians, stockbrokers, you name it."

"Why don't you go back?" Abe opened the car door.

Sam leaned over the front seat. "Are you crazy?"

Abe nodded, used to this, and tapped the bowl of his pipe against the curb. He stepped out of the back seat.

"Abe?" A burly man Abe recognized but couldn't name was crossing Twenty Second on his way to brunch. "You have a driver?" he asked, seeing Sam getting out of the car.

"I don't drive anymore."

"Why not?"

"I'm often preoccupied." As if to make this point, Sam took Abe's arm steering him around a pothole. "And when I'm distracted, I sideswipe parked cars."

"No kidding." The man clapped Abe on the back, then headed toward the house.

Abe followed. As he walked up the front steps, he patted down his tousled hair. For Abe, Sunday brunch was a manageable, not-too-intense way to see his mother. He came once or twice a month and stayed at least an hour. His presence was important; appearances meant a great deal to Jesse.

As he stepped down into the living room with the fourteen-foot ceiling, the walk-in fireplace, the lake and the mountain views, he checked his watch: 11:30 A.M. Okay, he would make the effort to stay until 1:00 P.M. The room was grand, yet somehow warm, even welcoming. Abe believed it was the interior woodwork. People said the walnut and mahogany were irreplaceable. There were at least thirty people today, and he recognized about a third, mostly regulars. He found his mother, talking in her up-close-and-convincing way with a former congressman and another man he didn't know. At fifty-six, his mother was still a classic Nordic beauty. Blonde hair framed a fair-skinned, blue-eyed face. It was a face men noticed—stunning and unforgiving. Jesse was tall and slender. She wore carefully chosen clothes from Milan, or Paris, or New York. She had a knack for making every touch count. He watched her move on. Jesse ruled the room—with a gesture, a word, a glance—a frosty Northwest princess who had grown into a worldy, gracious queen. She was as socially able, Abe knew, as he was maladroit. He wasn't ready to talk with her yet, so he stepped out onto the stone patio and lit his pipe.

What was on his mind was that woman, Corey Logan, who had come for an evaluation. She was angry, but she liked who she was; and she was confident—in a quiet, brave way. Not the usual prison bravado. What was so confusing was the call he'd had from her probation officer, Dick Jensen. He didn't know Jensen, but the guy had called to warn him about her...how she lied, how she fooled people...why would Jensen make that call? It was odd.

"Abraham," Jason Weiss' familiar voice interrupted his musing.

Abe turned and shook his hand warmly. Jason, a lifelong friend of his own deceased father, had been his mother's lawyer and confidant for years. Jason's suits were dark and expensively tailored. He wore a silk tie every day, and was the only Seattleite Abe knew who went every winter to Naples, Florida.

"I must have missed you last week," he offered.

"I wasn't here," Abe explained.

"My point exactly." Jason rubbed his ear lobe between thumb and forefinger. "So?"

Abe tapped the burnt ashes in his pipe into a flower pot. He knew what was coming.

"You seeing anyone?"

And then Jesse was between them, taking Abe's match hand, shushing Jason. "Abe, you owe me a call."

"What call?"

"I called you at the office."

"That's a paging service for my patients."

"Right. You've told me that."

He rubbed the back of his head. She had paged him to meet some famous artist's—was it Picasso's?—granddaughter. She meant well.

"She was lovely," Jesse noted ruefully.

And he was single, and forty-one. He looked toward the patio door. "Could you introduce me to some of your friends?" he asked, knowing she would like that.

At the door she nodded toward a fit-looking man, leaning against the walk-in stone fireplace. He was well dressed—charcoal suit, pale blue shirt, light gray on black cashmere tie—with a warm, engaging smile. "Our guest of honor," she said, "the next state attorney general, Nick Season." He had a face you would remember, Abe thought, strong and alluring. Jesse held him back to give him the low-down. "He's a crackerjack union lawyer— Boeing machinists, police guilds, restaurant workers, you name it.

Represents firefighters all over the state." She leaned in. When it came to presenting a candidate, she had perfect pitch. "He's got moxie, too. The man encouraged more than one firefighter's local to take women recruits."

As she detailed where Nick was going, he drifted. She took his arm.

"And he delivered union support to gay candidates when it counted. He plays hardball, but people like him because he sees both sides. And he's a little bit unconventional..." She squeezed his arm. "Like you. Look how his hair's a little long in the back."

Abe noticed that it was maybe a quarter inch longer than it ought to be. But this guy was not like him. No, this man was charismatic. Women wanted him, men admired him, and he knew it.

"The woman he's talking to, Fran Lipsom, is a publicist I brought up from L.A.," Jesse added. Then she moved him forward.

At the fireplace, Nick was patiently explaining to Fran, the publicist: "Seattle isn't Chicago, not even Baltimore. We sail, we chop wood when we're upset, a 'machine' is something we wash laundry with."

Fran shot Jesse a look Abe recognized—she could sell this guy, easy.

Jesse stepped closer. She whispered something in Fran's ear. They laughed together. Nick was already answering a local politician's question. Jesse and Fran listened in, plainly liking what they heard.

Abe turned away and tried to find a familiar face. Jesse stepped closer to Nick and steered him by the elbow toward Abe. "Abe," she called to him before he could get away.

Abe turned back. The candidate was smiling at him. "I'd like you to meet Nick Season," Jesse said to Abe. Then to Nick, "This is my son, Abe."

Nick extended his hand. Abe shook it. "I've heard good things about your work," Nick said.

"Don't believe anything my mother tells you," Abe joked. He realized too late he had been graceless.

"Your mother is innocent." Nick laid a hand on Abe's shoulder. "Actually, I heard about you from Detective Lou Ballard."

This guy did his homework, he had to say. Lou was a friend of his, and Nick had turned his gaff into a connection between them.

"You know Lou?"

"Worked with him when I was in the county prosecutors office. None better."

He was right about that, though Lou was unpopular. "I agree."

"Call me. Let's have coffee," Nick offered.

"I have to warn you, I'm a bona fide political liability. Honestly, I'm always saying the wrong thing. I'm afraid there's not much I could help you with."

"Let me be the judge of that." Nick smiled, shook Abe's hand again. "Think about it."

"Fair enough. Best of luck to you." Abe turned toward the patio. Nick Season had made a good first impression, no mean feat for a politician.

———

NICK WATCHED ABE SLOWLY lumbering across the living room. The big guy didn't like it here; you could see it in his expression, the way he moved. He was looking outside and fumbling around in his pocket for something. There it was. A pipe? He sensed Jesse drawing closer. Together, they watched him go out to the patio. "You must be proud," Nick said to her.

"I am," she replied, but only after thinking about it.

Nick glanced over at Fran. She wore a gray pinstripe pantsuit, like a businessman. Nick wondered if she was gay. Why else would a smart, connected L.A. gal want to work a campaign in Seattle?

Nick took Jesse's elbow. "That publicist you found, Fran, she's good." He watched Abe, outside now, looking around. "No, she's perfect. Thank you," he said to Jesse, eyes still on Abe. Nick saw smoke pluming from a trash can on the patio. He had to smile. The doofus had tossed his match into the trash and started a fire.

———

"CAN YOU IMAGINE WHAT it's been like for him? He's been on his own—in foster homes where they didn't want him, in juvie—for two years. He's gone to three different schools."

Abe sat behind his dark oak table listening to Corey talk about her son. It was Monday morning, and she was his first appointment. The brown leather chair was kitty corner from his desk chair, and she had grown confident enough to look at him. He saw how her blue-gray eyes brightened when she talked about Billy.

"The judge had no right to do that," she added.

"Was there another choice?"

"My friend Jamie."

"And?"

"She did time. For little stuff, years ago. She's a good friend and a good person, though. She took care of my boat. Billy wanted to live with her." She put a knuckle in her mouth. "He had a better chance with her."

"The judge had no choice."

"That's stupid."

He waited but she was done. "Perhaps," he said. The way she said it, though, he would bet she was right. "Tell me how it was to see Billy."

"About the best day of my life so far."

"Was he okay?"

"He's healthy, if that's what you mean. But no, he's not okay. Have you been listening to what I've been saying?" There was an edge to her voice.

"You're quick to anger."

"I guess."

"Why?" he asked.

"Wouldn't you be, too, if they framed you, took your child, then made you go to some guy who doesn't know you at all to decide if you're fit to be your own son's mother?"

He looked at her. "If I was framed, I'd be angry, and I'd tell someone what happened."

"I don't know what happened."

Abe made a note. If they framed her, why didn't she have any idea who? Or why? Why did she plead guilty? And if she was lying about that, was she lying about other things? He went back over the call from Dick Jensen, her PO. Jensen was mistaken. She wasn't a pathological liar, he was sure of that. Suppose she wasn't lying, just not saying? She's an evaluee, not a patient, he reminded himself. His job now was to confirm that she was a fit mother—she certainly seemed to be—then help her with her son. He looked up from his desk. "What did Billy say that makes you think he's not okay?"

"He said 'trouble follows you'." She pointed at herself. "And what must it be like for him when my trouble turns his life into a nightmare? Excuse me, but that's what happened."

"You're too hard on yourself."

"How can you know that?" she asked.

"It's an opinion, not a fact."

"I know what happened to Billy. And you don't know anything about it."

"Okay," he said. "Why are you angry now?"

"That's not anger, that's frustration or something."

"What's frustrating you?"

"You sure you want to hear this?"

"I'm sure."

She hesitated. "I dunno."

"Off the record then."

"The truth?"

"Please."

"Okay." She sat up straight. "You really don't know anything about Billy and me, or we would have been done here long ago."

"Why's that?"

"Because I'm a really good mom to him. The best thing for both of us is to be together. Anyone who knows us would see that. There it is. I know I shouldn't be saying it. But it's true."

Abe laughed out loud. "You could have saved us a lot of time."

"Not likely. From what I've seen, you guys bet on the tortoise not the hare."

"We do, don't we?"

She found his eyes. "You aren't mad I said it, or anything?"

"No." Her anger, he could see, was not directed toward her child. "I think you're a fit mother, Corey. I'll try to help you get your son back."

"That's good. That's great." Her smile, when it finally came, was open and warm. "Thank you."

FIVE

W HEN HE FIRST CAME to Seattle, Nick worked summers bussing tables at the Parthenon, his abusive great uncle's hole-in-the-wall Greek restaurant. It wasn't much, wedged between a sex shop and a used clothing store, but that first summer he was eleven, and it was all his so-called family had. The only good thing he remembered about the Parthenon was the fish soup. Every morning Uncle Nikos would send old Herminia, a deaf Greek peasant woman, to scour the market for fresh fish, produce, even spices. Before the restaurant opened for lunch, she'd have the soup pot simmering, ingredients coming together just so to create that wonderful smell that drew people from the street. Nick loved that smell and he had loved that soup. It was about the only thing in his loathsome great uncle's restaurant that Nick didn't hate. What he had learned, his first summer, was that just when Herminia's soup was simmering...just when the broth was rich, the fish tender, and the smell perfect...just when Nikos sat back with his morning ouzo, that's exactly when some pissed-off waiter, or an ungrateful dishwasher who couldn't even speak English, snuck over and spit in the soup pot. He had seen it done, and he had learned vigilance.

Nick was looking out the office window. He would announce his candidacy soon. Jesse Stein was going to manage his campaign, which was perfect. He could help her, state-wide. He could get out the voters in Yakima, Spokane, Port Angeles, wherever there were organized workers. And outside Seattle, the Democrats needed whatever help they could get. Then, after he won state attorney general—an accomplishment for a political newcomer—Jesse could introduce him nationally. A.G. was a sweet spot to take off from. High profile. You went after the bad guys, and you never had to cut anyone's budget. He planned to give Jesse Stein custom treatment—full focus—the kind of careful attention he lavished on his most important projects, or problems. She was perfectly positioned to help him. And if he delivered, she could give as good as she got. Maybe better. The woman had looks, brains, and clout, nationwide. She had been on top of his short list, and he had set it up carefully.

Now his campaign machine was up and running, ahead of schedule. The right people were saying the right things. His soup was simmering, just the way he liked it. But every time he tried to unwind, clear his mind, there she was—Corey Logan—spitting a nasty batch of phlegm right into the boiling broth.

He buzzed Lester. He would know where they stood with her.

Not that Corey could prove anything...and now, she'd had a taste of what could happen, and she had kept her mouth shut so far...but...but—whenever he looked over his shoulder—there she was, a scorpion with her venomous tail in the air. No! No, you can't have that! Not while you run for state attorney general. No, sir.

He heard Lester's cane in the hallway. When he first met him, twenty-one years ago, Les was an L.A. deadbeat with a bamboo cane. Nick, an undercover cop with an eye for the jugular, had caught the so-called deadbeat brokering a nine million dollar deal between South American businessmen and Iraq, trading U.S.-made bomb fuses for oil. Lester was a method-of-payment specialist, an expert in rough diamonds. He gave him a choice: ten to thirty in prison—or a quarter of, say, fifteen million dollars in diamonds. Then he bought him a new cane and a nice suit he never wore. Soon after, Lester told him about his epiphany—Nick was going to be king of something. Lester had been his right hand ever since. Nick swiveled in his chair, knowing Lester would get right to it.

"We own her PO," Lester got right to it. "Riley held his feet to the fire. The guy—"

Nick raised a palm. He didn't want to know. Riley, a short guy, could go too far. "So where are we?"

"Her PO has a past. Now, he's like a good guard dog. He'll bite her, we tell him to."

Nick didn't say anything.

"Her kid's pushing dope. He buys from an older kid in his foster home, Big Jimmy Raiser. We can lever that any way we want."

He glanced out his window.

"I saw her. Planted a seed. Told her you wanted her to work for me or disappear. My idea is we make her run, then tell the corrections guy to reel her in, send her back to prison. Two-time loser. No one listens. Whatever she says."

Lester rarely saw the easy way, especially if it meant being helpful. He didn't care; he didn't need Lester for that.

Lester handed him a file. "Here's the detail, who she sees, what she does. I got two people on it, and every now and then I touch her myself."

Touch her? He could only imagine. Lester had a gift for intimidation. He perused the file. Yes, Lester was hitting his marks just so. Something caught his eye…a name he recognized—Abe Stein. The guy was doing her psychiatric evaluation. Abe Stein?

Abe Stein. Dammit. Jesse's son. Clumsy, awkward guy looked like he couldn't do anything. Still. Bad luck? Coincidence? He loathed coincidence. Nick could feel his forehead heating up.

Lester was standing there, cloudy eyes unfocused. Nick watched Lester and stewed. Two, three minutes, easy. Lester's face gave away nothing.

"Les," he eventually said. He rarely called him that. "We've got a problem. We're going another way on this. I think you'll like it."

———

IN THE ALLEY BEHIND Billy's foster home, there was an abandoned shed where Big Jimmy hid his stash. The shed's rotted-out back wall sat against the alley, and under the corner Big Jimmy had dug a deep hole, set a wood plank over it, then covered it with dirt and rocks. In the hole Big J kept a green plastic garbage bag with one ounce baggies of marijuana inside. Billy would arrange to meet him in the shed to buy his weed. Jimmy was big—maybe 230 pounds—

and old, almost eighteen. He had lived in the foster home forever. Billy was sure their foster mother made him pay rent, or maybe she got a cut from Big Jimmy's deals. Same difference.

Every week Big Jimmy would replenish his stash, usually Purple Kush or Blueberry. Sometimes he had BC Bud, down from Canada. Billy never knew where Big J got his dope. He just knew that one day, maybe three weeks after he moved in, Jimmy had given him an eighth of an ounce to sell. After Billy sold it, he came back for more. Since joining the Chargers, he bought a one-ounce baggie every week.

Billy could buy one ounce for $250. He would divide that ounce into eight smaller eighth-of-an-ounce baggies that he could sell for $50 each, or $400 for that same ounce. At the Blue City he was such a reliable provider that his new friends fronted him enough for an ounce every Friday. He only did business, though, with Morgan or Dave. That was his rule. They would buy for the whole crowd: five baggies every Friday; three more baggies on Monday. They never even asked about his cost. Four hundred dollars a week was no money for this crew. He had seen Morgan buy a dress at Betsy Johnson for $495.

It was a sweet set-up. He was sure he could sell more but he didn't want to. He didn't want to be a drug dealer. What he was doing was helping his friends get high. And making enough money to keep up with them.

On Fridays, the Chargers practiced from 3:00 P.M. to 5:00 P.M., so he and the other guys didn't begin arriving at the Blue City until around 6:00 P.M. Tonight, Billy, Morgan, and at least ten of her friends, were going to her house to get high, eat pizza and hang out. Morgan had a great old house on Federal, and her parents were leaving at 7:00 P.M. for the weekend. When he arrived at the café, Morgan kissed him, putting her tongue in his mouth.

Billy kissed her back, glad that Morgan knew what she wanted and went for it. He was sure she had been with other guys. He'd had one girlfriend, an eighth grader who let him touch her breasts. That was it. And he'd been with an older girl one time. She made him come with her hand. It happened pretty fast. With Morgan there had been lots of kissing and touching, but it always stopped there. Still, he had bet she'd had sex, more than once, and tried things he had never done. So he let Morgan take the lead, cool, like sex was no big thing. Which was totally untrue.

"Good day?" she asked when they had finished a second kiss.

Billy liked how she was so thin and still had nice breasts, and her shoulder-length blonde hair always smelled good. At the foster home everyone had B.O. "Okay," he answered, not wanting to tell her that he had slept in a squat near the U last night. That he skipped school today. That except for his stop at the stash in the alley, he hadn't been near his foster home in two days. He had worked it out to shower at a teammate's house. He yawned. "Tired, though."

"Wake up, baby. 'Miles to go before we sleep.'" She ran her fingers along the nape of his neck.

He wanted to ask her what she meant by that, but Russ and Dave, two of the Chargers, sat down at their table. "Hey, Billy." Dave rubbed his shoulder. "You're the man."

"You coming to Morgan's?" Billy asked.

"I'm there." Dave tapped his fingers on the table, a drum roll. Under the table Billy discreetly handed him an envelope.

Dave pocketed it, high-fived Billy and moved on.

Morgan turned to Billy. "Where can we go before the party?"

He liked this idea. He also liked how Morgan always had a program, something bold. "Your house?"

"If we go to my house, my parents will make us clean up the basement for tonight. Besides, I'd like to see where you live," she said.

Billy could feel his neck tense up. "It's pretty far."

"Where?"

"Off Madison," he replied, casual.

"Madison Park?"

He stretched his long arms. "Near there, yeah."

"It's just one bus. Let's go."

He dropped his head. "My parents would creep you out."

"I bet you can handle them." His near hand was on the table. She covered it with hers.

"It's hard."

"You handle me. That's hard." Her hand moved to his thigh. "We've been together for almost a month, and I still don't know where you live. That's kind of weird."

He brushed his fingertips along the back of her hand. "Listen, Morg, my mom's kind of messed up. She can get really angry for no reason. It's like she just turns on you. I don't like to bring friends around or even to talk about it. It makes me, I dunno…it freaks me out."

"I'm sorry, baby." She kissed him again then whispered, "at least you turned out pretty cool." Morgan looked away, pensive. When she turned back, he recognized her purposeful expression. "Let's get high before the party," she announced, plainly pleased with her new agenda. "I bet we can use someone's car."

Relieved, Billy lightly kissed the back of her neck, a thing she liked. He was still tense, though. He would have to figure out a better story. Something that was at least part true. He didn't like to lie about his mom.

———

Corey hit redial on her cell phone, trying Billy again. She was sitting at her worn plank table, facing the fire. Her diary lay open in front of her. She had been writing about Billy, wondering where he was. She wanted to tell him their good news, how Dr. Stein was going to help. She left another message, her third of the day. Okay, she had to put him out of her mind. Corey began writing again, whatever came to mind:

I think I like Dr. Stein. He's not like anyone I ever met. He doesn't care how he looks or seems to be to other people. It's as though all he cares about is getting things right in his mind. When he's distracted, I think it's because he's working on some idea. But sometimes he just fades out, as if he's been alone too long, lost in the woods or something. I wonder why he doesn't put that big mind of his to work on that? I wish I could tell him what really happened. I'd like to see the look on his face then.
I have to be careful. Nick Season is out there, stalking. He's looking to strike again. I know we're in danger, though I don't know why. When I see Billy this week, we have to face this thing. I don't think I can wait until Wednesday. Why doesn't he answer the phone?

———

Billy and Morgan sat in Mary's car, smoking a joint. Mary was in the tenth grade, a total outcast. She and another outcast friend were regulars at the Blue City Café. They had wooden plugs in their noses, wore black clothes, liked punk music, and kept to themselves. Mary didn't hang out with the younger kids, but, for a joint, she would let them get stoned in her car. On Fridays she parked it at the Olympic Academy, in the empty lot behind the new gym, where no one would bother them.

When they'd finished the joint, Morgan kissed him again, a long leisurely kind-of-stoned kiss. He liked how, even after smoking a joint, her mouth still tasted fresh and minty, like candy. He put his hand on her breast, tentative, and she leaned into him. He put his other hand between her legs, his thumb just touching her panties. Billy wasn't sure what to do next; this was about as far as they had gone. He thought a lot about doing more. He had even stopped at Toys in Babeland, a hip sex shop on Pike Street, looking for ideas. Most of their ideas weirded him out.

So he wasn't ready at all when Morgan unzipped his pants then took his very hard penis in her hand. "Nice," she whispered. And just like that, she had it in her mouth. All of it. It felt unbelievably good. So good, Billy wondered if it was really happening to him. He opened his eyes. Uh-huh, yeah, it was.

SIX

COREY LOGAN. THE WOMAN was like some kind of obscure offshore virus, an incorrigible, possibly lethal infection. And now she was moving freely, zigzagging dangerously close to a sensitive, sterilized zone. Nick ran his thumb down the back of his lustrous black hair. It hung a quarter inch over his collar, a nod to another time. He touched it when he worried.

As a child, Nikos Sisinis was bold as a lion. On the streets of Athens he was a champion, a king. His father, an audacious con man, said his son had the "gift." That is to say, at the farmers market or in the lobby of the Royal Olympic Hotel, Nikos didn't miss a thing. In the alleyways the touts whispered that the kid was even smarter than his dad, who could multiply six numbers by six numbers in his head. For this boy, all things seemed possible.

Nikos' mother, a gypsy, died when he was seven. Four years later his father was killed, and eleven year old Nikos was sent to live with his father's uncle, the Sisinis family patriarch, in Seattle. Uncle Antoniou owned a Greek restaurant on a seedy stretch of Second Avenue. Antoniou "Tony" Sisinis was a scrawny guy with fish breath. And Uncle Tony hated gypsies, especially half-breeds. He had no use for wide-eyed young Nikos except for base unpaid labor and for sex. The youngster slept on a cot in the basement dreading his great uncle's footfalls on the stairs. The young lion understood that his vile great uncle was what he had, his prospective adoptive parent, his sole connection to this new place. And he had to learn English, become a U.S. citizen. He would put Uncle "Tony" out of his mind, bide his time. He could do that.

Before he turned thirteen, Nikos Sisinis was having feelings he didn't understand and couldn't control. At thirteen, he put a lug wrench through the windshield of his great uncle's prized possession, a '59 Mustang—three times—before admitting to himself that he had developed a weakness, an embarrassing, emasculating flaw. His weakness—his Achilles heel, as he saw it—took the form of unexpected, crippling anxiety attacks. And they were happening more often. Blindsiding him—a worrisome problem suddenly escalating to paralyzing anxiety. And when the anxiety came on, he was useless. Undone. Nikos, the ferocious Greek bull, morphed—in a heartbeat—to pissant pantywaist, raging lion to plaintive pussy, worrying obsessively about what could go wrong, playing and replaying endless bad outcomes in his mind. The thing was, to get where he was going—and he had his eye on real money, the big con—there would always be things to worry about. He had to take risks, he knew that much. So worrying about it was a curse. Here he was, Ares, the fucking God of war, unmanned.

Surveying his uncle's mangled Mustang, Nikos knew he had to fix this right away, or one day soon he would do something weird. That night, he waited for Uncle Antoniou to close the restaurant. Even then he knew to be discreet and assiduous. No one ever found Antoniou Sisinis. Nikos' times of unrelenting anxiety came less often, but they still came.

For the next three years he lived with his second cousins, marking time. He went to school and worked at the restaurant at night, waiting for his unmanly episodes to finally end. It was the end of the sixties, a con artist's candy store, and, for Nikos, proof positive that this was the land of opportunity. At seventeen, he was tired of waiting. Nikos ran away to L.A. where he changed his name to Nick Season. He finished high school then community college. For money, he went with older women. During these years he began to carefully manage one worry at a time. For the popular young gigolo, it was a revelation—if he removed a worrisome problem, took it off the table, one of his episodes was that much less likely.

———

AT TWENTY-THREE, NICK PASSED the LAPD tests and became a Los Angeles police officer. In time he was working undercover. He liked this work, and he was good at it. The way he put it to himself, he was a bad guy pretending to be a good guy pretending to be a bad guy. As he charted a course through the LAPD, he perfected his worry-managing skills. The key, he was learning, was to rend the worry from his life. Cut it out root and branch.

As Nick successfully managed his worries, he gradually regained his childhood poise and confidence. With time and practice, he was able to present himself as he wanted to be seen. The persona he artfully assembled was thoughtful and sincere. Above all, he shrewdly exploited his "gift." He worked to see what others actually wanted, and whenever possible, he gave it to them. By the time he turned thirty, he was well liked and a backstairs political influence inside the LAPD. At night, he went to law school. At thirty-four, Nick sold the Russian diamonds for fifteen million dollars. He was ready to return to Seattle.

Back in Seattle, Nick made detective. He finished law school, where his ruthless edge was honed razor sharp. Privately managing his most worrisome problems became easier for him at forty in the King County prosecutor's office, and, finally, routine at his high-profile Seattle practice of union-side labor law. When a thorny problem with his cousin Al was quickly resolved, fifty two year old Nick was reminded that it paid to eliminate a worry early on.

Nick ran his thumb down the back of his razor-cut hair, still worrying about Corey Logan.

———

COREY WAS DRINKING COFFEE at the plank table in front of her hearth, distracted. All weekend she'd had no call back from Billy. Her phone startled her.

"Corey?"

It was Sally, their CPS caseworker. Monday morning, 8:00 A.M. This couldn't be good. "What's up?"

"Billy's run off again. I got the message when I came in. He has been gone three nights. Do you know where he is?"

"No idea." Her trepidation was rising relentlessly, an incoming tide. "I was hoping to see him with you Wednesday, like you said."

"Can you find him?"

"I can try." She closed her eyes.

"Call me, anytime." She gave Corey a home number. "One more thing, I got a message to call your PO, Dick Jensen. You know what that's about?"

"No."

"You okay there?"

"No problems I know of." What was happening?

"Good. Find Billy. It's important."

"I'll call you." She broke the connection, tense.

Corey put down her coffee mug and hurried into her jacket. It would be windy on the ferry deck. She tried his cell phone again. Maybe he had turned it off or thrown it away. Near the sink, she found two Pepcid for her churning stomach.

She was zipping up her windbreaker when the picture window behind her exploded into her living room. She threw herself face down on the floor amid shards of broken glass. When she looked up, she saw Lester leaning through her broken window. The lizard bastard had smashed it with the heavy brass handle of his cane.

"Cat got your tongue?" he asked. When she didn't answer him, he offered, "goddamned cat must have gone right through your cheap, plate-glass window." Lester made a throaty sound, then he went around and opened the front door. Once inside, he took oversized photos from a large manila envelope and set them on her table. She rose warily to one knee, carefully sweeping aside broken glass. "Your kid's fucked," he said, oblivious to her glare.

She stood warily, eyeing this maniac as she slowly walked toward the table. On her table he had spread out pictures of Billy: with an older boy at his stash; with a baggie; dividing it up; putting the smaller baggies in envelopes; Billy and his girlfriend smoking a joint in a car; Billy and his friends getting stoned in some backyard.

She stared at the pictures: one, then another. She went for them.

The brass handle of the cane almost took her fingers off.

Corey faced him. "Are you crazy?" When he didn't respond, she added, "Why in hell are you here?"

"Off the radar screen."

"I am off the radar screen."

"Out of the country. Tomorrow."

What? "Out of the country?"

Lester tapped his cane on the floor, impatient.

"And if I don't?"

"Billy does his time. Felony drug time. Runs in your sorry family."

They knew just what button to push to make her jump out of her skin. "If you ever do that, I'll tell about you and Nick—"

"If you told your lies—" Lester stepped closer, and she felt the cane, hard, against the back of her knees. She buckled, stifling a scream. "If you ever did that—" He looked down at her. His watery eyes were dead. "First, we would explain that you were a pathological liar. A lying convicted felon with no evidence." He leaned in, looming over her. "Then, sometime later—maybe a week, maybe a year—Billy would become invisible, like his dad."

She was underwater. No, it was a black viscous liquid, like oil. Corey closed her eyes until she could breathe again. Then she stood, facing him. "Why are you doing this to us now? Why can't you just leave us alone? I keep to myself. I haven't said word one."

"You're a thorn." He stepped closer, his breath warm on her face. "If you're gone, I can pretend you're dead."

Okay, Lester was a troll who liked swinging cats around by their tails. But Nick had sent him here. Was Nick just trying to frighten her? "You think you can threaten me anytime, and I'll just do whatever you say?"

"Yeah, I think that."

She let it go. This was scaring her. "What about Billy?"

"He's the carrot and the stick. If you follow the program then he follows you. When I'm satisfied. Say a month from now. That's lucky seven for a whipped bitch like you."

Corey closed her eyes, then opened them. "And if he won't go?"

Lester made his churlish throaty sound. "We want him to go, he goes."

What had she done? Why was this happening? All she could think to do was find Billy. "Before I leave, I have to see him."

Lester wrote an address on the back of a picture, then handed it to her. "Nick's got a guy at the county prosecutor's office." He had her full attention. "If you're not gone tonight," he waved a gloved hand over the photos, "Billy's arrested before noon. At school." Lester's lips turned up, let's drown the cat. "One more thing. Dick Jensen is expecting you this morning at 10:00 A.M. He's heard you have consorted with known offenders. He's heard you left the jurisdiction without permission. He says you missed a meeting. He asked me if you have a firearm. I said I'd let him know. These are all violations."

As always, Lester had saved the worst for last. He was telling her he owned her probation officer, and Jensen could send her back to jail. Jensen had surely called Sally to say that she wasn't complying with the terms of her release. She wanted to scratch out Lester's watery, raisin eyes. When she didn't, Corey felt the blackness coming on. She fought back. "Goddamn you," she hissed. "You're—"

He ignored her. "Like I said, this is a sweet deal for you. You get to be with your son. If it was up to me, I'd see the both of you back in jail." Lester buttoned his threadbare suit and muttered, mostly to himself. "Up to me, I'd unleash the fucking dogs of war."

———

HER PROBATION OFFICER HAD a desk in a corner office. Corey waited on a chair in the hall. She watched him talking on the phone. Dick Jensen was at least sixty and round-faced. Even on the phone he had these ways of asserting himself when he didn't need to.

She was surprised when he came out of his office and motioned her to follow him. It was a little two-fingered summons. "Where'd you park?" he asked over his shoulder.

"The lot in back."

They went down the stairs to the parking lot. "Which is your car?"

She pointed out the black pickup.

"Keys?" He held out his hand.

"Why?"

"Vehicle search."

"Fine." She set the keys in his palm and watched him open her truck.

He checked the back, under the seats, then the glove compartment. She was right there, making sure he didn't plant anything. That's when she saw him pull an ID card she had never seen from her glove compartment. He hadn't put it there either. No, damnit, Lester had. This morning. Jensen showed it to her. It had her picture, but the name was Marsha Dunston. She didn't recognize the address.

"Where'd you get this?" he asked.

She was trying to stay calm. False ID was a violation of the terms of her probation. "I've never seen this in my life. Never."

"Be careful what you say. You're in enough trouble already."

"What trouble?"

"You missed a meeting." He opened his pocket calendar to show her an apparent appointment, circled in red.

"How did they get to you?" she asked.

"I beg your pardon, lady?"

"Lester Burell planted that fake ID. You know him? Big guy with a cane. And I didn't know anything about any meeting." She sighed. This wasn't working. His face was getting red. "Just get it over with."

"No problem. You're not complying with the terms of your probation." He turned and gave her another two-fingered summons, then walked back toward his corner office.

ABE HAD BEEN TREATING Nan Larsen, a real estate agent, for almost a year. She suffered from obsessive-compulsive disorder, which often made her irritable. Today, she was carrying a large bag. She opened it and proudly took out a vanity license plate. It said NOMODOE. Abe was listening to her slowly say "no more dough" when there was a knock on his office door. His brow furrowed as the office door swung open and Corey Logan marched in.

"I need your help," she said. "With Billy." And who was this woman? And what was that? A fucking license plate? "Right away."

"What?"

"They're setting me up," Corey explained. "They're saying I violated the terms of my probation."

"Who is this?" Nan asked. "This is my hour."

Corey shot her a look.

Dr. Stein stood up and started talking, kind of formal. "I'm with a patient now." He looked at his calendar. "Can this wait until one o'clock?"

She checked her watch—11:30 A.M. Was he kidding? She had to find Billy and leave tonight. "NOMODOE can wait until one. I'm not going back to jail."

"I'm sorry," he said. "Could you please wait twenty minutes, or come back later? I can see you for five minutes at eleven fifty or for fifty minutes at one."

She didn't know this person. "This was a bad idea," Corey said, and she walked out the door.

———

In the hallway Corey closed her eyes. Her head was spinning. She was lucky, she decided, that he was busy. What was she thinking? That he would help her? All she wanted was for him to be there if Billy got in trouble. Maybe talk with him. She had made up her mind. She had to leave Seattle. Jensen was under Nick's thumb, and he could send her back to jail. With the false ID, an apparent missed appointment, her so-called "attitude problems," and whatever else Lester would provide him, it was more than enough. Jensen had told her to come in again in two days. If she was still here, he would cut her off at the knees.

She would find Billy this afternoon, explain what she had to do. And what he had to do. They would stay in touch by phone. She didn't think Nick would bother him, and in a month they would be together. Billy would hate the idea of leaving, she knew that. Still, she had to give him the bad news today—whenever, wherever, she found him. Damn. She had lost half an hour coming here. And how had she been so wrong about Dr. Stein? She thought he liked her or at least wanted to help her. So why wasn't he there for her the one time he could really help?

She walked out of the waiting room and down the stairs. How could a guy face that sweet-and-sour smell every working day? Corey went out the front door, steaming. At the pet store she stopped to look at this great big turtle in the window, wondering how she had ever become so stupid about men.

———

ABE SHOWED NAN OUT at 11:50 A.M. Over time he had been able to help her be more comfortable with who she was. Days like today he caught himself wondering if that was a good thing. Abe grumbled, a gravelly sound, trying to clear his head. He had handled Corey Logan badly. He knew that, but Nan was a patient, and her needs had to be respected too. The problem was that Corey didn't understand how a therapist worked, how at certain times he had to be distant, neutral. When she came back, he would explain how awkward it was for him to be talking with both of them at the same time. He would explain why it was inappropriate for him to talk to her when he was with a patient. It was certainly uncomfortable for Nan.

He heard a noise in the waiting room and opened the door, hoping that Corey was there. She wasn't. What was there was a very large turtle. A note was taped to its shell. It read: "Hi, my name is NOMOHARDTIME. I can wait as long as you like." Shit.

———

THE ADDRESS LESTER HAD given her was on Federal Avenue. It was a three-story gray house with white trim and a white wrap-around porch. There was a black iron fence in front of a four-foot hedge separating the house from the street. At the gate there was an intercom. Corey wondered how Billy had ever come to be at such a fancy old home. On a school day, no less. Still, she was sure she would find him here. Lester had said she would.

The western edge of Volunteer Park backed up against the big houses on Federal. She went into the park, climbed a chain link fence, and dropped down into the landscaped backyard. There was a statue with water pouring out of its mouth into a pond with big stones, like this was Italy or France. She knew this yard. Yeah, Lester's dope-smoking photos. She crept to the back of the house, and looked through the kitchen window. Someone had left a plate in the sink. There were small daylight windows into the basement. She knelt and cupped her hands together to see inside. There he was, half-naked, asleep on an oversized couch amid soda cans, pizza boxes, and clothes strewn on the carpeted rec room floor.

The window was cracked open an inch or two, and Corey was through it in seconds. Inside, she shook Billy's bare arm. He raised his hands in front of his face: a frightened, self-protective gesture. When she let go, he rubbed his eyes.

"Why are you here?"

"We have to talk. Now."

He sat up. "I don't want to talk. I want you to leave me alone. Okay? I'm doing good. I don't want your trouble."

"You're already in it. Nothing I can do. I'm leaving tonight. On the boat. If I don't, they'll send me back to jail. And, even worse, they'll send you to jail." She threw the pictures in his lap. "What are you thinking? What are you doing?"

Billy looked at the pictures, one by one. "Who did this?"

"The same man who put me in jail, who do you think? For christsakes, who do you think is supplying your weed?"

"An older kid, at the foster house."

She shook her head. "He works for these people. They tell him what to do. They set you up. Do you see that?"

Billy fingered the pictures. "Oh man. Shit…it's because of you, isn't it?"

"Yes—" And that would haunt her. But right now it wasn't the point. "Billy, you're their best way at me, like it or not. So you have to be smart about this. What are you doing? Selling dope to rich kids? Staying at their houses?"

"You can lighten up, you know. Their houses are better than any other place I can hang out."

"I'm sorry. I really am, but right now we don't have time to work this out. Here's the deal. I'm going to get set up in Canada. You have to come join me in a month."

"And if I don't?"

"It's not up to you." She pointed at the pictures. They still scared her. "Billy, they know you're here. They gave me this address. These pictures could send you back to juvie, or worse. Don't make it any easier for them. What you have to do is go back to the foster home, work it out with Sally. I'll call you every night. Where's the cell phone?"

Billy took it from a pocket in his Chargers jacket, lying on the floor.

She waited until she had his eyes. Their problems were real. "Turn it on, okay?"

He did. "I don't want to leave here. Things are finally good for me. There's a girl I like—"

"And you're running away from your foster care, and you're not showing up at school, and you're dealing dope, and you're ignoring messages from your mom." Corey sat beside him. "I'm going to fix this. I don't know how. But I'm going to fix it." She let that sink in. "For now you have to stay clean for a month. You can still see your friends, but your dope-dealing days are over. Those pictures are a warning. These people can hurt you. Please be careful." She massaged his neck. He moved away. "Let's call Sally."

"I'll clean up. No drugs. I'll even listen to Sally. But I'm not moving to Canada. Unh-unh. I don't even want to leave Seattle."

"Billy, this is like getting cancer. I don't expect you to want any part of it." She didn't expect him to understand it either, a thing so perverse and humiliating. Corey closed her eyes, rubbed the back of her own neck. "There's no choice—you're going."

He turned away, faced the back of the couch.

She tried to imagine how it would feel to start over in Canada at fifteen, on the run. Nothing about it felt good.

Billy spoke to the back of the couch. "Jesus, mom. Why is this happening? Why? I mean, can't we do anything?"

"I don't know why it's happening now. And believe me, I don't know what else we can do." She hated her answer. Her face was drawn. "Your dad died because he underestimated what this man was capable of."

He turned around. "I don't need to know who he is, I understand that. But I need something...I dunno...something." He sat up. "Like why he hates us. Can you tell me that?"

"I can tell you what I think. A lot of it comes from your dad."
He nodded. "Okay."

"It's hard to explain. I thought about it a lot, though, at night in prison, when I couldn't sleep." She took a beat, aware that her explanation was important to him. "I know this is kind of round about, but…to start, I want you to imagine a very, very smart man. The thing is, he has no conscience. The way your dad put it—'a part's missing'. And he's totally, totally ambitious. Unstoppable. Picture some kind of rapidly evolving creature—a predator—a predator who can be one thing while he's doing another without anyone ever knowing it."

"That's too weird."

"Yes, I know" She pressed thumb and forefinger to the bridge of her nose. "But please hear me out." She lowered her hand. "You can't understand this guy in any of the normal ways. The next piece—and this is important—this man can fool anyone. On the surface he's charming, smart, fair, sincere…you can't imagine. And in some ways he is that person. But what you have to remember—always—is that when he smiles, even when he cries, he's on task, after something. He's a savage predator with a great big brain."

Billy's face was grim. "Like psycho?"

"Not exactly. He knows what's real. The thing is that no one knows what's real about him. He's very, very careful, what you'd call a control freak. I think that if you cross him, or even worry him, he hunts you down quietly…patiently."

"Which is why he has these pictures." He pushed them off the couch. "And knows all about me."

"I think so, yes."

"But why us?"

"Your dad figured out something he had done years ago. He tied this guy to a murdered Russian gangster, a gangster who had stolen millions of state-owned Russian rough diamonds. Your dad told me the bare bones of the story. To make a long story short, the same guy that's after us, he got away with millions in rough diamonds, and he got away with murder." She watched Billy stewing. She didn't blame him. "That's how he got his start, and now people believe he's this big upstanding success. He sees me as his weakness, his Achilles heel. And it makes him crazy. He can't stand that I know what he did, what he really is. He just can't stand it."

"Why didn't he kill you too?"

"He tried, in prison. I think that was part of his plan all along. Think how carefully he orchestrated everything that happened. He made it look like your dad disappeared with stolen drug money, and I was left holding the bag on a drug deal gone bad. That elaborate smoke screen doesn't work if I'm dead. No, he waited until I was in prison…waited until no one would connect my death with your dad's so-called disappearance. Only the murder-for-hire didn't work, and then I threatened to expose him if anything else happened to you or to me. I wrote down what little I knew, what I suspected, and he backed off. Until I got out, it was a stand off. Now, I don't know, something changed and I don't even know why. I don't…" Her voice trailed off.

Billy ran both hands through his long hair. "Can we go to the police?"

"With what? We have no evidence. None. Without your dad, we can't tie him to anything. And remember, he's this big shot. They'd believe him when he said I was just a crazy ex-con." She touched his arm. More than anything Corey wanted to be a mother who solved problems for her son. Instead, she kept causing them…awful problems that no fifteen year old should ever have to face…problems that left her teenaged son helpless and unable to move forward with his life…and she had saved the worst for last. "And if I ever did that, he'd find some way to hurt you."

———

ABE WAS ON HOLD for Dick Jensen.

"Jensen," a raspy voice said.

"Mr. Jensen. This is Dr. Abe Stein. You called about one of your supervisees, Corey Logan."

"Yeah. You doing the eval?"

"I am."

"So you know, she already missed a meeting with me," Jensen said. "She just didn't show."

"That doesn't sound like Corey," Abe reflected. "She's been punctual whenever we've had a meeting."

"Doctor, I found a false ID in her vehicle. I got a witness that swears she left the jurisdiction. I wouldn't be surprised…she just takes off."

"Why would she do that? She wants her boy back."

"Why? Who cares why?" Jensen asked, impatient. "Prisons are full of people who made bad decisions."

What? "She says she was framed. She says she's being set up again."

"Doc, how long you been working with felons?"

"Six, seven years."

"I been doing it more than twenty. Why is it I never get a guilty one?"

"I think you should give her a chance," Abe persisted. "She's a good mother and she wants her son back. She's motivated—"

"She stabbed someone inside with a pencil."

"Self-defense."

"Think about this," Jensen said, flat. "It's my nuts if she pencils you."

"You're wrong about this—" He heard a click. Dick Jensen was gone.

Abe dialed Corey's cell phone. He left a message to call, anytime.

———

THE BREMERTON FERRY PUSHED past the southern shore of Bainbridge Island, and the *Jenny Ann* rocked on its strong, rolling wake. Corey hardly noticed. She was below, stowing whatever she couldn't leave behind. Sally had come through. She had spoken to the foster mother at Billy's group home and organized it so that he could go back. Corey thought he would keep his cell phone on. At least she had gotten through to him; he understood that their trouble was real. Billy was, she reminded herself, a Logan, and Logans knew when to hunker down.

She would head north to the San Juan Islands, then on to the Gulf Islands in Canada. On the trip, she would have time to think—think about what to do, where to go, what to tell Billy. She had promised him that she would make things work for him. She would keep her promise, though she didn't know yet how she would do that. It would be hard to come back. Ever. If she left the country, she would be in violation of the terms of her probation. She looked for the pair of eagles that nested behind her cabin. She found the male, perched atop a fir tree overseeing their nest. Corey watched it, aware that the life she had always hoped for was fading away.

She checked her cell phone for messages, hoping for a message from Billy or Sally. No, there were two messages, though, both from the disappointing Dr. Stein. She called him back, and got his answering service, of course. "This is Corey Logan returning his calls...yes...tell him I said goodbye. I'm leaving town...yeah, tell him turtles like frozen beef hearts, the mini cubes."

Fifteen minutes later she was cruising between the fish farms, north, past Fort Ward. She would push on tonight until she was tired, not so wound up anyway. Tomorrow, she would cross the Strait of Juan de Fuca on her way to Canada. Corey opened a wheelhouse window. She wanted to feel the breeze on her face. The sea breeze and the smells of Puget Sound were things she could count on.

Her cell phone rang. She checked the incoming number, Dr. Abe Stein. She had nothing left to say. Corey let it ring.

SEVEN

"DINNER TONIGHT?" NICK ASKED Jesse. He was sitting at his desk sizing up the city's two new stadiums in the evening light. Black Safeco Field was practically airborne. The stout Seahawk Stadium would sink before it flew. *Beauty and the Beast*, he decided, in any kind of light.

"Wild Ginger," she fired back. "Eight o'clock."

"See you there." He hung up and then buzzed Lester twice. Why, he wondered, was he actually looking forward to dinner? Jesse, he realized, raised the bar, kept him on his toes. She played people like finely tuned instruments, and in her world she had perfect pitch. He was catching on, sure, but no one could make music like Jesse. And he was seeing how her world stretched from New York City to L.A. to D. C. to every damned Democrat who counted. Nick was thinking he would like to fish that big pond, too, when he heard Lester's cane.

Before he could turn around, Lester chimed in. "On her way. She'll slip into Canada at night on her boat."

"Good." Nick waited.

"I got a guy she'll check in with in Vancouver. I gave her three days to see him. Then I call Jensen, her PO, tell him she's skipped. He reports it, the door is locked. She comes back, she goes down."

This could work, Nick was thinking.

Lester went on, "Say we bust the kid. We bust the kid, what can she do?"

Nick touched his fingertips together, considering how to explain this. "In a good deal, one that works, one that lasts, all the parties walk away with something. You take away everything, there's always a risk." Even the meddlers—like environmentalists—you had to at least recognize them, give them a nod, or they'd find a way to queer your deal. He had learned that early on, and unionized workers all over the state had benefited from his understanding. He also knew that Lester liked to humiliate people, make them feel powerless. It made him good at certain things, not so good at others.

Nick watched him. He knew his answer wasn't working for Lester. Lester understood power, not relationships. Lester had no interest in relationships. "What do we gain?" he asked, patient.

"We own her. She knows it."

She knows it already, Nick wanted to say. Instead, he watched Lester's impassive face. If he told him to, Lester would walk right through that window. He deserved an answer he could work with. "Look at it this way...we bust the kid, he does hard time. She won't just let that happen. No, she'll come back at us. Somehow, somewhere, wanting to trade for her son. And the woman is no fool. The kid goes, we're done. We let her have the kid, she never bothers us again. You said as much."

In response, Lester took his cane, turned toward the door. As he was leaving, Nick heard him mutter, "Weak as water." And shaking his head..."fuckin' henhussy."

———

JESSE CHOSE ONE OF her favorite perfumes, a Bond No. 9, Eau de New York. It was insolent. Nice, she thought, for dinner with Nick. She felt a subtle stirring, both sweet and carnal. She sat down in front of her dressing room mirror. Feelings like these were uncommon for her, and she wanted to linger a moment with them. What was it about Nick? There was something intriguing behind those beautiful black eyes. It wasn't coarse, no, it was something she didn't recognize. And it touched her in a way that she barely remembered. Interesting. Jesse dabbed the Bond No. 9 on her wrist, her neck, between her breasts.

———

THE ONLY POLICE OFFICER Abe knew on a first-name basis was Detective Lou Ballard. He and Lou helped each other occasionally, though they rarely agreed on anything. Tonight he was having a drink with Lou at the Queen City Grill, a Belltown bar and restaurant. Though the neighborhood had become a trendy, singles destination, Abe still came when he could; he thought the Queen City Grill was among the most beautiful rooms in the city. Something about the dark woods, the muted colors, and the organization of the space and the light gave the busy restaurant an aura all its own, a warm, welcoming glow.

The detective slid into the dark wood booth. Lou was built like a pear. He always wore a tie, and every hair on his head stayed in place. "Doc," he offered, unenthusiastic.

Abe was nursing a single malt scotch. He wanted a favor, and he wasn't sure how to ask for it. "Thanks for coming."

"What's up?" Lou didn't like to chat. He took in the room. A habit.

"I made a mistake with a post-prison evaluee. She came to me for help, and I just wasn't there for her."

Lou ordered Grey Goose on the rocks and smiled meanly. "You want to talk about it?"

"Do people ever laugh at your smartass remarks?"

"Mostly they don't get 'em."

"What I figured." Abe went on, "I haven't been able to reach her. I talked with her PO, and he has it in for her. He actually predicted she would take off. Her message said she was leaving town. If she does that, it's the kind of violation that will put her back in prison. And make it even harder to get her son back."

"So? She knows that."

"That's just it. She's a smart, clear-thinking woman. This whole thing makes no sense."

"You sleeping with her?"

"What?"

"Fucking her. That would be a good thing, by the way."

"Of course not."

Lou shrugged. "Your life."

Abe ignored the comment. "Can you find out about Dick Jensen, her probation officer?"

"Sure, I'll ask around."

"Thank you."

Lou waited, cracked his knuckles. "You're the one supposed to be able to talk about things. What you do is choose the words—careful as you want—then go."

"Hmm," Abe grumbled, aware he'd been nailed. "Okay. Yeah. You're right. This is bothering me. As you know, I'm not very savvy about the way things work in the world." He raised a forefinger, afraid Lou would get off another wisecrack, something with "touchy-feely" in it. "I just don't like to make mistakes when people come to me for help. That's when I ought to come through. Something about this is all wrong, and I'm not sure what to do about it."

"I make mistakes all the time."

"And?"

"Don't overanalyze this. If you fucked it up, fix it."

"I'm not sure how. She's not returning my calls."

"Give me her name. I'll find her."

Abe wrote Corey Logan on a piece of paper.

"You know what I think?"

He braced himself.

"What I think is that psychiatrists always feel better when they get out of the office and do something."

"I hadn't thought of that," Abe admitted; glad to have a friend like Lou.

———

WILD GINGER, THE DOWNTOWN Asian-themed restaurant, began more modestly, across from a parking lot on Western Avenue. It was so successful that the owners expanded into this grand two-story space. Tonight Jesse and Nick sat in the high-ceilinged bar. Their table was beside a large window overlooking the street. A server unobtrusively set chicken, shrimp, and lamb satays, her preferred first course, on the table.

Jesse ignored the food, listening intently to Nick as he explained, "I liked police work. I liked L.A. I liked the action. But it wasn't a calling." Nick also liked that she was intense, focused, even when she listened. "In Greece, my dad was a union man. Way before his time. He died poor. Killed by the right-wing generals," he lied. His dad, a daredevil con man, had been shot in the face by a poorly chosen mark. Eleven-year-old Nick had been there, part of the con had come to grief. "Didn't seem right. Union-side law spoke to that."

"That's poignant. But you're affluent." She set down her satay stick, like punctuation.

"You checked?"

"Of course."

He wanted to tell her how much money he really had, watch her face then. "I'm a lucky investor."

"Don't be modest. You've built a powerful law firm, a strong financial base, and a very promising political profile."

Jesse had a look he hadn't seen before, almost vulnerable. "Nicky...may I call you that?"

And sultry. Sure of herself. Not even coy about it. Nicky? His name was Nick, from Nikos. Christ. He nodded.

"How old are you?" She eventually asked. She was looking into his eyes.

"Fifty-four." He wondered if this was some kind of test. Whatever it was, it made him wary. "May I ask?"

"Fifty-one," she shot right back.

Nick liked her style, he had to say, even when she blew smoke up his ass.

———

When his cell phone rang, Billy was sure it was his mother, but it was Morgan. He checked his watch, 8:30 P.M. He was in his room, a closet-sized area in the basement that he shared with Raul Peron, a twelve year old from Mexico with bad breath. Raul was still upstairs.

"Hey, Morg."

"I miss you. Can we get together later? Robin's got the car."

Robin was Morgan's older sister. She sometimes drove them around in their father's Lexus. "I can't. Not tonight."

"Come on, Billy. Why not?"

"My mom's been acting kind of weird. She won't let me go out."

"I'll come over there. I don't care if she's weird or not." Morgan made a kind of sexy breathing sound. "You won't be sorry."

"Jeez, Morg, I really want you to come, but it's not going to work tonight." He could hear Raul coming down the basement stairs. Someone was with him. He heard her voice—it was Jackie and she had her baby. She was harder to control than Raul.

"Who you talking to?" Jackie asked him after the door opened. Billy turned his back to them, trying to finish his call.

"Who's that?" Morgan asked. "Your mom?"

Raul was holding the baby. The baby started crying.

"Whose baby is that? Where are you?"

The baby was wailing now. Jackie was cooing to him.

"Got to go. I'll explain later." Billy clicked off the phone.

———

THE *JENNY ANN* WAS anchored in an island cove just south of Port Townsend. Corey sat on a canvas chair on her covered back deck. A single lamp hung overhead. Her diary was open on the table in front of her. She had been writing for a long time, trying to sort out these horrible days. She reread what she'd just written:

Why is this happening? I haven't even said the name Nick Season to anyone. I don't understand what's going on. What is Billy going to do in Canada? Start over, I guess, like I will. I have to find a job. How will I get papers? I'm a convicted felon who's violated the terms of her probation. I can't ever go back, not even sneak in for a weekend. What if Billy won't come?

Corey closed her eyes. This was going to be even harder than she had imagined. She thought of her own mother, holding off lethal, metastasizing cancer, working out a plan with her daughter to finish high school. That was hard. She wondered what her mom would have done now, in her shoes.

WHEN ABE CHECKED IN with his service after his 9:00 A.M. appointment, there was a message from Lou Ballard. He called him right back. He hadn't slept well, painfully aware that he had defined his job narrowly, safely, and missed the important thing: when this woman asked for help, she really needed it.

"Lou Ballard," the cop said, interrupting his thoughts.

"Abe Stein—"

"I had a man on Bainbridge check her house, talk with the neighbors. She has a boat, an old Chris-Craft cruiser. She took it out yesterday evening and she hasn't come back. I got the info on contacting her aboard the vessel. You got a pencil?"

Abe took down Lou's instructions for reaching her via the marine operator on VHF channel 16, the "hailing and calling" frequency. When he started asking questions, Lou said that if he met him at the SPD Harbor Patrol dock, he'd call the marine operator himself. When Corey responded, the operator could set up another channel for Abe to talk with her. He gave him directions. "When do you want to come?" Lou asked.

"I'll be there in ten minutes."

———

COREY WAS IN THE wheelhouse, sipping coffee, when she thought she heard her boat being hailed on her radio. She always monitored channel 16 when underway. It was standard operating procedure. When she heard another call for the *Jenny Ann*, she set down her coffee cup. Puzzled, Corey turned toward the radio.

"This is the *Jenny Ann*," she said over the static. The operator told her which channel to switch to for her conversation and signed off. Apprehensive, she switched to the designated frequency.

"The *Jenny Ann*," she said.

"This is Dr. Abe Stein. Please hear me out—"

"What? Why in hell are you calling me? How—"

"Corey. I made a mistake. I'm sorry. I want to help."

"Call my cell. This is being broadcast all over Puget Sound." She hung up.

Corey picked up her cell phone after the fourth ring. "There's nothing you can do. Just leave me alone."

"I'd like to meet you, talk with you. I'll come alone. Just tell me where."

"Why would I do that?"

"Because maybe I can help. At least with Billy."

She made him wait. He was right about one thing, she could use some help with Billy. At the very least, she would sleep better if he was there for Billy during the next four weeks.

Abe continued, "Let me talk with you. I won't do anything without your permission." And after a moment, "What do you have to lose?"

She was already weighing that. "I'll call you back. Answer your office phone in half an hour." She hung up.

———

LOU BALLARD WAS LEANING against the wall tossing cigarette butts out an open window to seagulls scavenging near the dock.

"Thanks, Lou," Abe said as he hurried toward the door.

Lou turned his way. "You know what you're doing?"

"I do."

"You want my advice?"

"Absolutely not," Abe called out over his shoulder.

———

ABE PICKED UP THE phone on the first ring. "Hello."

"I'll see you at the ferry terminal in Friday Harbor. Tomorrow."

"Friday Harbor? That's in the San Juan Islands."

"Uh-huh. Take the two-forty ferry."

"I have patients tomorrow."

"Are you coming or not?" Corey asked.

"Okay. Yes. I'll work it out. I'll be there."

"Can I trust you to come alone?"

"You can."

"And can you keep our meeting a secret?"

"Yes," he assured her.

"Drive off the ferry. Wait in the parking lot. I'll find you."

"Okay." He thought about telling her that he couldn't drive, that the judge had forbidden it. Too complicated. He would have Sam take him to the ferry terminal, then take his chances on the island.

"You feed the turtle?" she asked.

"No, I gave it back."

"Gave it back?" then louder, "Gave it back?"

Abe pictured her cracking that little smile.

———

BY SUNDOWN, THE JENNY *Ann* was anchored in a protected inlet on the east side of San Juan Island. Corey had taken her reliable old boat across the Strait of Juan de Fuca without incident. She felt better too. She didn't think Dr. Stein could do anything, but if he really came, wouldn't that be something?

She was sitting on her covered back deck, trying to decide whether to go clamming or grill a steak. She thought a steak would be easier. Still, the sandy beach, the sunset, a beach fire…her cell phone rang. She checked the number of the caller. It was Billy. Good, great.

"Hey, honey, what's up?"

"Nothing much."

"Okay."

"I've been thinking."

She waited, vaguely anxious.

"Could you come back with a different name? You know, as a different person?"

Right. She knew where this was going. "Billy, I know what you're thinking. And I wish it wasn't so, but you'll have to come to Canada."

"I don't want to do that."

"I understand that. But it's dangerous—"

"I have a life, too, you know," he interrupted. "And I know how to be careful."

She felt like crying. "It's harder than that. You're not safe there. We have no choice. I'm sorry."

Billy didn't say anything.

"I've been thinking too. I'll promise you this. Once we're together, we'll work out some kind of life that's good for you."

"Like what?"

"Like whatever you want."

"Sure. You're on some wanted list and I'm going to do whatever I want. I won't even be able to use my own name. Right?"

She would have to sort out their papers. She wasn't sure yet how. They might have to change their names, though—he was right about that. At difficult times she had learned to order things. Prioritize. Put off the things that she didn't have to deal with right away. She wasn't ready to answer his question yet. "Nobody's going to care that I'm gone. Now think about this. Vancouver's a great city. Better than Seattle. I'm going to get us set up there."

"I hate Canada, the way they're always saying 'eh?'"

"After we're settled, you could call your girlfriend, invite her to dinner in Vancouver," Corey suggested. "I bet we could work that out."

"And tell her what? That we move and change our names every so often for the fun of it?"

"You might think about telling her the truth. At least about living in a foster home, about your mom having been in prison. There's nothing to be ashamed of."

"Are you kidding?"

"You haven't done anything wrong," she persisted.

"Yeah sure. Listen, I'm late. I gotta go. Bye."

She was sorry she had said that about his girlfriend. Corey punched in his number then thought better of it and turned off the phone. She didn't want to crowd him. After he joined her, they would have time to talk about this, and much more. She wondered what his girlfriend was like, whether they were happy together. He was clearly trying to do the right thing by her. She could see that Billy was trying to be a young man his girlfriend could trust, even admire. It was a picture he'd had to paint for himself. He must have worked out a great many things on his own. He'd had no choice. He wasn't coming to Canada, she realized then. Billy wasn't going to come.

Corey lowered her head into her hands.

—

IN HIS BASEMENT ROOM, Billy was curled up on his bed. He could hear the television upstairs and the baby crying. It was cold in his room, and he pulled his ratty blue blanket over his shoulder. His mom knew what was what. She always had. But she was a trouble magnet. If he stayed, maybe he would get a job. Then, when he had some more money, he could take off. Get his own place. Yeah. Maybe Morgan would front it for him. She would think it was really cool to have a cheap one-room apartment, say in the International District. He wasn't sure that would work, but he knew he didn't want to be an illegal in Canada. That would be the worst. Always worrying. Working bad jobs for no money. No friends.

There were some things he needed to figure out. Like Morgan. He wanted to see her, tell her he was out of the drug business. It was a thing he had to do face to face. See if she was still his friend.

Morgan didn't like it when things didn't go her way, and he hadn't called her since she wanted to come over. She was smart, though, and there was something between them—this energy, this heat—that was different than he had ever had with anyone. He hoped she would stay with him, especially now.

He took two slow breaths, then called her up. "Hey."

"What's up?"

He heard the edge in her voice. Yeah, she was still mad. "Can I see you later?"

"I'm kind of busy tonight."

Payback. "Uh, I'd like to talk about some things."

"Sure. That'd be good. Yeah."

"Tomorrow, after practice?"

"Okay."

He let out a little sigh of relief. "See you then."

"Bye."

Billy put on his blue crew neck sweater. It was a little musty. He tried to wash it once but that turned out bad. Okay. He checked his money. He had $250 left. He worried what he would do for money when he ran out, since he couldn't buy from Jimmy anymore. Jimmy had leaned on him a little to buy a baggie, but Billy told him he was taking a break. When he did that, Jimmy backed off like he kind of expected it.

He would have to figure out how to tell Morgan that he wasn't selling anymore weed. He worried about that. She really liked to get high. Still, whatever else he did, he knew he couldn't buy from Jimmy again…ever.

Upstairs, his foster mother, Jean, was watching television. He could hear another noise, yeah, someone was doing laundry. He pulled the blanket over his head. He didn't know what to do about his real mom. She used to be awesome. When he was little, every summer she took him up the Inside Passage in their boat, just the two of them. They saw whales and bears and caught huge salmon and found some places where he bet no one had ever been. Stuff like that was normal for them. Nothing was scary. They would stay up late at night, she would tell him stories about the Greek gods, and they would talk about Moira, the Greek idea of fate. Until fate caught up with them. His dad disappeared. Since then bad things kept happening, and she was helpless. How could he follow her when she was, like, doomed? It was as if the most powerful of the gods had decided to punish her and the people she loved. If he were on his own, maybe they would leave him alone.

EIGHT

A T THE ANACORTES FERRY terminal, Sam pulled the Olds into the orderly waiting line. Abe got out of the car and walked around to the driver's side.

Sam had the window rolled down. "I think it's better if I drive. The judge, he's not going to like this."

"I'm driving."

"That's not so smart."

Abe opened Sam's door.

"In this country," Sam muttered, "even the psychiatrists need a psychiatrist."

"I'll be back tonight. Please meet the evening ferries."

The ferry ride to Friday Harbor took just over an hour, and it gave him a chance to review Corey's file. When he was finished, he knew no more than when he had started. Why was he here? He believed in her, as maudlin as that sounded, and he didn't want her to violate the terms of her probation. If she did that, she would be a fugitive, and Corey would have to carry that weight, one way or another, forever.

WHEN SHE SAW THE burgundy Oldsmobile with the nice white trim lurching into the Friday Harbor parking lot, Corey knew immediately that Abe Stein was driving that car. She didn't know how she knew; she just knew.

She waited until the ferry had unloaded. Then she waited another twenty minutes, watching Abe stew in the big Olds. When she was satisfied that he was alone, Corey knocked on his window.

He cranked it open.

"I'd better drive," she said.

"You were watching." Abe opened the door and slid over. "I'm not much of a driver."

She let it go.

Corey parked at the wharf where the *Jenny Ann* was moored. She pointed. "How about a boat ride?"

"I don't like boats. Is this necessary?"

"Yeah." He was wearing a sweater under his tweed sport jacket and Nikes. Better.

She helped him aboard. The *Jenny Ann* was a classic, hardtop wooden yacht. She kept the brass bright and the wood lustrous. The aft deck, where they stood, was covered. A wooden ladder went down from the enclosed wheelhouse and the covered deck. She leaned down and flipped on a light switch near the ladder. "You can go below, if you'd be more comfortable." She pointed the way down. Below there was a galley with a small teak table and two little staterooms.

He walked out on the deck. "This is fine. Where are we going?"

"I have to be sure this isn't some kind of set-up."

"Why would I do that?"

"Last time I saw you, you had five minutes"—she raised all five fingers, rubbing it in—"that is, if I could wait twenty minutes." She lowered her hand, her face serious. "I'm not used to anyone going out of their way for me. So make yourself comfortable."

Then they were underway. Corey looked back. Abe was clutching a post, his knuckles were white. Some time later he came through the cabin and up into the wheelhouse, where he sat down. She explained that the San Juan Islands were 768 fragments of a dying mountain range, the northernmost tip of the lower U.S. The island she was heading for was uninhabited. She slowed, then anchored in a protected cove with a white sand beach. He was relaxing a little, she could tell. Corey was sure that he had come alone. She didn't know why he had come, though. And she was tense, unsure of what to expect.

"What's the deal with the driving?" she asked, checking her anchor.

"I haven't driven in quite a while."

"Why?"

"I'm sure you've noticed that I get distracted, preoccupied. When that happens while I'm driving, I sideswipe parked cars."

"Are you serious?"

"Yes. The judge took away my license. He said I'm accident-prone. So I have a driver."

She smiled, just barely. "You, this guy who chooses every word carefully. Accident-prone? That's kind of funny."

"Why?"

"I'm wondering what that makes me?"

"Yes. I want to talk about that. That's why I'm here."

He wasn't exactly easing into it. She wasn't ready yet. Corey lowered her inflatable dinghy into the water then let down the ladder. "Let's go ashore. You've come a long way. But I still need a little time. And I'm going to steam some clams."

She had the clams in a beat-up, blue and white speckled clam pot. She helped Abe into the dinghy, then lowered the pot down to him. After he stowed their clams, she handed down a box with the rest of their meal. Corey rowed them ashore. Her strokes were long, efficient.

Fifteen minutes later she had a beach fire going, and she was pouring from a bottle of Scotch whiskey. She had worn her favorite blue and black plaid flannel shirt carefully tucked into freshly washed jeans. She had wanted to look good, even if she felt bad. Corey had given up on putting Billy out of her mind. They sat against a sea-worn log that had drifted onto the beach long ago.

"Can we talk now?" he asked softly.

He was asking if she was ready. Being nice about it. She was as ready as she would ever be. "If you speak up a little. There's no one around."

"Fair enough." He poked at the fire with a stick.

Corey felt bad. It was a cheap shot. She was still tense.

He didn't seem offended. "I do speak softly," he explained. "And, as you already noticed, I choose my words carefully. Even as a child, I only spoke when I knew exactly what I wanted to say.

I spent a long time learning why, but I still can't do much about it."

"I don't mind," she said truthfully, relieved that he was okay about it—pleased, too, that he had explained. "Why are you here?"

"First, to apologize. It's awkward for me when you interrupt me with a patient. But I handled it badly. I should have seen you right away. At least long enough to hear you out. I'm sorry."

"Did you like the turtle?"

"No one's ever done anything like that to me before."

"Pretty good, huh?"

"Pretty good?" The corners of his mouth turned up. "Yeah."

Corey smiled back. Yeah is right. They were quiet for a minute. She was enjoying the fire, the sea breeze, the whiskey. He seemed to be unwinding too, not in a big hurry, anyway. "Go on," she eventually said.

"I'm also, as you know, clumsy and inept at many practical things." He took a sip of his whiskey. "I compensate for this by trying to avoid mistakes with my clients. In your case, I hope I'm not too late."

She sat back against the log. He was honest about himself. And outside the office he got right to the point. She wondered again how—even on some remote beach—this careful, soft-spoken guy could be so intense.

"Corey, just tell me what you can. Start at the beginning."

"Why? I already told you what I could."

"No, I didn't ask the right questions. Like why you were framed, or why you couldn't tell anyone. I just wasn't getting it."

She had to say, he was right about that. She wasn't sure, though, how to tell it. Corey watched the fire until she saw a way. "Okay. Billy's dad, Al, knew this real up-and-comer. Long before I met Al, he did some off-the-clock work for this man. Al was in the U.S. Customs Service out of Seattle. This up-and-coming guy was a cop in L.A. He paid Al to ferry someone from Seattle to Vancouver. A man Al didn't know. Said it was a divorce deal. Al breezed right through customs with this guy. Several years ago, Al recognized the man he took out of the country. His file came up on a case Al was working. Apparently, the guy was a known diamond trader. Al connected this guy to the murder and robbery of some Russian diamond thief in L.A. It happened just before he ferried him out of the country." She sipped her drink. "Al told his old friend what he suspected. He asked this man for more money. The man—a big shot now—flat out denied it, and Al backed off. Seven weeks later, Al disappeared. I believe this man had him killed. Al was no Prince Charming, but he was in love with me. And he loved Billy. He didn't take off."

"I see. Go on, please."

Abe was looking at her now. His eyes were different. She could never tell him about Nick, she knew that much. "I hope you do see," she said truthfully. "I was busted the day Al disappeared. They made it look like he double-crossed me on some dope deal. Al stole a little dope, okay. Couple of ounces, max. Maybe I should have told you more about that. But we were small-time users, that's all. Someone wanted Al dead and me in prison, where they planned to kill me too. Twenty kilos went missing from one of Al's busts. They were stolen from the evidence locker. Ten of those kilos were added to our little dope stash. They said we already sold the other ten kilos. It was a smoke screen, a way to explain away what happened to Al and put me inside."

"And you couldn't tell the police that?"

"I did. But there was nothing I could prove. And no one believed me. I mean, we did keep dope on the boat, and it did come from that same bust. For christsakes, my fingerprints were on a box of stolen kilos." She hesitated. Talking about this still upset her. "That wasn't the worst part. That wasn't why I went along."

He held her eyes. "What was the worst part?"

"I was warned that if I didn't go along, or if I told anyone who I suspected, Billy would disappear too."

Abe lowered his head. "I should have guessed that," he eventually said. "And now?"

"They've put Billy in business as a dope dealer. They have pictures. They can have him arrested anytime." She added a piece of driftwood to the fire. "There's more. They've gotten to my PO. Nothing I can prove. But he says I missed a meeting I never knew about. He found a false ID in my car. I know someone planted that ID. Hell, I haven't had a false ID since I turned twenty-one. And Jensen, my PO, claims he has a witness who saw me out of the jurisdiction. He says I have attitude problems. And so on. His laundry list of made-up violations is enough to send me back."

"I talked with Jensen. He's certainly part of the problem." Abe tapped his pipe against the driftwood log, emptying it. "Who is this man?"

"I can't tell you that. Please don't ask me again."

"Why is he doing this now?"

"I don't know."

He sipped his whiskey, working on this, then looked at her. "Okay. Two years ago this man killed Billy's father, then he set you up, sent you to jail. He threatened to kill your son if you told anyone. Now, for some reason, he wants you back in jail or out of the picture."

"I can't prove any of it. There's no way to tie him to anything."

Abe shook his big head. "And I was making ridiculous psychological explanations. What an ass. I apologize." He furrowed his bushy brow.

Corey took a moment as she set two beach rocks, just so, beside the fire. When she was satisfied, she lowered the clam pot onto her rocks. Next, she carefully laid two foil-wrapped ears of corn on the fire. When she looked up, she knew he would be waiting. "You're not fast, but you did get there." She touched his arm. "If you let me finish cooking, we can eat."

———

THE BLUE CITY CAFÉ was not crowded when Billy arrived at 6:30 P.M. It was a school night and most kids were already at home. Morgan was waiting on a couch in the far corner. It was their favorite spot to talk, just the two of them. When he sat beside her, she kissed his neck, his ear, then his mouth.

"I missed you," she said. She kissed him again. He could feel her tongue this time. "You taste good."

Her teeth were really white. She didn't seem mad anymore, but he couldn't always tell with Morgan. He put his arm around her. She would take the lead.

"What's going on? Where were you the night I wanted to come over?"

This was not what he had wanted to talk about. "At home."

"I heard a baby crying," Morgan said.

"Yeah, my niece has a new baby."

"Your niece? How can you have a niece if you don't have any brothers or sisters?"

"She's—what?—my mother's sister's daughter," he lied. "So that makes her my cousin, I guess. And what is this? The third degree?"

"I want to know what's going on. We're at a crossroads here. You know?" She put her hand on his thigh. "I like how you are with me. How you see what's going on. And then how you take charge, without being bossy." She put her mouth near his ear. "I get that and I like it," she whispered.

He couldn't have put that into words until she said it. She was right, though, about what he did. And he liked that she liked it. He kissed her, a long kiss, hoping they could talk about something else.

After, Morgan ran her tongue along his lip. "I mean I want to know you. Meet your family. Okay?"

"Yeah." She was all over this family thing, and he was running out of excuses. He didn't like lying to her, even when he had to. "It's just that my family's kind of messed up." At least that was true.

"So? What do I care?"

He had to get her on to something else, anything. "I'm not selling anymore weed," he announced.

"Shit. Where are we going to score?"

"That's up to you. But not from me."

"This sucks." She sat up straight and turned toward him. "What the hell is going on? I'm not stupid, you know. All of a sudden everything's getting weird."

Shit is right. "Do you care about the weed?"

"Dammit, do you think I'm with you because you can get dope?"

"Dave and the other guys, they wouldn't give me the time of day if I couldn't score."

"I'm not them. You're not the only one that sees what's going on. Do you think I don't know that you lie to me?"

"Like what?" he asked, tentative.

"Like everything."

90

Billy felt his neck flush with shame. She was onto him. "What do you want to know about me?" he asked.

"Let's start with where you live."

———

ABE SIPPED HIS WHISKEY, watching Corey cook. She made it look easy. He would bet that she could break down the engine in her boat. He set his drink down in the sand then closed his eyes, rubbing them with thumb and forefinger. Eventually he picked up his scotch and looked out at the water. He was still reeling, he knew, from her revelations. What a frightening, lonely story she had told. How could he help? He hoped he could convince her to come back. How could he make that possible for her? He didn't know. But he had time, still, to work on it, if she was willing. He turned and watched her put together a plate for him—steamed clams, corn, coleslaw, bread, even melted butter. After she had fixed her own plate, they began eating.

"Really good," he said after his first clam.

"My mother and I often lived on the *Jenny Ann*," she explained. "We ate a lot of clams." Her face softened. "In those days, my mom would stay up late telling me about the Greek gods and the mortal heroes—their feats, their tragedies—and then we'd count the stars. She died when I was seventeen."

He finished a forkful of slaw. "Was your mother Jenny Ann?"

"Yes. How could you know that?"

"Watching you talk about her, how could I not know that?"

Corey tapped his glass with hers. "She was wonderful. I wanted to be that kind of mother to Billy."

He had been wondering about Billy. "And how is Billy taking this?"

"It's really hard for him. I'm afraid he's given up on me." Her expression turned grave. "I can't say I blame him. I don't think he's going to come with me to Canada. I don't know if I can handle that."

"Is that dangerous for him?"

"It could be. I would guess they'll let him be so long as I'm, as they say, 'off the radar screen.' But I don't really know. I don't understand why they're pushing me so hard now. I mean, I haven't said word one. There must be a reason. So anything could set them off—a mistake, anything—and Billy could go to jail, or worse. I never know what they'll do. What I do know is that it's an awful problem for me."

"How so?"

"I can't make a life for myself without Billy," Corey explained. "I won't do it."

He watched her irritably douse her corn with melted butter. "I see," he offered.

"I was hoping you'd help, be there for him when I'm gone."

"I'd be happy to talk with him." Abe didn't think it likely that he could influence Billy though.

"What do you think?"

"Another question first."

"Do you always have to know everything before you can answer a question?"

"If I can, yes."

"Go on then," she offered.

"Why didn't they make you disappear?"

"They tried. Those women in prison." She touched her scar. "After that I wrote a letter, gave it to a friend to send to the papers and the police in the event anything happened to Billy or me. I made sure the guy who framed me knew about the letter. He doesn't know what's in it. He does know that if I'm dead, people will take it seriously. Even an accident would put this man under a magnifying glass. He won't risk that unless he has to."

"So they won't kill you?"

"Not unless they have no other choice."

"Can you tell me anything more about this man?" he asked.

"Not without putting you at risk."

"I'll take that risk."

"I won't. You have no idea what you're dealing with. And please don't ask me about him again."

Abe stayed quiet, working with what he had. Here was a strong, savvy woman who wanted one thing in the world—to be with her son. Someone had made that impossible in Seattle. She wouldn't misjudge that. How could he help her to return home?

He would have to address her fears. One by one. Construct some kind of a safety net. If she ran, she would ruin her chances with her son. He knew that much.

She waited, watching his grim face. "Okay. Time's up. What do you think?"

"You may not like it."

She poured some more whiskey, raised her glass. "Do your worst."

He took a little more, too. "I think you should go back to Seattle. I think as hard as it is, you shouldn't give up your life. In fact, you shouldn't give an inch."

"Easy for you to say." She hesitated, lips pursed, petulant. "To tell the truth, you sound like my high school track coach. We always lost. He was expert at preparing his little lambs for the slaughter."

"Maybe, but hear me out. I may be naïve about the way things work in the world—I'm certainly not the man to fix your car—but I do know a good deal about how people work. Especially about the things they give up that could make them happy. Don't give up the chance to be a mother to your son."

"Then help me convince Billy to come to Canada," she said, terse.

He looked into their beach fire then turned to her. "Corey, if you violate the conditions of your probation and go to Canada, you'll be a fugitive. It will be impossible for you or Billy to lead a normal life. And you'll never be able to go home."

"I know that. Damn it. I'm asking you to help me. I know what would help too—having Billy with me. And I know I can't go back."

She was right; so far, he wasn't helping. Seattle wasn't safe. She couldn't go back unless someone changed something for her. Abe understood now why she got so angry. "How about this? Let's take a walk. Give me time to think about what you're saying, what I might be able to do, then let's talk some more. I do want to help you, and I understand that you're the best judge of how I can do that."

She stood. "Okay. Yeah. That sounds good."

ABE AND COREY WALKED to the tip of the island: a long, comfortably silent walk. Once there, she sat on a log while he picked out a driftwood walking stick. Eventually he asked, "What will happen if you go back home?"

"If I'm around, he's going to find a way to send me back to jail."

"Do you want to be in Seattle?"

"Like molasses." She shook her head. "Of course I do. My boy wants to live there. Our home is there. Agh—"

"I'll help."

"Are you crazy?"

"I don't think so."

"What could you possibly do?"

"I want you to give me twenty-four hours." He checked his watch. "I'll call you at six-thirty tomorrow evening."

"Accident-prone guys should stay away from this kind of stuff."

"Give me a chance."

"To do what?" she asked.

"Find a way to help."

She watched him, poking at the sand with his found stick. He really did want to help her. She still wasn't sure why. His mind was so different than hers. That could be good, though. And he was right about Billy.

"How are you going to do that?" she finally asked, wary.

"I don't know."

"You could make a mess, much worse than that fire in your office."

"I'm going to give you some options. That's all. I won't do anything you don't want me to do."

Be careful, she reminded herself. Oh, so careful. "You won't do anything I don't want you to do? You'll tell me what my options are before you do anything?"

"That's right."

She studied his face. "Uh, why would you do this for me?"

"Because when you needed help, I was off somewhere. And now, you've given me a second chance."

———

BILLY LOOKED AT MORGAN'S face. She was so—what?—fresh, shiny, eager, yeah, ready to take on whatever. He touched her cheek, wondering if she could ever understand what a foster home was like. "What difference does it make where I live?"

"I won't know unless you tell me."

"And if I don't?"

"I like you a lot. Maybe it's more than like. But I can't go anywhere with this unless you tell me what's going on. You're a smart guy. You understand what I'm asking for. I mean, c'mon, I'm not just this hot rich babe who likes to get high."

He laid long fingers between her shoulder blades. "I know that."

"Do you think what I do with you is just for kicks? That I'm, like, slumming? I know lots of smart, good-looking guys. I have lots of choices. But you know why I'm with you?"

When he was low, or worried, Billy thought it was mostly the weed, or that she liked how he was street-wise, like some kind of outlaw thing. Now he wasn't sure what she was getting at. He was still surprised that she wasn't mad about the drugs. "No, I guess not."

"Because you're not like other guys I know. You listen. You get what's what. You see what's happening. That's, like, rare in a guy."

Huh. He looked at the floor.

"Am I embarrassing you?"

"No, I'm sorry. I was just thinking about what you were saying."

"'Cause there's more. I've been thinking about this. You're considerate, too, especially when we make out." She took his hand. "And you think about what I say. Even when I'm going off about some weird thing you don't know about." She turned to face him and lightly ran her fingers across the back of his hand. "You've had to do hard things. I get that. And if you lie and pretend about it, I'm sure you have your reasons. But I still want to know about you."

Billy wasn't sure what to do. Since his mom went to prison, no one had really wanted to know about him.

She kissed him again.

What she said was really good. Still, there was no way she would understand. But he didn't want to lose her. "Morg, let me think about it. Okay?"

"'Til tomorrow. That's it."

"That's fine." He wondered if he could ever find a way to talk to her about his life. The things in his life could never happen to Morgan and her friends.

"Are you in danger? At least tell me that?"

Billy looked down. Too close for comfort. And there was something in her tone that made him uneasy. "No. I gotta go."

———

AT JESSE'S DINING ROOM table, six leaders of the African-American community were drinking San Pellegrino water and listening to Nick Season respond to their concerns about insufficient civilian oversight of Seattle police officers.

He paused, making eye contact with at least three of the six men and women. "Yes, I work with police officers all over the state. And I know them to be decent, hard-working professional men and women. I propose bringing you together with the ablest police leaders I've met to assess what we do right and what we do wrong. You should also meet with representatives from the review board and the office of professional accountability. We'll go from there to forming a committee to make specific proposals. You choose your representatives. Let's discuss who you'd like to meet with and how you'd like it to work."

The meeting was winding down and Nick knew he had won them over. He understood minorities, what they wanted. And he had paid his dues. For christsakes, he had marched in the early Gay Pride parades, even though he was afraid he would get AIDS. Even though it made him crazy that people might think he was gay. And it paid off. If you helped someone when they needed help, they never forgot it.

After the meeting was over, Jesse fixed him a drink—he liked Chivas—then sat beside him on the couch that faced the lake. She was drinking white wine, taking little sips.

"Well done, Nicky."

"Thanks. You set it up just right," Nicky, again. What was that about? He let it go. The way things were going, she could call him Zorba.

"Are we ready for tomorrow?" she asked, on task.

Tomorrow was the press conference where he would announce his candidacy, a formality, but important nonetheless. "I think so."

"Good." She changed her tone. "I've been thinking about you."

"Likewise." Last night she let him know she was interested. Then she backed off. Gave him hope then made him wait. Classy moves. Wasted, perhaps, on a former gigolo. "Tell me."

"I think you could be a power in national politics."

Perfect. "Aren't you going a little fast?" Nick asked.

"You go with momentum. And you've got it. I'm going to put together a dinner in New York City. Congressmen, maybe a senator or two, some national committee members."

He put his arm behind her on the sofa back. "You're unbelievable."

"Maybe I can get Bill Clinton."

"I'd like to meet him." Clinton interested him. The guy had spit in his own soup. He touched her shoulder. "Jesse, may I say something personal?"

"Of course."

"I don't want to do or say anything that could hurt our professional relationship, but I want to tell you that I've never met anyone like you. You're unstoppable. And smart. And very beautiful." He watched her enjoy that. "I won't say anything more if you don't want me to."

After a beat, Jesse put a hand on his thigh. He kissed her gently, already thinking about how to please her. He had some ideas about that. He had made a living bringing women her age to fervor.

NINE

J ASON WEISS, JESSE'S LAWYER, took a sip of his Maker's Mark. He was sitting across from Abe in front of the fire at the Fireside Lounge in the Sorrento Hotel. Abe had called Jason from the ferry, told him it was important, then suggested they meet at Jason's favorite bar, an opulent room with floor-to-ceiling Honduras mahogany paneling.

By 11:30 P.M. Abe had told Jason much of Corey's story. He didn't tell it as her version, he told it as plain fact. He never mentioned her name. He was waiting now for Jason to respond.

Jason set down his drink. "Abe, if this story is true—if—then there's only one thing to do. Take up golf. Apply yourself. Be a world famous psychiatrist golfer. Forget this other business."

Abe tried not to grimace. Jason's sense of humor was an acquired taste. "Could you explain that, please?"

"Why do you always need an explanation? I'm your lawyer, I protect your interests."

Abe sat back. Though Jason was famously cranky, he was also, Abe knew, kind-hearted.

"Okay. Put simply, life's too short," Jason finally replied. "This type of work"—he tapped Abe's knee—"this is not for a psychiatrist."

Abe pressed on. "Could you get me an appointment with one of the supervisors in Federal Probation who might be flexible about assignments? I want to get her a new PO, someone I know."

"Abe, when you wanted to work with the less affluent people, I got you the probation referrals. Yes?" He raised his silver eyebrows.

"No problem. This is different. Stay away from this. You're a doctor, a healer. Dealing with murderers is not what you think. It's not what you do. Listen to me, I know about this. This is not for you."

Abe knew Jason. He persisted, "I'd like to see him at nine o'clock tomorrow morning. And, Jason, there's one other thing. Judge Olsen is handling her son's dependency adjudication. I'll want to see him before four, if possible. I may need help with him. Could you please give the judge a call on my behalf?"

"What am I doing here, in this rainy place? I should be in Naples, Florida. Young people there, they listen."

"Thank you...thank you very much."

Jason tapped Abe's knee. "Be careful."

———

THE *JENNY ANN* WAS anchored again near Corey and Abe's picnic spot. Corey had dropped him off at the ferry dock then returned to spend the night. Now she was writing in her diary:

Abe's got this unexpected, kind of hidden, self-confidence. It's as though he believes that if he thinks about a problem carefully, turns it inside out and upside down, he can always find a way to solve it. He really believes he can help me. How can he even imagine a man like Nick? He's the opposite of Nick. Every word he says is what he means, or as close to it as he can get. I'd like to see him talk to Lester.

I'm really afraid. It started right after I dropped him at his car. I guess I got too excited at the idea that someone thought he could help. What was I thinking? Who was I kidding? How can Abe help with Nick? What if he makes Nick angry? Abe promised he wouldn't do anything I didn't want. I'll stop him tomorrow, when he calls, before he sets my life on fire. I have to admit, it was pretty cool when he said I shouldn't give an inch. What an unexpected thing from Dr. Abe Stein. Still, what can he do? I'm afraid he's going to disappoint me again, or worse.

———

NICK WORE A NEW suit he'd had custom tailored for his announcement: a lightweight Brioni, blue with faint chalk squares. His tie was dark red with tiny turquoise diamonds. His razor-cut hair just touched the back of the collar of his blue silk shirt. Jesse was standing beside him. She brushed her fingertips across his palm, flashed her megawatt smile, then stepped to the podium to introduce the next state attorney general, Nick Season. He knew she would shoot the lights out.

Jesse made him sound like Jack Kennedy. She compared him to Pericles. It was a good thing, Nick reflected, that Jesse hadn't seen young Nikos and his charming gypsy mother work the long con with his silver-tongued dad. He remembered an elaborate currency scam that their little family used to run on greedy tourists. He had to smile. Not even Jesse could spin that. Still, he had to hand it to her; Jesse was audacious. She took what she wanted, and getting it fueled her powerful engine, revved her up to be even more aggressive, to exercise her considerable ego and influence on his behalf.

He took in her well-dressed, well-preserved figure at the podium, thinking back to their lovemaking from the night before. In bed, she had been tentative, even coy. It took a long time to help her unwind. And when she finally let herself go, it was a big thing for her. After, she said he was as good as Warren Beatty. Young Warren Beatty, she explained, trying to flatter him. It was all Jesse to be with that guy. Still, talking about it was her first false note.

After the second time, Nick was pretty sure that he could help her let go, take what she wanted. New things. High-performance fuel, he was thinking, for her powerful engine.

He looked out at the crowd. Jesse held them in her spell. And it was a good turnout. Yeah. People wanted him to succeed. Behind the crowd he could see Puget Sound, the forested islands, the snow-capped Olympics. It was a beautiful morning. For the first time in a long while, his radar screen was clear. Corey Logan was gone, in violation of the terms of her probation. He wondered if they would put her picture in the Vancouver post office. In his mind, he crossed her off his list, like deleting an email. When he faced the press, his morning sky was clear and blue.

THE FEDERAL PROBATION OFFICE was on Stewart Street between downtown and Capitol Hill. As a released federal prisoner, Corey was under the jurisdiction of the U.S. Probation Office, which is part of the federal court system. There are supervisors within the probation department who pair an offender with a probation officer. Abe knew that Corey could be assigned a new probation officer by a supervisor. He also knew, before the meeting, that Corey had two things going for her: first, the supervisor Jason had recommended was open to assignment changes; and second, the PO Abe knew was very highly regarded by the supervisor he was meeting with.

The meeting, like many of his best meetings, was brief. Abe made it clear that he hadn't discussed this request with his client, but he wanted to suggest that she change her PO. He said the reasons were complicated and that there were confidentiality issues. Jason, however, had paved the way, and Abe's friend Ray Bailey, the probation officer he wanted for Corey, had poked his head in to help. Ray had said that if Abe thought there was a good reason to make a change, that was enough for him. The supervisor had said he would need to have the details if she wanted to make a change. But, basically, if Ray was going to handle it, there wouldn't be a problem. Before Abe left, the supervisor said, "I hear Jason Weiss has two piles of note cards on his desk. One is favors owed, the other is favors due. I hear he spends his days matching up the cards in those two piles."

"He'd be good at that."

"Tell him he owes me one."

Abe grinned. "For what it's worth, I owe you one, too."

At two o'clock, Abe was in Judge Olsen's office. Apparently, the judge played poker with Jason, and Abe had to listen to an elaborate story about how the judge won a large pot on a bluff. This meeting was neither short nor easy. Judge Olsen was feisty and careful. Abe had to give him Corey's name, in the strictest confidence, and then he explained why he felt she should be with her child and why that should be expedited. He spoke for ten minutes then answered questions. He did not discuss her past, nor the current threats, nor her location. The judge finally agreed to review the case as soon as he could get a report from Child Protective Services. He would see the mother and son within the week, he assured Abe, then he would make a decision. He asked Abe to write a letter making a recommendation to bring the family back together as soon as possible. Based on what Abe had told him, and assuming he agreed after seeing the mother and son, he said he was inclined to have them living together within a month. It was always good, the judge said, to have the child with his natural mother, provided she was fit. Good enough, Abe thought.

———

BILLY WAS WAITING AT the Blue City Café when Morgan came in. It was almost 6:00 P.M. He was sitting on their favorite couch, feeling kind of edgy. He had been thinking about what to say, how to say it. Nothing seemed right. He wanted to tell her about his family, but one of the things he had learned in his short life was that you didn't tell important things to people you didn't trust 100%. Especially when there could be danger. He trusted Morgan pretty well, but that wasn't nearly enough. He knew she could always dump him and act like she didn't know him. He had seen her friends ignore their ex-boyfriends, treat them like they were invisible or dead. And where would he be then?

He stood, took Morgan in his arms and kissed her before she could sit down.

"Nice," she said.

They sat side by side. He put his arm around her, then raised a forefinger to his lips to indicate that she shouldn't take over, that he had something to say. And he decided, then and there, to just say what he was thinking, no more, no less. "I don't know how to explain this. My life isn't like yours or like anyone's you know. There are things I can't tell you. Even if I wanted to."

"What does that mean?"

"That I can't tell you everything you want to know. That's real. That's just how it is."

"And I'm supposed to settle for that?" She pulled away from him.

Billy showed his palm, a hang-on gesture. "No, I'll tell you what I can. I hope that will be enough."

She sat back. "Me too."

"And I'm going to ask you not to talk about it with anyone, even if you don't like it. Will you promise that?"

"I guess...okay."

He was unsure where to begin. Get it over with, he decided. "I live in a foster home. It's a group home with five other kids. It's my third foster home."

Morgan began twisting a lock of her shoulder length blond hair with her forefinger. He had never seen her do that.

"Since when?" she eventually asked.

"Two years, more or less."

"But why?"

"My parents can't take care of me."

"Why?"

"I can't tell you that." She was blinking more often than usual.

"I don't get it. Are they criminals or something?"

He wasn't ready to get into that. "Leave it alone, okay?" Billy could tell he was edgy, not himself; he had never talked to her that way before.

"What can you tell me?" she asked, her voice tense now too.

"Between foster homes, I was in juvie—"

"Juvie?"

"It's the juvenile detention facility. Jail for kids."

Her forefinger was in her hair again. "Are you kidding?"

His teeth working on his lower lip was all the response she needed.

"What for?" she asked.

"They didn't have another foster home for me yet, so that's where they kept me."

"That sucks."

"Yeah, it was bad."

"But the group home you're in now is okay?"

Okay? What was she thinking? "No, it's not okay. The woman who runs it has us there so the state will give her money. She takes in laundry from an old people's home, and we have to wash it. The food is garbage. I share a room in the basement with a twelve year old Mexican boy who can't speak English. Our room's about the size of your closet. You want more?"

Morgan's right knee was going up and down. "You made your point."

Billy had never seen her lose her composure. Even in the car, when she showed him how to make her come with his fingers, she kept this nice little smile on her face. And her eyes were open wide. Now her eyes were almost beady, and her face looked weird—worried and, to him, disapproving. He wanted her to get this and she wasn't. She said she wanted to know him. Well, okay, he wanted that too. "I'm not sure I have. Look, I pretend to be like you because it's what you and your friends know. Well, I'm not like you, and it's not cool to be poor or get locked out and sleep under the freeway."

"What are you doing?" Her cheeks had turned rosy. "I'm trying hard to understand this. And you keep making it harder." She paused, working at collecting herself. "I mean, it's bad enough that you lied. What's the deal with this giant chip on your shoulder?"

Billy looked out the window. "I'm sorry I said anything."

She rose, teary now. "I'm sorry you took so long to say so little. I'm sorry you can't trust me." Then right in his face, "and I don't give a shit if you live in foster whatever." She turned, then turned back. "We could have been really good." Morgan tossed him a sad, goodbye look, then she walked out of the café, ready—it seemed to Billy—for whatever.

———

COREY'S CELL PHONE RANG at 6:30 P.M. This time she answered on the first ring. "Abe?" She was surprised she called him by his first name. It just popped out.

"Yes."

She wanted to say speak up, but she was in too much of a hurry. "Before you say anything, I made the mistake this time. I sometimes talk myself into things. I can't go back. It's just not possible. But thank you for trying."

"Please listen to what I have to say. Then you can decide what you want to do."

"I'd rather not. I'll just get upset. I'd rather talk about how we can get Billy to Canada."

"I'm going to tell you what I've done if I have to come back up there and find you."

"You're not listening…and you're like a pit bull."

"What is it the kids say, 'takes one to know one'?"

"Very funny. Okay. Get it over with."

"I have two things to report—"

"Can you speak up?" she interrupted.

"Sorry. There's good news. First, I met with a supervisor in the probation department. You can come back with a clean slate to a new probation officer."

She wondered if he was kidding or just exaggerating. Maybe he'd misspoken.

Abe went on. "This new man is someone I've worked with often. He's very good and no one will ever get to him. I didn't give anyone your name, so you're not compromised, whatever you decide. I'll be involved in any way you'd like—"

She interrupted him. "I don't believe you." Was he using some kind of psychology, or what? "I come back and—poof—I get a whole new deal?"

"Yes."

"That's not possible."

He ignored her. "There's more. I met with Judge Olsen. He's agreed to reopen Billy's dependency adjudication. I'm writing him another letter. He'll meet with you and Billy next week. He'd like to see you and Billy living together within a month."

Just like that? What was Abe doing? "Is this some kind of hen-headed mental test?" she eventually asked. Her voice was flat, suspicious.

She heard him laugh, which irritated her.

"No, it's true. You can rely on what I say. I promise you."

"C'mon."

"Please. You can believe me. I don't often make promises."

"There's got to be some misunderstanding here, or maybe some mistake?"

"No. I was very careful, very specific."

"Explain it one more time. Everything. Go slowly."

He did.

Corey let his words sink in. What if it was true? She went over it one more time in her mind, then she asked more detailed questions—all of which led to "are you sure?" Abe said, "yes, he was sure," many times, and after a while, she could picture his face, saying it. Could it be true? Eventually, she managed…"you, you really did that?"

"It was the least I could do."

Then—just like that—she couldn't breathe. And she was crying. Tears were running down her cheeks. "I can't believe this. And you—I'm sorry—but you promise this isn't some kind of shrink trick, some way to lure me back or something?"

"I do. You can rely on your new PO, and Judge Olsen will do what he said, so long as you and Billy say you want it."

"Just a minute, please." Corey stood. She wanted to remember how this felt. After a while she wiped the tears from her cheeks. "Please go over everything again. How you did it, every detail."

Abe did, starting with Jason, leaving out nothing. He ended with, "Here's the bottom line. You're free to come back. Your probation will be supervised by a fair and honest man. No one will put you back in prison unjustly. And you can raise your son."

She thought of Nick, what he would do. "And this guy, the one who wants me back in jail, what if he goes crazy?"

"I'd like to introduce you to Jason Weiss. He's been my family's lawyer for thirty-odd years. He's smart, well connected, and powerful. Tell him as much as you can. Between Jason and Ray Bailey—that's your new PO—I think this man will see he's been positioned. I don't think he'll bother you. He certainly can't frame you or Billy without opening a huge can of worms."

She'd have to think about this. "I need time."

"How long?"

"I need to talk with Billy. And I need to think about the risks."

"Please consider the consequences, particularly for Billy, if you don't return. They'll almost certainly ask the Canadians to extradite you. So even if Billy goes to Canada, you'll have to forge new identities. Live as fugitives."

"I understand that. And if I could really raise Billy at home in Seattle, that would be worth taking a risk for. What you can't know is what I'm up against. Or what my chances are of working that out. Even with your fancy lawyer. Can I call you in the morning?"

"Whenever you're ready."

"I'll call at nine o'clock," she said.

"I'll be in the office. I'd like to ask the lawyer to stand by. We'll only call him if you want to. But he can verify any specifics, answer any questions you have, and help with whatever you plan to do."

"I dunno. I never did too great with lawyers."

"Jason's very able. And not what you'd expect. I think you'll like him."

"Hmm." She was quiet, wondering how a good lawyer could ever keep Lester the hell away from her and Billy.

"I'll talk with you tomorrow then."

She made him wait. "There's one more thing. For a guy who can't drive, you're getting kind of wild and crazy."

"I am, aren't I?"

"Yeah. And it suits you." She paused. "Thank you, Abe. That's from Billy and me, and it's meant."

———

WHEN BILLY HEARD HIS cell phone ring, he hoped it was Morgan calling to give him another chance. Ever since she stormed out, he'd been sitting on the couch, arms outstretched, kind of out of it, stunned. He was trying to figure what went wrong. Replaying it in his head. Getting nowhere. He kept seeing her face—pale, like she had seen a ghost or something worse. It was the phone that brought him back to the here and now. He pulled it out of his backpack. And of course, with his luck, it was his mom, the one person he didn't want to talk to.

"Hi" was all he said.

"Hey, how are you?" she asked.

"Not so good."

"What happened?"

"I tried to tell my girlfriend the truth about where I live, and we had like this bad fight."

"I'm sorry—"

"I don't want to talk about it." And, he decided, since this was tell-the-truth day, he had something he better tell her too.

107

"Uh, mom, I don't know how to do this. So I'll just say it—I'm not coming to Canada." There it was. Falling through the air like this great big stone. It was harder to say than he thought it would be. Harder than telling Morgan about the foster home. He wanted a cigarette. "I can't do it. You do what you have to do, but I can't keep sinking in your trouble. I'm sorry." He hesitated. "You're the best, even when everything is against you. But things have gone totally bad. And I've learned to take care of myself. I had to." Billy tapped his fingers on his thigh. "I love you." He braced himself, afraid of what she would say.

After a moment. "I love you, too."

This was not what he expected. Not at all. He was sure she would be angry. He waited, tense, his fingers still working.

"I've been thinking about this a lot," she explained. "I understand why you don't think I can take care of you." Corey paused. "And, yes, we wouldn't have anything like a normal life in Canada. At least not at first. I can see where you wouldn't want that."

Billy didn't respond. For two years he had waited for his mom, hoping she could help him. And then, when he started lying and dealing drugs and pretending to be something he wasn't, he gave up on her. He didn't plan it. It just happened.

"But please don't give up yet."

It was like she was reading his mind. When he was little and they were together all the time, she used to be able to do that.

"If I worked out a way for you to live with me on Bainbridge, would you give me another chance?"

He wasn't sure he had heard that right. "Another chance? What do you mean?"

"The doctor I told you about. He met with the judge. The judge said we could be together in a month. At our house."

"Is this a joke?"

"That's what I asked when he told me about it."

"Why would he do that?"

"I talked to him about our lives. I think he understands what would be best for you and for me. And he's trying to help. You and I have to meet with the judge, tell him we want to be together. Would you do that?"

108

"Are you serious? What about the danger?"

"I'm working on that. The doctor got us a big-shot lawyer, and I'm talking with him tomorrow. He's also getting me a new probation officer, someone he trusts. I think we'd have a chance. If we could live together it would be worth fighting for, don't you think?"

Billy was quiet. This was the biggest thing he had given up on. "I'd fight for that," he finally said.

————

THE DRIFTWOOD LOG WAS a fine backrest and now it brought back good memories. Corey faced her beach fire, her yellow pad resting on her thighs, her diary on her raised knees. She ran her finger along the leather binding. It had been scarred and dirtied in its many hiding places. She reread the lists on her notepad. She was, she knew, circling this very hard, very dangerous decision. She opened her diary, picked up her pen.

> *Okay. This is too tempting and too dangerous. There are big pros—the idea that I could get PO Jensen, the monkey, off my back; that I could raise my son in our house; that I wouldn't have to worry about being sent back to jail. And the cons? Nick Season. Nick Season. Nick Season. What will he do when he finds out I'm back, I have a new PO, and I'm represented by this hot-shot lawyer? He'll lose it. He'll put me on his permanent elimination list. Sure, it might be eighteen months out. But when I get hit by lightning, it'll be his work. And he'll hurt Billy, too. A message to me that no one can connect to him. That's how he is. I have to find a way to strike some kind of a bargain. A truce. At least a stand-off. I just don't know what it is.*

She set the diary aside and poured herself a shot of Scotch. She had picked up a newspaper that morning in Friday Harbor. Corey sat back to read it. The sun was throwing reds and pinks off the clouds, and the evening sky was soothing. She took her time reading the national news, wondering whether she'd still care what the president said if she lived in Canada. She wasn't too interested in state politics, but Corey glanced at a story about Washington Democrats. Toward the end there was something…Jesus…Nick Season…oh my God…just like that her heart was pounding in her ears. She could feel bile rising in her throat. She closed her eyes, opened them. Nick Season was running for state attorney general!

She was breathing too fast. Her neck was a wet rope, knotted and tightening in the searing mid-day sun. She had read a book in prison about rapidly evolving lethal organisms. They couldn't stop themselves. State attorney general? It was his next evolution. Politics. Of course. That's why he'd put her feet to the fire. Off the radar screen is right. Shit. How could that jackal be state attorney general? He had wanted her out of the way before he made his announcement. He wanted her to violate the terms of her probation. Yeah. And now he thought she was gone. And the fork-tongued bastard would fix it so she could never, ever, come back. She reached for her diary.

What if, just once, I got ahead of him? I mean he thinks I'm gone forever. What if I sneak back? And then what if I have this lawyer put the whipsaw right to him? A new PO and a new lawyer. The lawyer could write him, tell him what's what. I wouldn't even have to tell the lawyer who he was writing to. He could write this letter on his fancy stationery addressed 'to whom it may concern.' And he could say in the letter that he didn't know who he was writing to, but Corey Logan was back in Seattle, that she had a new probation officer and a lawyer. He could say that she wasn't going to say word one about anything in the past. That she wanted to be left alone to raise her son. I would even promise, in my own P.S., that I would never tell anyone that I even knew him.

What if he sent Lester over? Or tried to frame Billy? Suppose this lawyer put Nick on notice that if they came at us—if there's even any kind of contact—he would sweat Nick in the press. Release the old letter. Updated. Tell the whole story. What I know, what I suspect. Everything. Nick would go crazy. But what could he do? He's a politician now. It wouldn't do for some fancy lawyer to take him to court, make accusations or even to raise questions in the papers. Especially if it raised doubts about his past, even if they couldn't be proven. He's running for state attorney general so the press would be all over it. Al, Lester, the Russian diamonds, all of it. I don't need proof. Not anymore. That's what I have to ask this lawyer. Will he deliver my message? Will he back it up? Will he put some real heat on Nick in the press? I can't go back without that. But I have good reasons to go back now. And, dear God, I'm tired of being afraid and bending to this twisted man's will.

Corey called Abe's office and left a message for him to call her right away. She wanted to talk with him before she got scared again and changed her mind. Her phone rang minutes later.

"Can you have your driver meet me at the Anacortes ferry terminal tomorrow morning? I can be there at 9:10 A.M. I'll meet you wherever you like. With your lawyer, please."

"Sam will meet the 9:10 ferry. I'll set up the meeting."

"And fill this lawyer in. You can tell him everything you know." She was quiet, hesitant. "Abe, I want to come home."

———

THE GUY LOOKS LIKE a lawyer, Corey thought when she first laid eyes on Jason Weiss. Fancy pinstriped suit, black and white silk tie, gray hair, a paunch.

They were downtown, at the Maritime Building, where Jason, a sole practitioner, had his spacious offices on the third floor. From the window she could see Bainbridge Island. Abe was moving Sam, his talkative driver, out the door.

After Sam was gone, Abe introduced them.

"Hi," she offered, shy.

Jason looked at her then bowed his head slightly. "My pleasure to meet you."

Fancy words, except that when he talked, he sounded like a street guy from NewYork City. And that bow, he had some moves. Yeah. She liked him right away.

Jason indicated a chair and she settled in. It was a comfortable burgundy leather chair, facing an old carved mahogany desk that looked like it belonged in some palace in England. Abe sat in a similar chair beside her. She turned to him. "See how nice his furniture is?"

He grinned. Stuff like that didn't get to him.

She set her notepad on the desk in front of her, serious now. Corey said, "Gentlemen," and she went over what Abe had promised her. After Jason confirmed her understanding, vouched for the new probation officer, and reassured her that she was not going back to jail, she worked her way through her list of questions—everything from the timing of the meeting with Judge Olsen to the mechanics of changing POs, to dealing with Sally, her caseworker. When she was satisfied, she would put a check beside the question and move on. The last thing she said was, "I don't know how I will pay you."

"Allow me this favor," Jason offered.

"Thank you, but you can change your mind after you hear what I want."

Corey explained just what she hoped Jason would do. And how she wanted him to do it.

When she was finished, Jason said, "You have thought about this, yes." A statement, not a question.

"Will you write the letter?"

"If you could tell me who this man is, it would help me to answer your question," Jason suggested.

"No. I'll only tell you if he moves on Billy or me. And I don't mean to be rude, but please don't ask me that again."

"You're not rude. You made it clear from the beginning that you didn't want to answer that question. It is I who has been rude, but I'm a lawyer." He shrugged.

"Can you help me?"

"Perhaps." He touched his fingertips together. "I can write a letter confirming that you will release certain information to me in the event that you are threatened, harmed, even contacted. I can detail the consequences of any act of intimidation. Certainly I can release your story to the press, though I can't say that it will help."

"Will he know who you are?" she asked. This was important.

"If he's familiar at all with the local legal community, yes."

"That's all I need."

"There's one thing you should know," Jason explained. "I'm willing to go so far as to write this letter. I'm willing, for now, to

112

hold a letter that you've written. However, both of these things I do with a misgiving. If it turns out that I represent this person, then I will not be able to represent you. Should this happen, I'll turn your letter over to another lawyer who you designate. And he or she will be your representative."

Corey thought about this. "I'll take that chance." After a moment she added, "Either way, if I ever have to tell you who he is, you're at risk."

"How so?"

"It's hard to know. I can't stay ahead of this guy. And if it served his purposes, he'd kill you both."

Jason's gray eyebrows came together above the bridge of his nose. "Let us hope then that the letter is sufficient."

"You can walk away." She turned to Abe. "Both of you."

Jason raised a finger. "You know what it is, a mitzvah?" And before she could answer, he offered, "It's a good deed." Jason stood. "I'll have the letter this afternoon, by two o'clock."

"Thank you."

"I suggest you send this letter via messenger service. Have them deliver it this afternoon," Jason said, rubbing his ear lobe between thumb and forefinger. "And make sure you get signed proof of delivery."

The meeting was over. "Welcome home," was all Abe said.

———

WHY HAD SOMEONE SENT him a letter from Jason Weiss via messenger? And why in hell did he have to sign for it? Nick pivoted in his ergonomic swivel chair so he could look out at the Sound. He didn't like this. Carefully, he eyed the envelope. It was Jason's envelope all right, but someone else had addressed it in longhand. He took the letter from the hand-addressed envelope. The typewritten letter was on Jason's stationery. The salutation was "To whom it may concern," which could be good. He shook off his worries—there had to be a good reason. He glanced at the first sentence and—Nick put a hand to his chest, wondering if this is what it felt like to have a heart attack. He took slow breaths— it didn't help. Damn it! Jason Weiss, Jesse's connected lawyer, the lawyer for his own campaign, was writing on behalf of Corey

Logan. She was not some obscure offshore flu—she was AIDS, Anthrax, and the Ebola virus, a fucking three pack. Satan's black seed is what she was. He should have known she would be back. Nick began to read:

To whom it may concern:

I am writing this letter on behalf of Corey Logan. She is returning to Seattle and believes that she or her son, William Logan, may be threatened, intimidated, or put in harm's way.

She has not told me who you are. She has no intention of ever seeing or talking with you again. She does not intend to communicate to anyone about you or your past. She has a new probation officer, a new lawyer, and the possibility of living in Seattle with her son. She would like to move forward with her life.

She believes that you may, in some way, attempt to interfere with her plans. Please be advised that any contact of any kind, from you or your associates, will result in her disclosing to me your identity, telling me what she knows about you, and what she believes you've done. Furthermore, it will cause the release of a letter that she has left with me, which, she says, details your history and her suspicions. At that time I or other counsel will pursue whatever legal and media remedies are necessary to guarantee her safety and her peace of mind.

Sincerely,
Jason Weiss

P.S. Mr. Weiss doesn't know anything. If you leave Billy and me alone, he never will. I promise to "stay off your radar screen." I'll never say a word to anyone. Please give Billy and me a chance to have a life. If you don't, I'll do everything he says in the letter and more. Al told me things. If I tell what I know, you have no future in politics. I know I can hurt you. Don't make me do that. I don't want to. You go your way, I'll go mine.

Corey Logan

114

———

A NEW PO? JASON Weiss was her lawyer. Jesse's lawyer, Jesse's confidante, representing Corey Logan? There was only one way that could have happened—Dr. Abe Stein. The shrink had pumped her up to where she was threatening him. Nick thought there might be steam rising off his skin. He watched seagulls flying west with the Bainbridge ferry. His pores still felt hot, so he counted the tall orange cranes, giant Chernobyl insects, gathering freight containers off the ships. He imagined driving his pick through Corey Logan's ear, in the one out the other. Sometime later his skin stopped burning and he started thinking again. Nick knew what he had to do. What he didn't see yet was how to do it. He buzzed Lester and stared out the window, working the problem. This called for careful planning, patience, and, finally, total surprise. Nick likened it to a terrorist strike.

He had to give her credit. She had boxed him in pretty good. She didn't know how good, he was pretty sure of that. They would have to wait for now. Until after the election, at least. Let her settle in. An idea was forming in the back of his mind. And, dammit, a rash, hot and itchy as hell, was spreading across his chest.

Lester's cane announced his impending arrival. Lester looked Nick in the eye and said, "That fucking cunt."

Lester knew she was back. Right. "Not another word." Nick raised a hand. He didn't want to dwell on it. His skin was heating up again. On to business. "I want history on Dr. Abraham Stein. Put Riley on it. Background only. Tell him to stay away from the guy, for now."

Lester's face was impassive. He set his cane against the desk, fished his Swiss Army knife out of his trouser pocket, and began cleaning his oversized fingernails with its tiny file.

Lester, Nick realized, was choking with rage. He hated failure, and, for Lester, inaction in the face of failure was unbearable, like impotence.

Though he didn't know—or care—why, Nick knew for a fact that today, right now, he wanted to get a rise out of his unflappable lieutenant. Just this once get under Lester's thick skin. The very idea of it was like a cool breeze. He made Lester wait. "How did you know she'd fucked with you?" he finally asked, stirring the pot.

Lester looked out the window. "Her boat. It's in Friday Harbor…I could sink it."

"No. She's become a different kind of problem. I'll have to think about this." Lester, he knew, hated waiting. Nick rubbed it in. "Patience. Tincture of time."

Lester cleared his throat, stifling god-only-knew what.

Nick took a moment to savor Lester's chafing as his own skin began to cool. He reached for Lester's cane, fingering the brass handle as he inserted another verbal bamboo splinter under Lester's newly cleaned nails. "She's got a new PO. And this high-priced lawyer, a heavy hitter."

Lester checked his nails, deliberate and stone-faced. "We can take the boy. Trade him for whatever."

The man was like a damned marble statue. Maybe his blood pressure had gone up. Had to. "Nothing like that. No." Nick saw his next move. He pictured Lester, bursting a blood vessel in his face, like some possessed African warrior, when he heard it. "Here's what we're going to do. I want you to get me a picture post card. Mountains, wildflowers, happy animals, maybe a stream. Wonders of nature. Something peaceful."

"I can have the kid in an hour." It was as if Nick hadn't said anything.

"You know, sunset over Mount Rainier. Eagles nesting on the Skagit River. Porpoises playing in the Sound. That kind of thing. Here's what we write on the card—'Hands across the water.' That's it." She would know who sent it, what it meant.

Lester didn't blink, he didn't breathe. Nick thought there might be a bead of sweat on Lester's brow. Maybe not.

Nick made him wait. "Have Riley write the book on Stein," he finally said. "Find a way at him. Something unexpected." He smiled warmly before twisting the knife deeper still. "First, the postcard."

Lester set his extra-large palms on Nick's desk, then lowered his massive frame toward Nick's face. His baggy blue suit jacket swung open. There was a Magnum in his shoulder holster. "You want a nature postcard?" He cleared his throat, taking his time about it. His forehead looked dry. "How about a grizzly, feeding on an elk carcass?" Behind his oversized glasses, Lester's rheumy eyes revealed nothing.

TEN

"**B**ILLY'S HOME IN TWELVE days," Corey announced. "The judge set the date." She raised a fist above her head, quietly triumphant.

"Yes!" her friend Jamie exclaimed, raising her paper cup of wine to the sky. Then even louder, "Yes!"

They were sitting on the beach in front of Corey's house. The tide was out, and Corey had made a beach fire near a sandy patch where she'd set two new Costco beach chairs. The sun had set, clouds darkened the night sky, and they had the long rocky beach to themselves.

"This is so great. You're about to start a new job. Billy's coming home. You've been home—What? Five weeks?" Jamie asked.

"Thirty-six days." It was July, though the night air was still cool. As they talked, Corey worked on an eye splice in wire—securing the metal eye loop to a heavier line that would ultimately connect her buoy more surely to its anchor chain. Just as the number of salmon entering a stream signaled the well-being of the watershed, her eye splice in wire was a pretty good sign that she meant to stay.

"And no trouble. You even like your PO. Chew on that." Jamie touched Corey's arm. "And how about Dr. Abe? First time I ever heard of a shrink making someone better." Jamie's smile was warm. She was a hairdresser, and tonight her hair was blonde and cut short, framing a cheerful face that men liked. "Did you have to fuck him?"

Corey shot her a look. "No. There was nothing like that."

"I don't get it."

"Just a good guy. He wanted to help." She turned toward the Sound, looking for her boat in the dark. She found it in the calm black water, resting at her buoy, stately. It was somehow reassuring. Beyond her boat the Bremerton ferry was making its regular crossing. All her lights were on, bright buoyant squares floating through the black night. "And as for the job"—she paused, sour-faced—"you call cocktail waitressing at a lousy bar a job?"

"You've got an attitude problem."

Corey pursed her lips. Jamie said what she felt and didn't avoid conflict. She was also her one true friend. They had fished together in Alaska. Tended bar together when times were hard. They had been single parents together, too. "Why is that?" Corey wanted to know.

"You think cocktail waitressing is beneath you."

"You know what it's like. The guys are always hitting on you. Maybe I'm just too old to like that."

"And you think if you were a lawyer, say, the guys wouldn't hit on you?"

"Not as much, no."

"We'll never know. Huh, babe?" Their laughter was drowned out by the sound of the ferry wake breaking over the Blakely Shelf. "How about fishing?"

"I don't want to be away nights after Billy comes home."

"You remember that Edmonds boat repair place? Larry's there now. He's always needing to hire someone. And he knows you can fix anything. I'll call him for you. He owes me. Done." Jamie touched her cup of wine to her friend's paper cup. "Now, damn it, I want you to listen up. You go celebrate, girl. Call the shrink. Call him. You like this guy."

"Christ, I can't do that."

———

"All started here, this very chair..." Max was saying as he tapped the old leather armchair with a beefy fist.

Abe never got tired of watching Max, listening to him. He was five foot ten inches, two hundred twenty pounds, not an ounce of fat. Eighteen years ago, Max Stern had left Tel Aviv for Seattle, where he had a cousin who exported U.S. industrial products. Max married an American woman and became a U.S. citizen. Until he got caught—or, as he put it, "backstabbed"—Max ran a lucrative ring of industrial thieves. After doing twenty-eight months for stealing machine parts and selling them to a Canadian mining cartel, he had to turn his life around. He couldn't go back to work. He was burned, and for the first time in his life Max was lost, unsure what to do or where to turn. His probation officer had recommended Abe. They had worked hard, twice a week for almost two years. This was Max's last session.

"You didn't like me at first," Max said. "I could see that."

"Try seeing this from where I sit. First thing you do, you tell me how to fix up—and I quote—this 'ratty old office'. Then you plant a large fist on my desk—'yes, it's well-built'—and knock over my coffee. While I'm trying to save my papers, you start taking apart my pipe tools."

"I did that?"

Abe smiled. "The second session, you asked me how much money I made a year, take-home."

"I was interested in that. You didn't make enough for me, that's why I ruled out being a psychiatrist."

"I remember. You had your own ideas about—what did you call them?—moneymakers?"

"Yeah, your classic franchise opportunities. Ahead of my time, too." Max grinned. His silver hair was combed straight back. He wore a three thousand dollar dark blue suit and a gold Rolex. "How about those Big Man Burgers? And then there was your all-weather solar panels, and finally, god forgive me, the Tropical Fish Emporium. Tell me you weren't worried."

"The tiny fish didn't seem quite right," Abe conceded.

"Not quite right?" Max had a twinkle in his eye, Abe was sure of it. "I mean for christsakes, remember what happened? You remember that day?" He raised a finger before Abe could say anything. "Me, I'll never forget it. Every fish died. Every single one. Belly up. I was doing something wrong with the air filter. Man-oh-man. I lost everything. I'm already paying prime-plus two on a loan from the kosher butcher. And now it's eight weeks—twice a week—I owe you." He sighed. "So believe me, I come in here that day, I'm ready to knock over a 7-Eleven. And I'm coming unglued, yelling at you how shrinks don't know anything about the world. You're just listening, like you always do. Nodding your head to some damn music I can't quite hear." Max set a palm on Abe's desk. "And then you asked in that funny, polite way exactly what I did know about? Remember that?"

Abe smiled. It had taken eleven months to get to that question.

"Hell, the rest is history—Worldwide Industrial Security... you get the credit, doc."

"No, Max, you get the credit." And he did. Max was financially savvy and streetwise, and he had worked hard. Abe had watched, in awe, as Max shrewdly built an international industrial security business. Within a year, he began acquiring small security companies in other countries. Abe especially liked that he was so unashamedly pleased with the results of his hard work, and with his life. He envied that, in fact. Lately Abe had been at loose ends. Sam, his driver, said he worked too much and called him Dr. Do-It-All. "You're a good man." Abe stuck out his hand. "I'm here if you need me."

Max took his outstretched hand, then pulled him into a bear hug. "That goes two ways, Dr. Stein."

———

ABE WAS SITTING BEHIND his desk, finishing his notes, when he heard a knock on his door. He checked his watch, 8:48 A.M., his next appointment was at 9:00 A.M.. He opened the door, preoccupied, and there was Corey.

"I waited 'til you were done," she said, wondering how such a smart man could regularly look like a television wrestler who had just taken a good shot to the head.

"Thank you."

"You good 'til nine o'clock?"

"You're a quick study."

"I've learned to watch how things work." She sat in her chair.

He stood, leaning his backside against the front of his table. She hadn't seen him since the meeting with Jason, several weeks ago. He had called her once to make sure that her probation officer was working out and that the meeting with Judge Olsen was set. "Billy's coming home. Nine days. The judge set a date. It's official." She pointed her forefinger at him. "You did that. Your letter... jeez, what a letter. Thanks."

He stood. "That's very good news," he said, sounding somewhat formal. "Congratulations."

"No one's ever helped me like you did." She waited. He had turned his back, looking for the right pipe. Not too great at taking compliments. She should have known that.

He turned back. "I think Billy's a lucky boy." He was choosing his words again. "I'm very happy for both of you."

She settled into her chair, hoping he would relax a little. Instead, he looked at his watch. "Well, thanks again." Corey stood. "If you ever need a favor, or say you just want to go fishing, I'll do what I can."

"Thank you very much." He shook her offered hand.

———

ON HER WAY DOWN the stairs, Corey considered picking up Chinese take-out later, sort of a celebration dinner. She pictured herself eating reheated food alone. At the pet store window she saw her turtle, back in its old place. She owed something to that turtle too. Maybe when Billy came back, they would buy it, give it a home. She reached into her coat pocket for her cell and she punched in the number. When Abe answered, she said, "This is Corey, is that you?"

"Yes, it's me."

"Uh, I've been thinking." She waited, hoping he would say something.

"About what?"

"Uh, Abe—may I call you that?"

"Yes."

She took a breath. "Bear with me here." Corey leaned against the brick wall, took another breath. "I'd like to invite you to dinner." And when he didn't say anything, she added, "Sort of a thank you deal."

She waited. And waited.

"Oh?"

"Well," she said, wishing he would help her along here. She could hear him, knocking that damned pipe against his big stone ashtray. She could picture him too, dumping out his ashes, making that lost-at-sea face that came on when he was thinking about something.

"When?"

"Whenever. Say tonight, so I won't lose my nerve. Or worry it to death."

"Tonight?"

"Perfect. I'll meet the six-twenty ferry."

———

Until Judge Olsen said he could come home, Billy didn't believe it would happen. Then, just like that, there were forms to fill out and meetings with Sally. His foster mother even stopped making him do laundry. He had seen his mom more often, and she was easier to be with. It was like they had sacrificed just the right animals (or—he couldn't help thinking it—offered up wondrous virgins) because the gods seemed to have lifted their awful curse. Now he and his mom were actually making plans for his homecoming. Nine more days. And he had this long list of things to do.

He was sitting on the worn couch at the back of the Blue City Café, waiting for Morgan. He had seen her only once since they argued. It was after a soccer game. They were friendly, in a polite way, but that was it. There wasn't much to say. He'd called her this morning, hoping that his new situation might give them a fresh starting point. He felt bad about their fight. He didn't know if he'd said too much or not enough. Probably both. Anyway, he had freaked her out—he knew that much—and then that, in turn, freaked him out too. At least he could invite her over now. She had agreed to meet him, reluctantly, after he promised he had something to tell her.

"Billy boy," his Chargers team mate, Dave, said, sitting down beside him, uninvited. "Got anything for me?"

"I'm out of the business," Billy explained. "I've told you that about ten times."

Dave made a don't-put-me-on face. "Find me a seller then." He tapped Billy's far shoulder. "You were a rising star—" Dave rubbed Billy's shoulder, a little too hard.

"Go fuck yourself."

Dave's fingers pinched some pressure point in Billy's shoulder. Billy grabbed Dave by the throat. Dave drove his fist into Billy's cheek as Morgan approached their table.

Morgan took it in. She knew both of these boys, and without hesitation she swung her heavy backpack squarely into Dave's face. It smashed Dave's nose and sent him sprawling back onto the couch. Dave howled, his hands on his bloody nose.

"Leave him alone, you sonofabitch," Morgan said.

A gaggle of high schoolers moved toward the fight. Betsy, the owner, threaded her way through the crowd calling, "Cool it! That's enough."

When Dave stood up slowly, ready to fight them both, Betsy firmly took his arm and gave him a napkin to stop the bleeding.

Dave leaned back, the napkin pressed to his nostril. He took a breath. "What's next?" he asked Morgan. "Your gardener and his Mex crew?" Dave raised his middle finger then he stalked off.

"What an asshole," Billy said. "Hey, thanks."

"Did he hurt you?"

"No. He's just leaning on me, trying to make me get weed for him. It's no big deal."

"He's pretty strong."

"Okay, he's strong, but he's just this puffed-up bully. A spoiled prick who likes to get his way. The real hard cases, they're not like Dave." He shook his head. "Un-unh."

"What do you mean?"

"He's used to pushing people around, scaring them. No one ever stands up to him. When he understands that I'd fight him— even if I got hurt—that I'd probably hurt him too, he'd back off."

"How do you know?"

"I don't know for sure. But he isn't scary. In juvie I had guys wanting me to join their gang. Older guys that shoot people. They were scary."

"What did you do?"

"I used my head to keep ahead of them. I stalled until I got out. I lied when I had to. Mostly I was lucky."

She sat back, watching him. "I've been thinking about you."

"Me too, about you."

"I meant what I said last time." She let that sink in. "I didn't like you because you dealt drugs. That was never it." She talked faster. "And you do have this huge chip on your shoulder. I mean, why do you have to hide who you are?"

"It's not so simple," he said.

"Why?"

"Let's not do this again." He bit down on his lower lip. "Could you, please, for now, just take my word on that?"

"I don't know if I can."

"Nine days?" he asked.

"Nine days. Why?"

"I have news. I'm going to live with my real mom. On Bainbridge."

"Your mom? Is that good?" she asked.

"Yeah. It could be really good. That's what I wanted to tell you."

"What happened?"

"Here's what I'm thinking. I'll be home in nine days. Would you come to see me there? I'd like you to meet her. And I think she can answer at least some of your questions."

Morgan took his hand. "I'd love to come to your house." She kissed him, using her peppermint tongue.

———

COREY WAS WAITING IN a long line of cars winding along the curb in the waterfront parking lot at the Bainbridge ferry terminal. She sat behind the wheel of her black pick-up, watching the foot passengers hurry off the boat. The 6:20 P.M. was a commuter ferry, and hundreds of people were walking to their cars. Tonight it was drizzling, and she saw a sea of umbrellas and folded newspapers held high working their way through the parking lot. She was worried now that he wouldn't come, that there had been a mix-up. He would have called her, she reasoned. But—wait…was that him, standing in the rain on the far side of the oncoming crowd? The guy was about the right size, but he was wearing a suit and tie she didn't recognize. Did he go home and change? And he had a bottle of something in a brown paper bag. The man was confused, she could see that; he seemed to be unsure where he was going to be met. No coat. No umbrella. No effort to keep dry. He was looking off toward Eagle Harbor now. Corey felt better. She knew this guy all right. She stepped from the truck, waving at him. "Abe, over here."

He saw her and ran in the rain to her truck. For a big guy, he moved pretty fast. In the truck he put on his seat belt, right off. "Thanks for picking me up."

"Thanks for coming."

They drove through Winslow in silence. Bainbridge Island was approximately twenty-eight square miles, slightly larger than Manhattan. Its population, however, was less than 25,000 people. Much of the island was rural, though there were areas of higher density, the largest being Winslow, the downtown area of the city of Bainbridge Island, where the ferry docked. Corey's cabin was at the remote southern tip of the island.

"Pretty," he offered as they moved through a more rural area toward Port Blakely.

"Yeah. When I was growing up, this wasn't built up at all."

"You grew up on the island?"

"No. Mostly, I lived on our boat. We had a slip in Seattle. We came over here when we could."

"I see."

Well, at least he wasn't any different when he came to dinner, Corey thought. She decided to drop the small talk. They drove south past Port Blakely, where she made an effort not to point out the old mill pond. At the bottom of Toe Jam Hill, she turned down the little road that led to her cabin. This wasn't a county road, so parts of it were better maintained than others. From time to time there was conflict among neighbors over speed bumps, property lines, new construction, etc. Corey hardly knew her neighbors, so she didn't know, and couldn't tell, what was likely an elaborate, contentious history.

Smoke was coming from the chimney of the cabin as they made their way down the steep driveway. She thought the cabin looked warm and welcoming in the rain. She parked the car between the steps winding down to the front door and her vegetable garden. "This is home," she said.

Abe looked out at the uninviting expanse of cold, grey, fogged-in Sound beyond her little cabin. "It's a long way from Seattle," he volunteered. They ran for the door through the rain.

Inside, she had moved her maple table to the center of the great room, where it was set for two. On the table, salmon filets were marinating in a shallow pan. Her well-worn couch, which she'd covered with a quilt, and a footstool she used for cooking sat in front of the brick fireplace. A grill was set over the fire. "I hope you like fish," she said, feeling awkward.

"I do."

She thought she saw him actually noticing the bag he held in his hand. Like the light went on.

"I almost forgot," he said. "This is for you." Abe handed her the gift he'd brought.

She unwrapped a bottle of Dom Perignon Champagne. "French Champagne," she said. "Isn't it?"

"It is."

"I never drank French Champagne."

"I can't think of a better occasion."

"Thank you. Will you open it? I don't know how."

She went to the kitchen area, where she took two water glasses and held them up. "This is all I have."

"They're fine. Could you bring a dish towel?"

She came back with the glasses and the towel. They stood in front of the fireplace. He had already unwrapped the wire that secured the cork. She watched him put the towel over the cork and begin to turn. It occurred to her that she'd made a big mistake. The guy couldn't drive. Maybe he couldn't open a champagne bottle either. Then—just like that—the cork popped off into the towel in his hand, and he was pouring the foaming champagne into their glasses. He raised his glass. "To you and your son," Abe said in his soft way. And then taking time to pick his words, "I envy him his mother. I envy you your years together."

She clicked his glass, feeling a little teary. "That was nice," she told him. "Really nice." She took a sip. "Jeez, this is good." Corey raised her glass. "Okay, I have one. To you, Abe…the most wonderful surprise ever."

When they clicked glasses again, he spilled some champagne on the floor. Embarrassed, he took the dishtowel and knelt to carefully wipe up the little spot. "Sorry," he softly said when he was done.

She ignored his spill, eyes on the fire.

Abe stood beside her, quiet, then he topped off both of their glasses.

She fingered the mantel, which was weathered and darkened with age. Corey remembered how her mom had patiently fashioned it from an ancient beam she'd pulled off some broken-down ship. "I wasn't sure you'd come," she eventually said.

"I'm happy to be here."

"I've never done this—" She pointed at the table.

"Oh?"

"You know—dinner. And French Champagne." She finished off her glass. "I wanted to do something nice for you. After everything you've done for me." She moved her hand, a gesture that took in the whole room. "Look, I know this isn't much—"

"It's home to your family," he interrupted. "That's quite a lot."

"Thanks for that." She touched his arm. "Why did you come tonight?" Corey didn't know where that came from.

He set his glass on the mantel, considering.

If she hadn't known him, the long silence would have been awkward.

"I thought about it, and I knew I wanted to come," he finally said. "And I was flattered that you asked. I admire you."

She raised her eyebrows, a question.

"It's many things," he explained. "The way you see things. Your directness. I especially like the way you make me feel—I don't know how to put this—with you I'm not quite so serious. Even when we're considering very serious things." He hesitated. "I'm fumbling around, scratching the surface, I'm afraid."

"Whoa, you admire me?" she asked, still in doubt. "I make you feel good?"

"Yes, yes."

"Huh." Corey took a breath, wanting to remember this moment. "Just so you know mister, that's a two-way street."

"Good." He tapped the mantel, obviously thinking about something.

She waited patiently.

"And the honest answer to your question is that I'm not sure why I came...I'm glad I did."

When he smiled, she said, "I'm glad you came too."

"Thank you."

She set her glass beside his on the mantel. Then, without even thinking about it, she kissed him lightly on the lips. When he put his big arms around her waist, their kiss turned into something more serious. This was not what she had meant, she thought, as his hands moved across her back. He was stronger than she imagined, though his touch was gentle. And then she couldn't think. She could feel her excitement building as he carried her to the couch.

On the couch she hurriedly unbuttoned his shirt. He was burly and hairy and, she realized, at ease. He undressed her, sure-handed.

Their lovemaking was intense. She especially liked that it was also generous. They were, in turn, responsive and demanding. Afterward Corey wondered if he was as surprised, make that mystified, as she was. She would ask him one day, for sure. Sometime later they made love again, beginning where they had left off. It made some kind of weird sense, she decided, that two misfits should do so well together in bed.

After she-had-no-idea-how-long, Corey lifted her head, wanting to see his face. She had drifted off and she was still a little drowsy. "You're awfully damn sexy. Never guess it looking at you."

"In my work I've learned that in matters of importance, appearances mean very little," he said.

Corey gave him a soft sleepy kiss, liking that idea. She gently tapped her finger on his chest, waking up now. "I have to say something. It's been more than two years since I've done this."

128

Abe covered her hand, considering this. "It might be a year I've been telling myself it's been a year."

She grinned at that, then lay her head on his chest. She closed her eyes. "I can't move."

"There's no hurry."

"What about dinner?"

"Whenever you're ready."

"Will you stay the night?"

"I'd love to."

"And what about tomorrow?"

"I'll cancel everything."

"You would do that?"

"I'd be crazy not to."

"Yeah, you would."

ELEVEN

WHENEVER NICK WOKE UP in Jesse's bed, he felt uneasy, even—though this was now rare for him—vaguely anxious. For years in L.A. he had gone with older women for money. And if he stayed the night, the price went up. But that wasn't the point. It had been a long time since he'd slept with an older woman, and it was bringing back memories he didn't like to think about. Memories of what it was like to be on your own in L.A. hustling. Especially if you were a worrier, a relentless worrier, as he had been. He would stay up nights, hidden in some abandoned car, worrying that he would be rolled or raped or worse. Some nights he couldn't sleep at all. On those nights he would think about how to make the worries stop.

This morning, more than thirty years later, he knew how to make the worries stop, and he knew that staying the night with Jesse was well worth putting up with a little uneasiness. The way he saw it, pleasing her was a prudent way to protect his candidacy. Nick likened it to term insurance—small premiums for big returns should something go very wrong in these crucial days before the election.

He looked around the huge master suite with the picture-perfect view of Lake Washington and the Cascades. No sign of her. He checked the clock: 7:30 A.M. Jesse was an early riser. She was probably working the phones already. Every phone in her house was set up for it—three lines, minimum. She was in the kitchen, he would guess. Calling her pals in D.C. or New York City. Nick rolled over and, yeah, he could see where she had two lines going. The woman always had someone on hold. On hold and liking it. He propped himself up against the headboard and stretched his muscular arms, thinking about this knowing woman.

Last night they were sitting on the couch, talking politics. He was feigning interest while he worried about Corey Logan and Abe Stein. Out of the blue Jesse asked, "Is something wrong?" She was onto him. "Is there anything I should know? Something you're not telling me? Anything at all?" No one was supposed to do that. No one. "Nicky, you're going to win. Don't play games with me. I'm your future and I hate surprises. Am I clear?"

Nick wanted to bitch slap her, the way she came on. He knew to sit on that. What made it even worse, though, he saw that she was right. Absolutely dead on.

He let out a slow breath, unnerved, even now, the day after. Since childhood he had played the long con. He was trained by professionals. No one could read him. Period. And now Jesse had seen right through him. Sized him up like he was a mark.

What it was, she had this nose for trouble—some kind of predacious instinct—the woman was always sniffing out what was wrong. And, he had to say, her smell test was state of the art. He stopped himself, sensing that he was too worried. Jesse and her cronies had rules, and she played by them. Jesse had *values*. End of the day, she just liked offense better than defense. It was her nature. She enjoyed that preemptive first strike; she liked to flaunt her colors. Okay, so let her strut. Yeah. He let out another breath. Sweet Jesus, you had to like her confidence. She did raise the bar. Good. So now it was his turn to step up. Okay, no problem, he'd explain his scent. She knew he was worried—fine—but she didn't have to know why. He looked into her eyes.

"Perfectly clear," Nick finally answered. "There is something," he admitted, lowering his eyes. "I have been worried. Mostly, I think, I've been worried about not meeting your expectations—professionally and personally." He looked past her out the window. "It's nothing more specific. I should have said something, but as you've noticed, I never quite get around to it." He fingered his silver cross. "I'm concerned that if I talk about my worries, you'll think less of me. It's a Greek macho thing. It's not a trait I'm proud

131

of. I'm sorry." As she touched the nape of his neck, he was still wondering how, precisely, she'd known something was wrong.

"Thank you," she whispered in his ear. Jesse rested her head against his shoulder. She closed her eyes, settling in. Nick realized he ought to get what he wanted while she was feeling so mellow. "Jess," he said softly.

"Hmm?"

It was always best with her to lay it out up front. That way, she could sniff around for the worst thing right away. "I'd like to meet your son."

She sat up, rubbed her eyes. "What?"

"He's a psychiatrist, isn't he? Does some work with the post prison population?"

"You've done your homework." She frowned. "Why?"

"Maybe there's a place for a man like that on our team?"

Jesse crossed her legs, adjusted the Native American beaded necklace she was wearing. "He's never been interested in politics."

"It wouldn't be political. He could help with policy. Prisons and sentencing, for example, are big issues, statewide."

She fingered her beads, considering this. "I'd love to see him get out, meet some people. But you don't know Abe. He's not the type."

"He doesn't know me," Nick said. "Give me a chance to talk with him. If he cares about these issues, I can find a way to plug him in. And I'd like to do something nice for his mother." And find a way at the meddling, clueless shrink. Stein was a pussy; he would bet on that.

"I'll put something together," she said. "And thank you, Nicky, thank you very much."

He readjusted the pillows, propping his back against the headboard. When he was satisfied, he closed his eyes. In his mind, Nick reran the rest of his evening with Jesse, frame by frame, until finally he was reviewing, and carefully assessing, their lovemaking.

Until last night, he had been playfully encouraging her, baby steps. Then last night, for the first time, he let her genie out of the bottle and, one by one, he made her wishes come true. So— he had to smile—Jesse, the splendid, strutting peacock, was discovering that she was a wanton woman. He opened his eyes, thinking that their brazen sex would only help him manage her. In his experience, when demanding, high-strung women finally let themselves go, they went crazy over it; they even loved the idea of it. It was a thing he could do for her, easy. And it was all the same to him; he didn't feel much, whatever they did.

Nick sat up and stretched his arms again. It had been a good night, he concluded, successful. It was time to focus on today's business.

He got out of bed, pleased. Then, just like that, he was back on Corey and Abe, worrying like some teenaged girl who'd missed her period. Like that girl, he should have taken precautions. And now Corey Logan was back in Seattle. Nick kept seeing Corey telling Abe Stein about him. Corey was a scorpion, striking at will, filling Abe's veins with her toxic venom. He looked over at Jesse's phone—three lines flashing. He considered the pros and cons of moving some clothes to her house.

THE LAST TIME ABE missed a day of work, it was for the Windstar Mediterranean cruise—a birthday gift from his mother. That was—what?—three years ago? Four? He could still feel the seasickness that came whenever the big ship swayed. His medication, which the doctor assured him would "give him sea legs," had made him dizzy and irritable. He jumped ship in Naples, where his wallet was stolen. Jason had to wire him the money to get home.

Abe heard a noise. He turned and saw Corey. She was bringing their coffee out to her small cedar deck. He watched her checking out the 180-degree South Sound view, aware that his luck had changed.

The morning was chilly and damp, and the hot coffee in its warm, chipped mug was perfect. Corey was watching the weather move in from the south. The fog lay about three hundred yards beyond the beach—puffy, cold, white smoke hovering three to four feet above the Sound. He sat on a wooden deck chair, sipping his fresh coffee, wondering if the fog was actually moving. She turned to set her coffee on the table beside him, then put her hand on his neck. She kissed his ear, his brow, and finally his lips. When she was satisfied, she sat on the deck, her back against his legs.

Abe watched her settle in. The way he felt was a thing he had forgotten, given up on anyway. Now he realized that giving up was neither intentional nor conscious. No, he had longed for this feeling but finally banished it to the "adolescent-feeling" graveyard—because he felt it so rarely, and hoping to feel it was a one-way ticket to black depression. But here it was, that feeling of well being that came when someone you wanted and admired felt just that way about you because they understood who you were and thought that was very damned desirable. She got who he was, the good and the bad, and he knew she knew what she liked. He put his hand on her shoulder, gently moving aside a strand of her curly black hair, touching her cheek. Corey wore jeans and a faded blue crew-neck sweater. She turned and moved between his legs, putting a hand on the nape of his neck, pulling his head forward, then arching her back and kissing him. It was a slow, leisurely kiss. Corey was, he decided, the sexiest woman ever.

The tide was out, and after finishing their coffee, Corey and Abe walked the beach, east to Restoration Point and then back to the western shore of the island. He had grown up in Seattle and been to Bainbridge often for social occasions. Still, the nooks and crannies of the Blakely Shelf were new to him. She introduced him to the plants and creatures of the tide pools, carefully explaining the sea life he was often seeing for the first time.

"Do you know Greek mythology?" she asked, tipping a rock to show him an orange sea star.

He bent to pick it up.

"It's better not to touch them," she said nicely.

Of course. Why didn't he know that? "Just a little," he answered her question. "I went to the British Museum and saw the Lapiths and Centaurs on the friezes from the Parthenon."

"The Greeks would like those back." She grinned. "My mother thought the English were pirates. After a drink she'd sum it up by saying the English eat spotted dick."

"What?"

"It's pudding."

He smiled. "I wish I'd met her."

"I told you how she used to tell me stories about the gods—she knew them all—Apollo, Dionysus, Zeus, Theseus, Pan the Satyr, you name it. Whenever I poke around in the tide pools, I think of the god of the sea. Blue-haired Poseidon, master of ships, the storm maker." She turned to the Sound. Abe watched her, wondering what she was seeing in the fog. Corey went on, "My mother was especially interested in Moira, or fate. She believed you could recognize it. When you recognize it, you just know what to do."

"For example?"

"For example—" She took his arm, whispered, "You."

He put his arm around her waist. "At least you recognized it."

"It almost got away from me. Really—we were hanging by a thread. Lucky for you it's unstoppable. No one can cheat Moira. No way."

"Is that so?"

"Yes."

Abe looked dubious.

"It is." She got a look he recognized. "Okay, Dr. Know-it-all, there's a paradox that proves it." She raised her palms. "Picture this…the king of Thebes has borrowed this divinely gifted hound, Laelaps. The king needs this special hound to hunt the Teumessian vixen—a blood-thirsty she-fox who can only be satisfied by the monthly sacrifice of a child." Corey turned to face him. "That's right. And to make matters worse—this vixen is divinely fated never to be caught. Never. Now the hound is divinely fated to catch its prey each and every time. Every time. No exceptions. You see the problem?" Abe nodded, he certainly did. "Okay. This contradiction rises straight to the heavens. Moira cannot be denied. Not for the vixen. Not for the hound. Zeus, in a huff, settles it—zap—he turns the hound and the vixen to stone." Her mouth turned up, just a little.

"Very nice." Abe envied her growing up in a family where such fine stories were passed from one generation to the next. Billy would surely know it, too. After a moment he offered, "Still, the people I see often let fate pass them right by. They miss opportunities. They aren't necessarily good at identifying things that they could do, relationships they could have, or new ways that they could think about their lives. Fate presents itself, and sometimes, they just don't see it. They let these chances slip away, unaware. With some people, I can help. What you call recognizing Moira, in therapeutic jargon, it's not unlike becoming self aware."

"That's a mouthful."

He grinned. "You're awfully sassy for someone who just explained Moira in two pithy sentences and a story about a fox and a hound."

"Just remember this. If you ignore Moira, you bring on Nemesis. Righteous anger." She leaned in then whispered, "You don't want that, smarty-pants."

He took her hand, warmed by her smile. "I'll remember." Abe was falling in love; he was sure of it.

———

COREY HAD HER DIARY open. She sat on the deck watching Abe gather wood for a fire. She wrote without thinking:

I've never felt like this about anyone. I have to pinch myself to be sure it's not some sappy dream. If it is, I hope I don't wake up anytime soon.

Corey put away her diary, She gathered supplies and went out to join him on the beach. It was, she reflected, her shortest diary entry, ever.

———

THE PICNIC AND A beach fire had been Corey's idea. They had wound up in bed again, and after making love, they were ravenous. So she had sent him off with an old newspaper and matches to gather driftwood and put together the fire, and now she was following him down with sandwiches, whiskey and any other beach fire paraphernalia they might need. A fire would be nice. The fog had rolled in, and it was cool on the beach.

At the landing, where her stairs turned to meet her deck, she stopped to watch him. He was conscientiously breaking twigs and rolling paper. Abe carefully organized the twigs into a boxlike structure on the paper, set a driftwood log behind the twigs, then lit the paper. The fire didn't catch. She watched him start again, meticulously rebuilding his fire, trying to get his twigs just so.

She loved the way he concentrated on whatever he did. Especially the way he concentrated on her. When they made love, when they talked, even when she was cleaning or cooking, he stayed tuned in to her, wanting to be present and responsive. Often she'd look over and find him watching—not in the usual guy way, no. What he was doing, she realized, was thinking about her, getting to know her rhythms, her way of doing things, her moods. He made her feel like it was her birthday party—that moment when the presents came on—every minute. "Wait up," she called out. "Wood's wet."

Corey stepped carefully down the stairs balancing her cargo. "You'll need this." She held out a can.

"Lighter fluid?" he asked.

"Gas."

"Gas?"

"Stand back." She poured the can of gasoline over his carefully constructed pile of twigs, stepped back, lit a rolled piece of paper and tossed it on the wood. The flames jumped three feet off the beach.

"I didn't know—"

From behind she put her arms around his chest, kissed his ear and whispered, "I know about this. You're excellent as is."

―――――――

MORGAN'S INVITATION TOOK BILLY by surprise. He hadn't expected to see her before the weekend, but she'd called him on his cell phone as he was leaving soccer practice. "I can't wait 'til Saturday," was what she said.

"What are you thinking?"

"My place, say four o'clock. My parents won't be home 'til late."

"I'm there." Thirty minutes later he was at her door. She took his hand and led him down to the basement.

The basement at Morgan's was a kids' place. There were futons, bulky pillows, colorful quilts, a widescreen television, this state-of-the-art music set up, two great big couches, and a soft, shaggy wall-to-wall carpet. Billy wasn't sure why, but in Morgan's basement he felt safe, even when they smoked weed.

At the basement door, she drew him into a leisurely kiss. Just like that, their kiss turned into something really intense, and then they were leaning against the paneled wall, taking off each other's clothes. "I want to make you happy," he whispered. And she kissed him all over his face and neck. He wasn't sure she had understood what he meant. But it seemed to excite her even more. And now he was so excited he worried he would have an orgasm before they even started.

She led him to a futon where they knelt and kissed again. Morgan lay back, pulling him with her, as she slipped a condom into his hand. "Let me," she whispered. He almost came when she helped him put the condom on. She knew how to do it, so it was really sexy. After, she slowed down, kissing his face and lips while he played with her. She had put his hands between her legs, helped him find the right spot. He had only done that once before, and he had been surprised by how much she liked it. Pretty soon she was moaning, holding him really tight, and then she started shaking. Was she having an orgasm already? It could be one but he wasn't sure. He worried then that maybe it was over, and he was too late. But when she was finished, she just took his penis and slid it inside her, and it was the best thing he had ever felt.

Afterwards, he kissed her tenderly then watched her smile. He was wondering what to say now—if he should tell her it was perfect, thank her, or what. Did she know it was his first time? Yeah, she had to know that. Did she really come? Wasn't that supposed to be harder? She was still underneath him. He couldn't even remember exactly how that happened. He rolled beside her. "Was that okay?" he finally asked, a little sheepish.

"Hmm," she settled in. "You like it?"

"Are you kidding?" He looked at her. "Could you tell it was, uh—you know—"

"Me, too."

He thought she didn't understand him. "No. No way."

"Yeah. First time, ever."

"I thought—"

"You don't know everything." Morgan ran her tongue along his lower lip.

"I'm sorry."

"You don't have to be sorry."

"Really?"

"Hmm-hmm." She held him to her. "In a little while we can do it again."

"This time it'll last longer," he said, sure and hopeful.

———

LESTER MET RILEY AT Shuckers, an oak-paneled seafood restaurant in the Fairmont Olympic Hotel. He didn't know why Riley wanted to meet there, but he knew how cranky the guy could get, so he agreed to meet him at the bar.

When he arrived, Riley was purposefully squeezing lemon on a dozen oysters arranged on ice in a silver platter on the bar. Riley was barely five foot two inches, which, Lester figured, was why he chose a barstool. He wore a white shirt, black slacks and a gray blazer. Square glasses with thick black frames were what you would remember about his face. You would never notice that his nose had been surgically reconstructed. His hair and eyes were brown, and he was thin, almost gaunt.

"Kumamotos, Kushis," Riley said, pointing out oysters to Lester with a thin silver oyster fork. The big man shot him a cloudy-eyed glare; Lester didn't want to hear about oysters. As far as he was concerned, Riley talking food was just one more thing he didn't give a shit about. Lester braced himself. Riley was about the only man he knew who could piss him off. And the smart-mouthed P.I. worked at it. He liked pissing him off. Still, Riley was good for digging up dirt and finding missing people. No one better.

Riley handed him a file. "Deep background," he explained. "Credit cards, insurance, bank statements, police records, so on and so forth." Lester looked over Riley's summary. Dr. Stein was boring. No bad credit history. Couple of professional associations. Ate out alone. Went to the office on weekends. A house on Capitol Hill, where he slept, and probably worked, when he wasn't at the office or eating out. No expensive hobbies. No health club. No vacations. Nothing except work. Not even an ex-wife. Couldn't even drive his own car. A sad sack of shit was what he was. "Whadda you think?" he eventually asked Riley.

"I don't get this guy," Riley confessed.

That was a fucking first. Riley always had some cockamamie theory about everything and everyone. "Give it a try."

"The man's depressed. Doesn't do much else but work." Riley shrugged. "You know anything about depression?"

Lester was getting pissed off. Oysters and now psychology. He considered putting the little silver oyster fork through the back of Riley's hand. Nail his hand to the bar. That would get him to drill down. He decided to give him one more chance. "How can we lean on him? Send him a message?"

"Hard?"

"Start slow." It was what Nick wanted.

"Break into his office. It's where he lives. Fuck it up. Maybe something squirrelly. That'll give him the jim-jams." Riley plucked a fat oyster with the little fork, then held it in the air. "Try one?" he asked.

Lester ignored him. He watched Riley dip the slimy, seeping oyster in horseradish shavings then dunk it in what he called a mignonette sauce. Some kind of vinegar and onion deal. Skanky. Fucking disgusting was what it was. Riley ate it slow—with his mouth open—just to piss him off, Lester was sure.

As he left the bar, Lester upended the silver platter, tipping Riley's skanky pussy food onto his lap.

———

FROM THEIR WINDOW TABLE at Chez Henri, Corey and Abe looked out over the Pike Place Market. They looked down through the orange neon market sign, past the green and pink neon fish, to the dark waters of Puget Sound. In the distance the familiar ferry boat lights, the great clusters of white squares, hovered above the black water following their orderly trajectory through the night.

She and Abe had been together for almost a week, and he had suggested this restaurant to celebrate. She couldn't spend enough time with this man. Corey wasn't working—she didn't start repairing boats at Larry's for another few days—and since their first night together, he had cancelled whatever he could. So these days and nights were an unexpected treat—an impromptu lover's holiday. When he wasn't working, they were at her cabin or his house on Capitol Hill. Yesterday they had gone shopping, and she had bought a simple black dress and new shoes to wear for dinner. Abe had somehow made her feel comfortable wearing these clothes and coming to this place. Corey was reading the menu, wondering why a restaurant in Seattle would have so much of its menu in French. She decided it didn't matter, since she didn't understand the descriptions of the food in English either. What she did understand was the prices—a green salad with some kind of cheese cost sixteen dollars. She looked around. White tablecloths, mirrored, beige-colored walls, cherry wood floors—this was the fanciest place she had ever been. She set down the menu, not sure what to make of all of this. When she looked at him across the table, Abe was already watching her, not at all self-conscious about it either. She took his hand, leaned in. "Place like this, do I have to eat fish?"

"Place like this, you eat what you want."

"Would you order for me?"

"Leave it to me."

"Nothing weird. Okay?"

He gently squeezed her hand.

Corey sat back as an intense-looking man with curly black hair arrived at their table and put a hand on Abe's back. He started right in. "Abe, missed you at brunch Sunday. I've been wanting to talk with you—"

Abe interrupted. "Mike, I'd like to introduce Corey Logan." And to Corey, "This is Mike Morris. Mike's a counselor at the Olympic Academy."

Mike smiled, a tight professional smile. He wore a black linen sport coat over a colorful Hawaiian shirt. His shirt was tucked into old gray Dockers. He looked her over. "Are you in the field?"

"Excuse me?"

"I was thinking that you might be a colleague."

"I saw Abe for an evaluation."

"I don't understand."

"I had to have a psychiatric evaluation to get my son back."

"Oh." Mike frowned, working on this. "I don't—"

"I'm on probation."

Abe took her hand, kissed it, lest there be any doubt about their feelings for each other.

"A client...on probation...no kidding." Mike patted Abe's shoulder. "Call me. Come to brunch tomorrow."

Corey watched him walk back to his table. "Friend of yours?"

He leaned in, finding her eyes. "What?"

She saw that certain twinkle that sometimes came to his eyes. It was a tell she was beginning to understand. "Sorry." She kissed him, a sweet sexy kiss, across the table.

———

Dinner was a three-course affair. Abe ate out a lot and he explained every dish as it came. He was pleased that she liked the rilette—potted guinea hen with coarse salt—and the hearty cassoulet with garlic sausage, lamb, pork and duck confit.

Corey took a careful sip of Armagnac. "I'm already used to this."

"I'd hoped you'd like it. I often eat out alone. This is a place I come when I have something to celebrate. I have a lot of good memories here."

She watched him nod to his friend, who was waving good-bye and mouthing, "Sunday brunch."

Abe thought back to the look on Mike's face when Corey said she'd been in prison. "I apologize for Mike."

"He's nosy."

"Yes, he is."

"Sunday brunch?"

"My mother's a big political fundraiser. She throws a brunch every Sunday. It's become a local political tradition."

"Tell me about her."

"She's very capable," he offered.

"C'mon—"

"Okay." Abe sat up straighter, readying himself to slog through the swamp that still sucked him down when he thought about her. "My mother, Jessica 'Jesse' Larson—Stein, is from a Northwest shipping family. The Larsons had it all—a house in the Highlands, a get away in the San Juans. They took turns serving on the board at Lakeside—the elite private school—and enjoyed skiing in Switzerland—"

"Nice."

"Not always. Her mother, Barbara "Bootsie" Larson, was a demanding, striving woman. Bootsie had her only daughter swim in the freezing cold waters of Puget Sound, off Richmond Beach, every summer day between the ages of five and fifteen. She believed it built character and purged impure thoughts. No kidding." He sat back, shook his head. "Jesse was valedictorian at Saint Nicholas—Lakeside for girls in those days. She went to Stanford, then on to Yale Law School. At twenty-eight my mother ran her own consulting firm, making and breaking big-time politicians."

"A powerhouse, huh."

"Yes, and that's a problem for me. Not long ago she tried to make me surgeon general. She's still angry that I told this confused presidential aide that there was some mistake."

"You? The cigarette guy?"

Abe raised his eyebrows, turned up his palms—an accepting, what-can-I-say gesture that summed up his stance toward life's unsolvable mysteries.

"I know you don't sail. Do you ski?"

"I hate heights and speed." He shrugged.

"Hmm." Corey wasn't done. "Mother like yours, smarter than everyone, connected. How is it you turned out—I don't know—the way you did?"

"My dad, the original Abe Stein." He nodded, his face lively again. "He was ten years older than my mother, a courtly, old-world, Jewish doctor. My father was a wonderful, complicated character. We used to take walks. I'd do most of the talking. And he listened. Then he said just what he thought. At home, though, he'd defer to my mother. She was just too much for him. Jesse decided he should marry her, and she kept on deciding—every last thing—for both of them. It was her idea to name me after him—he never would have done that otherwise. He died when I was thirteen. He just gave up. That's what I thought at the time, anyway." Abe stopped talking, done. He was trying to bring back memories of his father. What he remembered was a well-dressed, soft-spoken, patrician man who got along with all kinds of weird people. Even his mom.

"I'd like to meet your mom—though I have to say, I may not be what she had in mind for the surgeon general."

"Would you come with me to brunch tomorrow? It's likely the best way to get a sense of who she is."

"I'm not very good at fancy parties. I usually say the wrong thing."

"So what? You'll be the brightest star in the room."

"All right. Okay. Thanks." She finished her Armagnac, making a sour face as it went down. "Billy's coming home in less than a week. I'm nervous about that."

Abe took her hand.

"He asked if he could have his girlfriend over. I thought we could all have dinner together."

"Kids find me old-fashioned and, I worry, boring."

"You are old-fashioned." Her mouth turned up, just a little, pushing the patch of freckles that spread across her nose onto the gentle slope of her cheeks. "But you're not boring."

———

IT WAS A BRIGHT summer night, and Jesse watched Nick and Jason from her bedroom window. They were on the patio, working on a campaign idea that she'd asked Nick to present at brunch tomorrow. Jason knew that she and Nick were lovers. It wasn't a secret. She wondered what he thought about that. Jason would approve, she decided, if it made her happy. He was a realist and Nick, as Jason put it, was a man to watch. Her smartest political friends told her privately how Nick Season could be governor, in a heartbeat. What was it about Nick? The man had a keen eye for what people wanted. And when he could, he gave it to them.

He had done that for her. Sexually. To her surprise, Jesse's face and neck flushed red and hot. Before it passed, she smiled a lazy smile, deciding a hot flush beat a hot flash, any day. And she had reason to flush and to smile, ear-to-ear. Nick was giving her things she'd never allowed herself to ask for. With Nick she felt safe, even when—especially when—he tied her wrists to the bedposts.

He was tuned in—giving more when she needed it, backing off when it was too much, letting her take the lead when she wanted that. Nick had learned that she'd try new things, and that if she liked it, nothing was taboo. He was taking her places she'd never been. Places, at fifty-six, she had given up on.

And last night, his suggestion that Abe help with policy. How had he known she wanted that? She thought that Abe would like it too. So why hadn't she suggested it? Because, of course, if it was her idea, Abe wouldn't do it. Okay, Nick could ask him. Jesse couldn't wait to get them together. She wondered if Abe would see that she and Nick were lovers. Likely. Her out-of-step son didn't miss much.

She had seen how Nick used this talent on behalf of his clients. He was known for closing thorny deals. He was the ultimate closer, she believed, because he saw just what each side wanted most, what they couldn't live without.

She smiled again, thinking that he was also the ultimate seducer because he knew just what to tempt you with. Her smile faded as she grew unexpectedly anxious. Without knowing why, she was suddenly apprehensive about the sex, afraid of some price yet to pay for her unfettered pleasures, worried that Nick might be striking unholy bargains. She recognized her mother's disapproving voice, and Jesse abruptly set her worries aside, annoyed with her long-dead mother's lingering presence, and with her tone. If something made her feel so good, so intensely, she didn't have to jump to the most diabolically cynical interpretation.

Still, was she missing something about Nick? She couldn't tell. He had his secrets, she knew that, but so did she. And he was more ambitious than he let on, but that was true for her, too. And he was so good looking he could easily be with a beautiful younger woman. Then again, maybe he'd had enough pretty young women to want other things—like an adult relationship that worked in more complex ways. She understood that; she'd had more than her share of younger men. So what did that mean? He liked her and he liked what she could do for him. Good. That made sense. She liked helping him and he liked being helped. And he liked how smart she was, how quick. He was that smart too. It was a thing they saw in each other. And they looked so good together—when they walked into a crowded room, eyes turned their way. Yes, they had a certain chemistry together and if part of it was fueled by things they could do for each other—by a shared understanding of how things worked—so much the better. What adult relationship couldn't use a little extra octane? Especially seasoned adults. The starry-eyed stuff was long gone for both of them. They were players. She knew it, he knew it. Still, Nick could take her to the moon.

Did she ever, ever, have this with her husband? Jesse suddenly wanted to be sure that she wasn't deluding herself, that she wasn't just an aging woman with an ardent imagination. She remembered how hopeful and earnest she had been when she married. And yes, her husband had been a very good lover, gentle and genuinely pleased to do what she wanted. Still, over the years, they made love less often. And when they did, it was familiar, things they knew. No, sex with her husband had never been like sex with Nick. Nothing like it. Jesse felt the heat again at the back of her neck. She could let herself go with Nick; she had permission. And when her guard was down, when she was most vulnerable, Nick gave her things she didn't even know she wanted.

She decided to ratchet up the sex, see what else he wanted.

Jesse changed into a flowing black silk dress she had bought in New York. Twenty-five hundred dollars and worth every penny. She stopped at the mirror, adjusted her hair. When she was satisfied, she used the intercom line on her phone to buzz Nick on the patio.

"Dinner at Canlis?" she asked when he picked up. "Nine o'clock?"

"Absolutely," he replied.

"Jason?"

"Up to you."

"Let's make it a twosome," she said.

"Perfect. Can I fix you a drink?"

"A martini would be nice. I'll be down in a minute." She watched his handsome profile through the window, wondering how to please him. Unexpectedly, she was unsure.

———

ABE MADE THE PANCAKE batter while Corey squeezed the oranges. They were in Abe's small kitchen trying not to fall over each other. His kitchen was in the southeast corner of his cozy, gray and white wood house on Capitol Hill. It overlooked a postage-stamp-sized yard featuring a fish pond with no fish. Raccoons, he explained, had wiped them out. What Corey especially liked about Abe's home was the carefully crafted wood trim. Fine old walnut and cherry. Even the tiny kitchen had cherry cabinets. She stopped her squeezing when he raised his batter spoon and cleared his throat.

"This old man is trying to get his donkey across a bridge," he said. "And the donkey just won't move."

"What?"

"It's a joke. I'm telling a joke."

"A joke. Oh." She nodded. He had her attention.

"Now the man is pleading, screaming, cajoling. Nothing works...just then, as luck would have it, a therapist happens by and seeing the old man's dilemma, offers to help."

"Okay, so this is a shrink joke?"

"I suppose so. May I tell it?"

"Don't be cranky."

"Okay. Right. So the therapist, he explains to the old man that he will first establish trust, then understand the donkey's feelings, and thus, figure out how to get the donkey across the bridge."

"Is that what you were trying to do? Establish trust?"

"I didn't do a very good job, I know. And you're ruining my joke."

"So far it doesn't seem like a joke. It's more like a shrink-to-shrink kind of insider deal. And 'thus'? Did you say 'thus'?" She made a wry face. Was that a twinkle in his eye? "Never mind."

"Okay. The old man isn't at all convinced by the therapist, but at this point, he'd try anything. So he says, 'Sure, go ahead.' He watches as the therapist picks up a two-by-four and whacks the donkey on the backside." Abe raised his bushy eyebrows, pursed his lips, for emphasis. "The donkey takes off, running right across the bridge. The old man, confused, says, 'What about trust? What about understanding his feelings?' And the therapist nods and says, 'Yes, of course. But first you have to get his attention.'"

Not bad. "That's it?" she asked, deadpan, hoping to get a rise from this oh-so-serious storyteller. "You, the most serious guy I know, telling me that lame, loopy joke. And you did say 'thus.'"

He raised his batter spoon again. "You know it's funny."

Corey stepped closer and put her arms around his neck. She was in love, she knew that much. "You want to skip mom's brunch deal?"

"We can be late."

TWELVE

"THIS IS A MANSION, not a house," Corey said as she parked her black pick-up in front of Jesse's grand old Capitol Hill home. It was a brick Victorian Gothic with gray wood trim that sat on almost two lovely landscaped acres. A pair of brick chimneys rose from the steep slate roof. They got out of the truck and walked up the path to the front door.

"Brace yourself," Abe cautioned as he opened the fir door. Corey lingered at the door, taking it in. She loved the high ceilings, the walk-in stone fireplace, the old woodwork, and especially the far-reaching view of Lake Washington and the mountains beyond. This living room had surely been in magazines. Corey looked around the room at the guests. There were maybe forty people. She knew only two: Jason, the lawyer, and Mike, the curly-haired guy from the restaurant.

A striking, stylish woman was suddenly standing between her and Abe. She wore an elegant black designer dress. Whoever she was, this woman was a powerful presence. She was, well, classy, Corey decided. Corey turned to Abe, who was talking now to someone she didn't recognize. She felt a hand on her arm. "I don't know you," the expensively dressed woman said.

"No, we've never met," she replied as the woman looked at her. Corey wore light gray slacks, a white pullover, and a smart black jacket she'd bought recently with Abe. She felt underdressed.

Jason stepped beside them. "Jesse," he said to the stunning woman. Oh sweet Jesus, Abe's mom. Oh my God. Wow. I never would have known. Never would have guessed. Never. "Do you know Corey Logan?" Jason asked Abe's mom, interrupting Corey's thoughts. "She's a friend of Abe's."

"We were just meeting," Jesse said. "I didn't know Abe had a new friend," she added, and then Jesse was distracted by another guest. Jason led Corey down three steps into the living room. "Abe's a fine man," he explained. "The family's going to take some getting used to."

"The family?"

"The mother."

Abe's mother, yeah. Looking like a million bucks. Like she belongs on national television. Sometimes the apple falls a long way from the tree.

———

JESSE WATCHED JASON AND Corey step into the living room as she finished talking with Fran Lipsom, the publicist from L.A. When Fran left, she glanced over at Abe who was nearby talking with Mortimer Silver, a local psychiatrist and a friend. Jesse turned back to study Corey who was moving toward the patio now with Jason. Where did Abe find these women? This one had worked with her hands, Jesse guessed.

Mike Morris, the curly-haired counselor from the Olympic Academy came over. "Have you met Abe's new girlfriend?" Mike asked, when Jesse kept her eyes on the patio.

Girlfriend? Okay. Maybe it was a phase. At least he was interested in someone, she reminded herself. "She's not what I expected," Jesse said to Mike.

"Prison makes a person hard to read."

"Prison?"

Abe turned. "Mike, read my lips—dis-cre-tion—" he said slowly.

"I'm sorry," Mike said sincerely. "I didn't know it was a secret."

"It's not a secret." And to his attentive mother, "Corey was in prison. I did a court-ordered evaluation so she could get her son back."

"A son?" Jesse smiled warmly and squeezed his arm. "I'm glad you've met someone," she said. "We'll talk later," Jesse added, then stepped away to greet a couple at the door.

"Abe—" Mike steepled his fingers. This was important. "Abe, are you still seeing your analyst? I mean, kiddo—"

"I think my analyst had an affair with my mother," Abe interrupted. It just came out. An irresistible conversation stopper and, Abe reflected, a possibility he'd never considered.

"Sy?" Mike's eyes widened. "Sy? No kidding."

———

COREY WAS ALONE, NEAR the patio door. Jason had excused himself. Abe had come over, then left to use the restroom. She assured him that she would be okay, though she had to say, she didn't have a clue what she should do around these people. She was watching the party, wondering how people knew where to stand, who to talk to, what to say. They were milling around with apparent purpose, like bees working in a hive. These people were expert at this, she decided. They knew how to do this like she knew where to find fish.

Corey turned to the buffet table. In the center, a fancy baked ham was partially carved into slices that were attractively presented on an engraved silver tray that she would gleefully trade for her truck. Carefully arranged around the centerpiece were roast vegetables, steaming pasta with clam sauce, king salmon—Copper River, she guessed, the most esteemed and expensive of the Alaskan summer run kings—an elaborate cheese tray, pastries and oh-so-many things she had never seen before. She watched Abe, making his way back toward her from across the room.

A woman touched her forearm. "Hi, I'm Fran from L.A." Fran wore jeans and a v-necked cashmere sweater. "Jesse hired me to do the publicity for her candidate."

"Hello, I'm Corey."

"Enjoying the party?"

"Yeah. Sure."

"Did you hear about Sy?" Fran asked.

"Who?"

"Abe's analyst?"

"What?"

"There's no pressure," Fran said. "I know how hard it is to mingle after being inside."

Corey shot her a black look. "Are you loaded?" she asked.

"Sweetheart, that was friendly." Fran kissed her cheek and headed for the buffet.

"Do you know that woman?" Corey asked Abe, when he joined her again.

"No."

"How did she know I was in prison?"

"Mike Morris, the character from the restaurant, told my mother. She probably told that lady. Let's eat—we can go out onto the patio—then leave."

"Take your time. I'm okay." She took his arm. "By the way, who's Sy? And what's an analyst?"

Abe leaned in. "It's a little bit of a story." He covered her hand with his. "Let's eat. I'll explain later."

Abe led Corey to the buffet and handed her a plate. He pointed out some Jewish food he called chopped liver. It looked like lumpy liverwurst. "My father's family recipe," he said, and she decided to try it.

Corey was hungry and she took things she recognized first—roast vegetables, ham, linguini. Abe served her a cup of his mother's signature dish—some kind of cold creamy green soup. She set the cup on her plate and was adding a serving of chopped liver when Corey turned—and there he was...Nick Season...Nick fucking Season...running for state attorney general, not twenty feet behind her in the buffet line.

When she was fifteen, in the wilds of British Colombia, Corey had stepped between a sow grizzly and her two cubs. The mother grizzly charged her, stopping so close that she could smell the great bear's rancid breath. This was worse, way worse than that.

Nick looked at her with hard black eyes and smiled. Corey held Nick's gaze. She felt his pick, stabbing through her lower jaw, piercing the roof of her mouth. She considered going for his eyes with her salad fork, then realized that she couldn't move, she couldn't breathe. When Abe's mother adjusted a lock of Nick's hair, Corey felt her heart stop beating. When Jesse came to make introductions, Corey missed a step. She cried out, helpless as she lost her plate, splattering Jesse with vichyssoise, roast vegetables, steaming pasta. There were even dollops of chopped liver on Jesse's neck and in her hair.

"I—I'm so sorry," Corey stammered.

"My fault," Abe offered. "Clumsy, as usual."

"Don't be silly." Jesse smiled her megawatt smile, wiping her neck with a napkin. "Accidents happen. Enjoy the party. I'll be right out." She turned toward the kitchen. Corey bolted for the door.

———

IN THE KITCHEN, JESSE was using a dishtowel to wipe linguini with clam sauce and vichyssoise off her Italian dress. Nick came in all smiles. He could feel his skin, though, like it was sunburned. And he was pretty sure that there were hives on his chest. Big red suckers around his nipples. He had been too smart by half. What had she written? You go your way, I'll go mine. Why then was she here in Jesse's living room? Why then was she here with Jesse's son? Because Corey Logan was a tar baby that wouldn't come unstuck. Ever. And now the tar baby was fucking Abe Stein. Okay then. Set her world on fire. See if she came unstuck then.

"You look delicious." Nick shone his smile on Jesse.

"Who is that Corey Logan woman? Can you find out about her? She was in jail."

Nick took his time. This was where the great ones, the political giants, turned a liability into an asset. "Jesse, I know her," he calmly explained. "She got out several months ago, after doing two years. Go easy, she's as tough as you are."

"How do you know her?" And before he could answer, she said, "She's with my son."

"We'd better talk. Dinner?"

"Eight o'clock. El Gaucho." Jesse looked at her soiled dress, made a frosty face that deemed it hopeless, dropped the dishtowel in the sink, and went up the back stairs to change.

———

COREY WAS LEANING AGAINST her pick-up, gasping. When she finally caught her breath, she gagged, then threw up her breakfast pancakes. Abe was rubbing her back.

"Something I ate," she whispered when she could breathe again.

"Take your time. Do you want to see a doctor?"

Corey shook her head. She closed her eyes. Her mind was racing; she couldn't stop it. Nick was fucking Abe's mother! Abe's mother! Working her somehow. Her lawyer was Nick's friend. And one of his lawyers, for sure. How could this be happening? Shit. How? She hung her head.

"I can't see you for a while," Corey muttered, eyes open now. She was watching the door, waiting for she-didn't-know-what.

"What's wrong? I don't understand."

Nick opened the door, stood in the doorway. Double shit. She watched him. He would be wondering what she had told Abe. What she would tell him later. From here on, Nick would worry about her all the time. Her and Abe. Him and Jesse. Abe and Jesse. The whole set-up was wound too tight. In Seattle "off the radar screen" was no longer possible. If she stayed, their fragile truce was over. It was over already, she realized. She had to find Billy. Right away. If she stayed, Abe was in danger, too. Taking short controlled breaths, she turned to Abe. "I'm sorry."

"What can I do?"

"You do nothing. Nothing. You make a mistake, you maybe feel bad for a few days, lose a patient or something. It's not the same for me."

"What's wrong?"

"Abe, I like you. I may even love you. But I need to take a break. Sort some things out. I'm sorry."

"What happened in—"

"Nothing happened. Just let it go."

"Will you call me?" he asked, concerned.

"I don't know."

"What's going on? Something happened. What?" Abe put a hand on her arm as Corey moved toward the door of her truck. "Can we talk?"

"I don't want to talk now. Please don't argue with me about this. I need to be alone." Corey got in the truck. She saw Nick, watching her from the doorstep. Throwing her that silky smile. She looked down at Abe. "I'll be in touch."

"I'll wait for your call." She heard him say, in his kind way, as she drove off.

––––––

NICK WATCHED THE BLACK pick-up disappear. His skin was on fire. How could Corey Logan be with this man? How could that white trash bitch be with Jesse's son? How? Why? Goddammit! Dr. Stein, the scruffy-looking shrink, just stood there, a wilting doofus, a goddamned doormat was what he was. With a mother like his, maybe he liked being stepped on. Nick speed-dialed his cell phone. "Take the boy," he snapped at Lester. And after a beat. "Now, you fuckin' henhussy."

––––––

COREY DROVE SOUTH ON Nineteenth Avenue, clocking fifty miles an hour, easy. At Madison she turned left through a red light, causing an oncoming car to honk its horn, startling in Seattle. She tried Billy's cell phone. No answer. No answer at the foster home either. She was crying—close to panic. She worked to focus. She tried Billy again, he still wasn't answering. She left a message, "I'm on the way to your foster house. We're in danger. I think they're coming after you. If you're at the foster house, pack a bag and be ready to leave in five minutes. I'll pick you up then." She couldn't stop crying.

At Billy's sad-looking foster home, she left the truck running and ran to the door. She pounded on the door, again and again. Eventually the wiry woman with the pallid face and the red-rimmed eyes came to an open window covered by a rusty, wire-mesh grill. She looked at Corey, who was still banging on the door. "Are you crazy?" she asked.

Corey ignored her. "I need to find Billy," she yelled.

"He's not here."

"Where is he?"

"How would I know? And quit your damn banging." The woman turned away, muttering.

In the car, she called her friend Jamie at the hair salon. When Jamie answered on the third ring, all Corey said was, "I need help."

"What can I do?"

"Can you get a gun? Now?"

"Oh shit…I have a thirty-eight caliber at home."

"Meet me at the Blue City Café. It's between Pike and Pine, west of Broadway. I think they're about to move on Billy and me."

"I'll be there."

Corey tried Billy again. No answer. She left another message. "Meet me at the Blue City Café. Right away. Just do it. This is urgent."

Corey parked her truck on a side street. She ran to the café, checked it out through the front window. Billy wasn't there. She chose an entryway across the street where she could watch for her son, or Jamie, or Lester. She tried to think about something other than Nick Season's silky smile. And what he might do to Billy. She couldn't, she was sick with worry. Fifteen minutes later Jamie came running toward the café. Corey put thumb and forefinger between her lips and let out a sharp whistle. Jamie turned and zigzagged across the street to her friend. Jamie gave her a quick hug, handed her a paper bag. "It's loaded," was all she said.

Corey stepped back into the entryway and opened the bag. The .38 special was holstered. There was also a box of bullets. She checked the cylinder—it was loaded—then attached the holstered gun under her new black jacket at the small of her back. She put the box of bullets in her jacket pocket. "Thanks." Corey took Jamie's hand, anticipating her question. "You don't want to know."

"What are you going to do?"

Corey tried to stay calm. "Get Billy, then take the boat north."

"Canada?"

"Yeah."

"You need someone to watch your back? At least to the boat?"

"I'll be okay once I find Billy." And there he was, holding hands with that same girl, walking down Pine toward the café.

The rush she felt was as good as leaving her prison cell for the last time.

"Gotta go." She squeezed Jamie's hand. "I'll keep in touch."

Jamie took Corey's hand in both of hers. "You need anything, girl, anything at all, I'll do what I can. Your boy looks good. Godspeed."

"I love you, babe." And Corey was running across the street.

She intercepted Billy and Morgan at the entrance to an alley that ran behind the café. She didn't wait for pleasantries. "We've got to go," she said to Billy. "We've got to leave. Now."

"What? What are you talking about?" Billy looked confused, and unhappy to see her.

"Did you get my message?"

"Phone's off. Sorry." Billy glanced at Morgan, sharing something.

Slow down, keep it together, Corey reminded herself. She took Billy's arm. "We can't be here." She led him into the alley behind the café. Morgan followed. In the alley they stepped into the back entryway of the café. "You're in danger. I'll explain later. Let's go." Corey nodded toward the side street where her truck was parked.

"Who is this?" Morgan asked Billy.

"Another time. Please." Corey turned toward Billy. "We're leaving. Right now."

"Like hell," said Lester. He had a powerful hand, like a vice, on Billy's upper arm. Corey had no idea where he'd come from. Maybe he'd been waiting for Billy, lurking in an alcove somewhere in or near the alley. Billy couldn't move.

"Let go of him," Morgan said to Lester.

Lester made his throaty sound.

Corey stepped between Morgan and Billy. "Back off," she said to Morgan. "This is dangerous for you."

Something in Corey's tone made Morgan step back.

Lester pushed back a wide lapel so Corey could see his other hand on his oversized gun, unholstered inside his blue pinstriped suit. The gun was pointed at Billy. Corey nodded slowly. She got it.

"We're going on a trip," Lester said to Billy, picking him up by the arm with one hand. He pressed the gun muzzle into Billy's ribs.

Billy knew what it was, Corey could tell from the way he was biting down on his lower lip. Lester eyed Corey—a glare that plainly said she was an insect he could squash, whenever. "Say goodbye to your mom, boy," he hissed to Billy.

Morgan's mouth dropped open.

Corey raised her palms, nodding, acquiescing. She could feel her pulse pounding in her ears. "Don't hurt him. Please," she entreated. Lester ignored her. "Please," Corey repeated. He looked at her and closed one cloudy eye, a ghastly wink. She lowered her head, a final plea, her hands still in the air.

When Lester turned Billy toward the street, Corey drew the gun from the small of her back. She gasped as she shot a hole through his head—in behind his left ear, out his forehead. Blood splattered on the red brick rear wall of the Blue City Café, then the big man careened off the wall to the poorly paved alleyway and fell, facedown. Morgan was screaming. Billy was lying on his side in the alley where he'd been dropped.

Corey pulled him up. "We've got to get out of here." She turned and there was Jamie, blocking the entrance to the alley in her old Chevy, gunning the engine. Corey pushed Billy into the backseat. She turned back to Morgan. "Honey, take deep breaths," she called out. Corey jumped in front. And Jamie stepped on the gas.

"Fuck," Corey said. Her head was throbbing.

"Did you just kill that big guy?" Jamie asked, driving carefully toward the freeway.

"Fucking lizard creep. I hope so," Corey whispered. She worked to breathe.

"Jesus. I can't believe you did that. I mean Jesus Christ, gal."

"Our only chance," she managed to say, and then she was hyperventilating. Corey focused on her breathing—shallow, fast breaths, like childbirth—until she got it together. She turned to Jamie. "Can you take us to the boat?" she asked softly. "It's up north at Larry's for repairs. We have to get there before the police put this together."

"Can do," Jamie said. And when Corey turned her way, "I saw him slinking around in that alley, so I stuck around."

"Thank you. Thank you," she repeated.

Jamie turned north, onto I-5. "Got your back, like it or not."

Billy was in the back seat, head in his hands. Corey turned to him. "He was going to take you," she explained.

"Oh God." Billy shook his head, side to side. "What happened?"

"It's a long story. I'll tell you on the boat."

He bit off part of his thumbnail. "What about my friend, Morgan? I just left her screaming in the alley with a dead man."

At least she could reassure him about this. It might be the only thing she could reassure him about, she reflected. "Your friend didn't do anything wrong. She'll be okay."

"How can you know that?"

Corey could see how worried he was. "Honey, she didn't do anything. And she doesn't know anything. Right?"

"Not about, you know"—he made an impatient whirling gesture with his hand that was meant to sum up their improbable history—"this. No way."

"She'll be fine then. This is not about her."

Billy nodded. She could see that he got that. He was quiet for a minute, and then he was worrying again; she could see it on his face. "Shouldn't we be going to that lawyer who's helping us?" he asked. "You just killed a guy."

"He was kidnapping my son. There's nothing that lawyer can do now, anyway."

"What do you mean?"

"That lawyer is connected to the man who tried to take you. And now I'm a convicted felon who's shot someone. They're going to charge me with murder."

"This is crazy."

"Worse than that." Corey said. There was, she knew, good reason to worry. "The man I told you about, if he can find us, he'll try to kill us now."

THIRTEEN

ON JESSE'S PATIO NICK tried Lester's cell phone again. And again. No answer. No call back. He had sent him after Corey's boy several hours ago. Where was he? Lester always returned his calls. Right away. Even if the cold-blooded Neanderthal just breathed into the phone. Something was wrong. Nick's skin was still warm, and he was starting to sweat. Fran took his arm. "Nicely done," she said, referring to his presentation after the brunch. "Tough, yet warm, like your face when you smile." She squeezed his arm, insider to insider. "You've got a gift. I could help you with some new moves. And I'd like to see you tilt a little further left." Fran, he knew, was measuring him for something bigger.

"Thanks, you were a big help. It was your idea to emphasize immigration issues. They liked that." Nick smiled, thinking he had to get rid of this ball buster before he bit her tongue off, like Hannibal Lector did in that movie. He turned away from her, aware he was losing focus, drifting. Nick approached Jesse, who had changed into a smart black Italian designer pantsuit. She was talking to Jason near the door. He pictured Hannibal serving Corey Logan's brains to his head-shrinker colleague, Dr. Abraham Stein. Damn, he was drifting again, a sign that his anxiety was coming on. Nick wiped his forehead with a handkerchief.

"You okay?" Jesse asked, touching his arm.

"Something I ate," he explained. "Can I sit in the study for a few minutes?"

"Of course. You were great," she whispered in his ear. "You are great," she added. "Lie down. People are leaving. I'll check on you later."

On the way to the study, Nick's cell phone rang. It was Lieutenant Jim Norse, a police officer he had worked with for years. Early on, Nick had derailed an Internal Affairs investigation that would have cost Norse his job, at least. And then he used his considerable influence to help Jim rise through the ranks. Long before he made lieutenant, Jim was Nick's guy, period. He had called him to check on Lester. "Hang on a minute." Nick went into the study and closed the door. He sat on the couch, feeling better already. "Any word?"

"You sitting down?"

Nick loosened his tie, anxious again. "What's up?"

"Lester's dead. Shot."

Nick could feel the hives sprouting on his chest. And he was sweating, like a radiator overheating. Then he felt weak. Soon he'd be numbing up. His face, his feet, all over. At least then he wouldn't feel the weakness. He wondered if this was what it was like to lose a leg, or an arm. Lester, he realized, was an appendage. "What happened?" he asked, his voice a hoarse whisper.

"Some woman shot him in an alley south of Pine Street. One round in the back of the head. In broad daylight. Something about her son. The son's girlfriend says his name was Billy Logan. But the girlfriend's still in shock."

He used his handkerchief on his face while he regrouped. "Could I call you back, Jim?" Nick knew from experience what was happening. First came the anxiety, then the weakness, and, finally, no feeling at all. The numbness, he believed, was what his body did to hide his appalling weakness. He also knew that the weakness would get worse and worse, until it got so bad that he couldn't even speak. He pictured himself at a news conference in front of all these people. At the podium he was sweating, breathing really fast, and when he tried to talk, all that came out were raspy breathing sounds. Okay. He knew only one way to back off this crippling anxiety.

He lay down on the couch while he played, then replayed revenge fantasies in his mind. Nick wished he still had his lug wrench. He lingered on that, his lug wrench days. Time passed, maybe ten minutes, before he was back in the present, coldly replaying what he had just heard. And then he went full focus on Corey Logan. Putting her under his microscope. Everything he knew about the last weeks, about Abe Stein. After a while—he wasn't sure how long—something was surfacing, taking shape. He thought he could feel the tips of his fingers again, his toes. When Jesse opened the door, he pretended to be asleep. She turned off the lights and left.

Sometime later, Nick saw a way at Corey Logan. A way at Corey Logan and Abraham Stein. A way to clean up this mess. Cut it out, root and branch. He sat up, collecting himself, then he turned on the lights. Nick sat back down on the couch. He moved his forefinger along the hair hanging over his collar. When he was ready, Nick picked up the phone and called Jim back. "Corey Logan's the shooter," he said, more confident now. "You can bet on it. You have a file on her, she's a convicted felon. Could you meet me at the scene? I want to talk to the witness."

"I'll see you there, counselor."

"Thanks." Nick hung up the phone.

His feeling was back, even in his neck, so Nick knew the episode was over. It had been his first in many years, and it had only lasted about half an hour. It could have been worse, he knew, much worse. His debilitating episodes used to go on for hours and hours, and afterward he couldn't sleep at night. He went over his plan again, questioning, refining, then testing again. Ten minutes later he was retying his tie, readying himself.

Jesse cracked open the door. "You feeling better? I wanted to give you time to rest."

Nick smiled warmly, aware it was crunch time—when the great ones rose to the occasion, walked on water if they had to. "Yes, thank you. Please sit down." He waited until she sat beside him. "I couldn't talk before. I didn't have the full story. There's a serious problem." Nick took her offered hand. He focused on where to start. Jesse, he knew, had to come to this on her own. He began tentatively, "Here's what I know. Your son's new friend, Corey Logan, just shot and killed my legal investigator, Lester Burell." He stayed neutral, just the facts. "I called Lester right after we spoke. As you and I discussed, I asked him to find out what he could about Corey Logan. Apparently, he was following her son when she shot him in the back of the head. Maybe an hour ago."

Jesse was cold as a stone. "Are you telling me that this woman murdered your investigator, who was working at my request?"

"I think so. Yes."

"Why would she do that?"

Nick raised his brow, his free hand. He didn't know.

"I'm sorry." Jesse squeezed the hand she held. "Tell me what happened."

"It was on Capitol Hill, just off Pine. In an alley behind some café. There's a witness. I'm on my way. I'll call in when I have the whole story."

"What can I do?" she asked.

"Nothing yet. This is my department. Let me put it together. Go over the evidence. Talk with the witness who saw the shooting. I want to be sure I have it right before we do anything."

"Should I call Abe?"

"Not yet. Not until I'm absolutely sure it was her, and I know just what happened. I don't want to upset him unnecessarily." Or involve him quite yet. Nick touched Jesse's forearm. "Give me an hour."

––––––

IN HIS LIVING ROOM Abe was pacing. He had tried calling Corey three times but she wasn't returning his calls. Something horrible had happened at brunch. That disturbing knowledge had settled in his gut. Abe's cell phone rang, and a wave of relief washed over him. "Corey?" he said into the phone.

"Lou Ballard," his friend, the police detective, corrected him. "We have to talk."

Abe scowled. It wasn't like Lou to call him on a Sunday. "What's up?"

"Your girlfriend, Corey Logan. She just shot and killed a guy near Pine Street."

Abe sat, disoriented. "Are you sure?"

"There's a witness."

"Where's Corey?"

"We don't know. Maybe you can help. Where's her boat? Bainbridge?"

"I think so," he said, aware she'd moved it for repairs, covering for her without missing a beat. "I'm sure it was self-defense."

"The guy had a three-fifty-seven magnum. But it could have been holstered. We don't know. His gun wasn't fired."

"Can I talk with the witness?"

"Since when are you a cop?"

"I'm in love with this woman, Lou. Corey Logan didn't murder anyone. I promise you that."

"You can talk to me. At the station. Five-thirty."

———

COREY KEPT THE *JENNY Ann* on course for Port Townsend. At the picturesque port she would turn west, hugging the northern coast of Washington until she found a busy crossing of the Strait of Juan de Fuca. The other boats would give her cover. She knew this water, and she was confident they could cross the strait into British Colombia without a problem. After that, she would make a plan. Billy sat in the wheelhouse beside her, sullen. "Want to talk?" she asked.

"Why? We're fucked." He looked out at the Sound.

"Fucked is locked up in Lester's cellar. This is not fucked. This is free."

"Who's Lester?" he asked.

"Sorry. He's the man I shot."

"Did you have to shoot him?"

"Lester was going to take you. I couldn't let him do that."

Billy thought about that. "Why did you kill him?"

"It was the only way to stop him. The man's pretty much unstoppable, unless he's dead."

"He had a gun, didn't he? I could feel it."

"Yeah, he did."

'What if you let him take me?"

"These men killed your dad. They're capable of anything. So letting him take you was never a possibility. He'd have to kill me first."

164

Billy drummed his fingers on his thigh. "They'll be looking for us, won't they?"

"Yes."

"Can we hide?"

"I think so. At least for the summer. I know a place."

"And then?"

"By then we'll have a plan." And she believed that. A great weight had been lifted. Lester was dead. Nick Season's head games were over. This was war, and she'd protect her son.

"I need to call Morgan."

"When we get to Canada, you can call her."

"And say what?"

"Say whatever you want. Tell her what you know. You haven't done anything wrong."

Billy turned to her, looked her over carefully. "Neither have you."

She touched his shoulder, feeling pleased and proud.

FOURTEEN

NICK STOPPED TO CHECK out the crime scene: an alley south of Pike Street, west of Broadway. Squad cars had blocked off the alleyway, and a crowd of gawkers had gathered behind a SPD sedan at one end of the alley. He identified himself and walked over to the taped-off area where Lester had fallen. He could see where Lester's body had landed and where a slug had been dug out of the brick wall. There was nothing else he could learn here. He walked out of the alley, through the onlookers, and turned toward the café.

Morgan was wiping her face with a wet washcloth when Nick came through the front door of the Blue City Café. She tilted her head back and lay the washcloth over her face, ignoring the two policemen sitting with her at the round café table. The heavy-set one was reading over the notes in his notebook while his thin partner rewound a tape recorder. The policemen stood up when they saw Nick. He nodded. Since he had announced his candidacy, people were beginning to recognize him. Morgan glanced at him, then covered her face with the wet washcloth again, shutting out the world. Nick motioned for the policemen to leave them and he stepped behind her.

"It's okay," Nick said softly. He put his hands on her shoulders, massaging gently. "I'm here to help."

She let him work on her shoulders, her neck. He could see that this good-looking rich girl was used to special treatment. Morgan lowered the washcloth, found his black eyes. "Who are you?"

"I'm a lawyer. My name is Nick Season. I know the woman who shot this man. I'd like to help her." He stopped his massaging and sat beside her. She was crying now, really upset, which was good. "She's Billy's mother."

"That woman was really his mom?" she asked, still shaken.

"Yes. Corey Logan."

"Jeez." Morgan shook her head, as if unable to process this. "And what about his father?"

"He left them, years ago."

After a minute she asked, "Is Billy in trouble?"

"I don't know. Tell me what happened."

"I told them everything." She pointed at the policemen, standing near the door. "Maybe ten times."

"I know it's difficult. But you have to remember that a lot of police work is checking out details." She was crying again. He put on a sympathetic face. "My situation is a little different. I'm here to look out for Billy and his mom."

"Okay. Yeah." Morgan pressed the washcloth to her eyes. "I'm not sure just what happened. It was really fast."

So far so good. "Just tell me what you saw."

She set the washcloth aside. "This big guy grabbed Billy. He picked Billy up in the air with one hand. Like King Kong or something. Told him to say goodbye to his mom."

Nick looked concerned. "That must have been frightening."

"Yeah. It was."

"Did he have a gun?"

"I couldn't tell." She closed her eyes, opened them. "He had his hand under his jacket, but I couldn't see what he was doing."

Perfect. "And then?"

"He turned Billy toward the street. I looked away, toward Billy. The next thing I knew, there was a gunshot and the big guy was bouncing off the wall, blood spouting out of his head." Morgan grimaced. "Really gross."

"What happened next?"

"I was screaming. I guess I freaked out." She put the wet towel to her forehead again. "There was a car. The lady pushed Billy into the backseat. She jumped in front and then they drove away."

"Did you describe the car to the policemen?"

"Yeah. About a zillion times."

He touched her shoulder again, thinking this was going to work. "I'm sorry. I'll take you home."

"Can you do that?"

"No problem. Give me a minute."

"Can you help Billy?"

"Yes, I think so."

He stood and walked over to where the policemen were waiting. Lieutenant Jim Norse was chatting with them now. "Hey, Jim," Nick said when he got closer.

"Counselor," Jim replied.

"Looks like murder," Nick commented.

"Lester had a gun," the heavyset cop said.

"And a license to carry it. Fellas, he worked for me," he explained.

"That's what we heard. And that helps him. Still, we'll want to talk with you about what he was doing," Norse pointed out.

"Of course," Nick replied. And then, like an afterthought, "Was his gun fired?"

"No. But it was on the ground, beside him," the thin cop said.

"He's six foot four and solid. The gun's heavy too." Nick paused. "What do you think happens when a guy that big gets knocked against the wall and then drops to the ground?"

"What?" The big cop asked.

Nick watched the lieutenant's face as he worked this out. "Things fall out. Gravity," Norse eventually explained to his guys.

"Yeah." The thin cop nodded. "That could be."

"Did the witness see a gun?" Nick asked, feigning confusion.

"Not his, anyway," the heavier cop replied.

"The shooter's got quite a history," the lieutenant volunteered. "I brought her file."

"I'll take the witness home then meet you at the station. We can go over whatever you like," Nick offered. And nail this down. Once and for all.

"Sounds good. I'll buy you guys coffee," the lieutenant said to the two younger policemen. He led them to the counter and took out Corey's file.

Nick helped Morgan to her feet. "You're free to go. Have you called your folks?"

"Not yet. They're out of town. They'll be back." She checked her watch. "Jeez, it's already four-thirty. I've been here forever. They'll be back by five-thirty or six."

He considered this. "Would you like me to stay with you until your folks come home?"

"That would be great, yeah. Thanks," she added.

Nick led Morgan to the three cops. "I may be a little late. I'm going to wait with Morgan until her parents come home."

"You know where to find me," Lieutenant Norse said.

"And good luck," the thin policeman offered. His partner concurred.

Jim Norse gave Nick a thumbs up. "A.G.? It's in the bag, counselor."

"Thanks, guys." Nick smiled his smile.

———

"DAMMIT LOU," ABE BARKED. He was pacing in Sergeant Ballard's office. "Corey Logan didn't murder anyone."

"There's a witness. Logan's a convicted felon. She was carrying a gun, which is a violation of her probation. The vic's gun wasn't fired." Lou cracked a knuckle. When Abe winced, he cracked another. "She shot him in the head. The officers on the scene say it looks like she shot him from behind."

"I get the picture. Now, as a friend, imagine you're me—" Abe raised both hands. "I know, I know. Just try—and you know she's innocent. What do you do?"

"I find her. I find out exactly what in hell her story is—and it better be damned good—and then I bring her back." Lou shot him a hard look. "Find her, bring her back. It's her best chance."

"Can I talk with the witness?"

"Forget the witness. That's police work. Find Corey Logan. That's the best thing you can do."

"And if you find her first?"

"Don't start with me. If you find her, we'll talk." Lou opened his office door. "Keep in touch."

Out in the hallway, Abe sat down on a bench facing Lou Ballard's closed office door. There were people coming and going in the long hall, in and out of what seemed to be a bullpen of cubicles and several private offices. The door to the large corner office on his left was also closed. To his right there was a staircase that went down to the first floor. The clock on the wall said 6:15 P.M. Lou had been late, he realized, and he hadn't even noticed. He was that upset. And confounded. He had no idea at all how to find Corey. She was on her way to Canada in her boat; he knew that much. He hoped she would make it. The police would be looking for her, but she would know how to get past them. Lou wouldn't have asked him to find her otherwise. What a fool he was. He loved this woman. Something awful had started at his mother's brunch. He had no idea what. He shouldn't have let her leave without him. Easier said than done. Still…

Abe heard footsteps coming up the stairs. A man stopped in the hall, then sat beside him. Abe turned away, preoccupied.

"Excuse me," the man said.

He turned back, recognizing the well-dressed man, but not making the connection right away.

"Nick Season." The man offered his hand. "I was at brunch at your mother's today."

Abe shook his hand. "Right. State attorney general."

"Not yet."

"If you were at brunch, you're close," Abe noted, distracted.

"I hope so."

"I'm sorry, but this isn't a good time for me to talk."

"I apologize." Nick stood. "If there's anything I can do to be helpful, please let me know."

"Thank you. I may take you up on that." They shook hands again, then Nick was gone.

Abe took out his cell phone and called Jason, their lawyer.

Jason picked up on the first ring. "Abe?"

"Yes. I'm at the police station. Have you heard from Corey?"

"No. Nothing."

"You know what—"

"Yes, I'm afraid I do." Jason interrupted, uncharacteristically. "Your mother's in a state about it. Apparently, the legal investigator Corey shot was one of Nick Season's men, working at Jesse's request."

"Why would my mother do something like that?"

"She was checking out your girlfriend. For your mother that's standard operating procedure. You know this. Now she's worried that you, her only son, is romancing a murderer."

"That's crazy."

"So?" The question was rhetorical. Abe could picture the lawyer, pensive, rubbing his ear lobe between a thumb and forefinger. "She wants to see you."

"Put her off, please. Have you tried to reach Corey?"

"I've left messages at every number I have. I even left her my cell phone number. Not a word."

Why is that? Abe wondered. "I'm going home. Lou Ballard wants me to find her. I need to think about that. I'll call you if I hear anything. And if you hear from her, tell her that I have to talk to her." Abe broke the connection. He lowered his head. He was losing his bearings.

———

NICK WATCHED THE DOOFUS, sitting on the bench outside Lou Ballard's office. The guy looked like he had been gut shot. He would find out sooner or later that Lester had worked for him. So Nick hung back, reviewing the situation. He had anticipated this. The shrink was in his plan. And so was Lieutenant Norse. Riley was already on the case. Now it was time to talk to the lieutenant. When Abe lumbered down the stairs, through the reception area and out the front door, Nick went to a window overlooking the street. He watched him get into an old, burgundy-colored Olds. The shrink had a driver. Some wise-ass Chinaman. When he did his original work-up on Stein, Riley had tried to chat it up with the driver at a noodle place on Broadway. The Chinaman told him, "no English." When Riley persisted, the Chinaman said, "Bugger off, shitbag." Riley wrote it up in his report, word for word. No kidding. He must have liked the guy's attitude. Kindred spirit or something. Nick let it go. Lieutenant Norse was waiting.

———

ABE JUST SHOOK HIS head when Sam asked how it had gone. He didn't want to talk. Even Sam didn't have anything to say. Abe asked Sam to drive by the office; he wanted to get Corey's file. Under the viaduct, the street was dark. He went into his building, turned on the hallway lights and took the stairs.

His office door was unlocked. Odd. He waited a moment before turning on the lights. Not a sound. Maybe he had been preoccupied when he left on Friday and forgotten to lock the door. Stranger things had happened lately. He turned on the office lights. He had a clear view from his vantage point, and he could see that his office was empty. Abe stepped inside and looked around. The middle drawer of his file cabinet was open. He hurried over to the cabinet and leafed through the file folders. One file was missing: Corey Logan's.

Abe called Lou Ballard and told him what he'd found. Lou agreed to send someone over. "You want me to wait?" he asked.

"Are you kidding?"

"About what?"

"My guys find something—which I doubt—you'll ask too many questions and get in the way. Piss people off."

"Nice—"

"We'll call you if we need you," Lou interrupted. "Incidentally, you've found a really special woman." He broke the connection.

"And you're a horse's ass," Abe growled into the phone before he realized that Lou was gone.

Abe and Sam were silent during the drive home. Once there, Abe trudged to the steps, depressed and disoriented. He looked at his watch: 7:30 P.M. He hadn't seen Corey since about one o'clock, he was thinking, when a woman stepped out of the bushes. "Abe Stein?" she asked.

"Yes."

"I'm a friend of Corey's. She asked me to make sure you got this." Jamie handed him an envelope.

"Come inside, please."

"I have to go. It's not safe."

"You must be Jamie."

"You're as smart as Corey said."

"Can you get in touch with her?"

"No way."

"I need to see her."

"No way. She was sure on that."

"Can I get in touch with you if I need to?"

"No, I'm sorry. I have to go." And Jamie was off.

Inside, he looked at the plain white envelope. He recognized Corey's handwriting. His spirits lifted as he opened it. Abe read her handwritten note:

By the time you get this letter, you'll know that I killed a man. I had to do it. They were going to take Billy, and there was no other way to stop them. Please remember that because you will hear other things and they will be lies. You did your best, but you'll never stop these people from doing what they want. They do things you would never do, and no one ever stops them. So don't try and fix everything. Please. I love you, Abe. And if it weren't for Billy, I'd do what you wanted, even if I knew it wouldn't work. But I'm his mother, and I couldn't let them take him. And now it's too late to change anything. I'm sorry. Be careful. Goodbye, Abe. I'm so sorry. Corey

He sat heavily on his worn sofa, read the note again. He let it fall to the floor and buried his face in his hands. He felt the sweat on his forehead. He realized then that he was awash in sweat.

Abe tried to focus. He was completely lost. He had no idea what to do. None at all. Not even a next step. Who should he talk to? Jason? Lou? Lou had nothing else to say. Jason was a possibility. Still, why hadn't Corey turned to him for help? Jason was her lawyer. Why didn't she call him to explain why she'd killed someone? Why didn't she call me? He asked himself, yet again. Was it for the same reason she hadn't called Jason? And what might that be? She had her reasons, he knew that much. And Abe knew, like some kind of touchstone, that he had to trust her instincts.

He thought again about his conversation with Jason. Nick Season's legal investigator? What was that about? Why would Nick Season let his mother use one of his investigators to check out her son's girlfriend? Nick and his mother were lovers, Abe was fairly sure, and that might explain it. So okay, say he did. Why in God's name would Corey kill him? What had she written? They were going to take Billy, that she couldn't let them do that…Nick Season's investigator? Was Nick Season's investigator going to take Billy? Suppose he was…why? For godsake, why would Nick Season's legal investigator take Billy Logan? His mother would never want that. Could Nick Season want that? And if he did, why?

It hit him then, a two-by-four cracking squarely across his forehead. Abe felt like something had burst in his brain. Nick Season…Nick Season…it was as if he had fallen through ice into freezing cold water. What if Nick was the man Corey wouldn't name? What if Corey had something on Nick Season? What if Nick had framed her? What if the man running for state attorney general had killed Corey's husband and threatened to kill her son? Oh God. And her lawyer—the one person she hoped would protect her—represented Nick. And Nick was sleeping with her lover's mother. Shit. Was it possible? His mind was reeling. He pressed a forefinger to each throbbing temple. It was impossible, and it explained everything. Why she couldn't tell anyone, including him, who this man was. Why she didn't call Jason. Why she had fled the brunch to find her son.

Abe went over what little he knew. Nick had appeared at the brunch just before the problems began. Nick was at the front door as Corey drove away. He remembered Nick's offer to help him at the police station. Did Nick have someone steal Corey's file? It didn't feel like Nick. But that was the point, wasn't it?

What had Corey said—the guy was a "big shot" now and he could fool anyone. Nick was charming, even charismatic. And he had fooled his mother, no mean feat. He had probably suggested she use his man to investigate Corey. Oh God.

Nick had seen her with him at brunch. It must have made him insane. She was a problem that wouldn't go away. And now she was in his world, up close and personal. He imagined Nick, reading the threatening letter from Jason. Jesus, he must have freaked out. But okay, he sat on it because he had to. At least until after the election. It was a truce. He would stay out of her life if she would stay out of his. He could do that for several months. But seeing

Corey with his campaign manager's—his lover's—son, in his lover's living room? He couldn't bear that. No way. Corey wasn't just in his life—no—in his face is what she was. A violation. It was too dangerous. So he had to take a risk. Change the status quo. So he sent his investigator to kidnap her son. Made it seem like he was working for Jesse. And no one would ever believe Corey if she said Nick had her son. And she couldn't prove Nick had ever committed a crime. No, no one would ever believe her story. Especially now.

FIFTEEN

L IEUTENANT JIM NORSE HAD a corner office. It was Spartan—forest green walls, green felt blotter on the oak desk, brown wooden armchairs. The lieutenant was tall, with gray, crew cut hair, a neatly trimmed mustache and tortoise shell-framed glasses. Today he wore a plaid shirt, a navy blue blazer and gray slacks. "Business casual," they called it now. Nick thought lawmen should wear uniforms or suits. Norse, on the other hand, tried to keep up with police department fashion.

Though Norse was predictable, he was also very careful, which was perfect for Nick's purposes—point Jim in the right direction, and he would get there, unscathed. As far as Nick was concerned, Norse's singular distinction was his political acumen. The man could spin a nasty sow's ear into a fine silk purse. It was in his genes; there was no other way to explain it.

Norse waited on Nick, hands clasped on his desk, smile in place. Nick sat across from him, wondering how the lieutenant would spin it if he blew Jesse's fancy brunch all over his nice clean desk and on his spotless business casual blazer. Maybe ask him if he was feeling better. Nick made some notes in the growing file on Lester's murder. "Jim," he eventually said, setting the file on the desk. "We know who killed Lester—Corey Logan. Murder one."

"Yes, there's a warrant out on her."

"Have you considered bringing in her boyfriend, Dr. Abraham Stein?"

"For what?"

"He's the shrink who did her eval. He vouched for her, got her a new PO. Think about leaning on him. You might even tell him you think he's an accessory."

"I'll call him." After a moment he asked, "When?"

"Tomorrow. Yes. I'd sweat him on the phone," Nick suggested. "You could have him come in the next day. Press him about her file. And why don't you get a search warrant for his house and his office? Use the warrants if you need to."

"Of course."

Nick nodded. The end game, his time, had begun. "Now all we have to do is find her."

Norse leaned in. "How can I help?"

"I think she'll go to Canada. She's good on the water, and she knows where to hide. First off, let's get an extradition order."

"I can expedite that."

"Frankly, it's window dressing."

Norse squinted. "I'm not following."

"It won't help us find her." And she's not being extradited.

"I see."

"I have an idea how to find her," Nick offered. "If I may…"

"By all means," said Norse.

"The boyfriend. The shrink. If you set it up right, I think he'll lead you to her."

Nick watched Norse's face; he was putting this together. "I can put a man on him," Norse suggested.

"No, you don't want a cop. You want someone outside the chain of command. Someone who won't need a search warrant or turn back at the border."

Norse stood and looked out the window. "Riley?"

"He worked for Lester, on and off, the last five years. He already did a work-up on Stein. He'll want a piece of this. And he'll get it done."

Norse sat down again, still working on something. "Why are you telling me this?"

Nick sat back. "I think you should get the credit when he finds her."

"I see." Another moment. "Right." Jim frowned. "And if he oversteps?"

"Isn't that a Canadian police problem?" Nick asked.

"Mounties, yes. I'd think so, yes." Norse nodded, done with this.

"Another thing." Nick wasn't done. "It's best that the cops and the coast guard give him some room."

"I'll let them know I have an undercover man on it," Norse offered.

"Good. You take charge of this. I'd call Riley. ASAP."

Norse let out an audible sigh. "The last time we gave Riley his head," he leaned across his desk, "The bail skips came back in body bags."

Jim Norse was, Nick realized, what Lester called a "henhussy," his unkindest cut. He once told Nick why Jim Norse had slumped shoulders and a flat forehead. As a nod to Lester, Nick wondered if he could ask a question that would make Jim shrug his shoulders and then, when he told him the answer, slap his forehead with the palm of his hand. He could try. "Why would he do that?" Nick innocently asked.

"With Riley who can say?" Norse shrugged his shoulders. Nick beamed, imagining Lester's stone-faced delight. "The man's an enigma to me."

Enigma? Nick cut him a break.

━━━━━

JESSE WAS WAITING AT El Gaucho in a crescent-shaped black leather booth overlooking the large, dark room. The walls at El Gaucho were gray and mostly bare, the look was warehouse gone uptown speakeasy. A piano player was playing bluesy old favorites near the bar, pleasantly masking the din of the busy restaurant. El Gaucho served reliably good steaks at reliably high prices and featured tableside service, which Nick liked. Nick stopped to talk with a pair of local lawyers meeting with a Seattle Mariner. It was that kind of place.

"How do you know Corey Logan?" Jesse asked him as he arrived at their table.

He kissed her, a real kiss, then sat beside her. "She lived with my cousin Al. He's the father of her child." Nick was surprised when Jesse took a piece of cheese toast. She didn't like El Gaucho's cheese toast.

"Tell me more."

"Al was more than a cousin, he was a friend," he explained. "So I got to know her. I never trusted her."

"Why?"

"She came on to me, a couple of times," Nick confided. "Nothing you could prove, but you know it when you see it."

"This keeps getting worse. What happened between her and your cousin Al?"

"Al was a customs agent. He stole quite a lot of marijuana from one of his busts, and he and Corey went into business. Several months later Al just disappeared." Nick looked into her eyes, on his game, things coming together just so. "I believe she killed him, or had him killed. The drug money was never found. He must have suspected her because he told one of his customs buddies to check out his boat if anything ever happened to him. They found about half of the stolen drugs on board. Corey went to prison for two years. She just got out."

Jesse took another piece of cheese toast. "Why would Abe be interested in a woman like that?"

"She's a con artist. The type of woman who fools men. She fooled Al, that's for sure. Al wasn't the brightest crayon in the box, but he was a good man. I'm convinced she talked him into stealing from his own bust, then double-crossed him." He touched her hand. "She may have become sexually involved with Abe to make sure she got her son back. Or she may have had her sights set on more than that."

Grim-faced, she let this percolate. "I'm sure Abe doesn't get any of this. And he's not returning my calls."

"Let me think about that. I may be able to help."

Jesse turned away, then she turned back. "Thank you, Nicky." She took his hand again. And then she was crying. He had never seen her cry, and it interested him. She was feeling something he couldn't feel.

FROM THE BAR AT the far end of the large room, Riley Crabbe was checking out Nick Season and his fancy woman. He'd had a call from Lieutenant Norse, who wanted to meet in the morning. Lester Burell was dead and Lt. Norse was calling. That could only mean one thing. So he was watching Nick Season from across the dark room. Call it a precaution. And who was that woman? She was one snazzy-looking dame. And Nick Season, the next state A.G., was holding her hand. Nick rose, then walked to the men's room. From his table in the far corner, Riley watched Nick's profile as he made his way along the wall across the room. Though he recognized him from newspaper photos, this was the first time he had ever gotten a glimpse of Nick in person, up close. Riley felt a chill. No, it was more intense than that. He had it then, a word he'd wondered about. It was a frisson, yeah. His first.

THE CROSSING WAS UNEVENTFUL. Corey knew they would be looking for her in the San Juans, so she went the other way and fell in with the other boats traveling between Port Angeles and Victoria. At Victoria she would make her way north, staying in Canadian waters along the rugged eastern coast of Vancouver Island. Eventually she would cross the Queen Charlotte Strait to hide in the maze of inlets snaking through the wild country along the western shore of British Columbia. She and Billy had spent summers fishing and exploring among the islands, channels, and inlets off Queens Sound, and she knew where she wanted to hide.

Just after dawn Corey anchored in a protected cove near the Indian Reserve on the northern coast of Discovery Island. Billy slept below while she wrote in her diary:

> *I have hope that the worst part of our lives is over. I know that doesn't make sense, and I can't explain why I feel that way. But I do. Being with Billy again—here on this boat, at sea—has to be a big part of it. I'm trying to forget about Abe. I have to...*

She closed her diary and looked out at the lights of Victoria, Canada.

JESSE SIPPED HER MARTINI and looked out over the busy, dimly lit room. Below her a tuxedoed waiter was flaming bananas foster for a well-tanned, middle-aged couple. Tourists off one of the cruise ships, she decided. Not even her Jewish friends—who liked stewed prunes and almost any kind of cooked fruit—would eat something like that.

She was worried about Abe. How could it be that her son was with this woman? No one—no one—could upset her like Abe. Since he had been sixteen, Abe's choices had left her feeling distressed and deflated. She had worked to understand why. She even discussed it with her priest.

Put simply, her son had never been interested in the person he could be. He strove to avoid any kind of recognition. He flinched at success. He worked at obscurity. Abe was the opposite of ambitious, whatever that was, though he worked very hard. And he really didn't care how he looked—how had that happened? And his love life—well, why not fall for a treacherous convicted felon who likely murdered the father of her own son? Jesse had learned that anything she said would only make things worse. So she had tried to accept him. She really worked at that. He was her only child, and whatever he chose—however ill advised—she still loved him. She wanted him to love her that way too. But how could she accept Corey Logan? Sometimes Jesse thought Abe was deliberately trying to upset her.

No, she reminded herself, he just liked being an outsider. In fact, he liked being everything she wasn't. Her psychologist friends said that was normal. Still, it didn't seem fair. After all, there was so much she could do for him if only he'd let her. And he could make her feel loved and proud, if only he would try.

She watched Nick—so handsome, so poised—working the room with a touch to the shoulder and a warm smile, as only he could do it. Without warning, she was unbearably sad. Her son made her feel inadequate. He was the only one who could do that. Jesse felt herself tearing up again. She turned her mind back to Nick. He made her feel the opposite of inadequate. She wiped away her tears, hoping she could make him feel that, too.

SIXTEEN

A BE WENT OVER IT again. Lou, Jason, his mother, even Nick—all the people he had considered talking to. None of those conversations made sense; they were either impossible or unhelpful. Lou would laugh him out of his office. Jason would explain that even if the unbelievable accusation he was making were true—*if*—this was impossible to touch without evidence. And since he represented Nick in his campaign, he would have to pass it on to another lawyer. That was the last thing Abe wanted. His mother would dismiss him as being under the thumb of this murderous woman, or something equally unhelpful. And Nick, well, he couldn't even begin with Nick without confirmation from—and substantive conversation with—Corey. What to do was still, after all, up to her. He had to find Corey.

But how in hell was he going to do that? It had taken him most of the night but he had an idea. He checked his watch: 7:30 A.M. He called Max, his former patient, the security expert, at his home. It was a risk. Unconventional, anyway. But this was not a time to worry about convention. No, it was a time for risk.

"Max, Abe Stein here…Dr. Stein, yes…did I wake you? Sorry…I know this is unusual, but I need a favor…could you come to my house?" He gave him the address. It was, Abe knew, inappropriate. But it was his best idea. In the past year he had watched Max grow his company, Worldwide Industrial Security. In their sessions Max had described how he protected factories, warehouses, and people from theft and kidnapping. He did this in four—count 'em—four countries, including Canada. And he had clients in Vancouver, Abe remembered that. It was, at least, a start.

Thirty minutes later Max was pounding a sturdy fist on his front door. Abe let him in. Abe had slept in his clothes and knew he looked disheveled.

"You in trouble, ace?" Max said as he shook Abe's hand. Max wore an Italian gray chalk-striped suit.

"Not exactly. But I need help. I have to find someone. She's wanted for murder. I think she's on a boat in Canadian waters. I have no idea where. I think—"

Max put a hand on Abe's shoulder. "Slow down. You got any coffee?"

"Sure. Sorry."

They went into his kitchen where Abe poured Max a cup of coffee and sat across from him at the kitchen table.

"Cream, sugar?" Abe asked, an afterthought.

Max shook his head and took a sip. "First thing you have to do is pretend it's someone else has the problem, so you can calm down," he advised. "I mean if it was a patient had this problem, you'd sit there and act like it was no big deal."

"Point taken." Abe was tapping his fingertips on the table. He leaned in. "So listen, do you know anyone who can help me?"

"Uh, doc, I've never seen you so worked up. Who is this person?"

"Her name is Corey Logan."

"The gal in the paper this morning?"

"Yes."

"How do you know her?"

"I'm in love with her."

"Right. What was I thinking?" Max looked Abe over. And again. "Of course." He tapped two fingers on Abe's forearm. "Start at the beginning."

Abe explained to Max as much as he felt Max needed to know. He did not tell him about Nick Season. When he was finished, Max said, "I'll help you myself."

"How?"

"I'm not sure."

Still, Abe was relieved.

Then Max asked him about Jamie, the woman who had given him the letter.

"She's a hairdresser. And Corey's old friend. That's all I know."

"Tell me anything you can remember that they did together, whatever Corey may have said about that."

He took a minute. "Okay. Okay...she said they had fished together, and that they were single moms together."

"That's a start. Let's go to my office," Max suggested.

Abe nodded. He wasn't used to Max being ahead of him. Or maybe Max had been ahead of him more often than he knew. At the door he threw on the same tweed sport coat he'd worn the day before.

Max looked him over. "Dr. Stein, may I make a suggestion?"

"Sure."

"When you're facing the worst, it's a good time to look your best."

Abe looked down at his wrinkled shirt.

Max poked a finger through a hole in the pocket of Abe's sport coat. "No offense."

He smiled at Max. "None taken. Give me a minute."

———

ONE TIME RILEY CRABBE brought a bail skip back from Havana, Cuba. Another time he brought two mob guys back from Palermo, Italy. Recovery agents, commonly known as bounty hunters, all agreed that if you were on the run, Riley Crabbe was about your worst nightmare: an extra-smart, short guy who liked collateral damage.

Lately, Riley commanded big money, mostly private. The problem was that no one except Lester had been able to tell Riley what to do. So now that Lester was dead, Riley didn't listen to anyone. No, he came at things in his own kind of off-center, roundabout way. And once he had circled back, a couple of times, he would have his own certain, often unexpected, understanding. Fine dining, for example—who would have thought that Riley cared deeply about what, and where, he ate? He worked alone, traveling often. Surprisingly—to everyone except Riley himself—he had become a gourmet. He knew what he liked and why. And if you let him, he would tell you, chapter and verse. That's how he did things. And he was mean as a snake. That was Riley Crabbe, in a nutshell.

Lt. Norse met him at a downtown Starbucks. Riley had specified Sixth Avenue and Union Street, knowing that if you counted the office complexes, there were three or four Starbucks in and around the corner. So, Norse was late. He wondered if Norse would get the joke. Today, Riley wore a Mariners cap, jeans, and a plain black sweatshirt. At five foot two, he had a knack for blending in. He wore glasses or jewelry or hairpieces—as needed—and always dressed for the occasion. Riley said he was forty-seven, or forty-two or forty-five. He could go unnoticed at a formal diplomatic function or at a shelter for the homeless. On his best days he was almost invisible. "Riley." Norse shook his hand before he sat down.

Riley didn't answer. He didn't say much to guys like Norse.

"You heard about Lester?"

He nodded, just a tilt.

The lieutenant said, "Good man."

Riley thought he might gag on that.

"You could rely on Lester," Norse added.

"Yes. Lester had one human feeling," Riley eventually offered. "Bestial rage."

Norse looked confused.

Riley let him stew. As far as he was concerned, losing Lester was like losing a rogue grizzly who liked human flesh.

The lieutenant handed him a file. "You already know the guy," he said, and explained what he wanted him to do.

The way Norse explained it, Riley could see that someone had laid it out for him, step by step. Nick Season, had to be. Nick ran a tight ship. And Riley guessed that for a guy like Norse, carrying out Nick's instructions was an all or nothing deal. A dot over every i, every t crossed. Riley was certain it was the best deal Jim Norse had ever made. The powerful lieutenant would be a bicycle cop if it wasn't for Nick.

"We're bringing Dr. Stein in tomorrow. Put a little pressure on him to find her," Lieutenant Norse added.

Riley ignored this as he looked over the file. "In a boat...on that wild coastline...this one here's mostly art," he finally allowed.

"Art?"

"Art," Riley repeated.

"Fine," Jim said.

Riley nodded. He was a private investigator and a bounty hunter. Actually, a contract killer masquerading as a P.I. and a bounty hunter. If there was art in that, he was Michelangelo. "It'll be fifty," he said.

"And twenty-five on top of that if you find her in ten days."

Riley nodded again. "What's your cut, Looey?" he asked Norse, needling him.

"Watch your mouth, Riley."

"What are you going to do, bag man? Arrest me?" He cocked a thumb and forefinger then pointed it like a gun at Norse.

Norse glared at him, apparently speechless.

Riley wondered if the lieutenant was asking God why he had given some smartass, midget, douchebag a bigger brain than his. He hoped so. Riley winked, and then he was gone.

Thirty minutes later Riley was following Abe Stein and a beefy guy in a sweet suit.

———

COREY WAS TAKING THE *Jenny Ann* north along the eastern coast of British Columbia's Vancouver Island. She had just come past the mouth of the Cambell River, a famous fishing ground and home of the Tyee Club. The club had been founded back in the twenties. She had watched club members and would-be club members fishing at the mouth of the river. They were sport fishermen who worked to catch a thirty-plus pound king salmon, a Tyee, from a traditional fourteen-foot wooden dinghy within the estuary of the Cambell River. They had to fish without a motor, with single barbless hooks, and with twenty-pound test line, or less. There were further restrictions on reels, tackle, even leaders. They made it as hard as they could to catch the prized fish. Go figure.

Today there were large swells. Billy was below. She hoped he could sleep. She had been thinking about him, and she didn't like where her thoughts were going. Yes, he had to be with her for a while. Until he was safe. But after that? He wasn't wanted for murder. He could do things that she couldn't do.

Billy came up into the wheelhouse. His face was pale.

"You okay?" she asked.

"Been better," he muttered.

She guessed that he had gotten seasick down below. "Sorry," she offered. And when he didn't reply, she added, "We can stop if you'd like. I'll find a place where we can drop an anchor and maybe cook on the beach."

"I'm not hungry."

"Right."

Billy sat on the bench in the wheelhouse, opened a window and stuck his head out. He took deep breaths of fresh air.

Corey watched him, suddenly worried.

ABE WAS IN MAX'S conference room. Worldwide Industrial Security had half of the sixth floor in an older, downtown office tower on Second Avenue. From the conference room window, a person could see irregular-shaped pieces of Puget Sound in the varied spaces between the other buildings. Abe wasn't interested in the view; he was pouring over a map of British Columbia that was spread across the conference room table. He had never realized how many islands, channels, passages, and inlets there were on B.C.'s wild western coast. It looked like a labyrinth. How would he ever find her?

At the other end of the table, Max was talking to several of his men on the speakerphone. "I want to know what fishing boat she worked on...Corey Logan, right...when we find out what boat she was on, check if there was a Jamie something or another on that same boat...and I want Jamie's last name...then her address, home, and workplace...you got an hour." Max punched off the speakerphone. And to Abe, "How you doing?"

"Not so good. I feel like something's slipping out of my reach."

"It's worth the wait to find this Jamie. If she can tell us where Corey might have gone, it will save a lot of time."

"I'm sure you're right. It's just that I'm not very practical, and it's hard for me to think about how to find her," Abe admitted.

"Then don't think about it. I can read people. When the time comes, you'll know what to do. You'll do what you have to do. Period."

How could Max know a thing like that? The last time he'd heard Max sounding so sure about something, he was borrowing money to launch his "Big Man" burger franchise. He watched Max fingering his gold pinky ring. He was a good man, a friend, Abe realized.

———

NICK LOOKED OVER AT Jesse. She was sleeping in, which was rare for her...last night, there had been something different about their lovemaking. What it was, she was focused on him. Yeah, trying to please him, working hard. Letting him know that that's what she wanted. What could she do for him, she whispered, breathless, in his ear? Moments later, she was whispering again. So, finally, he asked her to play with herself while he watched—the least worst thing he could think of—acting like it was some kind of big deal for him. After she came, she wanted to drink him. And so he let her. Nothing too fancy, but it made her happy. As a gigolo, Nick had learned how to hurry, or to postpone, his climax. Last night he had hurried his orgasm. He wasn't sure why but he wanted to move this along. It made her suppose she had pleased him all the more. Nick wondered what all this was about. What was she thinking? He didn't get it. And something about being "pleased" made him feel uncomfortable, unpleasantly confined, like being trapped in a small space.

———

COREY TOOK THE JENNY Ann through a group of small islands then up a passage off Queens Sound. The passage wove through glacially gouged channels and inlets. There were myriad side channels, narrows, and islands to get lost among along the way. The inlets were actually deep fiords, plunging into the Sound from the forested mountains. This time of year the mountains were usually forest green, covered with old growth Sitka spruce, Douglas fir and coastal western hemlock; others had bare granite faces. This was wild country and it made her happy. Billy was finally asleep below. Earlier that morning she had seen an eagle pluck a rockfish out of the ocean and a big brown bear run off when he smelled her from the shore. Since then, she had spotted a pair of gill-netters, a gnarly old seiner and a pleasure craft, cruising the Inside Passage. Now she turned up the dogleg of a secluded channel. The shore was forested; a soothing green, and side channels came and went as she made her way northeast up the dogleg. A light fog, more of a mist, had settled into the near mountains. Several miles farther she found what she was looking for: a narrow, almost hidden passage that wove in and among a large group of good-sized islands.

Corey carefully took her boat up the passage, weaving among the islands for miles until she found a particular side channel. Five or six miles further, she turned toward the place she remembered—a calm protected spot, a U-shaped cove. It was in its own narrow channel off the side channel. The cove was carved out of an oval-shaped island that rose almost a thousand feet out of the water to form a dome-shaped hill. The oval-shaped island faced a larger flat island, shaped like an hourglass. Both islands were densely forested. The top of the hourglass created the narrow channel between the two islands. The stem of the hourglass faced the protected cove, creating a larger body of water. She had found this place many summers ago, when Billy was six. It had a little sandy beach where he liked to play, and they had anchored at this place for several nights every summer. At low tide it would still be deep enough, and there were places in the cove where they could beach their dinghy and make a fire. She knew where to find fish nearby, and they were far enough off the main channel that no one would ever happen by. Corey set her anchor.

When she was satisfied that the *Jenny Ann* was secure, she sat at her deck table and opened her diary. Something had come to her this morning, traveling through this remote wilderness—it was mostly a feeling—and she wanted to try and put it into words. She wrote:

*I've got my boy back. He's scared and confused. And so am I.
It's a new deal for both of us. This is what I wanted. And in this
unspoiled country, we finally have a chance to think. I'm not
going to screw it up.*

She was beginning to understand why she felt so good, in spite
of what lay ahead of them. If only she could put Abe out of her
mind.

————

ABE WAS IMPRESSED. MAX had found Jamie in less than two hours.
Internet magic, he had explained, was the key to his business
success. And, of course, therapy, he added soberly. And now they
were in his black Suburban in Ballard, not far from the docks,
watching Jamie through the window of the hair salon where she
worked. When she went into the alley for a cigarette, Max and
Abe followed. Abe called her name. Jamie turned.

"How'd you find me?" she asked them, testy.

"I'll tell you later," Abe replied. "Now, we need to find—"

"She didn't tell me where she was going. Besides, I promised
her I wouldn't help you. And I keep my promises."

"I can help her," Abe said. "I need to talk with her."

"I think she's heard that tune before."

"I love her," he continued.

"I'm sorry," Jamie said sincerely.

"I need to talk with her," he persisted.

"You already said that. I'm sorry, I really can't help you."

Max took her arm. "Ma'am—"

"Who is this guy?" Jamie asked Abe. "Look at that suit.
Cufflinks? Is he from Vegas?"

Abe rallied. "Max is a friend. He's helping me out. And he'll
help Corey if he can."

"Corey can take care of herself."

"She loves me."

"I know."

"So?" Abe raised his voice. Max shot him a look.

"So what is this? Love conquers all?" Jamie made a face. "Are
you kidding?"

"Sometimes you sound just like her," Abe observed.

"I wish I was like her. That woman can do what she wants."

"Help her, Jamie. Where is she?"

Max put an arm around Abe's shoulder. With his forefinger, he made a zip-it motion across his lips. Then to Jamie, "We're going to find her, with or without you. You could save us time though. Also, it took us maybe an hour to find you. The bad guys are going to find you, too."

Abe hadn't thought of this. He watched Jamie reconsider.

"Am I in danger?" she asked.

"I think you could be," Max cautioned.

Jamie turned to Abe. "What if I tell you where she might be and you find her? And then what if she thinks I betrayed her? Huh? What then? I'll take my chances with the bad guys."

Abe wondered how friendships like this got forged. He had never had one. "If Corey's upset with you, I'll take the blame. All I want is for Corey and me to be together, to deal with this together, whatever she decides to do. And I'll make you this promise; I'll let her decide. How can this hurt her?"

"I'm not smart enough to answer that." Jamie ground out her cigarette.

And that was that.

———

RILEY WATCHED THE GIRL walk out of the alley and back into the hair salon. Stein the shrink and the hard guy in the fine, chalk-striped Italian suit followed her. No one had mentioned the natty hard guy. Worldwide Security. Riley had checked him out. He made a few calls, and an hour later, he had a court clerk reading from the records of Max's trial. Riley took it from there. Apparently, Max had smuggled contraband out of Seattle until he was caught in a sting. Now he ran a legit security operation. If he had known about Max, Riley would have asked for more money.

The way they looked, he could tell they didn't get what they wanted. He would get it from her, if it came to that. When they were in the alley, he had planted his preferred tracking device under the Suburban. It was a tiny, self-contained, waterproof GPS device that provided twenty hours of motion-activated tracking. It logged position, date, time and stops. It made following them considerably easier. Besides, it was time he treated himself to a meal.

In his car, Riley thought about Abe Stein. He couldn't figure the doctor, a very careful guy who sideswiped parked cars. And the doctor didn't come off too polished, fashion-wise. No, looking at the guy you would guess college prof, likely an adjunct, down on his luck. And sad to say, the more he learned about Dr. Stein, the more it seemed like the man marched full time to his own, born-to-lose drummer.

Case in point—what was he doing with a girl like Corey Logan? Riley turned it over, then again. Had to be some kind of underdog deal. Outcasts find true love. He shrugged. Born to lose—S.O.L.—any way you cut it. The poor guy finally finds the girl of his dreams. And what happens? She dumps him and it puts him right at the top of Nick Season's shit list, that's what. Dumped is bad news. But baby, up top on Nick's list, that's the last place in the world you ever want to be.

Riley flashed on Nick—at ease, great smile—talking with the guy's mom. That's who the ritzy lady was—Jesse Stein—Dr. Abe's birth mother. Riley sensed that mom was Nick's cooze, his main squeeze. So Nick has to be doing her at the same time he puts a contract hit on her son. What kinda guy would do that? What kinda guy could do that? No wonder Lester looked up to Nick.

———

"Did you know she stabbed a woman in prison?" Nick asked Jesse. They were sitting in the living room, and he was trying to paint a picture of Corey Logan that would suit his purposes.

"So she's killed two people?" she asked.

"That we know of."

Jesse pursed her lips. "Why isn't Abe answering my calls?"

"I'd guess he's upset," he offered, liking this turn in the conversation. "You can understand that. And probably ashamed. The last person he'd want to talk with right now is his mother."

"I have to see him. Hear what he has to say about her. Abe's not stupid."

Nick nodded, sympathetic. "I've thought about how to help. Suppose I speak to Jason? He can reach Abe."

"I already tried that. Jason said Abe's not ready to talk."

"That may have changed. The police want to talk with Abe."

"What?" She pursed her lips again.

"I heard from Lieutenant Norse," he explained. "The police think Abe may know something. He vouched for Corey Logan. He replaced her PO. Apparently, he put his reputation on the line for her. He may even have lied for her."

"Oh no…" Her face began to fall. She kept it together, Nick thought, through sheer force of will. "What can we do?" she eventually asked.

"What if I offer to use whatever influence and resources I have to buy Abe some time with the lieutenant, then I could help him find her? Off the record. If he brings her back, he's the good guy. Maybe that will get him to sit down."

Jesse turned to him. "Why would you do that?"

"Because he's your son."

———

THE JENNY ANN WAS anchored in the softer water between a swirling eddy and the shore. In the circle of the eddy, herring were feeding. On the back deck of their boat, Corey and Billy were working on an eight-or-nine-foot stick. She had cut and whittled a long branch—maybe an inch in diameter—until one side at one end was smooth for about three feet, and now she was driving thin nails into that side of the branch. She drove them in very close to one another until there were at least fifty nails in the branch. As she nailed, Billy was cutting off the heads of the nails and filing them down into sharp points. It was something they had done before, and they worked well together. Billy was forty nails behind her. When all of the nails had been sharpened, they took their herring rake with them into the dinghy and Corey rowed them to the eddy where the herring were feeding on plankton. Billy stood in the bow while she rowed along the eddy. He thrust the stick into the swirling water, over the front of the boat, then pulled it back in a canoeing motion. With each stroke he skewered several herring—once he counted four—on the nails. In one fluid motion, he would shake them off in the back of the boat where she collected them in a bucket. Then he would thrust their herring rake into Queens Sound again.

When they had their bait, Corey rowed them back to the *Jenny Ann*. Billy raised the anchor and they were off.

———

"IT WAS A GOOD plan," Abe insisted to Max. They were back at Abe's house, eating turkey sandwiches.

"It didn't work. End of story." Max put up a palm before Abe could respond. "I got another idea." Max had his enthusiasm back. "Can you get a picture of her boat?"

"We'd have to break into her house."

"No problem there."

The phone rang. Abe answered it. "Lieutenant Norse? What's the problem? Yes, I know Corey Logan. Yes, I'm aware that she's in violation of the terms of her release. I'm positive she's not a murderer. That's not possible. I disagree. I see. I did disagree with her former probation officer, yes. I did vouch for her, yes. My letter to Judge Olsen is confidential. You already read it? No, I don't know where she is. Yes, her file was stolen. I've discussed this matter with Detective Lou Ballard. Detective Ballard is off this case? What? This doesn't make sense. Tomorrow? An accessory to murder? Me? What? What?" Abe carefully set down the phone; the lieutenant had hung up on him.

"They're going to give me the third degree about Corey," he eventually told Max. "The lieutenant said I was likely—his word—an accessory to murder."

"When?"

"Tomorrow."

"You got a good lawyer?"

"Yeah."

"Call him, talk it over, then relax, put it out of your mind. We can take a walk."

———

COREY AND BILLY HAD secured their boat at the dock in Bella Coola, a remote fishing and logging village, population 909, situated where the Bella Coola River met a long coastal inlet or fiord. A group of Norwegians had settled in nearby Hagensborg because the fiords along this coast reminded them of home. An assortment of often-used fishing boats were moored in the tiny harbor. From the remote harbor you could see eight-thousand-foot Mt. Nusatsun. Corey knew this place, and she led Billy to a marine hardware and general store not too far from the dock. They stepped inside the general store.

"We need to set a buoy," she explained to the storekeeper.

Billy had their list, which included twenty feet of chain, several hundred feet of rope, anchor shackles, two sixty-pound bags of dry premixed concrete, crates, a buoy, etc. It was what they needed to moor their boat in their hiding place. While Billy and the storekeeper checked off the items on their list, she picked out the other supplies they'd need.

Back at their hiding place they set to work, laying out their supplies on the *Jenny Ann's* back deck. After preparing the concrete, they poured it into two large crates to make cement blocks to anchor their buoy. While they waited for the concrete to harden, they set out the rope, the chain, and the various connecting eyes, shackles, and swivels, then took a break for lunch. When the blocks were ready, Corey spliced the rope to the chain at a swivel, then she attached the rope to the buoy and the chain to an eye set in each concrete block. Together, she and Billy managed to lift the two cement blocks they had made and drop them over the side of the boat. The chain, the rope, and finally the buoy followed the cement blocks over the side. Corey put her arm around him. They looked at their white buoy, floating smartly in their hidden cove. "It's a start," she said. "We'll be okay here."

"How long are we going to be here?" he asked with some attitude.

"Until we make a plan."

"And how long is that?"

She wasn't going to let him bring her down. "Let's get on it. I'm starting to think clearly again. In fact, I'm feeling better than I have in a long time."

"It's funny. I hate having to hide up here." His face softened. "But at least I'm not worrying all the time."

"Does it bring back memories?"

"Some really good times."

That made her feel better. "You want to barbeque salmon for dinner?"

"Yeah. Sure."

"Then we better go fishing."

As she took their boat down a side channel, Billy brought up the herring and their gear. He set up their rods then baited them with their herring. It was a familiar routine and he was good at it. Out of the corner of her eye, Corey watched her competent son. Coming back to this place with him was a second chance. She knew that in the way a salmon knows where it was born.

———

ABE WAS IN MAX'S private office calling his answering service. Out the window, he could see the Bainbridge Ferry leaving the ferry terminal. He turned away. When he punched in his code, he had a message. He had also been paged. Both messages were from Jason, who said it was important. Had Corey called Jason? Unlikely. He returned Jason's call. "Any word?" he asked after identifying himself.

"No, I'm sorry."

"I was about to call you. I just got a call from the police, a Lieutenant Norse."

"I know. I'm ahead of you and I have good news. Nick Season, your mother's candidate—"

"I know who he is," Abe interrupted, unsure where this was going.

"Yes, of course. The point is, he's volunteered to help you. Off the record. He has a large staff, police connections, and he spent years as a county prosecutor. He'll get Norse off your back— don't worry about that—and he'll help you find Corey. And, my friend, the Canadians would surely be pleased to help the next state attorney general of Washington."

"What does Nick have in mind?" Something about the fox and the chicken coop came to Abe's mind.

"He'll ask Norse to give you a week. During that time, he'll help you find her, however he can. He'll broker a deal with the prosecutor's office, if you'd like. Simply put, because of your mother, I think he'd like to do whatever he can."

Corey had it right; Nick was the devil's own instrument. And he was working hard at his nefarious business. Abe wasn't sure how he figured it out, but he saw what he had to do. "I'll meet with you and Nick and my mother tomorrow morning, say nine o'clock at the house. Will that work?"

"That will make your mother very happy. We can discuss all of this then."

"Thanks, Jason." Abe set down the phone, hoping that Max could help.

———

WHILE MAX AND ABE were riding the Bainbridge ferry en route to burgle Corey's Bainbridge house, Riley Crabbe was breaking into Abe Stein's Capitol Hill home. He planted a tiny micro transmitter in each of the three suitcases he found in Abe's bedroom closet. He hid one in the side pocket of Abe's carry on travel bag, a well-used duffle, and another in the spine of his hanging bag. The third he glued beside one of the wheels of a larger rolling case. He was in and out of the house in less than ten minutes. Riley was careful; a forensic detective would never discover that he had been there.

On the way to his car, Riley smiled as he picked a sunflower from one of Stein's flower beds. Tonight he wore jeans and a black crew neck sweater under a gray linen jacket. His shoes were sturdy, Timberland, with the Gortex lining and hard-ridged rubber soles. He was ready to sail, or hike, or eat dinner out. He liked working in Seattle. It was an easy place to go unnoticed. He liked that Seattleites were careful not to pry, slow to express their feelings, preferred consensus building to conflict, drum circles to cocktail parties. Riley got that look—he was way outside the box—and with a satisfied smirk, he tossed the sunflower into a trashcan.

In the car, he checked his messages. Jim Norse had called twice. Riley thought about calling Lt. Norse back. He knew just why he had such an uncharacteristically considerate impulse.

Nick Season was why. He kept flashing on the guy, like some kind of mind tic. So why, he wondered, was Nick Season messing with his mind?

Lester. Yeah, Lester—had to be. Lester was Nick's man. Nick had relied on Lester, his trusted lieutenant. And Lester got the job done. Riley had seen him do it. Riley, who never rushed to judgment, was certain that Lester was the most dangerous man he had ever met. Lester didn't have normal feelings. None. And you never knew for sure what the guy was thinking. Yeah, one time, Lester had picked him up by the throat and hurled him against the wall—just because he'd cracked wise about the big guy's vintage suit. Before Riley could reach his knife—and he was fast—Lester had that big Magnum more or less up his nose. He crushed the cartilage in his nose and tore both nostrils doing it. Messed him up pretty bad. It was the look on Lester's face that scared him though; the big man in the cheap suit really wanted to blow his brains out. No one had ever scared him like that. Ever. And here was the point—Lester had been scared of Nick. Bone deep. No kidding. So that put Nick at the top of this very nasty food chain. Though he'd never looked him in the eye, Riley already had a bad—a troubling—feeling about Nick. He sensed that Nick Season was big time, a true desperado. State attorney general. It made Riley think of the Old West, where every now and then some stone-cold killer got to be sheriff.

He called Norse. It was prudent.

———

ABE FELT HELPLESS INSIDE Corey's house. Still, the picture was where he had remembered it. Seeing her face made him worry, though. Was she safe? How could he find her? If he found her, how could he help her? He quelled his rising anxiety. "Will this work?" he asked, taking the framed photo of the boat off the mantel.

"Perfect." It was an old picture of Billy and Corey on the *Jenny Ann*. They were anchored in a cove somewhere in the mountainous British Colombia coastal wilderness. Billy couldn't have been more than six years old. Max studied the photo. "Nice boat," he said. He looked at the back of the framed picture. "Check this out," he said, showing it to Abe. On the back it said: Queens Sound, Summer, 2001.

"She said she used to take Billy up the Inside Passage," Abe said. "They'd spend the whole summer poking around Queens Sound on her boat."

Max put his hand up for a high five. Abe looked confused; he didn't know what Max was after. Max walked him through it.

"ABE WILL BE THERE at nine o'clock tomorrow morning," Jason explained to Jesse on the phone.

"Thank you, Jason. I'll see you then." She hung up and turned to Nick, who was sitting beside her on her living room sofa. "And thank you." Jesse gave him a long, leisurely kiss.

This was working, Nick was thinking. The soup was simmering, just so. And that meant he had to be vigilant. He went full focus on Jesse.

He kept coming back to last night, to Jesse whispering in his ear that she wanted to make him happy, whatever he wanted. It was all about him, she insisted. So he acted pleased that she was pleasing him—a double negative, a con within a con, since she couldn't ever please him—which left him twisted up like a pretzel. And the thing was, afterward, she was happy. Why, he wondered, was this happening? She wanted him to "trust her." What was that about? Jesse, he knew, could have about any man she wanted. Any man his age, anyway. So what was she after? What it was, he decided, was about wanting him to be a certain way. There was something she wanted him to feel. Not something he could name. It wasn't like winning or revenge or gratitude or solving a difficult problem, or even making big money. No, the feeling she was after was as strange to him as the mountains on the moon. He couldn't say just what it was. It made the skin on his chest hot. Crawly. Last night, before he came, he felt like he was trapped in a collapsing mine shaft.

They dug a fire pit on the beach in their cove. When they were satisfied, Corey and Billy set rocks around their shallow pit to elevate their grill, so they could cook their salmon over a wood fire. It was a small king salmon—maybe twelve pounds—that Billy had caught after a half hour of fishing. The now-this-is-really-cool look on his face when he landed their dinner made Corey smile. He had missed a lot of being a teenager, but fishing still seemed to be one of his favorite things. After he landed the fish, she worried that they were actually having fun. Maybe she wasn't spending enough time on their many problems. Was she denying how much trouble they were in? If she was, she decided, that was okay by her—for a while, anyway. It snuck up on her then, again, just as she was feeling better. She longed for Abe, a stirring, palpable longing. Time would help, it had to. While Billy filleted their fish, she ran the *Jenny Ann* back to their hidden cove.

Corey liked their hiding place. They were truly hard to find here, and in the unlikely event that someone happened up this out-of-the-way passage, she would hear them before they saw her boat. If they had to run, there were several ways out. They had supplies for at least another week, and she could rotate the marinas where they shopped and refueled. She decided to get, and fill, several spare gas cans, just in case. She turned into the narrow channel beside the hourglass island. It required her full attention. After tying up to their buoy, Billy rowed them and their dinner to shore. On the beach she prepared their picnic while he gathered wood and made a fire.

"How long can we hide here?" Billy asked, once he had the fire going.

"Let's see," she said, thinking aloud. "It's July. Weather wise, I'd say we have until early October to get our act together."

"I can't wait that long."

"Actually, I'd like to see you start school in September."

"I don't want to think about that."

His mood swings were mercurial. She couldn't blame him. "Why?"

"I already want to go back to Seattle," he said. "I need to explain to Morgan what happened."

"You like her a lot, don't you?"

He shrugged. "Yeah, I guess."

"I'm glad you've found someone like that." And she knew how hard it was to be fifteen—almost sixteen, she realized—and to be separated from that person.

"Lost her is more like it. What do you think she thinks about me now?"

Corey thought that over. "I'd guess she's mostly worried about you."

"I'm afraid she didn't know what was going down. I'm afraid the police will plant some other version in her head."

"I'm sure she's waiting to hear your version," she assured him.

"I'd like to give it to her. At least the part where I tell her that Lester had a gun, that he was going to kidnap me."

"Do you want to write her a letter, explain what happened? I'll mail it to Jamie from Victoria or Vancouver and she can re-mail it in Seattle."

"That's too complicated," Billy said. "Besides, I want to talk with her."

"Okay, I promised you that you could do that. Give us a few more days. Then, if we're still okay here, we'll make the trip to Port Hardy. I have things to do there. You can call her cell, give her the number of a pay phone in Port Hardy and have her call you back from a public pay phone in Seattle."

"This sucks."

"I'm sorry." Corey set their salmon on the grill. She watched her son. He was looking out into the mountains around them. In the twilight she could see a distant peak that was dusted with snow. And just like that, unexpectedly, she got a glimpse of what she should do. Her brow creased. And then there it was, again. She didn't like it, but she could see it. For maybe a nanosecond— less than a second anyway—there it was, in her head, clear as day. And it was the right thing. Somehow, she knew that. And it was time to say it. Past time. Damn. Corey felt an unwelcome surge of feeling. This wasn't what she had wanted. She had never even considered this. She closed her eyes, opened them.

"I'm starting to get it, Billy," she finally said, flustered. Corey organized her thoughts, trying to find a way to say this. She moved their salmon to the back of the grill, away from the heat of the fire.

Just get it out there, she told herself, and stick to the facts or you'll come undone. She sat up straight.

"Let's spend some time together, make a plan for me and a plan for you." She hesitated. "Maybe they don't have to be the same plan. I have to think about that." Corey massaged the bridge of her nose with thumb and forefinger. Then she softly said, "Maybe you can go back, even if I can't. There may be a way. Maybe that's the most important thing I can do for you."

Corey couldn't believe she had said it. But there it was, in full view. She felt worse and better at the same time, aware it was a sea change for her—this idea that she might have to make a life without him. She wasn't sure just how or why it happened. Maybe she didn't want to blow her second chance.

"Are you serious?"

"I'll work on it. I mean it." She paused, collecting herself. "Still, I need to be sure that you'll be safe, and I'll need to see you often. You may have to change your name. But you don't have to live your life as a fugitive in Canada. I can see why you wouldn't want that." And she could, even if it made her heartsick. "I'll get on it." She shrugged. "After all, I'm your mom." She knew it was right even though it went against everything she had hoped for. More than anything she'd wanted to share these tumultuous years before he was a grown man. She wasn't going to be able to do that. No. She turned away.

Billy came up behind her, put his arm over her shoulder. "Thank you," he said. "I know this isn't what you want."

Corey thought about what to say. The silence grew awkward. Eventually, she turned to him. "Here's what I want. One day I want you to tell your children how you ran away with their crazy grandmother. I want you to tell them how it felt on a summer night when you had to hide, when you didn't even know what your name was going to be…and I hope you'll say that you were scared, but that you knew it'd be okay because you and your mom had gotten pretty good at hard things…"

Billy leaned in. "No kid would ever believe the things we've done."

———

THEY WERE BACK AT Max's office where maps were spread out all over his conference room table. Max found the one he wanted and drew a circle around Queens Sound. There were maybe fifteen small ports in the circle—places like Namu, Ocean Falls, Good Hope, and Goose Bay—marinas where a boat could stop for gas, hardware and sundries. Then he called Vince Edwards, his man in Vancouver. "I know it's late, Vin. Client's here, you're on speaker." Max pressed a button on his phone before Vince could say anything. "Is there a detective agency up there we like?" he asked. "We'll need a man to work up north in and around Queens Sound. There's ten, maybe fifteen marinas I'd like him to check out."

"Yeah, sure," Vince eventually said. "It'll cost say three hundred dollars a day. And I'll let you know on the plane and the pilot."

"We're going to need one guy and a plane right away. Then, if we get a hit, we'll need to hire locals to stake out the marinas within striking distance until she shows. And we'll need to rent satellite phones."

Abe grimaced. Max waved him off. "I'm going to e-mail you a photo of the boat and the mother and son we're looking for. I'll also send you some more recent photos of them and go over particulars. We'll be in Vancouver tomorrow," he added.

"Just tell me when. I'll be at the airport."

"I'll be back to you. And Vinnie, my friend and I, we're going to need a seaplane with a long range and a good pilot."

"Done."

"I'll call you later." Max turned off the speakerphone.

"A seaplane? How much is that?" Abe was worried. This was going very fast. Fast was, he reminded himself, what he'd wanted.

"The one we'll need, I'd guess three thousand for a day."

"I can't afford that."

"I know. That's why I ruled out being a psychiatrist."

"You're not hearing me. I don't know where I can get that kind of money."

"You can get it from me," Max said.

"I can't take money from you." He couldn't—Max had been his patient. But he didn't want to slow this down either.

Max put a cigar-shaped finger on a detailed map of River's Inlet and the surrounding area. "Wherever she eventually shows up for gas or food, you and I go after her by plane. We'll be waiting in the area."

"Waiting where?" Abe asked.

"I dunno. A fishing lodge or something. I haven't gotten that far yet."

"I can borrow the money," Abe said, still on this. From where? My mother? A loan shark would expect less.

Max ignored him. "When you're looking for someone on the water, look from the air. You take my point." And before Abe could protest, he said, "Look. I want to do you a favor. You loaned me money when it mattered. So just go with this ace, even if it doesn't feel right. We can talk about it later."

"I'll pay you back," Abe said. He was borrowing money from a former patient. Certainly inappropriate, perhaps unethical. He could live with it. It wasn't very much to do for Corey.

———

COREY HEARD BILLY WASHING dishes in the galley below. He was so happy about their new plan that he had volunteered to clean up. It was, she thought, a nice thing for him to do. She went back to her diary, open on the table in front of her. Corey reread what she had written:

Something is very right here, and something is very wrong. The right part is how I saw what to do with Billy. The wrong part is how I can't see what to do about me. I don't want to change my name. I don't want to live in Canada. And I don't want to be separated again from Billy. Period. What I want is to live with Billy and Abe in Seattle. I can't see any way to do that though, so I have to move on. I get that, but getting it doesn't help. It's like being stuck in quicksand. Whenever I try to get out, I sink a little deeper. Okay. I'm feeling sorry for myself. It's time to move forward. I can do that. If I make a new life in Canada, Billy can meet me on his school breaks. And I have to let go of Abe. I can't see him again, ever. He'll want to fix this and we'll all get hurt.

How could he ever fix Nick Season? I have to stay positive and look to the future.

She closed her diary, holding back tears.

———

"I'VE GOT ANOTHER PROBLEM," Abe admitted. They were still in Max's conference room, facing each other across the maps on his table. The summer sun was setting behind the Olympic Mountains to the west.

"You?" Max was resetting the time on his Rolex.

Abe ignored him. "I'm meeting tomorrow with the man who's behind all of this. He's smart, powerful, very dangerous." He frowned. "Moreover, I'm sure he wants to kill Corey." Why was he so sure? He just was, though Abe knew he didn't understand Nick Season. "I need to see him now that I know what I know. I was told that he's offered to help me. I need to understand what I'm dealing with. Get inside his head. They expect me to take her side. My instinct is to play against their expectations. I'm not sure how to be convincing when I lie about Corey, especially about how I feel about her."

Max thought this over. "Okay. I see what you're after. Okay. You got one thing going for you—no offense intended—but you have this kind of distracted manner. You know, off...out there." Max shrugged, sympathetic; it was what it was. "You could crank that up, use it to help him underestimate you. If you come across weak, he'll be more likely to believe you."

Max, he was learning, had a knack for making people underestimate Max. "How does that work?"

"In your case, you can come on kind of awkward and uncomfortable. You know, be a wuss. What's your office word— anxious? Look at the ceiling like you always do. Admit that you're confused." Max paused, working on this, then he brightened. "Here's an idea. Make it clear that you're looking out for number one. Uncomfortable, anxious, and selfish. Yeah, showing selfish, he'll see that as weakness."

"The uncomfortable part I can do." Abe looked at the ceiling, unaware he was doing it, then back at Max. "Let's work on anxious and selfish. Suppose I tell him I'm really worried about the police. Worried that she set me up. Worried that my neck is out a mile. I can say that accessory to murder puts my life and my practice at risk. I'll ask the guy for his help. And in a situation like this, I'll sweat and stammer without even trying."

Max looked Abe over, then grinned. "My life and my practice...it could work..." He turned serious. "Whatever he says, though, no matter how convincing, it won't mean a thing. He already has his plans."

"I understand. If you were this man, what would you do?"

Max didn't hesitate. "If I was going to kill her, I'd have you followed. It's the smart move. You're going to find her."

"Will they find her without me?" Abe asked. He stood and looked out the window. He could see snow-capped Mount Rainier, glistening pink in the evening light.

"If we can find her, they can find her. And Jamie could get hurt."

Abe turned back toward Max. "I don't want to lead them to her." He was rubbing the back of his neck. This was a problem.

"I understand. Believe me, I do," Max added. "And it's a risk. But there's no better choice. None. She needs our help—"

"Even if she doesn't want it?" Abe interrupted.

"Whatever she decides to do, I can help her and so can you." Max waited for Abe to digest this. "And bear in mind that the best chance to throw them off is after we find her. When they think they're home free. When they think we're nothing to worry about."

"She's very able. If we do nothing, could she simply get away, out of their reach?" Abe wanted to be sure on this.

"Have you ever been on the run?"

"Are you kidding?" Abe chuckled. "And you, I gather, have been on the run."

"Couple times." Max shrugged.

Abe sat down again. "Why didn't I know this?"

"Why would you know this? You were my therapist."

Abe lowered his head and showed his palms—of course. "Go on."

"There are just too many ways to make a mistake. Say she's holed up in some wilderness anchorage. She's fine for weeks, maybe months, but what's she going to do this winter? How's she going to get papers? New identities? There's no way to do that without leaving a trail. If your guy can't find her now, he'll lean on the guys who do false IDs. If that doesn't work, he'll pose as a cop and check out all the high schools in Vancouver or Calgary with kids Billy's age who've entered the district this year. Then he'll run the names, check their histories. And then—"

"I get it," Abe interrupted, pretty sure Corey knew the score, pretty sure she was considering options. She'd have a trick or two of her own. "I still don't like it. If we lead them to her, and we screw up—" Abe paused. He couldn't bear that.

"Could happen. But consider the alternative. You said the people looking for her are smart. They've surely hired an able professional." Max touched Abe's forearm, then quietly asked, "What if you do nothing, and she and her boy get killed?" When Abe didn't answer, Max went on. "How about this? When we find her, even if she doesn't want our help, we'll set it up so she can still disappear. We can always create a decoy. If they're following us, we can be the decoys. At the very least, she won't be any worse off."

Abe wished he could be sure. There were, he knew, no guarantees. "Do you have an idea how we might help her, if, in fact, she wants our help?" he eventually asked.

"Not yet. We'll improvise."

This was like being on a creaky old roller coaster. "I see," he said, remembering Max's tropical fish disaster. "Should I be worrying?"

"Waste of time. We'll know what to do. You'll know what to do. I already told you that."

"You did—"

"You'll be okay," Max interrupted. "I know you. If you're with her, her chances get better." Max's expression turned serious. "What I worry about..." He leaned in closer. "In a deal like this, the smart thing, don't try to understand anyone's feelings."

SEVENTEEN

ABE WALKED INTO HIS mother's living room at nine o'clock sharp. Nick Season was standing beside the walk-in fireplace, all smiles. Abe shook Nick's outstretched hand. His own palm was moist. Jason was across the room, near the window, looking out at Lake Washington and the Cascade Mountains. He nodded at Abe. His mother rose from the burnt almond-colored leather couch facing the fireplace. She kissed his cheek then started right in. "I'm sure you have your reasons," Jesse said.

Abe put Nick out of his mind. "I think—" he looked at the ceiling. "I think I made a mistake," he quietly admitted.

Jesse hesitated, uncharacteristically surprised. "Really?"

"I can't see why she'd kill that man, or leave without giving me some explanation. I mean…I mean I helped her." He went on, grave, "I've left her a dozen messages, and she won't even return my calls. I don't know…my neck is out a mile."

"What do you make of it?" Jesse eventually asked.

"I'm not sure."

"What's worrying you?" she asked.

"I'm not sure how to put this." He wiped his brow with his handkerchief.

His mother excused herself, returned with a glass of water. "Take your time," she reassured him as she set the glass in his hand.

He drank some water. "Okay," he said. "It's possible—it's likely—that she shrewdly played her mark…I was her mark, yes, from day one." He took another sip of water. "And now, she's left me in the position where, if I don't bring her back, I could be an accessory to murder." Abe shook his head. "An accessory to murder," he repeated. "After all, I got her a new probation officer, and I vouched for her with a federal probation supervisor. I even wrote a letter to a judge on her behalf. And the prosecutor will surely find more." He faced Nick. "Frankly, I'm worried. I've handled this badly…inappropriately, at the very least. And I've put myself, and my practice, at risk."

"Don't blame yourself," his mother said, touching his arm. "She's a psychopath, a professional liar. The important thing is that you're all right, and that after everything, you're able to see her for what she is. Frankly, I'm relieved." She brushed some lint off the lapel of Abe's sport coat. "I was afraid you'd fallen head over heels."

"She fooled me." He nodded, uneasy that he was lying so ably. "I'm sorry to be so…so thrown. I really didn't get it."

Jason came around the couch to where they were standing in front of the fireplace. "She fooled me, too," he offered. "She did seem like a good person."

"Nick knew her," Jesse said. "He can tell you more about her."

"How did you know her?" Abe asked, aware that he wanted to smash Nick's face with the fireplace poker.

"She lived with my cousin, Al Sisinis." Abe feigned surprise. There it was, the missing piece. Corey had said that Al had done a favor for some big shot back when the guy was coming up fast. He pressed his handkerchief to the back of his neck as Nick went on. "We were close. Al more or less confided to me that he and Corey had access to stolen drugs," Nick explained. "When Al disappeared, I suspected that she had a hand in it. I think that somehow she killed him, or had him killed, and double-crossed him on their drug scheme. My guess is that Al was on to her, and he told one of his customs buddies to check out their boat if anything ever happened to him. That's the only reason they caught her at all."

"I had no idea," Abe confided. And, he realized, Nick was more than a pathological liar; he was another kind of creature entirely. He spun you into his wondrous ever-evolving web of lies.

"A police lieutenant, Lt. Norse, called." Abe went on, "He wants me to come in tomorrow." He looked over at Jason. "I think I should bring my lawyer."

Jason turned to Nick, a question.

"I know Jim Norse," Nick volunteered. "I'll ask him to give you a little more time."

"Thanks...that would be great." Abe hesitated. "Can you help me find her?" he asked, tentative. "My position is considerably improved if I help bring her back."

"I'll try," Nick offered.

"I'd like to see if we can't get her some kind of deal." Abe weighed this then said, "Maybe even get her into a long-term psychiatric facility."

"Interesting." Nick turned to Jason. "Do you think we could get the prosecutor's office to cut an unconventional deal?"

"If we can find her," Jason replied. "We can try."

"I was planning to look for her," Abe volunteered. "I'm leaving soon for Vancouver. I could use some help when I get there."

"Call me anytime." Nick gave Abe a business card. "My cell phone number is on the back."

"Thanks very much. I will...I'll be in touch."

"Perfect." Nick touched Abe's shoulder. "I'll back off Lieutenant Norse. So don't worry about that. And of course I can help if the prosecutor's office brings you into it." Abe recognized the proverbial stick. "The first priority is to find her." Nick went on, "If we find her, your problems go away." And yes, there was the carrot. "Then we'll work this out with Corey. I'm sure of that. The kind of trouble she's in, well, let's just say she'll see that we can help."

Abe eyed the poker. "Thanks. Thanks again," he said.

———

"THAT WAS GENEROUS. THANK you," Jesse said to Nick after Abe was gone.

Nick stood. "Jess..." He had started calling her that. "I'd like to see him on our team – consulting, special problem stuff. He's obviously insightful and very able." Mommy's little ladyfinger was what he was.

210

"Nicky, you'll be a great State A. G."

"Yes. I agree," Jason added. "That was very gracious."

"Thank you. You do someone a favor and—well—what goes around comes around."

———

"Did you shower this morning?" Sam asked him when Abe was seated in the front seat.

Abe realized he was still sweating. "Sorry, Sam. That was hard."

"Maybe you sit in back?"

"Right." When Sam pulled the burgundy Olds over to the curb, Abe climbed into the back seat and rolled down the window.

At the house, Abe showered and changed. He was thinking that he had to find Corey soon. Nick was too smart. Corey had said as much, but he hadn't really understood what she had told him until this morning. The man was actually two people all of the time. And no one ever caught on. Even his cynical, oh-so-savvy mother had no idea. None at all. How could a person do that? Something inside the man had to be dead, inhuman. He wondered if Nick ever allowed himself strong feelings. No, that kind of feeling would almost certainly get in his way, foul up his relentless shape-shifting. Hypersensitive to the world, hyposensitive to his own feelings. Abe rubbed the back of his neck. Nick Season was the most disquieting person he'd ever met. He was cut like a perfect diamond, a dazzling stone. He had Iago's gift for lies and no heart at all. A man like that, he had to have someone looking for Corey. A professional. He wasn't going to let this go. Un-unh. Never. Corey thought she could hide. Unlikely. Max was right—if they could find her, so could Nick. And then, when Nick found her, she would be on her own. He couldn't let that happen.

He remembered what she'd said about Moira, or fate. In his work a person's history, left unresolved, all too often limited his life, or, as the ancient Greeks might have put it, shaped his destiny. He knew that Corey would never be able to live the life she wanted, the life she deserved, if she wasn't free of Nick Season. Maybe that was another way to think about Moira. Perhaps because she was who she was, Corey was destined to confront Nick. And Abe understood that he could help her make that decision—or as she put it, recognize Moira—and then be by her side, one way or another. Was that his fate? It was, more than anything, what he wanted. He grabbed his overnight bag. He had packed it late last night. He had no idea how long he'd be gone.

———

RILEY SAT IN HIS car outside Jesse's house. After the shrink left, he had a hunch, so he just waited. First an older guy came out and went to his car. The guy wore a conservative dark brown suit, made for him in Hong Kong to minimize his paunch, he guessed, and a silk tie. Riley filed that away. Not fifteen minutes later, there he was, Nick Season, coming out of the house with mom on his arm. A handsome couple, Riley had to admit. Jesse Stein was, apparently always, one classy-looking chippie. And from a distance Nick looked like—well—Warren Beatty, yeah, only not so slick.

At the sidewalk they turned toward him. Seeing Nick up close for the first time, Riley sensed it right away: Nick was a jungle cat—a jaguar or maybe even a tiger. And he had been right about Nick and Mom Stein. He was sensing something else, though, something altogether more—what?—sinister, yeah, sinister. Okay, Lester had looked up to Nick. It was actually something more than admiration, he reflected. Yes, Lester, a monster by any measure, was somehow stirred by Nick. And frightened by him. Why would Lester—a fiend, a demon, a host of hell—be afraid of anyone? Riley squinted, then that out-of-the-box smirk crossed his face. Suppose Nick Season was spawn of the Old Gentleman himself, Scratch, the Father of Lies? Riley felt it, a frisson, his second.

———

"I OPENED MY HEART and groveled," Abe explained to Max. They were standing by the window in Max's conference room, looking down at a construction site. Beyond the site, Abe could see a freighter in the shipping lane. He turned to Max. "I always choose

212

my words carefully, and when I'm anxious—which I was—I sweat a lot. So to a guy like that, I was—what was your word?—a wuss? If I do say so myself, I was a total wuss." Abe sat on a near chair, aware he was wound pretty tight.

"Good. Excellent." Max sat kitty-corner from him at his conference room table. "So you lied—"

"Like Pinocchio."

"How did it feel?"

"Not so good. And he's so much better at it than I am. For this guy lying is the same as talking." Abe leaned closer, he couldn't stop thinking about Nick. "It takes your breath away. On the outside he's a sensitive, charming guy. I mean he's genuinely likable—imagine Jimmy Stewart or Paul Newman. On the inside he's a great white shark with an oversized brain."

"Uh, doc, suppose we do the headwork later?" Max quietly suggested.

"Right." Abe put his hand on Max's shoulder. "Okay…I told them we were going to B.C. I promised to keep in touch."

"Good." Max stood. "Hang on."

A minute later Max was back with a device that scanned for transmitters. Called a transmitter detection device, it had a wand or probe attached to a metal box. The wand could "sniff" for pulsed tracking transmitters. He scanned Abe—nothing. He had Abe run the scanner over his own hefty body. Head to toe. Nothing. "Let's check my truck," Max suggested.

Abe followed him into the elevator and down to the parking lot. Max located the GPS transmitter under his Suburban, showed it to Abe, then put it back. Next Max scanned his luggage in the back seat, the glove compartment, even the lock box he kept in the trunk. Nothing at all. Max leaned against the car. "Where's your passport?" he asked Abe.

"In my overnight bag. In your office."

They took the elevator back up to Max's office. Abe found his duffel and set it on the conference room table, where Max scanned it. After a minute he found the transmitter that was hidden inside the travel bag. "Not bad," Max said as he took the transmitter out from behind a seam in the side pocket of the duffle. He studied the little chip. "State of the art."

Max left the room. When he came back, he had another overnight bag. He put the transmitter in the bag. "When we find her, this bag goes one hundred miles in another direction."

"I'm lost," Abe confessed.

"Whoever's following you is a pro. He already knows we're going to Vancouver, so we leave the transmitter on the truck. When we find her, we'll have the pilot plant this on some other boat in some far-off place. A decoy. It'll confuse him."

"If he's good, he'll find us again."

"Yeah, he will," Max agreed.

"And he'll know we're onto him."

"Uh-huh."

"What's the point?" Abe asked.

"First, it buys us some time. Also, he'll see that it's a minor league play—pretty good, but not up to his standard—and I hope he'll sell us short. Then, when we find her, we'll make our play."

"What's our play?" Abe asked, thinking Big Man Burgers.

"Like I told you, we'll figure it out when we find her."

"I remember that. Right." Abe squinted. The cranky old roller coaster was inching over the crest of a harrowing run. Not so good for a guy who hated heights and speed. "Are we in danger?"

"Not until we find Corey."

NICK DIDN'T WANT TO be seen with Riley, but he had to talk with him. So he had Jim Norse arrange a phone call. Nick had a voice disguiser so he couldn't be identified if the call was recorded. The portable device was housed in a metal case that weighed about ten ounces. It allowed him to change his voice from male to female, or adult to child, with great ranges of bass and timber. Nick chose one of fourteen settings, a young man with a full bass voice. "Fill me in," was all he said into the phone.

"Your shrink is on his way to Canada. Today," Riley said.

"Today?" Interesting.

"Is there an echo or what?"

Nick waited, a beat. "I heard you were a smartass, Riley."

Riley changed his tone. "Sorry, just joking. But yeah, he's

leaving today with a fella calls himself Max. Max runs Worldwide Industrial Security."

"How do you know this?"

"Do I ask you how you practice law?"

Nick considered hanging up on the guy. Instead, he waited, not a word.

"Okay, sorry, I'll put a lid on it," Riley eventually offered. "I did the background on Stein for Lester, so I have access to Stein's credit card info. I confirmed with the airline."

Suddenly Nick missed Lester; he'd know how to put the fear of God in this smart-mouthed bounty hunter. "And?"

"If they find her, I'll find her."

"And when you find her?" Nick asked, aware he would eventually have to deal with Riley himself. Fine. It was like riding a bicycle, you never forgot how to do it.

"I need some advice on that."

"Simple is better. What are you thinking?"

"Okay. I'm thinking these old boats, they explode. A deal like that, in that wild country, it's like they never existed."

"Or they eluded you." Nick hung up.

———

AFTER CLEARING CUSTOMS, ABE and Max were met at the gate by Max's man, Vince Edwards. Vince was hard-bodied and gray-haired. His face was long and lined from thirty years of police work. Max made the introductions.

"We lucked out," Vince said after shaking Abe's hand. He pulled out a map and set it on a vacant check-in counter. Vince pointed to a remote town he had circled in Queens Sound. "They saw her boat here, in Bella Coola, two days ago."

"That's to hell and gone," Max noted, then he drew a larger circle on the map. "Hire a man at every marina within striking distance of Bella Coola—say seventy-five nautical miles. Is our plane ready?"

"Good to go. And you're set at this floating lodge. It moved last week to King Island." Vince showed them an island in an inlet off Queens Sound. "It's not too far by plane from Bella Coola.

Your first stop is here." Vince moved his forefinger to Dawsons Landing, a town on Rivers Inlet. "I've booked two rooms in your name. My guy will hole up there with your decoy bag. He'll plant the bag on a fishing boat and send it up some remote inlet when he hears just where you've spotted her."

"Perfect. Gimme a second." Max pointed to the men's room.

While Vince and Abe made small talk, a short, mustached businessman in a suit and tie asked Abe for directions to a downtown French restaurant. Abe said he didn't know, but his friend Vince might. While Vince gave the man directions, Riley Crabbe attached another transmitter to Abe's overnight bag.

———

NICK AND JESSE WERE at Bella, one of Jesse's favorite Seattle restaurants. The understated room was tasteful, the service was attentive, and the cuisine, outstanding. Nick liked how they paid careful attention to all the details. He understood the importance of that. And he especially liked how the chef didn't always do what he was supposed to do. How even though he was a Seattleite through and through, Bella's chef didn't hesitate to tell you what he thought. Nick swallowed his ego daily; the chef at Bella didn't have to do that. He envied the outspoken chef, Nick realized. And where, he wondered, was that coming from?

"What are you thinking?" Jesse asked, interrupting his reverie.

"I was thinking about your son, Abe."

"What were you thinking?"

"He left for Vancouver already. I was wondering why."

"Left? When?"

"This afternoon," Nick replied.

"Maybe his plans changed."

"Or maybe he's in touch with Corey Logan."

"Can you have him followed?" Jesse had that look he recognized, she was working on something.

"If you'd like."

"Please." She put her hand on his, squeezing gently. "Good..." She looked into his eyes. "Nicky, have you considered moving in?"

Like it was no big thing. He should have seen this coming. "Moving in?"

"Yes. Perfect." She was falling for him, fine. Still, she was a runaway train. "Part-time anyway," she added.

Nick turned this over, thinking you reap what you sow. "After the election," he said, buying time to weigh this carefully.

"That's what I was thinking too."

There it was again, that feeling, like being buried alive.

———

COREY AND BILLY SAT on the beach in their little cove. Corey had built a fire and they were cooking hot dogs on long whittled sticks. When Billy decided his was ready, she handed him a bun and a clam pot she'd used to carry condiments from the boat. He put mustard, a slice of pickle, chopped onions, relish and then ketchup on his hot dog.

"So when do we go to Port Hardy?" he asked after swallowing a big bite.

"Two or three days. I want to set up a meeting from there with someone in Vancouver who can get us some new IDs."

"How are you going to do that?"

"Jamie gave me a name. I'll call the guy from Port Hardy."

"Great."

"Do you miss your girlfriend?" she asked.

"Yeah. A lot."

"What do you miss the most?"

"At first I thought it was—you know—"

"Are you talking about sex?" Corey interrupted. "Jesus, have you had sex?"

"Jeez, mom, forget it."

"For christsakes, you're fifteen years old."

"So? So it's okay to be in juvie, but it's not okay to have sex?" he asked angrily.

She squinted. How old had she been? Seventeen? No, eighteen, at least. Billy was only fifteen years old. "No, it's not okay."

"Are you serious?"

"You're fifteen."

"So I can sleep under the freeway or in some abandoned building, but I can't make love with a girl I really like? Is that it?"

Billy looked at their fire. "Do you have any idea what it's been like for me? Do you? Any idea at all?" He glared at her. "At the first foster home, they'd lock me in the basement most nights. Guys beat me up in Juvie. They would have raped me if I didn't pull a shank." And then he was standing up, in her face and yelling, "I've had to take care of myself since I was thirteen. I was scared all that time." Billy walked away. And then he was crying hard, his face scrunched up, balled fists in the air.

Corey bit her lower lip. There it was. Things that could not be undone. He was right. He had grown up too fast. He'd had to. "I'm sorry, honey...you're right and I'm sorry." She went to him and put her arms around him. Billy let her hold him. After a while, he wrapped his lanky arms around her. And then she was crying, too.

ABE AND MAX TOOK a fifteen-minute taxi ride from Vancouver International Airport to a smaller facility known as the "South Terminal," where they were directed to an older twin-engine plane, a big-bellied aircraft that Max called a Goose. They taxied to a small airstrip and in no time they were airborne. Abe didn't like flying and small spaces made him claustrophobic. By the time they were airborne, he was sweating. Still, when they flew north of Vancouver Island along the British Colombia coast, Abe was dumbstruck. He had never seen this country. To the west the ocean was endless. To the east there were hundreds of islands in countless shapes and sizes, more channels, narrows, side-channels, straits and passages then he had ever imagined, soaring snow-capped mountains, vast misty forests and inlets—wide, deep glacial fiords gouged out of the rugged mountains. Occasionally there was a small harbor with fishing boats and a little town. Usually the only access he could see was by boat. He couldn't imagine how Corey found her way through these waters, but he had no doubt that she could do that.

They landed at a small airstrip not far from Dawsons Landing on Rivers Inlet. Max had called ahead and Vince's man was waiting. On the airstrip they gave him the empty decoy bag with the transmitter in it. He confirmed the plan. When he heard from them, he would plant the bag on another boat and send it out in the opposite direction. It would be easy to find an out-of-the-way inlet. He had the boat lined up already.

They took off again for the hundred-odd-mile run to King Island. The country was more of the same, wild and magical, though Abe was airsick. He tried counting islands but it made him nauseous. He settled back in his seat, eyes closed, summoning memories of Corey.

And then they were descending, making a wide circle over the Dean Channel, slowly turning toward the coast of King Island from the north. The Goose came through low hanging clouds, and Abe could make out imposing mountains, sparkling snowdrifts snaking down steep cliffs, then great waterfalls flowing down through the trees into the sea. Clouds were suspended in the forest, stuck in the trees on the rugged cliffs. What he couldn't see was a town, nor a landing strip, in this vast wilderness. Instead there were trees, and more trees, coming down from the rugged mountains then carpeting the shore. The pilot pointed out their destination, a floating lodge anchored in a cove at the southwest corner of this forty-mile-long forested island wilderness. The lodge, he explained, sat on a barge that followed the salmon during the fishing season. Then the pilot pointed out the second highest peak in British Colombia rising through the clouds. But where was the airstrip? Behind the lodge, out of sight? The plane was coming down toward the lodge, maybe ten feet above the water now. Where were they going to land? Abe grabbed Max's arm when the plane touched the water.

"Relax." Max patted Abe's arm as the plane skidded across the water. "She can land on her belly in the water."

The plane taxied on its belly to the edge of the great wooden barge that supported the floating fishing resort. A young woman was there to greet them. Abe's face was ashen.

———

ON HIS LAPTOP RILEY had watched the Goose fly past Good Hope. It had continued west across Rivers Inlet then landed near Dawsons Landing. He had asked the pilot of the seaplane he'd rented to set down some twenty-odd miles south, where he'd waited, tracking them. The signal had left the plane: gone into town, he presumed. Were they staying there? Or was it a ploy?

Max was good, he decided, but was he good enough? Unlikely. One way to find out. Riley adjusted the frequency on his receiver. A few seconds later his adrenaline kicked in. There it was. The second signal. Moving north. The overnight bag was still on the plane. Riley guessed what was inside—the meds, the computer, the toiletries, everything the oh-so-careful doctor needed. Yes, Abe Stein was on that plane. Riley was nodding to himself. They must have found the first transmitter. And now it was in some god-forsaken town about to go god-only–knew where. A decoy.

Airborne, Riley turned his receiver on again. He had his pilot follow the Goose. And less than an hour later he saw on his laptop where they had stopped on the far side of King Island. They had landed at a cove on the southwest corner of the island. "What's in this cove?" he asked the pilot. Riley pointed to a spot on his map, the southwest corner of King Island.

"Three days ago there was a floating fishing lodge anchored right there," the pilot replied.

Riley went back to his map. King Island looked to be about ten miles wide and forty miles long. He confirmed with the pilot that their seaplane could land off the near coast. "Let them settle in, then let's find a place to put down on this side," he suggested. "A spot where we can make our camp." The pilot had supplied the necessary camping gear. It was part of their arrangement.

Maybe half an hour later Riley saw the Goose. It passed overhead, not ten miles from where his own plane had landed. The signal wasn't on the plane, though. No, the signal wasn't moving at all. It was coming, strong and steady, from the far side of King Island where they were staying. The second device had gone unnoticed. Riley cracked a smile. No one ever looked for a second transmitter in the same place as the first one. That was human nature.

EIGHTEEN

THE JENNY ANN TIED up to a dock at the all-but-abandoned town of Ocean Falls at 11:45 A.M. Accessible only by seaplane or boat, Ocean Falls had been built at the beginning of the last century, and for fifty years it was a boomtown with bars, hotels, indoor swimming pools, even taxis. In 1980, when the pulp mill closed, most of the people had already left the area. At one time home to 6500 people, the last census set the population at 37. Today the local hotel, once the largest in British Columbia, sits abandoned with a Merry Christmas sign still hanging in its ballroom.

Corey had a phone call to make. She pointed out the Rain County General Store where she was likely to find a phone. It was the kind of town, she mused, where you might meet a black bear foraging down Main Street. Out of the corner of her eye she noticed a man leaning against a storage shed, looking their way. He wore reliable rain gear and seaworthy boots. He could have been a local but her antennae went up. When she turned away, Corey kept her eye on his reflection in her side window. She saw him back into a doorway, out of sight. Was that some kind of a phone in his hand? Corey didn't like the look of this. "Got to go," she whispered to Billy, and they left abruptly. She steered their boat north, and then west, and then south again, hoping to disappear among the islands until they reached their hiding place. She went over it again and again. The guy could have been waiting for his girlfriend, or just skulking around. Hell, who was she kidding? Something was wrong.

———

MAX GOT THE CALL at 11:52 A.M. Their plane was waiting. By noon he and Abe were airborne. Vince had supplied them with detailed maps of the area and luckily, Ocean Falls was not far. By the time they came over the town, the *Jenny Ann* was long gone. Corey must have spotted their man, they guessed. He had said on the phone that she left in a hurry. They had anticipated that they might scare her off, but there was nothing to be done about that. Now they had to find her. Max studied the map. He was wearing camo and packing a side arm. He circled a dense maze of channels, straits, and islands. "Let's check this out," he said to the pilot.

Abe had binoculars and he was scanning each and every waterway for any sign of the *Jenny Ann*. Nothing yet. He could feel his heart pounding, and he was nauseous from the turbulence.

"You okay, buddy?" Max asked as the plane followed a deep gray channel that cut its way through countless forested islands. The pilot turned south over a smaller side channel. Abe didn't answer, he was too busy checking out every passage.

As the pilot circled back to the main channel, Abe turned to Max. "Am I okay? …Are you kidding? I'm scared of heights. I hate flying. I get airsick. I can't swim—"

Abe opened the window of the little airplane and stuck his head out. Max grabbed Abe's belt from behind.

With his free hand, Max put a handkerchief in Abe's palm. "Hah…love—ain't it grand," he muttered.

The plane banked sharply to make another pass. Abe was resolutely back on the binoculars. The pilot turned off the main channel again. He was leaning out the open window now, scanning every waterway. Nothing.

The pilot came back to the main channel and angled southwest, cutting again across the maze of islands and side channels. Abe methodically moved his binoculars north to south. No sign of them.

The pilot was angling northeast now, crisscrossing the waterways below, working the grid. Abe swept again, west to east. He spotted a purse seiner, casting its nets at the mouth of an inlet.

The pilot made another hard turn then another southwest run. He scanned a small group of islands that were separated by a side channel from a larger island with a steep granite bank. There was something moving, yes, between two small islands. Abe leaned out the window, focusing. "Yes!" he cried out, fist clenched, watching Corey's boat flying southwest down the side channel. "There she is!"

The pilot took the plane lower still. Clearly, Corey had seen them, for she was racing around an island for an even smaller passage. The pilot tried to cut her off before she could make the abrupt turn up an even narrower channel. Too late. Corey made the passage and the plane had to climb into a hard turn. The pilot tried to follow her, but she was hugging the steep bank of the narrow channel.

"Can you come in low in front of her?" Abe asked.

"Are you serious?" Max just looked at Abe. "You are serious. Damn, was I right about you or what? Wear a lifejacket."

Max strapped the lifejacket over Abe's shirt as the pilot brought the plane around again. Max took the binoculars, focusing on the boat. "Doc, her boy's just brought up a twelve gauge."

Abe ignored him. He leaned out the open door, waving, as the plane came toward the boat. Corey fired a warning shot and the pilot climbed out of danger. Max's hand on his belt kept Abe from falling out the door.

"She's nuts about you," Max said.

"One more time," Abe insisted.

"I'll have to touch down on the water and drop you well out of range," the pilot explained. "It'll be ice-cold when you hit the water."

"Just do it." Abe said as the plane circled around again.

———

COREY WAS WORRIED. HOW had they found her? If she could make the next passage, she knew a place where they could hide. But she had to keep them away long enough to disappear. She guessed the guy hanging out the open door had a gun. And if the pilot was any good, the shotgun didn't have the range to bring them down. She watched the Goose turn toward her again. She gunned the engine and raced around an island. When the Goose anticipated her move, she handed the wheel over to Billy. "Head between those islands." She pointed out the passage. Corey took the shotgun.

She trained her shotgun on the approaching plane. The guy was hanging out the door again. The plane was on the water, slowing. What were they doing? She flipped off the safety. And then the big guy flew out of the plane, tumbling head over heels into the icy water, as the pilot raised the flaps and put the Goose in full throttle. The plane rose and swerved away sharply, out of range. Corey ran and grabbed the wheel. The man ahead of her in the water was wearing a lifejacket, yelling and waving his arms. She slowed. Christ, he couldn't swim. And there was something odd about the way he flailed in the water. Dear God. Abe. Unmistakably, wondrously, Abe.

NINETEEN

COREY SAT ON THE *Jenny Ann's* covered back deck, wondering what this man who couldn't drive had gone through to find her. And then there he was, shivering and looking silly with a faded turquoise beach towel around his waist and one of Billy's scraggly old soccer sweatshirts tightly covering his torso. His hair was still wet and he had a blanket draped over his shoulders. She made a place on the bench beside her and motioned for Abe to sit. When he was sitting, she handed him a mug. "Hot soup," Corey said and put her arm around his shoulder to help keep him warm.

Abe shivered and watched Billy, who was at the wheel, taking the boat north. He sipped his soup. Corey tightened the blanket around him with her free hand.

"He's a good-looking boy," Abe offered when his shivering finally slowed. "Seems to have his mother's quiet competence."

She gently squeezed his shoulder, so, so glad he was here.

They were moving through a mid-sized channel, staying close to a long, crescent-shaped island. Abe turned to the wild shoreline. On the shore a steep green wall of trees rose straight out of the ocean where the glacier had carved out this channel. On the island side they passed an inhospitable rocky beach fronting dense, dark green forest. She pointed out a bald eagle perched on a driftwood log that had washed onto the desolate beach.

"This is all new to me," he said. "It's exhilarating, and daunting."

Corey held him close, kissed him lightly on the lips. "I love that you found me, even if it's thickheaded and dangerous, and you use words I don't understand."

Abe kissed her back, a tender kiss.

"You're freezing," she said. "Your lips are freezing." She wrapped the blanket more tightly around him and rubbed his back and arms with both hands. "That water you jumped into was fifty degrees, mister."

"I'll be okay," Abe said, taking one of her hands. He set his mug on the deck. "There's a lot to sort out. Most of it quite dangerous. I get that now. But first, Corey, there's something that I want to say...that I came up here to say. I—"

"I know what you want me to do, and I'm not going to do it. So can we talk about something else?"

"This is something else," he explained.

"Another plan?" she asked.

"No. Something else entirely."

"Like what?"

"Just a question. One question."

"Okay, one question." She leaned in, her mouth close to his ear. "Don't ask me to go back," she whispered. "Okay?"

"Fine. May I ask my question?"

"What?" Corey pursed her lips, readying herself for trouble.

Abe turned to her, full face. "Will you marry me?"

"What?" came out again, much louder.

"Will you marry me?"

Corey looked at him, still shivering underneath his blanket. She had heard him but she wasn't tracking. This wasn't possible. "I can't," was all she could think to say. And then, "I won't go back. I mean it."

"I'll find a way to live with you, wherever you choose to live."

"Do you have any idea..." Her voice trailed off. She couldn't marry him. She was on the run. And even with the best intentions, he would never be happy running with her. She pressed her palm to his back, unaware she was doing it. Never.

"Just think about it," he eventually asked. "Let's talk about it again in a few days."

Corey closed her eyes, opening them as she turned to him. "How can I possibly think about it?" she asked. And then she was crying, sloppy tears streaming down her face. She couldn't marry him, no. But it was really something that he'd asked. She cried for a while then Corey put both arms around his neck. "How I missed you, Abe."

"Likewise," he replied, kissing her teary face.

Billy slowed the boat and Corey disentangled herself. "Be right back," she said, wiping her face with her sleeve.

Abe watched Corey grab their buoy. She was helping Billy tie up when the Goose circled for a landing on the bigger water on the far side of their little dome-shaped oval island.

———

JESSE LAY HER HEAD on Nick's chest. They had just finished making love and she could hear, even feel, his pounding heart. The skin on his chest was warm and flushed. "Did I make you happy?" she softly asked.

"Hmm," he replied. Nick ran his fingers through her mussed hair.

Jesse felt good; she liked making him happy. And she was getting better at it, she hoped. She would offer something new, and he would just smile that terrific smile. Tonight, she had asked him to shower with her. In the shower, he made her come before she took him in her mouth. Later, in bed, she asked him to have his way with her—anything. And they finished with rough sex, at her suggestion. It wasn't the first time for them with the riding crop, and she had learned that he knew just how far to take her. Still, it was unmistakably forbidden fruit, and, with Nick, that made her feel sexy. When it hurt, she would beg him to stop, while she imagined the look on his face and how well she was pleasing him. Once inside her, he came quickly—which, she decided, meant he must have really liked it. Still, there were times during their foreplay when she caught this far-off look in his eyes. Like he was somewhere else. What was that about? But each time, almost as if he knew she was watching, he would do something wondrous for her, and she couldn't think about it anymore. Afterward though, when she came back to that look, it was still troubling. She was hoping that one day he would be able to lose himself with her. Utterly. Unconditionally. He would have to trust her. But he could. And maybe then his far-off look would turn to something blissful. She wondered why she wanted that so much. She didn't know. It was so unlike her, these intense, confused feelings. Without warning, and to her, inexplicably, she asked herself: was it love? The idea of that made her apprehensive, and then she felt suddenly giddy, a feeling she could barely remember.

——————

Abe, Corey, Max and Billy were sitting on driftwood logs that Corey and Billy had set on the beach around their fire pit. Max had just joined them—he had hiked over the top of this island carrying their gear from the big-water side where the Goose had landed. Now they were talking.

"Am I hearing you right?" Corey asked. "You knew you were being followed? That you might lead them to me?"

"No better choice," Max said.

Corey stood. "Yeah there was a better choice. You could have stayed the hell away."

"We found Jamie in less than two hours. How long do you think she'd keep your secret while they broke her fingers and toes?" Max asked. "Or hurt her child?"

"Goddamnit." She turned to Abe. "I told you—"

"Corey, I know who's after you," he interrupted. "I made the connection to Lester. I met with this man, along with Jason and my mother. I get what you're up against. And he's going to find you, with or without us."

Corey's hands were on her head, pressing down. "How did—"

"We'll talk about it later. He has no idea that I'm onto him. But I understand the problem now. And I made a judgment that I'd rather be here with you than have you face this problem alone."

"You made that judgment?"

"I did. I love you. Max can help you in all kinds of ways. I can help you too." Though he didn't yet know how, or how to convince her. "And we have the jump on them. They don't know that we know we've been followed."

"That's a big fucking relief," she snapped.

"I understand why you're angry, but please bear with me. You have some choices."

"Are we okay here?"

"I think so. We found a tracking device in my overnight bag. That device is now transmitting from a fishing boat out of Rivers Inlet. It's going up Draney Inlet, over a hundred miles south of here. Whoever's following us should be checking out that fishing boat tonight," Abe explained.

"This sucks." It was Billy's first contribution to the conversation. He turned away, toeing the dirt.

Corey put a hand on Billy's shoulder. Abe was aware how very unhappy she was. And he was suddenly worried that he'd made another mistake. "If you want to leave right now, you can," he offered. "But—" Abe weighed finishing his thought. "Sooner or later they'll find you."

Billy mumbled something. It sounded a lot like "fuck."

"What's the alternative?" Corey eventually asked.

"Let's work on this together until morning. See what we can come up with. If we come up short, I only hope you'll take me with you."

She looked at Abe, plainly miserable. "Here's the deal. Billy and I leave in the morning at six-thirty sharp. Just the two of us. And you promise to leave us alone."

Abe looked at his watch, it was almost 5:30 P.M. "If that's what you want," he said, hoping against hope that somehow, in the next thirteen hours, they'd find their way.

———

RILEY WAS PLEASED WITH the boat, a well-worn twenty-four-foot Osprey. The pilot had arranged to have it brought down from Bella Coola. This was the first time Riley had it on the water. It had a small cuddy cabin, slept two, and moved like the wind. There was room to store his scuba gear, and he was protected from the weather. He especially liked the cleverness of features like the walk-through transom door and the live well. Most important, in this boat he looked like he belonged on this water. It was a sensible boat, the kind of boat the locals understood. He could be on his way to fish or just cruising the Inside Passage.

He had a good idea where they were, though he hadn't seen them yet. The second GPS signal had begun moving around noon. They had flown from the fishing lodge to a place he had found on his map. The GPS wasn't moving anymore. It was in between a larger hourglass-shaped island and a smaller oval island. They were at her boat now, had to be. He turned the Osprey toward the oval island.

On his detailed map, Riley could make out the U-shaped cove where they would likely be anchored. A side channel ran between the two islands. He adjusted his course, guessing he would be at the top of the side channel in fifteen minutes. He had thought about drifting in close at night. But in these narrow channels they would see or hear him before he was ready. No, the more sensible plan would be to put ashore well above them on the larger hourglass island then pack his gear down. Once he was just north of them, he would make the swim across the channel. He would cross the channel underwater in his cold-water scuba gear. After dark no one would notice him. At her boat he would attach the explosives to the bottom of the hull. He would set three separate charges of C4, a powerful, plastic explosive that could be detonated underwater from a remote location. It wouldn't be hard to make the boat, and everything on it, simply disappear. He didn't like the idea of swimming in these waters at night. But it would be a short swim, and he had logged more than his share of hours underwater. Scuba diving was one of a few sports where a man of his stature wasn't at a disadvantage.

He liked that he could put his Osprey ashore far enough north that they would never hear it or see it. It would be easy to pack his gear along the shore to the best crossing point. It was a thorough solution. No loose ends. Done with this job. After, he would take a long trip. And if he never saw Nick Season again, it would be too soon. Riley checked the boat's little clock. Okay, almost 7:30 P.M. Twilight ended at 10:31 P.M. He checked the location of the transmitter—it hadn't moved in over an hour—and anchored the Osprey in a protected spot near the northwest tip of the hourglass-shaped island.

———

ABE AND COREY SIPPED whiskey and watched the setting sun splash pinks and reds on the clouds from the back deck of the *Jenny Ann*. It was 8:30 P.M. He was smoking the same pipe he had smoked when she first came to his office. She remembered how even the outside of the bowl was charred. They heard the Goose taking off, then saw it flying overhead toward the fishing lodge. She took a slow breath; there went their emergency exit.

They had been talking nonstop without success, and she had finally signaled him that they needed a break. Abe had asked Max to excuse them so that he and Corey could have time to discuss certain aspects of this privately. The Goose flying overhead had quieted them. "I see patients, I'm a diagnostician. I just didn't get it," Abe offered when the Goose was out of sight.

"Hon, you only see a man like Nick after something goes very sour. Not when he's on his game." Corey watched the lines in his face reconfigure in that familiar way that meant he understood her. And she was sure he did. She was very happy he was here, even if she was scared. Even though she couldn't see a way to be with him.

"Still…I didn't have a clue. And I thought my mother was so tough, so capable. Nick has her eating out of his hand."

"He's expert with tough women."

"I'm sorry. Of course you'd know that."

"Nick puts himself inside your mind, however he wants you to see him; most nights I can't see my way clear." She wondered if that would ever change.

Abe tapped his pipe on the deck rail, emptying the burnt tobacco into the ocean, then he set it down. "I'd like to talk about that."

"I bet…" She touched his face. "Not now. We've got our hands full with finding your—what did you call it?—*Opportunity*." Corey was having second thoughts. This guy couldn't drive, he sideswiped parked cars, for christsakes. "We've been round and round this mess for hours. I'm not seeing anything."

He hesitated, then asked, "Would you please consider coming back to Seattle? There has to be a way."

"Is that your big idea?" And before he could answer, "If you won't let that go, I'm leaving now." She tensed at a noise.

"Are you frightened?"

"Frightened? Every time I hear a wave lap against the side of my boat I want to wet my pants."

———

RILEY ROWED HIS DINGHY to shore. He pulled it into the trees and began hiking down to check out Corey Logan's boat. He had no trouble following the shoreline south until he found what he was looking for. From the spot he'd chosen, Riley trained infrared binoculars on the Elco Cruisette. It was a fine old wooden boat, well maintained and newly painted. The venerable cruiser was moored to a white buoy in the little cove he had pinpointed on his map. The clouds had rolled in, but he could still see a light on the back deck, and yes, there was a light on in the wheelhouse. The Chris Craft looked stately, a remnant of another, more elegant time.

Riley was in the trees, on the shore of the larger island looking south toward the cove, maybe three hundred yards from the *Jenny Ann*. He increased the magnification on his binoculars, and he made out two people on the covered deck in back—yes, the S.O.L. shrink was unmistakable and the woman was Corey Logan, had to be. She looked just like her picture. S.O.L. was looking relaxed, smoking a pipe. Riley smiled. The shrink did live up to his nickname. The pro was there too, wearing camo: Camo Max in the wheelhouse with a teenaged boy. Perfect.

He had studied the tides and currents, and Riley had decided to swim to the boat from the north. He would start above the neck of the hourglass and swim south into the cove. Coming from the north, he would have the main current behind him. On the way back, he would also swim south and come ashore below the neck of the hourglass, well below where he put in. The currents would be with him both ways. After he came ashore, he would hike north to return to his starting point. He had seen their plane leave, so presumably the four of them planned to stay onboard. Maybe take the boat north in the morning. In any event, they had no other way out. He returned to the Osprey to begin his work.

———

ABE WAS SITTING ON the teak bench that ran along the port side of the old boat's covered deck. His back was against a post and his legs were stretched out on the bench. He checked his watch: 10:00 P.M. Corey was taking a break below, where Max and Billy were playing some videogame on Max's BlackBerry. They had agreed to regroup in ten minutes. They were still spinning in circles, getting nowhere. Their discussions had been unproductive. No, frustrating and, finally, irritating. They were stuck, unable to come up with a plan beyond cut and run in the morning. He had decided to try again to convince Corey to reconsider Seattle. And if she wouldn't—which was likely—ask her to take him with her. He doubted that she'd agree to that either.

———

RILEY PACKED HIS GEAR in his little dinghy, then rowed to shore. He hiked south with his gear until he found his spot. It was 10:15 P.M. as he sat down to organize his gear and wait. At 10:30 P.M. he packed his explosives—enough to make the boat and the people on it evaporate—then put on his wet suit and his tank. Training his binoculars on the cove, he could see lights through the fog, shapes on the back deck. Max and the boy were likely in the galley. He adjusted his tank, then threw himself into the cold black waters of Queens Sound.

The underwater currents made the swim a little more difficult, a little longer, than he had anticipated. Still, there was no problem. Ten minutes later he could see an anchor chain. Perhaps thirty feet beyond the chain Riley saw the bottom of the *Jenny Ann's* wooden hull.

———

ABE SAT UP STRAIGHT, listening carefully to the night. He heard the waves, the reassuring sound they made lapping against the side of their wooden boat. Nothing else at all.

Earlier, he'd imagined he heard a sound on the water, but when he looked over the rail, all he could see was smooth, gently rolling blackness. Clouds covered the moon, fog was settling in, and visibility was poor. He took a breath, wondering if there was another way to think about what they might do.

When Corey came up again, Max was with her.

"I thought you said we'd know what to do," Abe said to Max, tense now.

"Sometimes it takes a while," Max admitted. "Let's focus again on how he's going to find us."

"It's almost eleven," Abe said, checking his watch. They had been over and over the events of the last few days. They had considered things that Abe might do in Seattle. Places where Corey and Billy might be safe. Max had volunteered to double back and try to track down whoever was hunting them. After all of this talk Corey was more determined than ever to run as far and as fast as she could. And she was angry that they had forced her hand in this way. Abe sensed an impasse, and reluctantly, he went to the worst case, a place where, his mother used to say, his Jewish father liked to linger. "What if he's already found us?" he asked.

Corey was pacing, anxious. "...okay...yes...let's assume he has."

"How could he find us so quickly without a transmitter?" Max asked.

"Knowing who hired him, this guy will be very good," Abe pointed out. "World class."

Corey sat. "Maybe he placed another transmitter that you never knew about."

"We checked everything," Max replied. "We found his transmitter. Last night we went over the clothes on our backs. Even the plane. We were clean."

Abe was pacing now, drawing on whatever resources he had left. "Corey's on the right track. Assume this guy's smarter than we are. What if he placed another transmitter later? You know, long after the first one. Maybe even days later." Abe thought this over.

"Where would a smart guy do that?" He looked up at the sky, he scratched his head. "Where?" he mused aloud.

It was painfully quiet until Abe muttered, "shit" and lumbered like a great bear down to the galley. "Shit!" he yelled from below. Abe came back up, carrying his overnight bag. "I screwed up. A smart guy puts it the same place as the first transmitter. A place we had already looked. We didn't check this bag a second time."

Corey turned. "You mean he's out there right now? Damnit, are you—"

"There's no time," Max interrupted her. "We have to get off the boat. Now!" He was already collecting gear.

Corey pulled the inflatable dinghy to the beach side of her boat and rowed Billy to shore. Abe looked and listened for any sign of a watcher. Nothing. Below, Max hurriedly checked the galley one last time. He propped up several cushions near a porthole and set Billy's soccer team cap on the top one. Then he moved a lamp close to the porthole. Finally, Max turned on the radio and the interior cabin lights. On his way to the dinghy, he hung a jacket on a cleat on the covered deck.

———

WHEN COREY PULLED ALONGSIDE, first Abe and then Max slipped quickly and quietly into the dinghy. The inflatable was on the protected beach side, out of sight from the far shore. When they were safely aboard, they pushed off from the *Jenny Ann*.

In the darkness Corey and Billy carefully pulled the dinghy into the woods and wiped their tracks off the beach with leafy branches. When they were finished, they hurriedly led Abe and Max farther into the trees. They chose a course up the hillside that they knew would take them over the island. Corey took the lead, carrying her twelve-gauge with both hands in a bird-hunter's ready position. Billy carried a small duffle holding clothes, Jamie's gun, their first-aid kit and his mom's diary. Abe followed Billy with a garbage bag full of clothes. They had left the "goddamned overnight bag" in the galley.

Max brought up the rear. He was wearing his side arm.

No one said a word.

Just below the top of the island they stopped in a small clearing. They had come about half a mile, Corey guessed. Hidden in this clearing, they had a good view down to the cove. They would wait here until first light, about 4:30 A.M. in late July, then they would call the pilot via satellite phone to pick them up on the far side after sunrise, an hour later. In and out as fast as they could do it. When they got to a safe place, they would regroup, sort out options. The four of them sat, tentative, waiting for they-didn't-know what. In the distance they could see the *Jenny Ann.*

They were quiet then, as doubts fed on themselves until nothing was clear and prickly tentacles of fear began to find their purchase. Corey watched her boat. The *Jenny Ann* rocked quietly in the cove. From so high and far, it was a buoyant little jewel lit from within. She wondered how it had come to this. She had been caught in the vortex of this thing, swept up by people and events beyond her control. Corey raised her eyes to the night sky and thought about Moira. She watched the northern lights streak across the vast starry sky—an unforgettable punctuation mark—as the quiet, eerie night exploded in one great crescendo of fire, thunder, and cascading debris. And the *Jenny Ann* was gone.

Corey gasped, a desperate guttural sound, as the unimaginable image was branded, red-hot, onto her brain—shocking, successive explosions shooting fire, water and all manner of boat debris high into the night sky. It was as if a powerful underwater volcano had erupted, spewing like a horrific fountain, and then it was over. One moment the *Jenny Ann* was there, tranquilly moored for the night, and then she was a plume of smoke, a burning fuel slick peppered with flotsam and jetsam and a lone white buoy.

Corey watched the burning slick, stunned. She bit down on the back of her thumb. Billy took her other hand. Abe and Max sat on the hillside beside them, struck dumb. Her boat, a thread, a primary color, woven through the fabric of her life, was gone, vaporized. Corey shut herself down, a thing she had learned to do in prison. She closed her eyes, working to suppress any and all feelings. She let go of Billy's hand and quietly moved off to sit by herself.

Abe sat beside her and put his arm around her shoulders. She couldn't respond. She moved away, just slightly, and he knew to let her be.

Fifteen minutes later they heard a boat coming down the channel. A light from the boat played across the water. Corey shuddered. The explosions had been so powerful that there was, literally, nothing left of the *Jenny Ann* except shards of wood floating away with the outgoing tide into the strong currents in the channel. In the deeper channels there were subsurface as well as surface currents that shifted with the tides. The floating debris would be carried away then dispersed by the various currents. Anything that wasn't buoyant would be sucked under, then carried out to sea. There would be no sign of her boat, or anything that had been on it, by morning. The light scanned the sandy beach and the tree line. Corey said a silent prayer, oh-so-glad they had hauled the dinghy well into the woods. The boat stopped and a dark shape cut loose their white buoy and hauled it on board. It was a ghoulish moment. Then the boat—Corey thought it was an Osprey—made a U-turn and checked out the cove and the beach again. And again. The boat circled one last time. Then, apparently satisfied that no one had survived, her captain turned into the channel and sped north.

Corey took Abe's forearm, aware now that they might actually survive. She tried to measure the magnitude of what had happened. Of what had almost happened. She couldn't. She couldn't even think clearly. Would any of this have happened if Abe hadn't come? How could she run without her boat? Why hadn't he listened to her? Why? And then Corey began to hit him with her fists, raining blow after blow against his face and chest. He pulled her close as she cried and cried.

———

Nick was in his office when his phone intercom buzzed. "Who is it?" he asked his secretary.

"Lieutenant Norse."

"Put him through." Nick picked it up. "Nick Season," he said into the mouthpiece.

"I heard from our undercover man," Norse said. "Bad news. He says they disappeared without a trace. No way he can find them."

"What exactly did he say, Jim? Word for word."

"Okay, word for word." Norse hesitated. "He said, and I quote, 'They're gone. Disappeared without a trace. Sorry to be the bearer of bad news.' End quote."

"And then, Jim, what did you say?"

"I said, 'You're sure there's no way to find them? You've tried everything?'"

"And the response?" Nick asked.

"No way. No sign that they were ever here."

Riley must have blown up the boat in that remote wilderness with all of them on it. Perfect. Nick felt light headed; this was too good to be true. "Did he leave a number?"

Norse gave it to him. "Thanks, Jim. If he can't find them, no one can. And let's do him a favor. Don't tell anyone that he struck out. He'll appreciate that."

"If you say so. No problem."

Nick hung up. He set up his voice scrambler, went to a secure line, then he called Riley. "Norse said you couldn't find them," Nick said after Riley picked up.

"The lieutenant has the brains god gave a halibut," Riley replied.

Nick waited. "I understand they disappeared without a trace."

"As we discussed."

Nick felt his skin cool down, a rare event and a sure sign he was feeling good.

"One thing," Riley went on. "I'm going away. Taking a long break. I may retire. Will you watch my back?"

Nick knew what he was asking. Riley had cleaned up a terrible mess, it was true. And if anything happened to Riley, Nick was sure that Riley had set it up so that it would hurt him, too. No, he'd let him go, for now. It would be best to take care of this particular loose end later. "Don't come back," Nick said and hung up.

Nick sat back in his desk chair and considered what to tell Jesse, how to tell it. He would ease her into it. Yes. He would help her construct a story about how Abe ran off with Corey and Billy to parts unknown. By now they probably had new identities. Yes, the man was—what?—beguiled. He hummed a song—"Bewitched, Bothered and Bewildered." Damn, he was singing; he had to be feeling good. Jesse would jump on this, try to find Abe, the whole nine yards. Good. A distraction. There was nothing to find. Their trail would end somewhere on the wild B.C. coast where Corey, apparently, had taken Abe on her boat and disappeared. They could be anywhere up the Inside Passage, or back in Vancouver. Who could say? It would give Jesse a project other than him, which was important right now. He had to slow her down, redirect her. She was wanting things he couldn't ever give her. And sooner or later she would call him on that. So it was getting harder to manage her. And she was becoming even more demanding. Most nights, the woman was on him like a nasty rash. Wanting to "please him," as she put it. Like she was doing something for him, some kind of big favor. When, in fact, she was forcing his hand. She was a mark who asked him to "trust her." Who wanted him to "lose himself with her. Unconditionally." What was that about? Before Jesse, he couldn't imagine a mark—and his women were marks, Jesse most of all—ever thinking anything like that. And Jesse wouldn't be satisfied with anything less. More and more what he felt when she was "pleasing him" was worried, inching toward asthmatic—a condition he first treated with a lug wrench on Uncle Tony's '59 Mustang. Shit. She had waited until his soup was simmering, just so, and then she spit—no—she pissed in his carefully seasoned broth. And she liked pissing in it. That was the problem. So... Nick tapped his desk with his fingertips, sensing just where he was. Yeah. After the election, he would have to cut her loose. Make it her idea. He felt better. Okay. Until then, he had to back her off a little. Changing Jesse's direction, however, was like turning a battleship. A project like this would keep her on task through the necessary turning radius.

TWENTY

THE PILOT DROPPED THEM below a fishing cabin, more than a hundred air miles northwest of Bella Coola. The sturdy, weathered structure was tucked away at the tip of a pear-shaped island near the Fiordland Provincial Recreation Area, a 225,000-acre mountainous wilderness of islands, inlets, fiords, waterfalls, rivers and glaciers. The remote cabin sat on a bluff several hundred yards north of an unexpected sandy beach. Beside the cabin was a sparsely wooded field, and the pilot pointed out brambles at the edge of the field where they could pick blackberries. At the end of the long wind-swept beach there was a creek where salmon came to spawn. From the beach you could look across the wide inlet to a sheer cliff climbing straight into the sky. It was a gray misty day, and in the dull light the island looked dreary, even bleak.

The little cabin was accessible only by air or water. Max explained that his man Vince had rented it from a hunting and fishing club. Abe was sure of one thing: so long as they were dead, no one would find them here.

After settling into the cabin, they went to the beach where they gathered wood and set up a fire for cooking. Abe and Billy set a grill over the fire on four big stones. Corey was going to cook steaks, which the pilot had picked up with their other provisions at the Klemtu marina.

Abe had asked Max to give the three of them some time alone. They agreed that unless one of them called on the satellite phone, Max and the pilot would pick them up in four days. And now, finally, Abe and Corey were sitting beside the fire on a driftwood log where they were sipping whiskey and talking. The tide was out, and Billy was digging clams down the beach.

"Are you still angry?" he asked her.

"Angry and sad. I lost my boat." And she had felt unstable and disoriented ever since, as if some essential piece of her emotional operating system was missing. "That didn't have to happen."

"No, it didn't. I'm sorry for your loss." He looked glum. "I should have found the second transmitter sooner."

You found it, mister, that's the point, though she wasn't ready to tell him that just yet. "I'm still in shock and second guessing everything."

"So am I. With hindsight, I would have handled this differently—" He stopped, looked at the sky then back at Corey. "I know that doesn't help you. I'm sorry. I screwed up. I can't undo that."

She could see he was being awfully hard on himself. "The silver lining, we're dead, which is the best news ever." She had realized that resting in Abe's arms, waiting for dawn. And eventually her anger was paired with a more hopeful feeling.

"It certainly gives you some time."

Yes, it did. Still, she wasn't about to let him off the hook. "Do you get it now?"

"I do," Abe said. "But there's no excuse for putting you and Billy in danger."

"It was frightening."

"Yes, it was. I wish I'd been—I don't know—smarter. I should have assumed that Nick would be a step ahead of me. It's who he is."

"I'm going to pretend I'm you. Here's what you would say—your way, soft and slow—'Don't be so hard on yourself.'" She nodded. "Babe, you felt you had to come. I can understand that. Even if I didn't like it. Give yourself a little credit—it worked out... you know I'm right." She went on, "You said it yourself. We were already in danger. You just jumpstarted the whole deal. And in the end you came through—you did—even if you cut it awfully close. Let's not dwell on what could have happened. I mean—c'mon— those women could have killed me in prison. Lester could have taken Billy. You know?"

"Thank you for that." He hesitated. She saw a subtle shift in the lines on his face.

"I knew I had to be with you. It was the single most important thing. I just knew that. I can't explain it."

"I get that. Sometimes you just go full bore. I killed Lester without a second thought. I never even considered consequences. I mean I couldn't let him take Billy, whatever the risk, whatever the cost."

"Max says it's usually like this. That you don't even get it until the last minute. That your best chance often comes when you're about to lose everything. He believes you have to go after it, or you never get that chance." Abe shrugged, he wasn't sure. "As you can guess, he didn't explain that bit about the timing until this morning. Still, I should have known just how good Nick's man would be."

"And I wish I'd told Al not to bring up the past with Nick. I wish I'd known that if he did, Nick would kill him and frame me. But that's the point. No sane person ever sees what Nick's capable of."

"Point taken." Abe sipped his whiskey. He was watching her in that way that only he could do.

"Do you get it now about Nick?" she eventually asked. "What I've been dealing with?" She felt hugely—hugely—relieved, just to be talking with someone about Nick. It was as if she had been dragging this great anvil behind her in the sand. She'd even gotten used to it. Now, just like that, it was gone, cut loose, and for a moment, Corey felt like she could fly.

"Yes. And you've had to live with this alone, all of this time."

"I wanted to tell you, Abe, you can't imagine."

"I understand why you couldn't tell anyone."

"I had to kill Lester. I had to take Billy. Do you understand that?"

"Yes, yes I do." He shook his head. "I can only imagine your horror when Nick turned out to be my mother's lover...my God. And then Jason turned out to be his lawyer."

"It was a low point," she admitted.

"A nightmare is what it was." Abe turned to her. "Do I have this right? After you left my mother's brunch, Nick told his man

242

Lester to take Billy. Lester grabbed Billy, you killed Lester. Then, of course, you had to run."

"That's pretty much it." She could see on his face that it made perfect sense. Someone got it. What a fucking sea change.

"I'm sorry I was so slow to see this."

"No apologies necessary. You didn't know. And no one gets it about Nick. Ever. That's the point." Corey poked at the fire with a long driftwood stick, thinking about her future, looking for a way, any way, that Abe could be part of it. "Are you aware of what you've just given me?" she asked.

"I'm not sure what you mean."

"A clean slate. I'm dead. I can change my name and start over. I'll live in Canada and I won't have to look over my shoulder because Nick won't be looking for me. You can go back, you'll have to invent a story. We'll have to figure it out."

He nodded. "I could have been on the far side of the island when the boat exploded. A horrible accident. Let's work it out when and if we have to."

"Okay. Good." She lay her stick on the sand. "After I'm set up and its safe, you could come visit, or we could meet someplace else in Canada. Maybe Montreal, I've never been to Montreal."

"I hadn't thought of it that way. And if it's what you want, I'll meet you in Montreal anytime. Or, if you'll have me, I'll disappear with you, live with you in Canada. I mean that…" Abe fussed with his pipe, then he softly asked, "Can I raise another possibility?"

Shit. "No, I can't go back."

"I think you can," he said.

"Why? So Nick can kill Billy and me? Why are you doing this? Don't you get this?"

"I do get it," Abe insisted. "And I know I've made mistakes. But please hear me out. This is a complicated and critical decision. Even if Nick believes you're dead, Corey Logan will still be wanted for murder. I'd like you to listen to what I have to say."

Double shit. Corey stood, stoking their fire again. She sat back down. "Why can't you just let this go?"

"Because there's such a terrible cost if we do that. Consider what you're giving up. Don't you want to be in Seattle with your son? With me?" He persisted, "Wouldn't you like to clear your good name? Imagine never having to look over your shoulder, never having to worry about Nick, or fake identities, again. Wouldn't you like to get married in your own backyard?"

"Of course I would. You know that," she snapped. "But I can't."

"Why not? Because Nick Season says you can't. You have the right to live the life you want to live. Don't give it up for that son of a bitch. Hell no. You don't have to do that." Abe leaned closer. There it was, those laser-like light blue eyes. "It won't be easy, but together, we can figure out what to do. You and I can do this. We have to."

"My God, what are you thinking? This isn't like psychotherapy." She held his eyes. "We can't 'figure it out' or 'work on it.' It's not a head game. We have no evidence. Nothing. Nick's a foolproof liar and a stone-cold killer. And he's going to be Washington's state attorney general."

"And he has to be stopped." Abe looked into their fire. "It's not just about what you'd have to give up…think about what he'll do if he ever finds out that you and Billy are alive. And though you might be okay for a year, or even two, eventually, he'll start to wonder. And then to worry. It's who he is. You've told me that. And then he'll never stop checking. He'll have me followed. Every year, he'll run your prints, and Billy's, through some Canadian database. And that's just the beginning…unless we stop him."

"And how do you propose to do that?"

Abe's bushy brows furrowed in a "V" until they almost touched. "I understand the problem now." They touched. Corey had never seen that. Very cool. He meant business. He turned to her, full face. "To begin, I'll comb my hair and look this devil in his shiny black eyes."

What? What was that? Corey was dumbstruck. Eventually, she softly mouthed, "What?" And louder, before he could answer, "Aren't you afraid of him?"

"He's very frightening, and I'm painfully aware of what's at stake. And of course I see how very dangerous he is and yes, that scares me." He scowled. "But I have other feelings that are even stronger than my fear."

"What does that mean?"

"What I'm afraid of, what keeps me up at night, is losing you. Nick wants to kill the person I love most in the world. That makes him my archenemy, my nemesis. What I feel for Nick is inexhaustible rage." He tapped his pipe against the log, emptying it into the sand, then he carefully set it down. When he looked up, his expression had turned fierce. Abe took both of her hands. "Nick Season be damned!"

"You're being crazy." She had never seen Abe like this.

"No, I'm telling you how I feel. I want to marry you Corey. I want to live with you and Billy in Seattle. I want to go to parent night at Billy's school. I want to take you guys to dinner at Tulio and for pizza at Via Tribunali. I want to fish at your favorite spots near Bainbridge—"

"He'll kill us all." And Abe was really scaring her.

"I have to keep that from happening."

"This isn't a storybook. Nick isn't like anyone you know. And this isn't an insight kind of deal. Look what happened the last time you tried to help. They almost got Billy, and I had to kill someone. Look what almost happened last night. This time you and Billy and I, we could all die. Do you understand that?"

"Yes, I do. But I won't let that happen."

"Won't let that happen?"

"No, I won't."

"How?"

"I'm working on that. "

"Working on it? How? You're going to comb your hair? Look this devil in his shiny black eyes? What is that about?"

Abe considered her question. "It's a way of starting."

Corey put her head in her hands. She didn't know what to say.

———

DINNER WAS A RESPITE from the difficult decisions they were facing, and Abe took the opportunity to get to know Billy a little better. Not surprisingly, he had his mom's keen sense of humor and a sharp eye for what was going on in his world. At one point Abe asked him about the Olympic Academy, where Morgan and some of Billy's soccer teammates went to school. Abe was curious about

Olympic because he had worked with young people who went there, and his mother's friend, Mike Morris, was a counselor there. "It's okay," Billy said, "if you want to pay a lot to feel bad about having money or wanting to be mainstream."

Abe had sensed something like that, though he couldn't have put it into words.

They ate heartily—salad, corn on the cob, bread and, for a change, steak. Although the steak was good, Abe missed grilled salmon. He hoped he'd have the chance to eat bright wild salmon harvested from these very waters. It seemed likely. After leftovers were cleared and burnable trash tossed into their fire, Billy left to continue fishing the little stream nearby. Corey and Abe stayed by the fire to watch the sun go down. They were both preoccupied.

She picked up right where they had left off. "I don't get this. Why aren't you more afraid?"

"It's not that I'm not afraid." He hesitated, wanting to get this right. "I think it's more that I can and will do things that scare me. It's what I tried to say before. If the stakes are high enough—and in this case they couldn't be higher—I'll manage my fears and I'll do what I have to do."

"And you can do that?"

"I think so." He nodded. "I've worked hard to be able to do that."

"Worked hard? I don't understand," Corey said.

"When I was a boy, I was afraid of so many things. I'd stay home at night because I was afraid to walk the streets in the dark. I was bullied at school and afraid to tell anyone. I was afraid to be home alone. As a teenager, I couldn't stay in a relationship with a girl. And so on. When I finally got help, I said that what I wanted was to learn to do the things that scared me."

"What was that like?"

"It took a long time, even with a good therapist." Abe hesitated. "At first, you work to understand why you feel what you feel. There's lots of talking about that. Then there's one failure after another. It's discouraging. But you just keep after it. The fear is still there, and it's real, but at some point you're ready to take a chance again, try a worrisome thing. And little by little you begin to do things you thought you could never do. There are lots of setbacks, but when that happens, you talk about what's holding you back and how you could handle it differently, and eventually you try it again." He tossed a pebble into the fire, remembering how hard that was. "And then sometime later, maybe years, you begin to see how you've grown stronger. It's incremental change, baby steps, but the time comes when you know you can do hard things, even if you make mistakes. Nothing makes you stronger than successfully doing hard things. You, of all people, must know that."

"I do. I do understand that." She leaned against him. "Abe I love you. You're the finest, most courageous man I've ever met. But that's not enough this time. This time, if you fail, I'll lose you."

"You'll lose me if I don't try. Don't you see that? I'm willing to do this—likely the hardest thing I've ever done—because if I don't, I'll never be able to be with you." Abe nodded; he had wrestled with this. "We'll be sitting in a restaurant in Montreal, wondering why we never tried. It will always be there—when we're wishing we could have dinner with Billy and his girlfriend, or go to his college graduation, or see Billy's newborn child. You know that and I know that."

"Do you have any idea of the risk you'd be taking? Abe, you'd be risking everything." She took his hand, wanting to make sure he understood this. "Everything," she whispered.

He turned to face her. "That's the point. For the first time in my life there's someone worth risking everything for."

She buried her face in her hands again.

———

THE SUN HAD SET. Billy had come back with two bright silver salmon, then gone to their cabin to clean them. After he left, Corey and Abe took a walk down the beach. On their way back, they collected driftwood to build up their fire. When they were satisfied with their beach fire, they sat and watched hot red embers disappear into the great northern sky. The night was cool, the sky sprinkled with more stars than Abe had ever seen. Corey pointed out where the northern lights periodically splashed the starry night sky, and her heart ached for her boat. Before long they were back in intense conversation.

"Billy and I will disappear," she suggested. "Then, when I'm set up, say six months, max, I'll call you. By then, I'm hoping we will have fallen off Nick's radar screen forever."

"I think that's unlikely. But if that's your decision—and I know that, finally, it's your decision to make—I would like to go with you and Billy, if you'll have me. Whatever the risks."

Could Abe start over as a different person? What about his patients? His house, his friends, his colleagues, his life in Seattle? Would he be willing to give up all of those things? And if he did, was he aware he could never change his mind, never go back without putting her and Billy in danger? Did he have any idea what it meant to be a fugitive? How would it make her feel if he did give up everything? This was complicated. "I need time to think about that."

"Okay. And please, think some more about coming back." He put another piece of driftwood on their fire. "You don't have to decide now, but please think about it."

"Why do you keep raising this?" She turned to him on their log, eyes steely now, a frustrated glare. "Do you even have a plan? Something specific?"

"First, we get you and Billy to a safe place. Next, I flush him out, then I have to be ready."

"Is that your big plan?" she asked, incredulous.

"So far, yes. I've thought a lot about going to the police or to Jason, but without proof, there's nothing they can do. My friend, Sergeant Ballard, he'd insist on backing me up, one way or another. If that happened, we'd never flush Nick out without hard evidence."

"The flush him out part I know you can do alone. What about the ready? How do you do that?" she asked softly.

Abe's eyes locked on. "I'd have to be ready to kill him."

"Oh my God. Oh my dear God," Corey just stared at him, aghast. "Abe, you're a doctor, a psychiatrist. You're a man who lives in his mind. Have you ever even fired a gun?"

"No," he admitted. "Never."

"Do you intend to hire someone to do this?"

"No, I'll have to do it."

"Why?" she asked.

"Because Nick doesn't understand who I am. He doesn't know what I'm capable of." Abe furrowed his brow. "So I'd have a good chance."

Was she dreaming? Shit. "You mean you'd murder him?"

"No, he'd have to make the first move, then I'd react," he explained. "Reacting, it's what I do in my work, it's what I know."

"You're being—what's your word?—unrealistic, yeah. Totally, completely unrealistic."

"I don't think so." He took a moment then asked, "Do you agree that I'm a cautious person? That when I focus on a problem, I work to see it clearly? That I don't deny those aspects of it that may not suit my purposes?"

She nodded. These things were true.

"When it matters, I assess situations very carefully. I worry about things. I weigh risks. If I'd been a Jew in Europe before World War II, I would have fled. And I would have been among the first to see why I had to do that. This is different. I've been over it and over it. We can do this. Nick Season can be stopped."

"Abe, you're scaring me." She touched his face. Jesus God. She didn't want to lose Abe, too. "I can't let you do this. No. I'm out. I love you and I love how you love me. But you can't kill Nick Season. Even if you're not afraid of him. No way. I mean that. No way. Period." She could see in his face that he wasn't taking no for an answer. "Abe, you have to let this go. Now I need some time alone. I'm sorry, babe." Corey stood and walked down the beach.

Abe fired up his pipe. He watched her disappear into the darkness under the streaky northern lights.

COREY WOULD ALWAYS REMEMBER the next day. At breakfast Abe cooked pancakes and acted as if everything was fine. She appreciated that, especially since he knew she'd been tossing and turning most of the night. Later he asked Billy if he'd like to take a walk. To her surprise, Billy said, "sure." Corey watched them walk off, then she took out her diary. There was a table on the porch where she could see the water and think about what to write. She set herself up. After several minutes she began to write down her thoughts:

Abe is confusing me. He's so smart and so well meaning that I want to believe him. But how can he possibly stop Nick Season? It would be easier to stop the Alien. I can picture Abe's answer—"well, that woman did stop the Alien." Right, but only after—what was it?—five or six people were killed. And she didn't have a choice. She would have cut and run in a heartbeat if she had a way to do that, any way. And—here's the point—I do have a way.

Another thing. Abe really believes that we could have it all. Everything. Where does that come from? I've never had that. Ever. I never even let myself imagine what it would be like anymore. It only makes me sad. I mean how many times have I wanted to kill Nick Season? Wanted to clear my name? How often have I hoped that Billy and Abe and I could live together? A million? But then I ask myself—what if one or both of them died? What then, goddamnit?

What about the alternatives? I don't think Abe could disappear and start a new life with me. He'd always regret it. He already said that we both would. But he could come and see me after I'm set up, after I have a plan for Billy. This is bothering me—I promised Billy that he'd be able to go back. But even if he had a new name, a new identity, what if Nick, or one of his people, ever came across him? What if Billy was arrested? They must have his prints on file. If Nick knew that Billy was alive, he'd come after both of us, big time.

Shit. I wish I was smarter. And I wish I wasn't so used to being afraid.

What should I do? If only I could see my way clear. Unless I do, unless I feel it in my gut, I can't go back. I won't. Abe's intentions are so good, but he's way too hopeful. He wants things to be a certain way so he clutches at straws. I've been burned before by hoping for the best. With Nick, it's smart to plan for the worst. Period.

———

SHE FOUND BILLY AND Abe several hours later, near the creek, building a sea aquarium. In his meticulous way, Abe was packing sand and seawater into a beat-up waterproof crate they had found in a shed behind the cabin. They had set the crate on a flat patch of beach. It was a bright sunny day and Billy, shirtless, was gathering sea life near the creek. Next to the crate she could see where he had set out shells, mussels, even a sea star. In the crate she saw rock crabs and a sea anemone. The tide was out. Near the mouth of the creek, she realized, there must be a saltwater tide pool. Yes, she could see it now. These two guys worked well together, she thought. She went down to the tide pool where Billy was rooting out sea treasures. Under a rock they found a little black eel, a sculpin and an interesting shell. While Abe worked, fixing up their aquarium, she asked Billy, "Do you know what's going on?"

"Sort of. I'd like to know more."

"Abe wants us to go back, face the monster. Maybe even kill him."

"Do you have a chance?" Billy asked.

"Abe thinks so; I'm not so sure."

"I like Abe," he said. "He's okay."

"I'm glad you feel that way. I think so, too."

"What are you going to do?" he asked.

"As hard as I try, I can't see a way to go back. It doesn't feel right. It's just too dangerous," she told him. "What do you think?"

Billy thought this over, tapping his fingers against the side of his leg. "I think you ought to trust your instincts. They're good ones."

"Thanks. That's pretty much where I came out, too."

———

AFTER A LEISURELY PICNIC lunch, they finished their sea aquarium and carefully carried it back to the cabin. Abe proudly set it on the porch.

"If you pick some blackberries, I'll make a pie," Corey offered. She pointed toward the blackberries at the edge of the field. It was a sparsely treed field that sprawled almost fifty yards down the bluff before disappearing into a slew of blackberry brambles that fronted an inland forest. "The berries should still be a little tart, which is perfect."

Billy didn't hesitate. "I'll get a pail." And he was off.

Corey watched him run to the shed. This afternoon he was still a kid who loved his mom's blackberry pie.

When Billy came back with the pail, she saw them to the door. "Make a lot of noise, so you won't surprise a bear."

Abe shot her a look.

Corey nodded, she meant it. "Singing should work," she added as they headed toward the brambles. She stayed behind to make the pie crust.

Corey watched Abe and Billy from the window, singing loud scare-the-bear songs, laughing and filling the pail. She was putting the crust in the pan when she glanced out again. She saw Billy slip on something and almost fall, barely holding the pail upright. She was smiling at how he'd saved their blackberries when she saw his pail of berries fly through the air and she heard Billy screaming. Corey flew out the door and down the porch steps. She ran out onto the field where she could see Billy near the brambles, flailing his arms wildly at swarming insects. She put it together instantly: Billy had fallen on a wasp's nest, yellow jackets that commonly build their nests in the ground. And now the wasps were everywhere and Billy was covered with stinging yellow jackets. Corey ran toward him, yelling incoherently, beside herself, unsure what to do. And then out of nowhere, there was Abe, hauling Billy over his shoulder and running like hell across the field. They came charging out of the field onto the bluff's rocky edge, both of them covered with yellow jackets now, and without breaking stride, Abe jumped into the freezing cold water with Billy slung over his shoulder.

Corey ran to the edge of the bluff. When they came up for air, she could see that the wasps were gone. Billy was having trouble breathing, she could hear him gasping for air. Abe was flailing in the cold salt water of the deep, glacially gouged inlet. He was being carried into the deeper water.

That's when she remembered that Abe couldn't swim.

Corey dove from the bluff into the icy water.

And she decided to marry Abe.

TWENTY ONE

COREY WAS SUPERVISING DINNER preparations. They were at their usual spot on the beach, gathered around the fire, working quietly. Billy and Abe had cortisone cream smeared all over their arms, necks, and faces. Billy had been stung six times. Abe, four. They had each taken an antihistamine then napped, and now the worst was over. They were lucky that Abe had reacted so quickly.

Grilling on the beach was becoming a regular event, and they had fallen into a routine. Billy filleted the fish, prepared the marinade, then organized a basket of plastic forks, paper plates and whatever accoutrements they needed. Abe prepared the side dishes—tonight it was coleslaw and baked beans. Corey made the fire, cooked, and was pretty much the boss of everything. It wasn't right until she said it was right. Tonight, Abe thought, she was especially feisty.

"I know it doesn't mix with your medicine, but pour one shot for each of us," Corey said, after everything was assembled and approved on the beach. She handed Abe their bottle of scotch. Something was up, he realized, she had her spark back. "Pour one for Billy too," she said.

"Scotch? Are you kidding?" Billy asked.

"Add some water." She handed him their water bottle while Abe poured him a drink.

Corey waited until everyone was settled in. "I have something to say," she announced and raised her glass. Abe watched her, curious. "First, to the two best men I know." She touched Billy's raised glass then Abe's.

Corey turned to Abe. "My next toast is a little more complicated." She looked, apparently distracted, at the sea—the similarity to his own preoccupied looks was not lost on Abe, though she would likely argue that—then back at him. "It took me a while to get this. I finally saw it this afternoon. It was when you grabbed Billy the way you did, then jumped into the ocean even though you couldn't swim. I mean you had no chance at all—none—of getting to shore on your own. But I believe that somehow you knew that I'd get you out of the water safe, one way or another. And you were absolutely right." She nodded, hitting her stride. "When I dove off that bluff, I knew I was not going to let you drown, no way. And I think that's what you've been trying to tell me—that if we go back, you're going to get me to shore. One way or another. That you know you can do that. And for reasons I can't put into words, I believe I can count on you. Well, only a fool would walk away from that." She clicked their raised glasses. "Abe, I'd like to be your wife, if you'll still have me."

Abe felt lightheaded. He knelt beside Corey, who was sitting on their driftwood log and put a hand on the log to get his bearings. He couldn't. Still, Abe reached into his pocket and took out a little box, which he set in her hand. "I've been carrying this around for a while. It's gotten wet a couple of times. Sorry," he said, self-conscious.

She opened the box. The blue velvet inside was faded, rough and salty from the ocean. Corey took out the diamond ring. "Oh my God," she whispered then put it on her finger. Abe started to say something. "Shush," she said. "Not yet." Corey stood, admiring the ring on her finger then raised her glass again. Abe and Billy raised their glasses too. "I want to marry you, Abe," she reiterated. "But here's the deal. I want to do it in my own backyard. And I want Billy right there. Then I want to live with both of you in our own house in Seattle. Can we manage that?"

Abe felt this great swell, feelings he wasn't used to having coursing through his body. "We can. We will," he eventually said. Corey sat beside him. "You've made me happier than I've ever been," he whispered in her ear.

"Uh, do you guys want some privacy?" Billy interrupted, looking out to sea.

"We'll keep it under control," she promised.

"Mom, that's really gross."

———

BARELY AN HOUR AFTER saying yes, Corey's giddiness was gone. In fact, she was sure she had just made the biggest mistake of her life. They had finished a celebratory dinner, done their clean-up, and now she and Abe were sitting around their fire working on logistics. They had agreed to confront Nick together. There was no way she would let him do it alone. That was non-negotiable. Beyond that, it was pretty vague. Billy was off fishing for tomorrow's dinner. Corey had sent him after sea-run cutthroat or rockfish, for a change.

So far they didn't have much of a plan. She kept thinking about how Abe had said he would comb his hair and look this devil in his shiny black eyes. He said that about Nick Season. What was that? How was that going to bring down a cunning, murderous, about-to-be state attorney general? She watched him throwing pebbles at their little beach fire. Billy fished along the shore.

"Will you teach me how to use a hand gun?" Abe eventually asked her.

"I don't have many bullets. But we can try."

"I have Max's gun and four extra boxes of bullets," he offered. "He said I could keep them."

"You were all over this, weren't you," she reflected. "Even before you found me."

Abe turned to her. "It's all I've thought about since you left. Especially what to do when we came back."

How could he even know how to think about that? And how had he known she would agree to come back? "Are you sure you want to do this?" she asked him again. "You can change your mind. You don't have to prove anything to me. We can disappear somewhere in Canada together."

"I'm sure."

How could he be so sure? Where did that come from? It made her think of Moira. If this was what Moira felt like, she didn't care for it at all. "Tell me what you're thinking we should do then," she eventually said, working to stay positive. "I know you're way ahead of me. Tell me how you want to do this."

"First, I talk with my mother. Tell her the truth about Nick."

"Your mother?" Corey was getting antsy again. She set a piece of driftwood on their fire. "That's the plan—the shrink tells the truth to his mother?"

Abe smiled. "I should have seen that coming."

"Cheap shot, sorry. I'm a little tense." That was the goddamned understatement of the year. "Go on."

"She's going to come unglued when I tell her about Nick," he said, resigned. "But I'm sure I can convince her to set up a meeting. I'm going to tell her we want to work it out with Nick, then go our separate ways. She'll want to be there. She'll insist."

"That will flush him out, as you put it, I can guarantee you that." Corey could just imagine Nick's fury when he learned that they were still alive, that Abe was onto him too, that Jesse was about to learn the truth about him. He would tell Jesse, sincerely, how we could come to an understanding, work this out, while he fitted all three of them for a black hole. "He's going to come out of nowhere at that meeting. He'll try and kill us all."

"Exactly." Abe nodded. "He'll have no choice."

"And you think you can stop him?" Corey's face gave the lie to her positive tone.

He went right on, apparently oblivious. "What he won't know is that we're expecting that. And we have to be ready for it."

Ready. How? "Do we want help? Max? Jamie?" she asked.

"I don't think so. I think anyone else at all tips our hand. I think we're counting on Nick being overconfident. Sure he can take me down."

Corey made a wry face. "I don't think that will be a problem, babe. No offense."

"None taken." His brow furrowed into that "V." "I'd guess that it's you he'll be primarily worried about. And you're surely the one he'll want to hurt—to punish—the most." Abe stood, pensive. He watched Billy making long effortless casts along the shore, then turned back to Corey. "So if I'm right, you're the one he'll focus on. He'll neutralize you, one way or another, but I don't think he'll want to kill you yet."

"How do you know that?"

"I can't be certain." He hesitated. "But don't you think that for someone like Nick, it's very rare that he has the opportunity to show his true colors? Don't you think he'll want to savor the moment?"

She bit down on her lower lip. "You mean kill me slowly."

"No, I'm afraid once you're helpless, he'll want to demonstrate how easily he can hurt and humiliate you. Before he kills—" Abe sat back down beside her. "It's likely the only time he allows himself to vent his rage, to actually feel it. He'll want to show it off, parade it in front of us. In his mind, killing you will come later."

Abe was inside Nick's head. How had he done that? That had to be completely creepy. "I'm not feeling good about this. Un-unh." She stood now, watching him, her back to the setting sun.

"Bear with me. Please. I've thought about this—believe me—I've turned it inside out and upside down. And if I'm right, this is his moment, when he can finally flaunt who he is. It will be an irresistible opportunity for Nick to shame my mother, his fancy benefactor, and to inflict his revenge on you and me, the interlopers." In the waning light, his face was grim. Corey was mesmerized. Abe went on, "The perfect diamond, this man without feeling, will reveal its flaw. He'll want to tell us how he played you, how he used my mother. And I think he'll want to make both of you watch him taunt me, watch him humiliate me."

Corey pursed her lips. That sounded like Nick. Eventually she offered, "If he did that, it would make me feel helpless. No, worse."

"He'll understand that. And he'll prolong it. Nick will want to tell us who he is, what he's done, how he's going to kill us all." Abe looked up from their fire. "I'm guessing he'll parade around liked a rutting tom turkey, fanning his tail."

"I can picture that." She touched the scar on her neck. "Yes."

"At some point he'll see that I'm beaten down, not a threat. Remember Nick thinks that I'm weak. He doesn't see me as a fighter. He thinks that he can kill me anytime."

"Hon, he has reason to think that," she said, suddenly miserable.

"Then it's time you taught me to shoot."

"I'm not feeling too good about this." Corey was losing her nerve. She sat back down beside him, hoping he'd put his arm around her. He did. She lay her head on his shoulder.

"You don't have to feel good," Abe suggested. He held her close. "You have to teach me to shoot."

That would be good.

———

IN THE MORNING THEY set up two-by-two foot wood squares against the hillside behind the cabin. Max's gun was a 9mm Beretta. Right away, Abe had trouble with the safety.

"Like this," Corey said. She clicked off the safety, located on the left side of the gun, with her thumb. She explained how to breathe, how you squeeze the trigger as you exhale, then she showed him her two-handed grip and her stance. She fired two rounds and hit two wood squares.

He nodded. "You make it look easy."

"Take your time. Remember your breathing. Hold the gun as tightly as you can. You can't hold it too hard. Let it tremor." She waited until the gun was shaking in his hands. "Get used to it now. Under stress, there's going to be some tremor for sure. Now back off, just a little, then squeeze —don't pull—the trigger. You'll get the hang of it."

Abe shot the hillside full of holes.

Before it got too discouraging, she suggested they find Billy and take a walk. Billy was eager to do something, and the three of them explored the island for hours. The sun shone through scattered clouds, but among the trees it was cool and dark. They found the remains of an old mine and saw a Sitka deer. From a hilltop they saw osprey and a pod of orca whales surfacing in the cold gray Sound. When the sun disappeared and the mist turned to rain, they went back to make a fire in their cabin. Corey kept thinking how these days might be the last time the three of them would ever be together.

They'd made their plan. Abe would call his mother. He hoped to call before the pilot picked them up. There was no reason, he explained, to prolong this awful business.

"Will you be ready?" she asked.

"If I'm not, we'll postpone the call."

Corey hugged him as hard as she could. After a slow breath, she gamely added, "Let's just do this before I have a fucking heart attack."

Abe proposed that he set up the meeting with his mother in Vancouver. They could meet with Nick the following evening. She suggested that they meet on an island she knew among Canada's Gulf Islands. It was uninhabited and only accessible by boat. At the tip of the island there was a sand spit. Not even eighty yards wide at high tide, the spit was nothing but sand covered with huge driftwood logs. At the very tip, less than a mile out, was a warning light that blinked at night. They could meet near the light after 7:00 P.M., the four of them, and independently verify that no one else was there. If another boat approached, they would see it long before it arrived. Max would rent a boat for Abe and Corey at the nearest port. At another port he'd rent one for Nick and Jesse. It was a short trip from either port, and both Nick and Jesse were experienced on the water. Whatever happened, it would happen on that lonely stretch of sand. They had three days to prepare. Corey was worried that she and Abe would die on that sand spit. Before she could articulate her worries, Abe put his arm around her and pulled her close. "We're okay," he whispered. "I can do this."

She had no idea where that confidence came from, or what to say.

The second shooting session went a little better. Abe was learning to control Max's Beretta. By the end of their third session, he could hit a two-by-two-foot square from fifteen yards most of the time. It was a start. They had two more days, Corey reminded herself.

TWENTY TWO

J ESSE WAS WORKING IN her rose garden when the call came on her
cell phone. She liked to prune when she was worried, and this
morning, she'd been pruning for over an hour. Abe was in over
his head, she was sure of that, and Nick was distracted. He wasn't
even staying the night tonight. What was that about? She'd have
to talk with him.

She didn't recognize the caller ID number and was going to
ignore the call when she realized that the area code of the incoming
call was from British Colombia, Canada. "Abe," she said, into the
phone.

"Yes, it's me."

"I've been trying to reach—"

"Just listen," he interrupted. "I need a favor. I want you to
come to Vancouver this afternoon. Come alone. Check in at the
Four Seasons. I'll contact you there. Do not tell Nick—I repeat,
do not tell Nick—that you're coming or that you've talked with
me. You have to promise me that. I mean—"

"What's wrong with you? Are you all right?"

"Just promise me that you won't tell Nick."

"Yes. Fine. When will you call?"

"It's ten-thirty now. You can be in Vancouver by three this
afternoon. I'll call every hour starting at four o'clock. Can I count
on your promise?"

She pruned a Peace rose. "You're acting strangely."

He ignored her. "If you tell Nick, the damage to our relationship
will be irreparable." His tone was emphatic. "Do you understand?"

"What?" Something was very wrong. "Are you serious?"

"I've never been more serious in my life." And after a moment, "Do I have your word?"

"I promise," she assured him. "See you this afternoon and I'll be expecting an explanation."

"Don't forget what I said." Abe hung up.

Jesse looked down over Lake Washington, then she pruned another rose and considered the unprecedented phone call. She weighed telling Nick about it. No, not yet. Abe had never threatened her before. He was up to something, and before she told Nick, she'd better find out what.

———

MAX AND THE PILOT arrived as scheduled. The sun was shining and the sea surrounding their pear-shaped island was more green than gray. On the beach, Abe told Max the details of their plan. It made Corey nervous to talk about it, so she helped the pilot pack their gear. Max interrupted him often to ask questions and to offer advice.

When Abe was finally finished, Max said, "Didn't I say when the time came, you'd know what to do? Didn't I say that? From the get go?" Before Abe could reply he advised, "Be yourself," and patted him on the back.

On their way to Vancouver, via the Goose, they dropped Max and Billy at the port town where Max would rent their boat. Abe and Corey went on to check out the sand spit where they hoped to meet Nick and Jesse the following evening. It was exactly as Corey had described it, a gently curving, narrow spit of sand—little more than eighty-five yards wide at its widest point, and, she pointed out, the tide was still rising. The spit was covered with large driftwood logs. The strip of sand formed a natural breakwater. They walked the length of the three-quarter-mile-long spit. Together, they chose a spot for the meeting. Not too far from the tip of the sand spit, three large weatherworn logs formed a misshapen U. The bottom of the U was the largest of the logs. It was at least thirty feet long and fat enough to sit on comfortably. The sides of the U angled out unevenly, and it created a large enough space for Abe and Corey to spread out, to put themselves on either side of Nick. Finally, the only access was up the narrow spit or by plane or boat. They could see in every direction, and no one could hide on the spit or surprise them in some other way. Abe said it was a good choice. Corey couldn't help worrying, but she didn't say anything.

Abe had his handgun, the 9mm Beretta. He took it out, positioning himself behind one of the logs.

"Your grip," she said. "Remember your grip."

He made an adjustment.

"Shoot that log." She pointed at the far side of the U.

She could see the tremor in his hands.

"Safety!" she called out.

"Right. Sorry." Abe carefully released the safety then put a round into the log.

She sat on the log that formed the other leg of the U, so that she was facing him. She had her revolver, the same .38 she had used to kill Lester. "It's not too late to change the plan. I could take the shot. Hell, I could shoot him when he steps onto the beach."

"No, it's a good plan." he nodded.

Corey looked skyward for a sign—she didn't know what—then back at Abe.

He came over, took her hand. They discussed possibilities for half an hour. Their conversations always came back to the same thing—they would both be armed, and Abe would likely have an opportunity, one chance, to make his move. She was the decoy—Nick would surely disarm her. Nick had to make the first move though. That was his advantage; they couldn't kill him before he showed his hand. When they were finished walking through various scenarios, Corey went back to the plane. She said she was antsy. In fact, just being at this place made her want to jump out of her skin. Abe walked the spit again, stopping finally to walk around and inspect the logs at their designated meeting place one more time. When he was satisfied, he joined her in the Goose.

———

TWO HOURS LATER THEY were at the motel in Vancouver that Max had reserved for them. Their suite had a Jacuzzi tub, a steam shower, a large bed set under a mirrored ceiling, a full bar, a basket of fruit and a bottle of champagne, compliments of the hotelier. The "Romeo and Juliet Suite," it was named. Corey thought the whole deal was pretty sweet. Billy was with Max, safe.

Corey poured champagne for both of them. She raised her glass. "For the first time in my life, I have no fucking idea what to say."

He shushed her with a kiss.

Abe reached his mother half an hour later. Max's man, Vince, had volunteered his office suite for their meeting. Abe arranged to meet Jesse there at five.

The office set-up was nothing much, but it had a conference room and a pot of coffee. The windowless conference room had white walls with sixteen—Abe counted them—paintings of different kinds of ducks. Exotic species, he thought. There were four paintings artfully arranged on each wall. Vince, he guessed, was a duck hunter. Abe walked around the room looking at ducks and scratching his scraggly suggestion of a beard. He hadn't shaved since he first arrived in British Colombia, six days ago.

He was sitting at the conference room table thinking about duck hunting when his mother came in. "You threatened me. I hope you have a very good explanation," Jesse said, breathing all of the air in the room.

"I asked you to come because there's something we need to talk about."

"There are several things we need to talk about. But why are we talking about them here? Why did you forbid me to tell Nick? I don't—"

Abe held up his hand, stopping her mid-sentence. "This time, I'm going to talk. I'd like it if you'd just listen." He held her eyes. "Please listen carefully. Since Corey left, I've been lying to you. The reason I've been lying is to protect her from Nick Season."

"What are—"

"It's important to me that you focus on what I'm saying and please don't interrupt." He recognized her chilling look; she was unsheathing her skinning knife. "Nick's fooled you. He's an extremely dangerous psychopath. He killed Corey's boyfriend, the father of her child. His man Lester was going to kidnap her son when Corey killed him."

"Impossible—"

"Mother, brace yourself. What I have to say gets worse. Much worse."

"You sound awful." And after an appraising glance, "You look awful."

He ignored her. "This is horrible for all of us, believe me. I suspect that you love him, and that makes it especially hard for you. I'm not going to mince words though. Nick tried to have Corey killed in prison—"

"How do you know this?"

"She told me."

"And you believe her, without proof?"

"I do. Absolutely. In fact—"

"Abe, please...please," she implored. "Won't you just consider that an unstable felon could be telling you very clever lies?"

"She's not—"

Jesse held up her palm—my turn. "She killed her boyfriend for drug money. Nick had nothing to do with it. And his man Lester was following her son at my request when that woman shot him in the back of the head."

"I don't ask that you believe me. I ask that you trust me enough to hear me out. This one time, forget about how things look. Just listen, just listen to your son."

His mother looked him over again, searching for he didn't know what. He saw the light go on. "Is it a sexual obsession?" she asked.

Abe let that blow right by. "Try and understand. Nick's man tried to kill us all just five days ago. He blew up Corey's boat, thinking Corey, her son Billy, and I were on it. I'm lucky to be alive."

"Nick's man? Do you have any proof at all?"

"No," he admitted. "But—"

"She's a convicted felon and a murderer. I'm sure this woman has many dangerous enemies."

"I love Corey. I'm going to marry her." Abe watched his mother's face freeze, as though she was refusing to process this. "Nick lies all of the time. Effortlessly," he explained. "It's what he does. He fools everyone. I know he's fooled you. I know how hard it is to believe what I'm saying. But mother, I'm sure of these things."

"Can you prove any of this?"

"No."

"Do you have any evidence?"

"Corey's version of events is evidence."

"I see." Her face softened. "Abraham, you spend your days telling people what they imagine—what they fantasize—is as important as what actually happened." He recognized her tone, firm but fair. It often followed "Abraham." "It's possible that this convicted felon's fantasy is not real."

She was unreachable. As a kid, he called it her ice queen mode. As a psychiatrist, he recognized Jesse's very own high-style denial. She was in love with Nick—some kind of unreciprocated, imagined love—and she couldn't give up that fantasy. So they were at an impasse. "I'm sorry but we're getting nowhere. Here's what would help me. Please tell Nick that I know about him. All of it. Tell him I want a meeting, a deal. I'll bring Corey. I've chosen an island in Canada where we can meet. I've arranged for a boat for Nick. Tell him to come alone."

"If I set this up—if—I'm coming."

"Just the four of us then," he insisted. "I'll want your word on that."

Jesse didn't respond.

"Will you set up the meeting? The place, the marina where you can pick up the boat, it's all detailed in these instructions, including a map." he handed her an envelope. "Would you do this for me?"

"If you accuse him, there's no turning back. I won't be able to help you later."

"Help me now."

"Why are you doing this?"

"I'm trying to be with the woman I love. Nick doesn't want me to do that. In fact, he thinks I'm dead. Watch his face when you tell him you talked with me. You might catch a glimpse of the real Nick. And please be careful, this man is dangerous."

She was glaring again. "Do you take me for a fool?"

Abe was suddenly weary. The stakes were so high, and his mother couldn't even hear him. "You're being foolish, yes, but I can live with that. If anything happens to Corey, though, I'll never forgive you."

And may God forgive you, she said with a disagreeable look. Then Abe watched her weighing options.

"I'll set up this meeting," Jesse eventually said. "Just the four of us. Let's damn well see which of us is the fool."

———

AT THE MOTEL ABE found Corey sipping champagne in the Jacuzzi. She invited him in. Sometime later they were entwined on the oversized bed. Every so often Corey would shift their position so she could watch them in the mirrors on the ceiling. Their lovemaking was necessarily talkative. It was also punctuated by laughter. Afterward she lay with her head on his chest. He had his hand on her back.

After a while he asked, "Did you enjoy watching?"

"Yeah, sure. You?"

"I never got a chance."

"I was a little piggy, is that what you're saying?"

"Piggy? Did you hear me say piggy?"

She ignored his question, tapping his chest with her fingertips. Her anxiety was coming on. She fought it back. "Jacuzzi, champagne, lovemaking under the mirrors. I feel like a prisoner on death row getting her last meal."

"Hardly."

"You know just what I mean. And if you want the mirrors next time—which I know you do—don't be sassy."

"Okay, fine."

Lighthearted wasn't working. "So?" she whispered.

Abe turned to her. "My mother was difficult, unpleasant, and unconvinced, as expected. But she'll set up the meeting. And she'll be there."

"When she tells Nick, I'd pay to be a fly on that wall."

"He won't let on. That's his whole deal."

"Yeah, but he'll be so pissed that his heart might just stop."

The corners of her mouth turned up. "Blow up like an overheated car radiator. Wouldn't that be something?"

"We can always hope."

She fought back another wave of anxiety. Corey wanted a distraction, anything. "Are you going to shave?" she eventually asked, gently running her finger along his scraggly beard.

"Yes."

"Why?"

"When you're facing the worst, you want to look your best."

What? This guy didn't care how he looked. "Did Max tell you that?"

Abe chuckled, a familiar rumble. "Sassy, that's sassy."

———

JESSE AND NICK WERE at Canlis, a family-owned special-occasion restaurant that over the years had become a Seattle institution. She had chosen this restaurant to tell Nick about her meeting with Abe.

After their cocktails arrived, she simply repeated what Abe had said about him. Between sips of her martini, Jesse made sure that Nick heard each and every accusation. Then she told him how Abe and Corey wanted to make some kind of deal. Nick didn't seem upset. Throughout, he was at ease, listening carefully, concerned. He asked questions when he needed clarification. He encouraged her to explain with as much detail as she could, which was helpful at this confusing time. In his low-key way, he made it clear that the accusations were unfounded and that he'd explain why whenever she was ready. Nick certainly wasn't surprised that Abe was alive. Where had Abe gotten that idea? Rather, he seemed surprised that Abe had found Corey. He was especially glad that Abe wasn't hurt when Corey's boat exploded. "It sounds like a drug smuggling vendetta," he opined. When she sat back, finished, Nick simply covered her hand with his. His drink was untouched. "I'm sorry," he said. "That must have been horrible for you."

Jesse nodded, sullen, as a large crab leg and two plates were unobtrusively set in front of them. She felt worn down—no—

cranky. She was in a thankless position, passing on her son's poisonous accusations against her lover. Jesse sat up straight in her chair; cranky or not, she had to deal with this. She decided to ease into it. She picked at her appetizer then looked up and said, "This isn't like Abe. Something about this is wrong. Could she have some kind of sexual hold on him?"

"That would make sense." He tasted his whiskey. "She certainly played Al that way." He paused, seeming to remember something. "Al was captivated by her, spellbound."

Go slowly, she reminded herself. Don't jump to conclusions. She watched him, so poised. He even ate his crab assuredly. Although she wasn't at all persuaded by Abe's version, she would have to be convinced by Nick's answers. She had to be sure. "I've got to ask this." Her face hardened. "Abe's my son. He's always been an odd duck, but he's never been stupid. Is there anything else I should know?" She found his eyes. "Something about this isn't right. Is there anything at all you should tell me?"

Nick set down his fork, took a measured breath. "I understand the question. And you're right to ask it. No one knows this. And God knows, I'm not proud of it. Frankly, I'd hoped to spare you this. In a moment you'll understand why." He leaned in. "Jess, I have an idea why she's focused her lies on me. Here's what you don't know—Corey Logan and I have a history." He hesitated. His expression changed, something dark, even bleak, rearranged the lines on his face "This next is between us, okay?"

Jesse nodded. Here we go.

"My problems with Corey Logan began sixteen years ago." Nick took another moment, collecting himself. "She seduced me, and we had an affair," he pulled away, wary. It was instinct, Jesse judged—this was rancid. "Even then, I knew it was a mistake, but Corey Logan can be irresistible, and relentless, when she sets her sights on a man. That's not an excuse, it's an explanation." His eyes were restless; talking about this obviously made him edgy. "She set her sights on me soon after she met Al. I broke it off within a month. Long story short, she doesn't like rejection."

Damnit. It was the first time, Jesse was certain, that one of her lovers had been with the same woman as her son. So far she was glad Nick hadn't said anything. She rubbed her temples to keep her head from aching. No, she didn't like this at all. "What happened?"

He drew closer, confiding, "She kept calling me, showing up places where I'd be. She threatened to tell Al, who was a dangerous hothead. My cousin Al was a hard guy with a hair trigger, and she knew just how to set him off. I realized that there was something about her that wasn't right. So I paid her off. Five grand to make it go away." His face was long, unbelieving, even now. "Paying her off was the biggest mistake I ever made."

"How so?"

"When Al came back to her, over ten years later, I heard from her again. This time, she said if I didn't pay her twenty grand, she'd tell Al about our affair. Even worse, she insisted that I was the father of her child..." Nick closed his eyes, opened them. "She threatened to tell Al, who believed the boy was his. She said she would tell him that I had known about the child and that I'd abandoned my own son." He raised his hands, a gesture of helplessness and frustration. "It was her kind of thing. Corey said she had DNA tests—she actually kept my toothbrush—that would prove it. Though it was unlikely I was the father, I couldn't take that risk, so I paid her off again."

"I'm not following."

"Think about it," he said, his tone patient. "Her timing was perfect. How could I ever go into politics with an enraged customs agent out to destroy me in the press and an unclaimed illegitimate child—which could possibly be confirmed by DNA testing—hanging over my head?"

"It's true. Even the rumor of an illegitimate child is a political train wreck." She thought of John McCain, upended by that very rumor in the 2000 South Carolina primary, "Proven or otherwise, abandoning your own child, it's a non-starter." Jesse sensed where this was going, and she saw that Abe was in trouble. And why Nick had hoped to spare her this.

"Six months later, Al disappeared—he had scored the drugs for her and she had no more use for him. The surprise was that he'd laid a trap. If anything happened to him, one of his customs buddies was supposed to check out her boat. She never expected to get caught with the drugs. Never expected to go to jail."

"And you thought, finally, she'd leave you alone."

"Yes," Nick said, looking angry for the first time. "But then she showed up at brunch with Abe. She was using Abe in exactly the same way she'd used Al. I'm sure you see that."

She nodded. This was what was worrying her.

He went on, "She chose him because of my relationship with you. It's her modus operandi. She'd targeted me again. And this time she had even more leverage because I'm actually running for office. Infatuating Abe was the key. It's the way her mind works. She believed that if she threatened me with telling Abe, her spell-struck lover, her scandalous lies, I'd have to pay her off. I'd have no choice." Nick took a good hit of scotch. "I can't even guess how much she was after this time. The woman has the conscience of a black widow spider."

"So she bewitches one guy to blackmail another." Jesse frowned, mulling this over. "That's diabolical, but it makes a weird kind of sense. This is helping me. I'm beginning to see how her predacious mind works." And it was apparent why this woman had chosen Abe. First, because he was her son. The threat to Nick was implicit. And, she thought, he was easy prey. Abe was inexperienced with women, and underneath it all, oddly romantic. It made him vulnerable to a woman like Corey. "Is Abe in danger?"

"Not yet. She needs him for leverage," he explained. "Lester upset her applecart. She wasn't expecting him, and something went very wrong. And now she's in trouble and she's hoping to cut some kind of deal. That's why she told Abe her lies and sent him to you. She's hoping to walk away from murder one."

"She's not stupid," Jesse observed, though she felt violated. She looked into Nick's eyes. There was another question she had to ask. "Why did she kill Lester?"

He hesitated. She could see that he was focusing. "I can only make an educated guess."

"I'd like to hear it."

"Okay." Nick settled in, pensive. "Here's how it could have gone. Lester knew the whole story. When she went to prison, he did some background work on her for me. That's why I sent him. I'd bet he followed her son to find her. In his notes it said that her boy was a drug dealer. He even had proof—photos.

Say he confronted her, tried to back her off. He may even have threatened to turn in her son. It's likely she showed her gun, which is a violation of her probation. He knew her probation officer. Lester would have threatened her if he had a way. He may have pushed her too hard." He took another sip of his drink, looking uncertain. "Knowing Lester, he wanted to send her back to prison. And knowing Corey, she wasn't going back to jail. I don't know just what he did to set her off. After the brunch she would have been wound awfully tight."

She was a bad seed. And she was wound too tight. And now Corey Logan was pulling the strings on her son. Eventually Jesse said, "I can only imagine how you must have felt when this harpy shows up at brunch with my son. Damnit, I don't know what to do. And I'm worried about Abe."

"You have reason to be worried," Nick said, before he excused himself. She watched him thread his way toward the restroom, stopping at the odd table to chat or pat someone on the back. He had been forthcoming with her, which couldn't have been easy, and the story he told was so sordid that it rang true. Was there some kind of quid pro quo in life? Was Abe somehow paying the price for her happiness? She recognized her mother's voice.

———

IN THE MEN'S ROOM Nick studied himself carefully in the mirror. Nice. No tells. He had put the lid on, stayed focused. Even though he wanted to stick his crab fork in Jesse's eye, right through it. Instead, he stepped up. He unbuttoned his shirt—the hot, itchy rash on his chest was gone. He smiled, enjoying the moment. Jesse had actually called Corey Logan a harpy. Perfect. A harpy was a foul creature, half woman, half bird of prey. Uncle Nikos used to call his mother that.

Nick checked the mirror again. He looked good. He was speeding a little, he could tell—something bright in his hard black eyes—but on a roll, red-hot. He was thinking Michael Jordan, game seven, at the buzzer. A sow's ear to a silk purse. Floss to gold. Father of her child? He was walking on water.

———

JESSE WATCHED NICK APPROACH their table. He stopped to talk with a couple she hadn't noticed, women friends of hers. He pointed her out and both women waved. Before he sat back down, Nick gently touched the back of her neck. It made her feel good.

Their server appeared and both of them ordered Copper River salmon. "Jess, I think I can convince Abe that she's lying," Nick said after their server had left. "At the end of the day what matters is what really happened. And the truth is that Corey Logan killed Al. Just like she murdered Lester. Yes, I slept with her, and I'll always regret that. But that's the only mistake I've made. She may lie to my face, but she can't change what happened."

Jesse sensed he was doing better. Maybe talking about this was a relief for him. Her own neck and shoulders were tensing up. More alcohol, she hoped, would help. "Will you cut some kind of deal?"

"First let's call her bluff. After she knows where she stands, we'll hear her out, see what she wants. Remember, she's wanted for murder. If she'll agree to a long-term psychiatric facility, and if she'll tell Abe the truth, I'll go to bat for her." Nick held Jesse's eyes. She could see that his black eyes were sure now, steady. "The key is that Abe must see her for what she is."

"Thank you." She finished her martini, hoping that Nick could accomplish that. It would be a measure of the man, she realized. If anyone could persuade Abe, Nick could.

He squeezed her hand. "Don't worry about this. It'll be over tomorrow night." He smiled at her, shifting gears. "Jess, I owe you an apology. As you undoubtedly know, I've been distracted, preoccupied. Now you understand why. It had nothing to do with you. Because of Abe, I've been keeping you out of this. I was hoping that after she killed Lester, Corey would disappear, that Abe would never find her." Nick ran his thumb down the back of his razor-cut black hair. "I hoped that because she was wanted for murder, she wasn't coming back. I didn't want her to work her black magic on Abe. And honestly, I didn't want you to know about my embarrassing past with your son's lover. I have nothing to hide except an unfortunate sexual liaison sixteen years ago. I hope you understand."

"I understand that you hoped it would go away. And you knew that it would be distasteful for me. I still wish you'd told me sooner. But I appreciate that you've told me now." She ordered a second martini. "Let's not let this be an issue between us."

"I appreciate that." Nick touched the back of her hand with his forefinger. "I should have told you when I first put it together, right after the brunch. I should have known that a woman like Corey never goes away. I was foolish. With hindsight, I can see that. Now, at least, it's out in the open. We'll settle this tomorrow night, once and for all. In the meantime let's think about other things. Why don't we make a night of it? After dinner we can go to your place."

Jesse felt so much better. And another martini would only help. She would let him take care of her tonight. "That would be perfect."

TWENTY THREE

M AX HAD RENTED A car for Corey and Abe, and Corey drove to the marina where their boat was waiting. She wore jeans, a t-shirt and a blue windbreaker. He wore baggy khakis, a beige flannel shirt he liked and his favorite tweed jacket. Corey's gun was holstered at the small of her back. Abe wore a shoulder holster. He was clean-shaven. She thought he looked pretty darn good, all things considered.

Their boat was a twenty-three foot 220-hp Wellcraft Walkaround Cuddy. It was primarily a sport fishing boat, smaller and not as seaworthy as the Osprey that they'd seen through the mist on that ill-fated night up north. Corey had picked it because it was the best available option for their short trip. The white fiberglass Wellcraft could make the sand spit in about an hour. That would put them there about 6:15 P.M., half an hour early. Max would call when Jesse and Nick left the other marina. One of his men was holding the keys to their boat, and he would only give them the keys when he was sure that the two of them had come alone. If they brought anyone else along, he'd leave with the keys, and the meeting would be called off. Nick and Jesse had about the same distance to travel, maybe a little more. Corey untied their mooring lines, and then they were off.

The satellite phone rang. "They just left," Max said. "Just the two of them. No one followed them." Their boat, he told Abe, was yellow and white, a Bayliner. "Nice-looking couple," he added.

That put them right behind them. Abe broke the connection without a word. He was readying himself.

An hour later Abe could see the sand spit. It looked exactly as it had the day before. The wind was blowing and waves were breaking on the exposed shore. She put the cruiser in neutral while he checked the spit out with binoculars. It was a barren, curving ribbon of sand scarred by large driftwood logs. "Not a soul," he said.

Abe felt Corey's hand on the back of his neck. When he turned, she kissed him longingly. Their kiss lasted quite a while. "You okay?" she eventually asked.

"I am." He nodded.

She pointed out a yellow and white Bayliner, maybe five minutes away. "Buckle up, babe, it's show time."

The curving spit formed a natural breakwater, and Corey took their boat to the protected side. She anchored, then rowed them to shore to their designated spot.

Abe walked around their meeting place, checking it out. When he was satisfied, they sat facing each other, each of them on a leg of their U-shaped logs. They watched Nick anchor the yellow and white boat beside their own, then row Jesse to shore in their dinghy.

Abe felt a wave of fear course through him. He knew when it was cresting—an overwhelming, apparently endless moment of panic—and then it washed through, leaving him clear, centered. Ready.

———

COREY WATCHED NICK AND Jesse approach. Jesse waved. Nick was all smiles. Corey kept her eyes on Nick Season. Nick sat Jesse on the log that formed the bottom of the U. He didn't sit, he knew he was flanked. Instead, Nick paced, walking between Corey and Abe. He wore dark slacks, a button-down blue shirt, sturdy boots, and a lightweight gray sport coat. She saw the outline of a gun, holstered on his hip. Corey thought he looked like a cop.

Nick paced for several minutes. He kept his eyes on the water, showing his back to her and then to Abe. Corey guessed it was meant to reassure them. It made her even more frightened.

When Nick stopped pacing, he was facing Abe. He took charge right away. "Jesse filled me in on your conversation," he said to Abe, his tone friendly. "And I'd like to clear up whatever misunderstandings we might have. I think I can see a way to settle our differences and to help Corey come back to Seattle. Are you willing to hear me out?"

She watched Abe do his thing, look away, mull this over. While Abe was crafting a careful response, Nick sat beside him, blocking Jesse's view of her son. This was not going as planned, Corey knew that already. It was way too fast. What was Nick doing sitting next to Abe? And before she could think what to do, Nick had his pick in Abe's ear. From her seat on the log, Jesse couldn't see it; Corey could see it though, picture perfect.

"Throw your gun in the water," Nick said to Corey. Christ. This had already gone to shit. Abe had said he'd go after her first.

Nick shot her a look she remembered; he would kill Abe if she made a wrong move. "Now," Nick ordered.

Corey did as she was told. She walked deliberately to the water and tossed her .38 into the ocean, hoping against hope that Nick wouldn't figure Abe for a gun.

"What the hell are you doing?" Jesse asked Nick, standing now. "Take that weapon out of his ear. Nicky!"

"It isn't what it seems, Jess." Nick pulled a .38 Colt Detective's Special from the holster on his hip. He pointed it at Corey, then he took his pick out of Abe's ear and slid it back into his belt. "Give me a reason," he whispered to Abe. "I'll kill her. Sure as sunrise." Jesse sat, shooting Nick a make-me-a-believer look. "Just give me a minute to disarm these people," he said to her. "I don't want anyone to get hurt while we talk."

"Lie down in the sand where I can see you," he ordered Corey, pointing his gun at her. "Right in front of Jesse."

Corey walked toward the longer middle log, where she lay face down in the sand, praying that Abe would make his move soon.

Jesse was watching, plainly unsure what was happening.

"I'll want your gun too," Nick said to Abe, standing him up at gunpoint. He opened Abe's jacket with his gun barrel, revealing Abe's holstered weapon. Abe never had a chance. Corey said a silent prayer. Nick walked him past Jesse and Corey to the water.

Reluctantly, Abe tossed his 9mm Beretta into the water.

Jesse was shaking her head. "Good God. What were you thinking?" she asked Abe, who ignored her.

We're dead, Corey thought. Fucked. Abe's big plan was useless now, dog meat.

Nick kept his gun trained on Abe. "Hands in the air," he ordered. "Turn around, face the boats."

Abe raised his hands and turned his back to them.

Nick stepped closer and whispered in Abe's ear, "If you turn around, for any reason, I'll do your sweetie in the back of her head. Like she did Lester."

"Nick?" Jesse asked.

"Bear with me, here. I just want to make sure that no one gets hurt."

Before Corey could think what to do, she felt Nick roughly cuffing her hands behind her back. The cuffs were too tight.

"Nicky, that's enough," Jesse said, standing again.

Nick was back behind Abe, ignoring her. He pressed his gun to Abe's spine. "Don't move, doc. Don't even think about moving. Take slow breaths, try to relax," he whispered.

Then Nick turned and walked to where Jesse was standing. He smiled at her. "You know, I hate the name Nicky." He watched her face turn red, then, without warning, Nick savagely slapped Jesse to the sand. When she tried to get up, he kicked her in the stomach. "I hate that name," he repeated. "Ridiculous bitch," Nick added, then he cuffed Jesse's hands behind her back as well. Jesse was fighting for breath.

Nick pulled each of the women up by their hair and their handcuffs, then sat them roughly against the log at the bottom of the U. Jesse was gasping and crying. Abe was still standing, back turned, hands still high in the air. Corey was working to get her feet under her and thinking fast.

Nick turned to Abe. He walked around to face him. "Did you think you could play me? Did you think you could threaten me? Did you think you could fool me? You?" Nick asked, each question louder than the last. Before Abe could answer, he cracked him in the mouth with his gun butt. Abe staggered back toward the near log, then Nick pistol-whipped him, smashing the gun against Abe's head and face two more times before Abe fell to the sand, blood covering his face. Abe curled himself into a ball, protecting his head as Corey and his mother watched.

Corey cried out. She would have to do something soon. Nick looked ready to kill Abe.

Jesse was still gasping, making incoherent, guttural noises.

Nick watched Abe curl up in a fetal position. "Regular fucking warrior," he said, then he laughed. He smiled at the women. "Okay. Now we can talk." He was pacing again. As he paced, Nick would look down at the cuffed women then over at Abe. He stopped where Abe was curled up in the sand. As the women watched, he kicked Abe, firmly planting the toe of his boot in Abe's side, a vicious blow. Abe cried out. "You scared, doc? Bet you never said boo to a goose. Bet your mommy trimmed those nuts early on. You're not a fighting cock now, are you, bucko?"

Corey had managed to get her feet underneath her butt and was squatting now.

"Did you know that your mother's a whore?" Nick asked Abe. "She'll do anything. Did you know that?" He kicked Abe again, his boot glancing off the back of Abe's head.

"Please, stop. Please," Jesse pleaded. She was close to hysteria. "Please. I beg you. I'll do whatever you say."

"You still want to please me?" Nick asked Jesse. "Try squealing like a pig, you blue-blooded sow bitch." Nick kicked Abe in the stomach.

Corey started screaming. As Nick turned, she rose suddenly and kicked him in the groin as hard as she could. He went down, breathless. Jesse rose carefully. She still had the presence of mind to kick Nick's gun away. Nick stood up slowly. He took one step before Corey cracked her head into his face. Nick yelled, blood spouting from his broken nose. He fell to his knees.

Corey knew what she had to do. Abe couldn't help. She couldn't pick up the gun; her hands were cuffed behind her back. Jesse was useless, cuffed and panicked. She had to kick Nick's bloody face in. Nick was on one knee, collecting himself, holding his handkerchief to his bloody nose. His free hand was at his waist, and he was working to breathe slowly. Corey chose her moment. As she shifted her weight, Nick sprung like a panther, grabbing her hair, pulling her off balance. And before she could deliver her kick, she felt Nick's pick under her chin.

Nick raised Corey to her toes. He stood behind her. He held the pick under her chin with his right hand. Nick caught his breath then he looked at them, one at a time. He wiped his bloody nose on his left sleeve. "What were you thinking? Don't you get it? Don't you get it?" he asked again, louder still. With the pick in Corey's lower jaw, he turned to Jesse. "Lie facedown in the sand," Nick ordered her. "If you move again, you'll die slowly, after your son."

Jesse lay facedown in the sand, making raspy sounds.

Nick punched the thin needle-nosed instrument through Corey's lower jaw into the roof of her mouth. Corey rose again on her toes, gasping. Nick pointed at Abe and walked her closer on her tiptoes. "There's your big man, your studhorse, sweetie. Take a good long look."

Abe had pulled himself onto the log, where he had collapsed again. His face was battered and bloodied.

"Al looked like that before he died," Nick said. "Did you know that Al begged for his life? Do you think Abe's going to beg?" Nick kicked Abe in the side again. Corey thought she heard a rib crack. Abe rolled off the log, onto the sand on the far side.

Nick put more pressure on the pick and Corey gagged. She could feel blood, pooling in her mouth. Nick called out to Abe, "Come on out, beefcake, or I kill her right now." He raised the pick. Corey gasped. How could Abe have ever been so sure? How had he convinced her to do this? Why had she ever gone along with him? How was Billy going to manage?

Abe raised his bloody head above the log.

"Did Corey tie you up, doc, boss you around?" Nick asked. "She always liked her men weak as water." He raised the pick higher still. Blood came out of Corey's mouth, running down her chin.

Abe struggled to stand up. His eyes were on Corey. They were not the intense, smart eyes she remembered. They were bloodshot and lifeless. His face was despondent, bloody and torn. He used one hand to prop himself up on the log, which almost reached his waist. "I'm sorry," he mouthed to her, then Abe looked down at the sand, humiliated.

Corey cried out as Nick pulled out the pick, letting her drop to her knees in the sand. He picked up his gun and motioned to Abe.

"Come on over here, Sir Lancelot," Nick said. He faced Abe across the log, less than fifteen feet away. "We're going boating." He laughed again, then turned to Corey. Nick gestured with his gun for her to move toward the water.

Corey guessed Nick's plan. He would kill them—his pick through an eardrum—then cut the fuel line and set their little fishing boat on fire. Eventually, it would blow up with all three of them on it. A boating accident. And Nick would get away with it. He always did.

Nick turned toward Abe, gesturing again with his gun for Abe to move along. Abe looked at his mother, lying in the sand. She was gasping for breath, and crying out, panic-stricken. Nick glanced toward Jesse. How Corey hated his triumphant look. In that instant, Abe brought his right hand up from behind the log with a handgun in it. Corey thought her heart would explode in her chest. Time virtually stopped. It was the longest second of her life.

Nick must have sensed something. When he spun back toward Abe, his gun raised, Abe fired two shots. Two-handed grip—9mm Beretta held tight. Two in the chest. Centered. Blood sprayed the salty sea air. And Nick went down. Flat on his back, arms spread. The earth stopped spinning on its axis; Corey was sure of it.

Corey wondered if she was dead. This was some kind of dead person's dream. She stepped over to where Nick was lying in the sand. Blood was seeping from two holes in his chest. He tried to reach for her, but he couldn't even move his hand. He could barely move his fingers. Was this a dream? Corey kicked Nick's gun away. This didn't feel like a dream. No. She took a breath. No, this wasn't a dream. Corey turned to Abe and yelled at the top of her lungs, then she ran to him, crying. Abe held her, still cuffed, in his arms.

"I asked Max for a second gun," he quietly explained. "I hid it in the log the last time we were here. I couldn't —"

"Not now." Corey kissed his battered, bloodied face. "Thank you," she whispered between her tears. "Uncuff me so I can take care of you."

He put an arm over her shoulder, so she could help him walk. She helped him to where Nick was lying in the sand, dying.

Abe knelt beside Nick, who had blood running from the corners of his mouth. Nick was immobile. Nevertheless, Corey planted one foot on each of Nick's hands, just to be sure. Nick's keys were in his jacket pocket. Abe took them out, moving slowly. Carefully, he uncuffed Corey. It was slow work because his eyes were swollen, and blood still flowed down from his brow onto his eyelids. After Corey was free, Abe knelt in the sand beside Nick, using his tweed jacket sleeve to wipe the blood from his brow. It wasn't working. Corey rubbed her sore wrists then, using her teeth and her right hand, she tore a piece off the bottom of her t-shirt. She used it to wipe the blood off Abe's brow then his eyelids. When Abe could see again, Corey uncuffed Jesse.

Jesse sat on the sand, disjointedly weeping and fighting for breath. Corey helped Jesse sit on a log. On the log, Jesse lost any semblance of self-control. She wrapped her arms around herself, wailing and sobbing inconsolably.

Abe stared at Nick.

"You?" Nick finally sputtered at Abe, uncomprehending. He gasped.

Abe took a breath, wiping his brow again with Corey's torn shirt. "I get it about you, Nick. Think about that. How could I possibly understand you and still be anything like I'm supposed to be?"

It was the last thing Nick ever heard.

Corey put her arm around Abe's waist and helped him sit on a different log from his mother. She just wanted to be with him. She took back the piece of cloth she'd torn from her t-shirt to clean more of the blood from his face. He would need stitches, but she knew it didn't matter. Not now, anyway. Eventually she asked, "It's over, isn't it?"

"Yes, it's over."

"It was even worse than I imagined."

Abe tossed her a trace of a smile. She could see that it hurt. "I couldn't tell you. It was the only way I knew to stay ahead of him."

Corey got that. She didn't know what would have gone down differently if she'd known. Something would have, though. And that was Abe's edge. Her not knowing made Abe's apparent defeat vividly real.

"I had some trouble with the safety, behind the log…"

"Shh," she shushed him. "You're my hero. Forever. You did what you said you'd do. I don't want to know the rest."

Abe put his arms around her then whispered, "We did it."

Corey lay her head on Abe's shoulder. Abe had made Nick think what he wanted him to think, then the shrink who couldn't drive put Nick Season down like a rabid dog. It took her breath away. "You did it, babe."

RILEY WAS HAVING DINNER at Tulio, an Italian gem in the Vintage Park Hotel. It was one of his favorite restaurants. Tulio was warm and welcoming, the food was excellent, and the staff, unusually able. The restaurant had old dark mahogany, upholstered booths along the wall, a cozy bar and informal dining area with a red-brown and black-splashed—with white patterned tile floor and tables covered with white tablecloths. The bar opened out onto the street if the weather permitted. When the corporate owners redecorated the dining room, they didn't destroy its charm. Riley credited local management for that.

He was organizing grilled onions and oyster mushrooms on a splendid veal chop when they came in. Born-to-lose Abe Stein, Corey and Billy Logan, and the girlfriend. He was haunted by these people. They were stalking him. A constant reminder of his inadequacy. He had seen their name on the reservation book at Chez Henri. He had seen them at Shuckers. He should have known that they would come to this place.

Never, ever, had he misjudged people so badly. He watched them. Corey Logan had taken down Lester Burell, for christsakes. That should have been a clue. And S.O.L. Stein had killed Nick Season. Drove a stake through the devil's black heart. Riley thought about that often. How he'd misjudged the goofy doctor. How Nick must have underestimated him, too. The doctor was a demon killer. How could he ever presume to kill people like that? People? Hell no. Immortals is what they were.

On his way out, Riley bought them a drink.

ACKNOWLEDGEMENTS

THE AUTHOR WOULD LIKE to thank: Brad Bryant, Tyson Cornell, Dorothy Escribano, Sarah Fisken, Ruth Grant, Steve Grant, Suzanne Harris, Arlene Heyman, Brendan Kiley, Robert Lovenheim, Kenneth Millar, Dave Miller, Marianne Moloney, Kate Pflaumer, Brian Phillips, Mike Reynvaan, Rebecca Riley, Avery Rimer, Robert Rohan, John Sargent, Jack Swenson, Andy Ward, Bernard Weissbourd, Bernice Weissbourd, Ben Weissbourd, Emily Weissbourd, Jenny Weissbourd, Kathy Weissbourd, Richard Weissbourd, Robert Weissbourd.

M